THE NEVER LIST

DL WHITE

BOOKS
BY DL WHITE

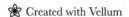 Created with Vellum

This one's for me.

THE NEVER LIST

10. RIDE A ROLLER COASTER/FERRIS WHEEL
9. PLAY AN EXTREME SPORT
8. TRAVEL BY PLANE
7. EAT AN "EXOTIC" FOOD
6. GO SAILING
5. SWIM IN THE OCEAN
4. PET A COW
3. BE DARING
2. HAVE SEX
1. FALL IN LOVE

CHAPTER ONE

Content warnings: attempted robbery/assault and references to the attempt

ESME

"Try online dating, they said. It'll be fun, they said." I rolled my wrist to glance at my watch for the fourth time in the last half hour, staring out of a fogged-over window with my arms folded over my chest.

From my seat at a cozy table for two, my view was a parking lot. A light rain hadn't kept the residents of Vinings, Georgia, an Atlanta suburb, from frequenting neighborhood eateries and watering holes arm in arm, with peals of laughter rising over the piano music droning from the speakers above my table. I watched them hop over puddles to make their way to the strip mall filled with burger joints, a vape store, an Asian market, and Bistro, a wine shop serving small plates with accompanying wine flights. Steamed mussels, crab fondue and stuffed mushrooms served with white wines and garlic chicken lettuce wraps, stuffed pasta shells, and bruschetta served with red.

I wished that I'd declined this date invitation. It was too late in the evening. I had TV shows to watch. I'd *just* met him on a dating site. Wasn't it too early to meet a man in person?

But my cousin, O'Neal, talked me into agreeing to meet him. Now I was sitting in a dimly lit, romantic restaurant.

Alone.

"This was a bad idea," I muttered aloud. "I tried to tell O'Neal, but you can't tell him nothin'."

"Excuse me, ma'am?"

I nearly jumped out of my skin at the interruption of my low volume tirade. A man stood next to my table, bent slightly toward me. I took in his fresh cut, the lush curls of his beard, soft brown eyes and mahogany skin. I loved the scent of a man, and this one smelled delicious, like sandalwood, rich vanilla and laundry detergent. Coupled with his subtly expensive taste in fashion—wool slacks, crisp button-down dress shirt, and dark jacket, I could forgive him for being so *very* late if he was my date, but he looked nothing like the photos of the man I'd chatted with the evening before.

"Do you mind if I take this chair?" He gripped the seat across from me, already beginning to cart it off with him as if I'd said it was fine. "We're at the table behind you."

I squinted at him. It wasn't like I was using it; it was his audacity to assume that he could just take it.

"Yes!" I said, louder than I'd planned. "I mind very much, actually."

He straightened, his actual height taking my breath away. I stood 5' 9" and relished a bona fide big and tall man, not a man who bragged about his height but wouldn't make it over six feet unless he borrowed Prince's heels.

"I only need one chair, and you're alone."

"I'm *not* alone."

He glanced around, dramatically searching one end of the restaurant, then the other. "You look alone to me, ma'am."

2

I bristled. "Who are you calling ma'am? I'm obviously waiting for someone."

"How would I know— whatever." He emitted a grunt that assured me he was not pleased. I could not manage to care. "You could have just said no. All that attitude was unnecessary."

"Why wouldn't I have an attitude with a man who waltzed up to my table and started taking chairs? Where is my date supposed to sit?"

"What date?" He snickered, then went back to his table.

The waitress stopped to ask, again, if I wanted to order anything. I handed her my glass, asked for a refill and the check. I'd take my time, waiting to slip my credit card into the slot, then drawing out signing the slip. Maybe, in that amount of time, my date would show.

Ten more minutes and I am out of here, I promised myself. I'm missing my shows, messing around with this fool.

Usually a Thursday night — really any weeknight meant a swing through somebody's drive-thru or placing an order for delivery and hours of escapist books or TV. I rarely missed my shows. I was more of a homebody than most homebodies, but, as my mother phrased it during our most recent conversation-she from the Phoenix Omni Resort and Spa, me from the swing on the wraparound porch-the man of my dreams couldn't fall into my lap if I didn't take my lap somewhere.

My cousin, best friend, and housemate, O'Neal piled on, encouraging me to try meeting new people through a website. "You don't do bars; you don't do clubs or sports. You can sift through men and meet somebody virtually before you have to meet them in person."

After some arm twisting and internet searches, O'Neal created a profile for me on BlackSinglesMatch, the most reputable site with a robust personality assessment and what seemed the least number of shady profiles.

Almost immediately upon pimping myself out to the world at large, I'd begun receiving messages.

Hey, Sistah. U R cute. Call me.

"Call him?" I'd asked O'Neal. "For what? Just straight from the internet? What are we supposed to talk about?"

"Ignore him. He don't want nothin' but nasty chat and you —" He cut himself off before completing his thought. "Anyway, who's next?"

I must know you, my Queen! I will like for you to be my wife. Please contact me immediately.

"Next."

Hey, sexy. Welcome to the site. I like what I see, and I know you'll like my nine inches of long, hard—

"Damn!" O'Neal cringed. "I'm sorry. I didn't know it was this bad, Es."

"What do you mean, you didn't know? You put me on this site, and you've never used it?"

O'Neal's grin was as wide as it was salacious. "I get plenty of women the natural way."

"I'm calling it! I'm done." I deleted each message that had popped into the inbox, but for every note I deleted, two more arrived. "It's like feeding time in the shark tank! I'm fresh meat."

"Wait, wait!" O'Neal stabbed the monitor with the tip of a finger. "That dude in the suit. Third one down. Click on him!"

I cleared the screen until only one chat request existed.

What's up, beautiful? I'm Chris. How are you this evening?

"Full sentences and no innuendo. I'm in love."

"Hold up, Es. Check his profile," urged O'Neal, pointing to the link. I did so and was rewarded with a photo of a broad-shouldered bona fide cutie in a designer tuxedo. His smile was wide and pearly white, his skin a perfect toasted almond, his hair a thick mane of locs that went past his shoulders, and his eyes were a soulful deep brown.

I skipped down the list of attributes: 6' 3", works in

finance, lives in Atlanta metro, single, no children. The caption read *My cousin's wedding. I clean up nice.*

"Aight. He's not an uglass mofo. See what this Chris is about." O'Neal picked up a bowl of roasted edamame and balanced it on his taut belly as he slumped in the chair next to me.

"Hello, Chris," I typed, after accepting his chat request. "I'm Esme."

"Hello," came the response seconds later. "How's your Wednesday coming along?"

An hour later, O'Neal was making appreciative noises at Instagram models. And I was still chatting with Chris.

Like me, he worked with numbers, so he was analytical, but he was also funny, getting in a quip or two during our spirited back and forth. I was comfortable enough to share details about life, work, family. Chris was warm but less forthcoming. I didn't want to push, though. I would learn about him as we got to know each other.

"I hope I don't seem too forward," he wrote, "but I wondered if I could buy you a drink tomorrow?"

The message came through after a longer than usual pause on his side. My stomach dropped, and I clutched O'Neal's arm, making sure he read the message. "He wants to meet!" I squeaked. "Tomorrow!"

"Ok," he said. "Pick a place. Tell him to meet you." Then went back to his phone.

My jaw dropped. "Seriously? Would you meet a woman that you just—never mind. I know the answer already."

"It's a public place, Es. Meet him. Let him buy you a drink. Plus, you won't be sitting at home. Win-win." He pointed at the screen, then waved at the keyboard, gesturing for me to type. "You'll be fine. Do it, Es."

"Hey, no pressure," Chris had typed after I didn't answer right away. "I'd like to talk face to face, you know. See if there's chemistry."

Chemistry. *Tuh.*

I checked my watch again, glaring out of the window as if I could summon my date to show up, then at the open app on my phone. My inbox was a desert. I was sure I saw a tumbleweed blow through. No messages. No *'hey, running late, I'll be there in ten minutes.'* In fact, Chris hadn't been online all day.

I had to tell myself what I hadn't wanted to tell myself. I'd been stood up.

I slipped my card back into my wallet, anger roiling anew that I'd spent $23.99 on a little Beef Crostini appetizer and a drink that I didn't even like. I could have bought a bottle of wine at Publix and had a dollar menu dinner on my couch and enjoyed it more. I stalked out of the restaurant, already mentally delivering the scathing speech I would give him when he inevitably contacted me. They always came back.

I crossed the parking lot, hearing only the staccato rhythm of my heels. The sound of sneakers scuffing the pavement caught my ear too late to adjust for the impact of a body crushing blow. Someone was all over me, grabbing for my bag, attempting to yank it away. I screamed, holding onto the straps with both hands.

He pulled; I pulled harder.

He yanked; I yanked harder.

Items flung from inside the bag and scattered across the parking lot. He gave a hard pull and grunted, "Let go, bitch!"

"No, motherf—"

A fist came into contact with the side of my head. My vision dimmed; the parking lot spun. I felt my grip loosen.

Through the ringing in my ears, I heard the restaurant door swing open, footsteps, and a cacophony of garbled voices. Then a scuffle, forceful grunts, and a meaty crunch that could only be a fist meeting a mouth. I felt the thud across the pavement as a body hit the ground, mere inches away.

I pushed myself up to get a good look at the man that laid

on the pavement, arms and legs splayed. He wore dark jeans and sneakers, and someone had pulled his hoodie back. I didn't recognize him, but I knew who he was. I'd have laughed if my head wasn't pounding.

I hadn't been on a date in years, had never arranged a date on the Internet, and got mugged.

"Ma'am?! You ok?"

A figure hulked over me and a hand entered my field of vision, offering help. I smacked the hand away and maneuvered to my feet. On shaky legs that grew stronger by the moment, I collected the items that had flown from my bag.

"I'm… fine," I stammered. "If I just… can get… I want to go home."

I stuffed my things into the bag and pulled out my keys. I wanted to be where I should have been all night long, on my couch eating popcorn and watching my usual Thursday night lineup.

"Ma'am?" The voice called after me. "The police are on the way."

I limped toward my car, parked a few spaces away. My ankle stabbed with every step and the right side of my face throbbed. Once I reached it, I unlocked the door and fell into the driver's seat. I was still dizzy, but the fuzzy edges were becoming more defined.

All I knew was that I needed to get out of there. I reached to start the car but was startled again by a knock at the window. I looked up and winced. It was the guy that had tried to take my chair. I started the car and rolled the window down.

"Yes?"

"Hey, girl," he said, grinning down at me. He leaned against the car, his arm resting on the hood, rather easy-going for having just knocked a man unconscious. "You did a lil bob and weave on the way to your car. Are you ok?"

"I'm fine. I think. Thanks for your help. That was you, right?"

"Ah, it was no big thing," he replied. "But I'm not sure you should drive, ma'am. He got you good. Maybe you–"

"Stop calling me ma'am," I snapped. "I said I was fine. I want to go home."

"Ah, ok. You just always have an attitude." He pushed out a couple of sarcastic chuckles. "Anyway, the police are on the way. You should stick around."

"I'll stop by the precinct tomorrow. I think I know who that guy is. Now move before I run you over."

He made a sucking noise with his teeth but stepped back. I pulled out of the space and directed the car away from the lump of man still lying in the middle of the parking lot, and the crowd that had gathered around him. The sky was already glowing with the red and blue flashing orbs of police cars approaching.

CHAPTER TWO

Esme

By the time I eased the car into the garage, I was lucid. And livid.

I had almost been mugged. I knew my mugger. Sort of.

I should have stuck around to inform the officers at the scene, but I was embarrassed. I'd been stood up, wasted an entire evening and was attacked. I was in no mood to tell Cobb County's finest about how someone pegged me right away as the perfect mark.

I grabbed my bag, inspecting the straps where he had pulled it. It was Louis Vuitton. Authentic, not a knockoff. I had just decided it was worth every penny that my mother had spent on it.

I entered the house through the kitchen door and hung my keys on my designated hook. Every light on the first floor burned bright, the TV blared at two notches above an acceptable decibel, and the kitchen was a mess: all signs that O'Neal, a flight attendant for Delta, was home.

As if on cue, O'Neal rounded the corner from the living

room in his usual at-home wardrobe: a sleeveless tank that showed off his chiseled biceps and loose basketball shorts. When I wore loungewear, I looked like a scrub. O'Neal's effortlessly casual look was goals.

"Aight, gimme the rundown. How'd it go?"

He slid onto one of the bar stools that lined the counter while I stood in front of the freezer, letting the cool air soothe my face. The skin around my eye was already puffy, and I considered calling in sick to work the next day. I plucked a handful of ice cubes from the bin and stepped back to let the door close, careful not to turn too far toward O'Neal.

I made a noncommittal noise as I pulled open a drawer, rooting around for the box of Ziploc bags and dumping the ice into one as soon as I pulled a bag from the box.

"I don't like that sound. Was he ugly? Bad breath? Did he even look like his picture?" He clicked his tongue. "You got catfished, huh?"

"I didn't get catfished. I mean, I don't think this was technically a catfish."

"Say more. And why are you putting ice in a bag, Es?"

Knowing I wouldn't be able to hide it forever, I turned so my cousin could see the swelling and redness down the right side of my face.

"Oh, shit!" O'Neal leaped off the stool, reaching me in seconds. He cradled my face in one hand, poking at the growing lump on my temple with the other. "What happened?"

I winced. "Ouch, O'Neal. It feels like it looks."

"Ooh, sorry." He grabbed the baggie of ice and applied it to the angry red lump. "So, what went down? Did he do this? And if so, tell me he's in jail, because if he isn't, I'm about to fuck him up."

"I don't need you to fuck anyone up." I stepped around him, taking a seat on one stool. O'Neal sat next to me. "I got stood up. Kind of."

He cocked his head to the side. "Nah. Do men do that shit? He ain't say nothin'?"

I recounted my evening for him, from arriving at Bistro to find that my date wasn't waiting to meet me, to the testy conversation with the man that wanted to take my chair.

"I sat there for an hour, O'Neal. No messages, no apologies, nothing. When I got sick of waiting, I left. That's when I got jumped. He went for my bag, and when I wouldn't let go, he hit me. I went down and…"

I shook my head, switching the hand holding the makeshift ice pack. "That guy who wanted my chair came out of the restaurant and knocked him out with a single punch."

O'Neal's eyes were wide and getting wider. "What did the police say? You pressed charges, right?"

"I don't know what they said. I left."

"You left the scene? And… didn't call the police."

"They showed up as I was leaving."

"One more time... you left before you could file charges?"

"And tell them what?" I switched hands again, wincing as I applied pressure to the wound. "I set myself up to get robbed by some guy I met on the internet. So they can write that down in their little spiral notebook and make shitty jokes about the dumb ass chick that got played by an internet con man? That *you* encouraged me to meet, I might add."

"Ay, don't start. You asked for my help."

"You helped me right into a concussion."

"It's not like I introduced you to one of my friends, Es. So, you're going to let him get away with it?"

"No." I exhaled, resigned. "I'll call the police station tomorrow. I can give them what I have on him, even though what he told me was probably made up. Maybe they can get something from the website. And there's the guy that beat him down. I'm sure they got his statement."

I stifled a yawn, then another. Adrenaline had worn off,

and I was delirious with exhaustion. "I'm going to call it a night. I've had enough of today."

I picked up my bag, headed through the living room and up the stairs. Since I bought the house from my parents while they traveled the country in a decked-out RV, I got the first choice of bedrooms. I took the master because I was home more but also because it had an ensuite bathroom with a garden tub and Jacuzzi jets.

I dumped the bag on my bed and headed straight there, salivating at the thought of soaking this night away.

I turned on the faucet to fill the tub, tossing in a bath bomb to soften and scent the water, and pinned up my shoulder-length hair. I undressed, unbuttoning the silk blouse I had picked out especially for this date. I peeled off the camisole and the lacy bra that my date would never see, but I felt confident and sexy in them. I unzipped the brand-new black pencil skirt that had been rubbed in spots from my encounter with the concrete. Disgusted, I tossed the skirt into the dry clean pile in my closet.

As I pushed my panties down my hips, the doorbell chimed. O'Neal's flight attendant friends were prone to visiting at all hours of the night and staying until sunrise. Occasionally, I had to step over slumbering figures sprawled out on the living room floor.

I turned off the faucet, stepped into the bath, and turned on the jets, sinking deep into the steamy, soapy water. I exhaled a breath I felt I'd been holding for hours. Since before I left work and headed to Bistro. Since I arrived and my date wasn't waiting to meet me, and since I had sat alone at a table and 8:30 came and went, 9:00 came and went, and there was no Chris.

I should have expected something to go wrong. It was too good to be true from the beginning. I'd heard the long-winded moans and complaints about online dating, about how there were more scammers and men looking for sex than the genuine article looking for love.

I'd been so smug, having met a handsome gentleman right out of the gate. We'd have a romantic first meeting and look deeply into each other's eyes. Months down the line, he would drop to one knee at some romantic locale to propose. I would say yes, and we would have one of those cute stories you see on those commercials that run nonstop from New Year's Day to Valentine's Day.

I blew scented bubbles away from my face. Now I had a story about how my first online date tried to mug me.

A soft tap-tap at the door interrupted my pity party. "What, O'Neal?"

"There's a man here, asking for you."

I sat up, searching my brain for any person I knew that would stop by without calling first. I didn't know any men that had a reason to stop by at this time of night.

"You sure it's for me?"

"He has your wallet; he showed me your ID. His hand is all bandaged up. Es, I think he might be the dude that knocked that guy out!"

I could have kicked myself. I hadn't even checked my bag when I got home. I was not in the mood to see or talk to anyone, not even to thank a stranger for finding my wallet and bringing it to me.

"I don't want to talk to him. Get his number. No, wait! I'm not calling anyone. Get his email address. I'll send him a thank you."

"I'm not your secretary. Get out of that tub and come thank this man for coming to your rescue and delivering your property to you!"

O'Neal stomped through the bedroom, down the hall, and back downstairs. Defiant, I took my time drying off, throwing some clothes on my body and a pair of slides on my feet before descending the stairs to greet the Good Samaritan who had interrupted my relaxing bath.

O'Neal was on the couch, intently listening to the man comfortably seated in the chair across from him. The TV was still on, but he'd at least turned the volume down. The conversation came to an abrupt halt as I entered the room. As he drew to his full height, I was reminded of his distractingly attractive features. One sleeve was unbuttoned and rolled up to the elbow. One hand was indeed wrapped in gauze and tape.

"Uhm. Hi, again."

"Hello, again," he returned, then angled his head to look at my face. "Ooh, he got you good." He raised a hand as if he was going to touch me, but I bobbed out of reach.

"Yeah, he got me good. You have something of mine?"

He turned to pick up a compact wallet that matched my bag. "I saw it after the officers left the scene; it slid underneath a car. I figured you'd need it."

He handed it to me. I unzipped it and looked through it, not even trying to be surreptitious about checking the amount of cash still left and that all the credit cards were there. Satisfied, I glanced up to find him mid-smirk.

"Considering what you've been through tonight, I won't take it personally that you thought I'd take something from you."

"Yeah, well, thanks. And uh…" I gestured to his wrapped hand. "Sorry about that. I hope you're not a surgeon or anything."

"Nah." He flexed the hand, regarding it with a casual glance. "Looks worse than it feels. I put the responding officer's business card in your wallet. Call him at the precinct. They'd like to know what you know about this guy."

His lips bent into a smile as he slid his uninjured hand into his pocket. Something about that smile made parts of my body stand at attention, making me glaringly aware that I'd pulled a thin, summer weight t-shirt over my full breasts. I folded my arms over my chest.

"Did you see what happened?" O'Neal asked. "Somebody left the scene, so she has no idea."

"Aight, so here's how it went down." His face lit up, becoming entirely more animated. "From where I was sitting, my view was the parking lot. I watched her go out. The dude was in black; hoodie, cap, sneakers. He came up behind her, grabbed the bag, but she wasn't letting go."

He glanced at me; I didn't know what my face said, but he interpreted it as an urging to continue. "Anyway, I got two fellas to come outside with me, and right as I opened the door, he pulled his fist back—"

He mimed the move for O'Neal's benefit. "Cold cocked her. Next thing I know, I'm running right at him. Scuffle-scuffle. Then he tried to hit me. I gave him all I had. He was laid out, didn't come to until the cops showed up and tried to cuff him. It was a trip."

O'Neal listened to the story with wide eyes and an open mouth, his gaze moving from me to him and back.

"The paramedics checked him out. He's fine. They took care of me, too, though there wasn't much to take care of."

He wanted me to know that he wasn't hurt much. My hero.

"He's being booked, I'm guessing. I made a statement, so I hope it was enough to keep him there." He eyed me. I stared back, not taking the bait.

"Yeah, well… whatever your name is—"

"Trey Pettigrew. Nice to meet you." He extended the hand that wasn't wrapped. I ignored it, leaving my arms crossed.

"Trey. I appreciate your help. Thank you for bringing my wallet. But I feel as bad as I look, and I've got a mean headache coming on. I'd like to call it a night."

"Yeah, sure. I wanted to make sure you got your wallet. You mentioned that you knew the guy?"

I tried to swallow the lump that had suddenly risen in my throat at the thought of Chris and the utter embarrassment of why I was at Bistro. "I had a date tonight. I met this guy at a... an online dating site, but he didn't show. As you know."

An eyebrow rose, letting him know that I remembered how rude he'd been.

"Anyway, it looks like he was waiting for me. As soon as I got away from the entrance..." That sentence could finish itself.

Trey's lips pursed as he nodded. "Yeah. The officers at the scene were saying this is the third attack like that this month. This guy lures women out after dark, then he doesn't show up, and when they leave, they get mugged. You didn't read about that?"

"No, I don't get *The Mugging Times*. Where would I read about that?"

He chuckled, clearly finding humor in my tragedy. "I don't know, ma'am. You get the AJC paper, right? Or online? If I was going out with a guy from a dating site, I'd be checking into that kind of thing. Just passing along some knowledge."

"Thanks for the knowledge. I'm from the school of hard knocks, apparently." I pointed at my face, my swollen eye, my bruised cheek. "I'm all learned up for the day."

"I'm just saying—"

"You're just saying goodnight." I stalked to the front door and swung it open wide. "Thanks again."

"Uh huh." Trey stood immobile for a few beats before he moved toward the door. "You might want to see a doctor, by the way."

My brows hiked. "About?"

"That stick up your ass. Good night."

He stepped out of the house and down the front steps toward a dark SUV parked in the driveway. I wanted to shout a parting shot but couldn't think of one. Instead, I slammed the door and stomped back toward the stairs.

"I don't want to see or talk to another living soul tonight. You hear me, O'Neal?"

"What was all of that attitude about?" He asked, ignoring my statement. He hadn't moved from his spot on the couch, where he stared at me like I'd grown another head. And antennae.

"I don't have an attitude. Why does everyone think I have an attitude? I'm going to bed."

I huffed, bounding up the stairs.

"Sleep tight," O'Neal called. "Tomorrow? We gotta talk."

CHAPTER THREE

Content warnings: references to mental illness.

Trey

Vincent Karl, Vice President of Pettigrew Construction, walked into my office and planted himself in a chair in front of my desk. Without a word, he waited, one foot resting on the opposite knee, a ring-laden finger tapping rhythmically to whatever was playing in his head.

As one of Pettigrew's first employees, Vincent was my father's right-hand man. He knew the business forward and backward, but that didn't give him carte blanche over my office.

"Why haven't I heard about how the meeting went last night?" He asked, apparently tired of waiting for me to acknowledge him.

I rolled my eyes up, working to keep my facial expression neutral. "You could do me the courtesy of knocking and waiting until I give you permission to enter. What if I was doing blow in here?"

Vincent laughed. "Nobody calls it blow, Trey. You're too square for that, anyway."

I laughed, dropping my pen and gliding my chair back. He had a point. "You would never bust in on my father. Don't do it to me. If I have to lock the door—"

"I have keys to every door in this building. But fine, I'll knock from now on. Tell me about the meeting with Miller. And about what happened to your hand."

I flexed my wrapped fingers. My knuckles were still swollen and stiff, but the skin seemed to be already healing. I had all but forgotten about the incident the night before that interrupted a dinner meeting.

Last night's tapas and wine affair was supposed to be a casual chat about combining two companies: Pettigrew, a mid-size commercial construction company, and Miller Design, a small but enterprising boutique architecture firm. More to the point, Pettigrew was about to swallow Miller Design. Whether it would be a friendly or hostile takeover was up to Thomas Miller.

"I had an altercation. Not with Miller," I clarified. "A young lady was attacked in the parking lot. Then the ambulance and the police showed up, and I had to give a statement. I found the young lady's wallet and took it to her."

"Why are you telling me this long, pointless story?"

"Because you asked what happened to my hand."

I stood, stretching my arms and twisting from side to side. I'd been in the chair for hours. It felt good to get up and walk around, to feel the warm afternoon sun beaming into the office through the window. I moved around the desk and slid onto the corner, near the chair Vincent sat in.

"And because I was stuck dealing with the police. We'll need to reschedule."

The downturn of his mouth, which was more pronounced than usual, said Vincent was disappointed. "We're no closer to signing is what you're saying without saying."

"That is what I'm saying."

I pulled at my tie, loosening the knot, then unbuttoned and rolled up my shirt sleeves. I couldn't seem to get used to the uniform of a business professional— stiff and starched shirts, expensive ties, designer slacks, and suit jackets. The transition from field crew to stand-in CEO felt as if it had been overnight, though I'd taken over for Pops a few months ago. I still hadn't settled into the new job.

"Saul won't be happy to hear that."

"I'm not looking forward to updating him. That's why I'm waiting. I hope to have better news later today. Any word on the bid for the new county hospital?"

Vincent shook his head, frowning. "I think it's way off, but we don't want to take chances. We need at least a handshake agreement with Miller. We won't get enough time to merge companies, and we need—"

"To say we've built healthcare facilities. I know, Vincent. I know."

"And of all the acquisition targets, Miller is the most profitable, the most organized and smack in the middle of our price range."

"I know that, too," I assured him. "Why are you repeating things we've said in every meeting?"

Vincent's face darkened, his cheerful smile gone. "Because, son, you don't seem to remember. This was the last project your father launched, and I don't want to see it go down the drain because you're too afraid to make a move. If I need to step in—"

"No." I stood, stepping around Vincent, the chair, and the entire subject.

Saul "Pops" Pettigrew put his heart and soul into his company. He hired me to work summers during high school and while I attended Georgia State University. Once I graduated, Pops began showing me the ropes, teaching me what it took to grow a business and how to keep that business innovating.

Three months ago, Pops collapsed and had to be rushed to the ER. Stress, a high salt diet, lack of exercise, and working non-stop for the last thirty years were contributing factors to his heart attack. While he survived, he'd been ordered to take a long break, and my mother was hearing nothing of her husband doing anything resembling work for at least a year.

One day, I was in polo shirts with the Pettigrew logo on the breast, in khakis or jeans and steel-toed boots, roaming job sites, keeping projects on course. In the blink of an eye, I had a closet full of suits and ties, starched white collared shirts and shoes that made my feet hurt. And I was being asked to take over the company.

Temporarily.

That's how he'd sucked me in, promising that it wouldn't be a permanent change. He would be back to work as soon as he was medically cleared. And, if I did well, I could move to any other position in the company. I could even design a new role if I wanted to.

Months later, though, the arrangement seemed to change. Pops had been using words like *retirement* and *successor*. He'd asked me to think about taking over permanently-a word that would have made me run six months ago.

And maybe Pops knew that. He also knew that I wouldn't want to let him down.

I strolled to the end of the office that housed a mini-fridge stocked with soft drinks and a cabinet full of liquor, plucking a glass from the stack in the corner. After a questioning glance at Vincent, I set a second glass on the counter. I chose a nice cognac that had been a gift from a client, splashed two fingers of the liquor into each glass. I walked back to the desk, handing Vincent his mid-afternoon taste, as he liked to call it.

Vincent was my antithesis. Vincent had a business degree and an MBA and had made a career as the right hand to the CEO of Pettigrew. He lived in satin-lined designer suits, silk ties, and shiny shoes. He'd never worked on a crew, never worn a steel-toed boot, never scaled the side of a building, never created art with dirt, bricks, cement, and steel. He was all business—proposals and spreadsheets and phone calls, not hard labor. He set foot on a Pettigrew construction site when it was time to cut the ribbon.

It was no secret that he hoped to take over the company when Pops retired. It was also no secret that Pops didn't see it for him and was instead grooming me for the position. True, I wasn't ready to fill such big shoes. But I wasn't ready for Vincent to have an *I told you so* moment, either.

"Pops asked me to handle this deal. He expects me to make it happen. I'm going to do it. I might not do it like you want me to or like he'd do it, but it'll get done. Alright?"

"So, what now?" Vincent asked, smacking his lips after enjoying a few healthy sips from his glass. "When's the next meeting? You'll need to have an upside to tell Saul."

I took my time answering the question. It wouldn't be the answer he was looking for, so there was no sense in rushing it. "We haven't scheduled our next meeting. Miller has been avoiding my calls all day. Hasn't responded to my email. I think he's going soft."

Vincent made a sound, an ominous rumbling from his chest. "That's bad news, son."

I nodded, stroking my beard, sipping my drink. Things would work out. I would make sure they did.

The sun was beginning its descent below the horizon when I pulled into the driveway of my parent's home, a rambling stone structure in a north Atlanta, well-to-do suburb, steps away from the lush greens of Atlanta Golf Club. I hadn't made it good out of the SUV before the front door swung open.

My mother was barely five feet tall, so her sleeveless yellow maxi dress brushed the sidewalk. She grabbed two handfuls and pulled it up as she marched along the brick path from the house to the driveway.

"I was about to call security and have them force you out of the building. You know Saul has to eat on time because of these medications—"

"It's alright, Mom. I'm here." I leaned in to press my lips to a warm cheek. She smelled good, like peaches. "I'm sorry for showing up late. I was on a conference call. I wanted to have something good to report to Pops."

I bent closer and made a show of taking a long, loud sniff. "Did you make peach cobbler?"

She cocked her head back so she could look me in the face, and so I could see her terse expression, but I detected the smile that wanted to bend her lips. "And do you have good news? He's had a nice day, and he doesn't need any stress."

"I know what kind of condition he's in. It's all good news. Now, can we go in because I also smell chicken and red potatoes?" I sniffed again. "Maybe some green beans?"

She laughed and turned back to the house. "Putting that big old nose to good use."

"Using it for its God-given purpose."

My childhood home had looked like the pages of Southern Living for as long as I could remember. The color scheme changed yearly, but purple was Mom's favorite color. This year, the decor was lavender and coral with a mint accent. I once called it purple, green, and pink and got a smack upside the head.

I followed Mom through the house, letting her lead me like I didn't know where I was going. We ended up in the kitchen, the epicenter of family activity. Mom could burn, as the kids say, and she liked to burn at least two if not three times a day. Years ago, Pops surprised her with the Viking range of her dreams. She only watched cooking shows on TV and famous chefs, to her, were rock stars. She would live in the kitchen if she had her way.

"I thought we'd eat out on the patio. Saul is already out there."

She nodded toward the pair of glass doors off of the kitchen and beyond them to the paver patio. A glass table was already set with four places and a sunny sunflower centerpiece. Pops was in his usual chair, content with a book in his hand and a glass of ice water at his elbow. The four outdoor lamps that flanked the table were already lit, casting a glow over him.

"Mom." I turned. "Four place settings."

"Yes. Missy is coming."

An eyebrow shot up. "I can't give him bad news because he can't handle stress, but Missy is coming to dinner."

She handed me a dish of mini ears of corn on the cob. "He wanted to see his daughter. I invited her. She said she would come. I set a place." She lifted her hands in a surrender gesture. "Come on, we're waiting on the corn."

Pops' head rose as I stepped through the patio doors and he slipped a bookmark into the pages. He had been looking well lately. Bright and alert eyes, healthy, deep color, no longer gray and sallow. He was a big man at 6' 6", 300lbs, but the trauma of the heart attack had taken some of his bulk. Over the past few months, he had put weight back on. His silver hair had been cut and lined, and he wore a white Pettigrew polo and jeans.

Pops was all about not looking like an invalid. As soon as he could dress, he refused to wear the pajamas and fleece pants I had bought him. Jeans were as casual as he would go these days.

"Hey, old man. You good?"

"Evening, son." He made a move to stand. I rushed to

him, urging him to sit with a clap to his shoulder. He relaxed again, picking up his water glass for a sip. He smiled as he set the glass back down. "I'm feeling fine. Glad you could come. I've been alone with your mother all day. Torturous."

Mom clicked her tongue while she busied herself around the table. "Do not listen to him. The world's worst patient has been in a mood all day."

"And you're late. She was about to call you a name."

"Those drugs he's on are making him delusional. Come on, Trey. Sit. Eat. Talk with your dad so he can stop talking to me."

I pulled a chair out and sat. Mom dished up a roast chicken breast, red potatoes, and green beans and set it in front of him.

"Tell me about Miller," he said, picking up his fork and a knife. "Weren't you meeting with him last night? And what happened to your hand, son?"

I had taken off the bandages to let the wounds breathe. My mother gaped at my raw knuckles and jumped up from her chair. Then she was hovering, poking, and frowning. "What in the world? Did you hit someone? Are they still alive?"

"It looks worse than it feels. Yeah, he's still alive and hopefully in jail."

I relayed the story to my parents from the brief conversation with the woman at Bistro to her attack and later, finding her wallet and deciding to take it to her.

"Well, I'm sure she was shaken up." My mother was back in her seat and listening to my story with rapt attention. "To have some strange man show up at her house late at night? You're lucky she didn't greet you with a pistol."

I laughed at that. The only pistol Esme Whitaker seemed to have on her was her mouth.

"Anyway, Pops, by the time I finished with the police, Miller had left."

Pops grunted, slamming his fork onto the table. "Trey, if that bid comes out and we don't own Miller–"

"We won't have a chance of winning it. I know."

The constant need to remind me of what was on the line was wearing me thin. Pettigrew was well-positioned to win the construction business for a new county hospital if they could show experience in healthcare construction. We built commercial structures–schools, grocery stores, parking complexes, shopping plazas, the occasional office building. The healthcare field required additional steps to meet codes and guidelines.

Miller's line of work was clinics and hospitals, not only small buildings but state-of-the-art facilities. With his staff's expertise and software, coupled with the Pettigrew name, we were positioned to bust into a new business vertical. I wasn't about to screw that up if I could help it.

"I have good news. I spoke with Miller late this afternoon, and we've rescheduled our meeting. I thought he might have been going soft, but he wants to talk about contracts on Monday morning. We're on track."

At this news, Pops seemed to relax. He picked up his fork and poked two green beans on his plate. "Maybe I should put Vincent on this one. There are other things you could take care of."

Bristling at the suggestion, I bunched up my napkin and tossed it onto the table. "With all due respect, Pops…"

"Vincent's just more of a shark. A closer, if you will."

"You gave this job to me. You told me you wanted me to do it. You wanted my hands in it."

He lifted his glass and sipped from it, then licked his lips as he lowered it back to the table. "I tell you to set up a meeting and get a deal brokered with Miller. You whittle away that meeting time sticking your nose in where it doesn't belong."

"I should have just sat there? That man could have killed her."

"I hope the young lady is appreciative, because if you've cost us thirty million dollars-"

"Trey is right, Saul," Mom interrupted. "We didn't raise him to be a do-nothing type of man. If Pettigrew doesn't get this bid, another one will come along."

The vase of flowers and all the dishes jumped when Pops slammed his fist down on the table. "Dammit! When I start something, I finish it! I want this deal done. If you can't do it, I'll bring in someone who can. Do you understand?"

"Yo. I got it, Pops." I reached for him, clasping his shoulder. "Breathe. You can't get worked up like this."

"Saul, please," pleaded Mom.

Pops inhaled deeply, closing his eyes. The lines across his forehead regressed. "I'm *fine*," he muttered. "I want this shit done, and I don't want to hear excuses."

He paused for a breath and then said, "I thought you made cobbler."

"I'll get you a little. And some frozen yogurt."

Mom rose from her chair, shooting me a dirty glare for half a second before heading back into the house. I watched her pull a pan of golden brown, bubbling cobbler out of the oven, then reach into the cabinet for three bowls. As she opened the freezer door, a willowy figure appeared.

My heart seized in my chest as if I was the one recovering from a heart attack.

Melissa, or Missy, as she liked to be called, had been a charming child, full of personality and boundless energy. She didn't sit still for any length of time. She was disruptive in her classes, aggressive with her friends and classmates, prone to fits of fantasy and then long, sullen, and quiet phases. She rarely slept and often refused to eat, rapidly cycling through moods.

She saw family doctors, then psychiatrists, was prescribed one medication and then another. They treated symptoms and tried to curb behaviors, but Missy was admitted to the children's ward at Brownwood Residential Center in

Birmingham, Alabama. I saw Missy every few months until she turned eighteen when she left Brownwood since they couldn't legally keep her.

Missy found life to be difficult given an extensive treatment plan. She couldn't maintain employment long enough to support herself, so Mom and Dad had been taking care of her. Keeping Missy well was as much a stressor as running Pettigrew had been.

Missy smiled, wrapping her arms around Mom and chatting away. Her hair was wrapped in a brightly colored scarf. She wore a black tank top, a long black skirt, and sandals. She looked much better than she'd looked the last time I had seen her, but that had been at the hospital. Missy didn't deal well, emotionally, with Pops' condition.

She bounced through the door and around the table to throw her arms around Pops as he rose to greet her. He grinned as if he'd opened a million-dollar check and dropped a long, loud smooch on her cheek.

"How's my baby girl?"

"I'm fine, Pops." She grinned, pulling at her hair. "Sorry, it's been so long. I've been busy."

"Busy? You?" I couldn't resist lobbing the question across the table.

She smirked, taking the seat across from me. "Hello, Trey."

"Missy. How are you?"

She dished up a plate of now cold chicken, potatoes, beans, and corn. Mom came out of the kitchen to take the plate and warm it up. "I'm alright. I'm on a new cocktail of meds. My psychiatrist seems to think—"

"You know you have to take them, on schedule, for them to work, right?"

Her lip curled as she shot an ugly look across the table. "Don't start with me, Trey. I'm doing the best I can."

"A familiar refrain. You don't do much but spend our

parent's money. The least you could do is check on your father and not have to be summoned to dinner."

Missy stood, leaning across the table, pressing her palms into the glass. "Fuck you, perfect son, who's never had to deal with anything tougher than a hangnail in his life. You have no idea what it's like to live with this illness—"

"Trey. Melissa." Mom eyed us both with a nod toward Pops, who was already digging into a bowl of warm peach cobbler and a dollop of frozen yogurt. Friday night was the only night Mom would allow him dessert, and he wasn't squandering his portion.

I backed down, opting to keep the peace for Pops' sake.

A few hours later, I took my leave, giving Pops a hearty handshake and dropping a kiss on Mom's cheek. I climbed into the driver's seat of my SUV and started it up. My eye caught a flash of a card stuck in the cupholder. I picked it up and turned on the interior lights.

Esme's Costco Membership Card. It was the only card, besides her driver's license, that had a photo on it. I had used it to verify that the wallet belonged to the woman involved in the altercation in the parking lot at Bistro. I should have put it back into her wallet, but I forgot. Besides, it was expired, so I didn't figure she'd miss it.

My mind traveled back to the encounter the evening before. Her eyes were full of fire, and her mouth full of sass. Full lips, cocoa skin, expressive eyes, and a body that reminded me I hadn't had a date or anything close to romance since before I took over Pettigrew had my rapt attention.

I fingered the card, rubbing my thumb over the image encased in plastic. I wasn't vain, but I saw my face every day. Rugged, a little more handsome than the next guy, warm eyes, friendly smile, thanks to two years of Invisalign, and a growing wardrobe of fashionable pieces that GQ said a metropolitan man in power should have in his closet.

I looked the way I'd aimed to look when I put effort into

evolving myself. I had spent a considerable amount of time and money molding my body from an unremarkable, average shape to a physique that I was proud of.

I worked too hard to go unnoticed. I laughed a little, remembering the way her eyes flared and her lips pursed when she spat scathing sarcasm at me. She'd noticed. She didn't *want* to notice, but she had.

I turned off the interior lights, put the truck in reverse, and backed away from my childhood home.

"Suit yourself, Ms. Whitaker."

CHAPTER FOUR

Esme

I lounged on O'Neal's bed, watching him pack for another trip. His ability to squeeze so much clothing into a miniature suitcase was a real-life game of Tetris. Aside from the uniform that he wore on the aircraft, he picked out a few extras for a mid-week excursion, a fringe benefit of a career with an airline.

"How many days this time?"

"Seven. Tuesday, I work LAX to Milan." He stopped packing long enough to gloat. "Then three days off. I'm trying to meet up with a baddie at MXP. She doesn't speak much English, and I don't speak any Italian, but I know *yes, more* and *harder* in every language."

"You have a girlfriend in Milan?"

'Hell no, I ain't got no girlfriend." He gave me the usual side-eye before heading back into his closet. He pulled out a pair of North Carolina blue track pants that looked amazing against his deep skin tone. "The ladies love O'Neal Whitaker.

France, London, Greece? I love Greek women, and they love Black men."

"You know you're a fuckboy, right?"

He ignored me as I leaned back against his pillows, being careful not to drip water from the ice pack onto his bedding. I'd called in sick after all and hoped to get the swelling to go down by Monday. I did not want to be the center of attention and the subject of office gossip.

"Where else do you have "baddies" waiting for you to hit a couple of days of layover time?"

O'Neal removed the leisurewear from the hanger and folded it into a tidy square before squeezing it into his bag. "If Delta flies there, I got a Boo there. I text to let them know when I'm coming through." He shrugged, so nonchalant about worldwide hookups. "If we can get together, we get together."

"And by get together, you mean–"

"Just what I said. Get. Together."

He turned back to the closet, this time surveying his collection of footwear. O'Neal loved shoes — designer slides, Italian leather brogues, the latest Jordans, and more pairs of casual footwear from his favorite designer, Bruno Magli, than I could count spilled over from his closet storage system onto shelves that lined the walls.

"I keep telling you, Es. It's a good gig. I can still get you on."

I shook my head without even thinking about it. "You know I need one foot on the ground at all times."

O'Neal frowned at me. "You could do it. You don't want to."

"No, I can't. There's a difference."

"You'll forget you're even in the air. If something was gonna happen–"

"Aht! Stop!" My free hand shot out in front of me as if that could guard me against the words he was about to say. "I

34

don't know how you can even get on a plane. My parents are in an RV, and I'm nervous about that, let alone in a plane."

"Your parents are fine. How are you the only one in your family that has never been on an airplane?"

"I was on an airplane once," I mumbled.

I reached for a decorative pillow that coordinated with the brown and cream palette of O'Neal's room. I leaned onto it, seeking relief for my arm, which was tired from holding an ice pack to my face for hours.

"You mean that time our families tried to go to Disney World together? And you screamed bloody murder as soon as the pilot pushed away from the gate. Your mom had to get off the plane with you."

"Shut up. I was scared!" I protested but laughed along with O'Neal. It was funny now. When I was six years old, not so much.

"Aunt Carol had to put you on Amtrak. You didn't show up for two days!"

"Whatever." I lobbed a pillow at O'Neal, giving him plenty of time to duck, then retrieve it from the floor and toss it back. "It was a pleasant ride."

"You are too old to have never flown, Esme. You are too old to have never done a *few* things."

His eyebrows rose and his mouth curved downward into a disapproving line.

"Don't start. It'll happen when it's meant to happen."

"At what point can it happen if you run eligible men out of the house?"

I groaned. "Don't start with that, either."

"Look, I'm impressed that you even went out on a date because you do nothing but work, watch TV, and read books. How are you going to meet someone with your nose in a book?"

"I go to the bookstore. I might meet a book lover."

O'Neal dropped a pair of Magli and Adidas into his

suitcase before heading to the bathroom to retrieve his shaving kit. "Listen, the other night was a lot, I know. But that man not only took out your attacker, but he also drove all the way out here to bring your wallet to you."

"He could have dropped it in the mail. Left it on the doorstep. Gave it to the police. You don't even know that it was out of his way." I shifted, as my arm was falling asleep again. "I bet he thought he was getting something for his trouble."

O'Neal rifled through his shaving kit for a few seconds before zipping it and tucking it into the full compartment. "Would that have been so bad? He was funny. He's got some style. And he was flirting with you, Esme. Hard."

"You wouldn't be begging me to give him a chance if you were with me at Bistro."

"From what you told me, Es, you were rude, too. Don't act like you don't have Resting Bitch Face."

"I do not have–"

I stopped protesting when O'Neal snapped his fingers at me. "You *do*. He was probably very polite when he asked if he could take the chair. How was he supposed to know that you got stood up?"

"I thanked him. What else was I supposed to say?"

"He was flirting too hard for you to run him out of here the way you did. Couldn't you offer him a little something? As a reward for saving your life?"

At that, I rolled my eyes. "I should fuck him because he brought my wallet over here? He did not save my life, O'Neal."

"You can fuck him for no reason if that's what you want to do. But it doesn't matter; you could have been warmer to him. You ice men out, Es."

He zipped the carryon case closed and flopped down to lounge next to me, stuffing the pillow I had thrown behind his back. "Remember when your parents sold you this house, and

I moved in to brighten your life? We said that you'd take this time to get out there, to let your younger, handsome cousin show you how to get social..."

"My younger, handsome cousin got me out there. I got social. I joined a dating website and got mugged. Why should I keep listening to you?"

"It was *one* date." He sat up, resting on one elbow. "You're scared of men now?"

"No, I'm not scared of men! I work with men, I'm friends with men, I *live* with a man."

"Don't get loud with me. Cousins don't count."

"Whatever. I love men. I don't have to be nice to that one."

"You gotta figure some things out, Cousin. That mentality will keep you from living life and accepting people into your world. Your entire existence is Shonda Rhimes TV shows. Shonda can't write your future."

"See, that's where you're wrong. She'd do an outstanding job writing my future."

O'Neal took any opportunity to rant about my lack of life experiences. I was the complete opposite of my thrill-seeking cousin. There were so many things I'd never done.

Fly in an airplane.

Swim in the ocean.

Have sex.

Not that I'd never seen a man that made my entire body thump. Trevante Rhodes walks among us. Being the baby of the family and somewhat of an awkward, unfortunate-looking duckling until I was well into adulthood meant that I bloomed late in life.

I was in my twenties before I grew into my "negro nose" and, at the urging of my older sisters and cousin, began investing in my skin and doing more with my hair than tucking it under an unimpressive wig or pulling it into a bun. When I earned my MBA, my family gave me cards to several clothing stores, gifting me thousands of dollars. I roped my friends into helping me shop to accentuate a large bust, thick thighs, and a high, round ass.

"You dress like Whoopi Goldberg," O'Neal had declared, right before he swept all of my roomy, floor-length kaftans into a bag. He was so happy to drop them off at Goodwill.

My closet was now bursting with dresses made of rich, indulgent fabrics that flattered instead of hid my shape and pants tailored to fit. My drawers were full of the softest, frilliest things that had ever touched my skin. What I couldn't do to my coils and now unblemished skin, my sister, Jada, could handle at her salon.

I was coming into my own at work, too. I'd been promoted to Senior Contracts Administrator at Benning Mergers & Acquisitions Consulting, which didn't bring much prestige, but it meant more money, more responsibility, and that they could assign me to bigger and more lucrative case profiles. My boss was an ass, but I could handle him. I hoped that I could prove my worth and move out of his department.

The last leaves of my bloom had everything to do with my heart, and, by consequence, my body. I guarded my energy fiercely and waited to have sex for a defined reason. I didn't want to give any part of myself to someone who wasn't invested. I refused to get close to someone who didn't genuinely care for me. Boys in high school and young men in college were more concerned with getting off than my self-worth.

The longer I said no, watching men be cool with walking away instead of finding out how they could hear a different answer, the easier it became to say no. And here I was, about to turn 40, and still saying no.

I was afraid, but not in the traditional sense. Sex didn't scare me. I was, in fact, primed for it, more than ready to meet *him* if he was a handsome specimen that produced lusty thoughts and ride him over the virginal rainbow. I just didn't want that ride to be all about him.

My fear lied in meeting a man who didn't know or care what it meant to share a deeply intimate part of myself with him. And until I met him, the answer would have to be no.

O'Neal wasn't wired that way and would never understand.

"Did you watch last week's Insecure yet?" I asked, desperate to change the subject. "I've been waiting for you to be home so we can watch."

He was already getting up. "Yeah, then I have to get in the bed. I have a 6 AM flight. Will you pop some popcorn?"

CHAPTER FIVE

Esme

The voicemail indicator on my desk phone pulsed as I got to my cube on Monday morning. My box was usually empty, so something big was happening, and I was already behind.

I dropped into my chair and lifted the phone handset, tucking it between my shoulder and ear while reaching for the keyboard to log onto the network.

"Esme! I've been looking for you. You're needed in the Great Room. Right away."

Reese, my boss' assistant, stood outside my workspace, prim and proper in a dark pantsuit and three-inch heels. Her long hair was twisted into its usual chignon, and her jewelry, as always, was understated. Pearls today.

I glanced up, voicemail droning in one ear. The Great Room? That was the big conference room at the opposite corner of the floor, decorated in overly southern tones. I was definitely behind.

"I just got in. I was out Friday, and I'm catching up–"

"No time," she barked. "Grab a notepad."

I took the advice, swiping a half-used pad and a pen from a jar I kept at my desk before following Reese through the hallway to the other side of the suite. The partners and senior staff worked in plush offices and meeting spaces, not cookie-cutter cubicles where they expected the contracts staff to pump out paper.

Though they had promoted me, I still did the heavy lifting of detailing the pertinent points of an acquisition, whether it was a friendly coming together or a hostile takeover. Partners didn't care what I learned in my MBA track, or what I'd read that morning in a business journal. I was a highly paid clerk, which got under my skin.

"What's this meeting about?" I whispered, keeping pace with Reese's long strides. She was 5'10" in stocking feet, most of which was muscled, runner's legs. "I didn't have time to listen to my voicemail."

"An acquisition," she answered. "The client wants to keep it friendly if he can help it. There are millions of dollars on the line if this doesn't go through." She smiled, bringing softness to her brusque demeanor and naturally husky tone. "No pressure."

I inched a hand up to feel my face, to make sure the swelling was still undetectable. I had spent the weekend with bags of frozen vegetables pressed against my skin and avoiding O'Neal's not-so-gentle teasing about Trey Pettigrew.

I'd closed my account at BlackSinglesMatch as soon as I'd made it back to my computer that night. I wouldn't be going back online soon. As I had told the investigating officer from the local police department, I wouldn't be prey ever again if I could help it.

That included even thinking about a man that could joke about my black eye.

I purged all thoughts of Thursday night and the incident from my mind as I pulled open the conference room doors.

My boss, Ethan Byron, and a guest were seated at one end of the long table, casually chatting with porcelain coffee cups and saucers in front of them. Scattered across the table were stacks of binders and manila folders stuffed with documents.

"Gentlemen," I greeted them as they stood, nodding to Ethan before extending a hand to our guest, a salt and pepper haired man with sparkling blue eyes, a George Clooney-like appearance and a firm grip. Ethan waved me toward an empty seat.

"Esme, meet Thomas Miller, President of Miller Design. He is negotiating an acquisition. He wants to make sure he's working from a power position."

I nodded as he continued unfurling the events to date. When he finished, I swiveled my chair toward Thomas Miller, who had contributed clarifying details to the overview.

"Esme is one of our senior associates," Ethan said. "I think this project would be a great proving ground for her. Should be cut and dry, but if it isn't, she'll know how to work you through it."

"Was the deal always contentious?" I asked Thomas.

"Not at all," he replied, lips pursed while he shook his head. "I began work with the CEO earlier this year when we got the news that a bid was coming down the pipe for a 328-bed facility. That's a large project for the design alone. And we don't build, so we'd have to subcontract the construction. I reached out to a potential buyer to gauge their interest in purchasing my company in the efforts to jointly submit for this bid."

Miller paused, picked up his coffee cup, and drained it. The cup wasn't back in the saucer more than a few seconds before Reese swept in to fill each cup, including mine. When I caught her eye, she winked at me.

"When the senior Pettigrew fell ill, I put this deal to bed, in my mind. Then I got a call that his son had picked up the reins, and he'd be continuing the deal if I was still amenable.

We'd use Miller experts to expand their design department, use their team to construct what we design. Should have been a beautiful marriage of companies."

I didn't hear much past the familiar name. "Did you say Pettigrew? As in Trey Pettigrew?"

His eyes lit up. "Any history with them?"

"Let's just say that we're acquainted."

Miller pushed a frustrated sigh through thin lips. "Trey is difficult. Argumentative, a stickler for a certain price point. It seems like he's trying to impress his father, and I'm not interested in that performance. We can do great work as one company, but I want my team taken care of. Most of them have been with me since the beginning. That's where you come in."

"Of course," I responded, with a solemn nod of my head. "Concessions should be made to compensate furloughed employees. Offers should be made for severance and health care continuation, and then there's the subject of shares and–"

"You're speaking my language." Miller smiled, which brightened his face. If I wasn't mistaken, his shoulders sagged a bit in relief. "Let's get together and hammer out the salient points. I'd like to carve out space for you at our offices. Vinings is twenty minutes from town on a good traffic day, and we never have a good traffic day. Pettigrew drives to my office for our meetings."

I glanced at Ethan. Junior associates could not work offsite, and though I'd been recently promoted, this was my first project in my promoted role.

"Of course, Thomas," Ethan offered without hesitation. "Whatever you need, for as long as you need it."

"Or until the retainer checks bounce." Miller chuckled, then checked his watch. "Speaking of bad traffic days, I've got a meeting. I'm afraid I need to leave now to make it on time."

He stood, reaching for the suit jacket he'd shed, and hung on the chair behind him. "I've requested your full-time help, so you'll report to my office in the interim. We'll set you up with access and a space to work. I can have my assistant send directions."

I stood and offered Miller a parting handshake. "I was in that area for drinks last week. I'm sure I can find Miller Design."

He slipped into his jacket, smoothing down the lapels. "What restaurant?"

"Bistro," I answered. "Do you know the place?"

His expression darkened as soon as the word left my mouth. "Know it? I witnessed a mugging last week, right in the parking lot."

My heart thumped a beat so hard that it almost threw me back into my seat. Thomas Miller had been at Bistro the night I was attacked. That meant that Trey had been meeting with Miller when he tried to take my chair. And that he left that meeting, leaving multiple millions on the table, to rescue me.

I almost... *almost* felt bad about how much Pettigrew money I was about to spend. But not enough to turn down the job.

Was I interested in dating Trey? Not really.

Was I interested in spending Trey's money and making him come correct? Oh, *absolutely*. This would be fun.

"See you in the morning, Mr. Miller. We're going to make a great team."

As soon as Thomas Miller left the room, I turned to face Ethan. His cheerful, easy-going demeanor had disappeared, and the stone face with the ever-present divots of irritation between his eyes had replaced it.

"Was this assignment your idea?"

"I think we both know that it wasn't." He scoffed, scowling.

"What aren't you telling me? What's going to trip me up?"

"You've been in and out of human resources, whining about the opportunities we haven't given you. Now you're whining about an opportunity to serve as a senior consultant. Do you want the project or not?"

"Ethan, I'm just asking–" His expression told me that any argument would be a waste of my time. I threw up my hands in defeat. "I'll do what I can to close it."

"Just do the job, Esme. Mind your business and write the contract so Thomas can close his deal." He stood and buttoned his jacket before stepping around the table. "And don't fuck this up by thinking too much."

CHAPTER SIX

Trey

Weekends were for resting, but my mother had me at the house and in the yard, completing the honey-do list she'd normally set out for my father.

Like many middle-class families, I didn't grow up with maids to do the housekeeping and staff to manage the garden. Though my parents could be considered wealthy now, they were set in their ways and mired in routine. They set aside every other Saturday for taking care of the outside of the house. Mowing the lawn, weeding the garden, washing the windows, spraying down the driveway, painting the garage door.

More than once, I offered to pay for someone to take care of things for them, but they wouldn't hear of it, so I took it as a compliment that they wanted to see me and trusted me to do things around the house since Pops couldn't do it.

I also used it as an excuse to get a home-cooked breakfast.

I did so little resting that by Monday morning, I was beat,

so I was relieved to receive an email that rescheduled my early Monday meeting with Miller Design to Tuesday morning.

I slept late, lounging in bed for a few extra minutes with a cup of coffee and my tablet. I liked to check the newspapers, the markets, and any personal email before starting my day.

Pops' words from dinner on Friday night had rolled through my head all weekend, like a record player on skip. I could not fail to bring this deal home. I spent Monday locked in my office, my desk line on Do Not Disturb, getting all of my ducks in a row, all of my talking points laid out.

When I strolled into Miller Design at the stroke of nine o'clock on Tuesday, I was more than ready.

I stopped at the front desk and signed in, then headed for the locked door that separated the offices from the reception area. The receptionist usually buzzed me through, and I went to Miller's office.

"Oh, actually," she said, her mousy brown curls springing around her face as she stood. "Mr. Miller requested that you wait here. He'll come to get you when he's ready for your meeting."

I strode back to the reception desk and stood in front of her. Her gold brushed nameplate read Jenny Collins. The longer I studied her, the more uncomfortable she became until she reached back for her chair and resumed her seat.

"Jenny, is it?" She nodded. "Mr. Miller set a meeting for 9 AM. I am here. I am never, ever late and yet I'm told that I'll be…" I waved a hand casually in her face. "Waiting until he's ready to see me? Just hanging out here in the waiting area like I'm an average vendor and not a potential buyer. That's the situation?"

"Yes, sir," she replied. "That's the situation."

So, it's like that.

Miller was making a play for power, first by moving our meeting, then making me wait. I urged myself to remain neutral, to not play the game. It wouldn't give him any points. I was writing the check. Whether or not Miller wanted to admit it, the control was on the Pettigrew side. I was ready to use all available resources to bring the companies together, with or without Miller's help.

I turned on a heel and headed to guest seating, a gathering of chairs that were modular and sterile in design. Miller thought his interior decorating skills were avant garde and chic industrial. It was boring and dry. White, steel, wood. Boring.

Pops thought a leader should stand out. Be bold. Make yourself seen and heard. Pettigrew signs were a bright yellow, an unmistakable icon on top of the refurbished factory that housed the business; a beacon of pride outside of any construction site.

The locked door clicked and swung open. Miller strolled through it, wearing a gray suit that matched the color of the walls. His slim build moved toward me, a hand outstretched. Thomas wasn't one to raise his voice or speak out of turn. Like his building and his taste in décor, he was plain and unemotional.

The guy creeped me out, honestly. No one was that calm, especially when someone was trying to take over your company.

"Sorry to keep you waiting. I had a last-minute meeting." He gripped my hand and pumped it a few times before he began guiding me toward the door. "You know the drill."

"I'm hoping we can hammer out these details you're stalling on. My father is not pleased with how long this has been dragging out."

Instead of walking us to his office, Miller was strolling down one hallway, up another, to a side of the building I'd never visited before.

"I agree. I'm eager to get things wrapped up." He stopped in front of a closed door and grinned, his eyes sparkling. My gut twisted with foreboding. "I'd like to introduce you to someone."

The door swung open, and Miller stepped inside the room, blocking the view. I dropped my briefcase into the nearest chair, expecting to shake the hand of a board member, an attorney... hell, he could have introduced me to Chuck E. Cheese, and I'd have been less surprised than to see Esme Whitaker seated on one side of the table.

Esme stood and offered a hand across the table. "Mr. Pettigrew. How nice to see you again."

My mind went blank at the moment that I saw her. Her hair in a bun, her full lips a deep red, her dress a short sleeve, rose and heart print that clung to her shape like... *Mmmph.* It was so nice to see her again.

I had been so used to her face popping up in my mind with a frown on her thick lips that I was taken aback at her smile. Sarcastic as it was, it was prettier in person than it was on the card I had taken from her wallet.

I glanced at her outstretched hand and hesitated long enough to see her smile falter. Then I bit out a laugh and took her hand in mine, giving her a friendly squeeze. I didn't know why she was standing in front of me, but my day had just become interesting.

"Ms. Whitaker," I greeted her. "An unexpected pleasure."

The lines of confusion across Miller's forehead were comical. "You said you didn't know Mr. Pettigrew."

"We met briefly last week," Esme offered. "He rescued me from the attacker at Bistro."

Miller's face brightened, then frowned, deep lines forming between his eyes. He sank into a chair. "That was you? So you... are you alright?"

"I'm fine," she answered. "And ready to work." She sat, then clicked a pen and hovered the tip over a blank page in her notepad. "Shall we?"

Miller cleared his throat and pushed his chair forward.

"Trey, I've retained the services of Benning Mergers & Acquisitions Consulting. I don't want to leave anything on the table. No loopholes. Ms. Whitaker will work with you to paper a deal that benefits both sides. I've made my negotiable and non-negotiable terms clear. I expect I'll be conferencing with her from time to time."

He clasped his hands, gazing at me with an arrogant stare that made my fists clench, then throb. I wanted to pound on Thomas Miller like I'd pounded on Esme's assailant last week.

"Once the bid comes out, we'll take some time to put together a proposal and submit. So long as we paper our deal before then, we're in the clear. If we don't have an agreement on terms before we submit…"

Miller unclasped his hands to spread his arms and hunched his shoulders in a helpless gesture. "We have no deal. I can't waste more time on this. Miller won't go under if we don't get to the proposal stage. Neither will Pettigrew. I won't sign an agreement that isn't beneficial on my end. I've spoken to my board of directors, and they're not inclined to sell the company over my objection. This is your last chance to pull this deal together, or it goes down the drain."

I fixed my gaze on Esme. The upturn of her lips was a dead giveaway—she was enjoying this. Not only was she working for the other side, but the knowledge that she stood between Pettigrew Construction and a lucrative contract must have turned her crank.

I unclenched my jaw, glanced at Miller, then at Esme and back to Miller. I gave a single, resolute nod.

"Let's get started."

Vincent's high pitched hyena laugh carried out of his office and, I was sure, down the hall to the offices of the other company executives and the area where our Executive

Assistants worked. I didn't see what was so funny, but as I joined Vincent in his office for our afternoon taste, his laughter had risen from an amused chuckle to a brash, loud cackle.

"So, to recap," he got out amid gusts of laughter. "You met this woman last week when you played Captain America. Come to find out, she's working with Miller? Boy, you don't have no kind of luck!"

He slapped his knee and wheezed. I worried that he'd stopped breathing for a few moments. He pulled at his tie, loosening it at the neck while taking a healthy swig of Scotch.

"Are you done?"

"Sorry, sorry." He brought his glass to his lips and tipped it back while he tried to regain composure. "I'm trying to imagine you working with this woman who isn't your biggest fan to start with. Then having to update Saul when you tank this deal because she's got a vendetta against you."

"It's not a vendetta," I argued, pointing with my glass. "It's a misunderstanding."

"Mmmmm," he hummed while he sipped more liquor. "She didn't misunderstand that you thought you had turned on the charm, and instead, you turned on the hose."

"Don't you have any work to do, Vincent?"

"Your father asked me to keep an eye on you. I'm doing my job right now. We should have nipped this in the bud last week. Speaking of Saul, what are you going to tell him?"

I got up and paced the space between Vincent's desk and the windows, squinting into the rays of the evening sunset. I'd come back to Pettigrew after my meeting with Esme and Miller and headed straight for Vincent's office to download the day's events.

"I'm not going to tell him anything," I announced.

"Not your best idea, Trey."

"I'll tell him when we're about to file ownership papers. It'll be a funny story about a bump in the road."

He turned, leaning forward and grasping the edge of his desk. "Trey…"

"It's well and good for you to want to stress my father out, but I'm not going to do it. Not a word. He'll get worked up, and I'll never hear the end of it from my mother."

Not to mention that he wasn't impressed by my heroics, claiming I'd stuck my nose in where it didn't belong instead of following orders. If he heard that last week's distraction was working to Miller's benefit, it might send him back to cardiology. After which, he would throw me off of the project, if not out of the company. And destroy any hope for my future.

CHAPTER SEVEN

ESME

"O 'Neal, when you get out from under... or over... or... out of... dammit, when you're unentangled, call me! I have an update you will not believe. I hope you're having a good time!"

SiriusXM Hot 100 tuned back in when I pressed the end key on the steering wheel. I was still giggling about my day. I had been prepared to work into the night, but soon after Thomas left us to our negotiation, Trey picked up his copy of the proposed agreement and said he'd take it to his office to read and make notes.

"I'll be in touch," he said, before stalking from the room and down the hall. A few minutes later, Thomas came back.

"Well. That was interesting." I relaxed, leaning back in the cool leather chair. "How do you gauge his reaction to the wrench you've thrown into the process?"

"I knew he'd be unhappy. I don't know what the repercussions will be. He might pull out."

"Hmmm..." I mused, thinking it over, then shaking my head. "He'd have given up already if he could."

"You're right." Miller paused, then smiled, but he tried to tamp down his apparent joy. "Senior must still run the show from his sickbed."

"I'd say that you should expect something underhanded, but you've already predicted that he'd try to go around you. Knowing that he can't go above you to buy out the company was the final blow."

Thomas nodded, rubbing his bottom lip with his thumb, his forehead creased. "I hope you're right. I want this deal, but only if we do it the right way, which isn't the cheap way."

"I agree." I closed the lid of my laptop and began gathering up notes, files, and supplies. "I expect Pettigrew to come back tomorrow with a marked-up document. And he'll be ready to fight."

"Are you ready to fight?" Asked Thomas. "I watched that attack last week."

"No worries, Mr. Miller," I assured him. "I'm fine and ready to fight."

"Good. Very good." He nodded, then pumped his fist before walking out of the room.

I had stopped at the neighborhood grocery, put away the food, and was putting together a homemade pizza when O'Neal returned my call from his hotel room in L.A. I waited until he left on a trip to do the grocery shopping, because while we split the grocery bill and shared food, O'Neal ate more in a day than I ate in a week and somehow stayed slim enough to rock the hell out of that Delta uniform.

"Was he surprised? What did he say when he saw you? Were you nice to him, Es?"

"I think it shocked him to see me. And I was very nice," I

added. I sprinkled a few diced vegetables around a pre-made crust covered in sauce and a layer of cheese. " I was cordial. Polite. Businesslike."

"You mean dry. You didn't give him anything to work with."

"He said it was nice to see me again."

"I told you that man was flirting with you. Was he nice to you?"

"He was ok. I think he's used to getting his way, and Miller isn't rolling over."

"Just remember... eventually, this deal will be over. Think about what comes after that and treat him accordingly. Don't kill the vibe."

I laughed. "What vibe?"

"The *I need a man* vibe!"

I laughed again. "Technically, I don't need a man."

"You're right. *Technically* you need dick."

I opened the oven door and slid my pizza inside. I shut the door, then set the timer and settled onto a stool at the counter with a glass of Stella Rosa that I liked and didn't cost me $20.

"You're talking like I'd let him get near me."

"You don't have to date him, Esme. You just need him to do a job."

"I don't want to *not* date him, either. I don't need a fuck buddy."

"Why are you trying so hard to be difficult, Es?"

"Why are you dictating who I should fuck? You've never thought twice about anything? You're just... fearless, out in these streets?"

"Fearless, my ass. I'm a Black man in America. Fear is a feeling, and I don't live by it. I do what I want."

"I'm never going to believe that you get scared, bungee jumper. Roller coaster rider. Airline attendant. You love giving up control and letting whatever happens happen. I can't live like that."

"Because I don't see it as giving up control. Yeah, I get scared. And then I get over it. I get up and get on that plane every day, knowing it could be my last flight. I take control. I don't let fear keep me from a great job that I love. And the benefits I love more."

His sinister cackle made me laugh.

"By the way, I won't be over, under, inside my Italian Baddie until Wednesday. Tonight, I'll be with Roxane."

"Who's Roxane?"

"A honey I met on the leg from Houston to LA. She has a long layover, so we're going to… layover."

"Well, damn, player. Is she cute?"

"Puppies are cute. Kittens are cute. This girl? Nah, shit. This *woman*? She's got those Michelle Obama arms. You know what I mean?"

"I tap out when you bring the forever First Lady into your sexcapades. So you're going out with Roxane tonight, then spending three days with what's her name in Milan?"

"Giorgi is her name. But yeah, I'm kicking it with Roxane tonight. We're about to get something to eat. Before I get a bite to eat, know what I mean?"

"O'Neal!" I scolded through laughter. "I'm telling your mother."

"She don't wanna hear your gossip about her baby boy. But for real, though, Es. You don't have to jump out of an airplane or anything but decide that you're going to stop being scared of shit. Make it a goal, or a part of that intention setting thing you do. Make a list of things you need to stand up to before you turn forty. Find a way to live your life."

"Eh. I will think about it."

"Mmhmm. I feel you rolling your eyes at me through the phone line. I nag because I care."

"Yeah, yeah," I responded, though I was rolling my eyes. "Love you. Fly safe and wear condoms."

"Always, Cousin. Love you."

We signed off, and I pulled the earbud from my ear. While waiting for the pizza to cook, I basked in the silence of the house since O'Neal was gone. He had been getting on me a lot lately about all the things I'd never done.

I asked him to do so, but he didn't have to go that hard.

I had never been to Six Flags over Georgia because I was afraid of roller coasters and heights.

I didn't go to waterparks or the ocean because I couldn't swim. I couldn't swim because I was afraid to go underwater. O'Neal had even offered to take me on a buddy pass to an exotic locale of my choosing, but I couldn't muster up enough courage to get on an airplane.

Ten things I've never done, I mused.

I reached for a notepad near the phone and humored O'Neal and myself. I already knew what number one would be… so I started at ten.

Twenty minutes later, I munched on pizza and went over my list.

Then laughed at it, tore it off of the notepad, and shoved it into my pocket because that list would never see the light of day. When O'Neal was home next week, I would show him, and he'd be proud. I would pretend to be ready to knock some of them off. Then he would leave on another international flight, or he'd be occupied by another woman, and we would let the conversation fade into the atmosphere like always.

After dinner, I put away my leftover pizza. I loaded my plate and wineglass into the dishwasher before heading upstairs. Aside from the usual creaks and moans of an old house, it was dark and quiet. Just how I loved it.

I hit the second-floor landing and walked down the hall, touching each of the photos that my mother had left hanging on the walls. Portraits of my sisters, twins who were ten years older than I was, my parents, our extended family, including O'Neal and I were evenly spaced visual mementos of the Whitaker family.

My parents had planned for one more child after my twin sisters, but despite trying for several years, nothing happened. As soon as they'd settled into parenting and had considered childbearing days to be over... *oops*.

I could admit that I was a spoiled baby and an overprotected child. By the time I was old enough to want things, my sisters were old enough to indulge the baby. I played the baby of the family card expertly. I wasn't naturally adventurous, and they never pushed me to explore.

Raising two children had taught my parents a few things. Namely, that they were tired. So the easier my life was, the easier their lives were. But working hard for things builds character and I learned early that the easiest way to not make mistakes was to not take risks.

Which is how I had ended up with a ridiculous list of things I had never done and was too afraid to try.

In the past few years, though, my life had changed. Encouraging my parents to sell their house to me, and the chain of convenience stores they owned to a conglomerate, then buy that RV they'd been eying for years, and take the tour of the country that they had always dreamt of taking were among the first steps.

Soon after I bought the house and my parents set off on their cross-country adventure, I invited O'Neal to move in. He was always in the air, and it didn't make sense for him to have an apartment. And I wouldn't have to live in a big house by myself.

I entered my bedroom, painted a sunny yellow that took up half of the second level of the house. The room used to be smaller, but once Jada and Jewel moved out, my parents had the second level remodeled, expanding the master bedroom. On one end, floor-to-ceiling bookcases and an old but so comfortable chair flanked a gas fireplace that I loved to curl up in and read. Much to O'Neal's annoyance, I was perfectly happy to spend a weekend in the corner of my bedroom, a fire over my shoulder and a book in my hands.

The other side of the room housed furniture— bed, mirrored dresser, five-drawer bureau, TV stand, and a flat-screen TV. If I didn't have to leave my room to eat or go to work, I would live there. This *also* annoyed O'Neal, who was rarely home even if he was in town. If we weren't cousins and hadn't grown up together, I wasn't sure if we would even get along.

I roared a loud yawn, pulling off clothes as I aimed for the bathroom. The folded list that had been my dinner entertainment popped out of the pocket of the jacket I'd worn that day. I picked it up, unfolded it, laughed at it again, and tossed it into my bag.

Maybe I could stand to knock a few easy items off of the list.

I reached into the shower and turned on the hot water, letting the room fill with warmth and steam before stepping under the pulsating shower head. Grabbing a bottle of my favorite gel, I lathered up a bath puff and, as was my habit during my evening shower, reviewed my day, mentally picking out the high marks as I scrubbed the day away.

Trey's face, full of shock and surprise? A high.

I rinsed off, pulling the shower head off of its holder to spray the suds from my legs and feet.

My conversation with O'Neal bubbled up again, and his assumption that I would let Trey Pettigrew do anything to me, let alone share my first sexual experience, since I would sit on the opposite side of the negotiation table, standing between him and several million dollars. Sex would be the last thing on his mind.

Well, it *should* be the last thing on his mind.

I'd be lying if I said it was the last thing on mine.

Damn you, O'Neal.

I pushed away a nagging desire to see Trey outside of that windowless conference room for reasons that had nothing to do with work. It wasn't appropriate to imagine his muscular frame, his long face, his beard, those soulful eyes that seemed to say so much, even more than those lips that might feel nice as they moved down my neck, across my shoulders, down my body...

I shook my head to clear it, but my overactive imagination did not obey the command. I pulsed at the mental image of him kneeling before me, one of my legs hung over his shoulder, the soft curls of his beard tickling my inner thighs. I could almost feel the flutter of his lips against the delicate skin at my core, inching closer to where my heartbeat thumped a powerful rhythm.

The power of the mind was... strong. My daydreams produced images and sounds, causing my body to convulse and a jolt to speed down my spine. My knees buckled so quickly that I reached out for something... anything to hold on to. I nearly pulled the wire shower caddy off of the wall.

In a few moments, I regained my composure. When my lustful fog had cleared, my resolve had returned: Trey Pettigrew was, technically, the enemy.

No matter how many orgasms my daydreams about him produced, I absolutely could not even entertain getting close to him.

CHAPTER EIGHT

Trey

M iller had thrown me for a loop.
I wasn't ashamed to admit that. Not even out loud, as long as I was alone. I hadn't expected an additional person to be added to negotiate terms, let alone the warmth that washed over me when I walked into the room and got an eyeful of Esme.

Esme with the halo of loose curls that had pulled from the bun she always wore.

Esme with the deep brown, silky tone, and the long lashes, and the lips that pursed just so when she smirked at me in that way that said she knew she was under my skin.

Esme, with those patently dangerous curves that carried the feather-light scent she wore.

Esme… who was working with the enemy.

Pops would surely lecture me about trusting people before they'd earned it, about not predicting a sideswipe. I thought we could settle up together, but Miller was more wily and agile than I'd taken him for. I wasn't Saul, who slept, ate, and breathed this business. Miller knew that.

It didn't matter, though. I wasn't a fool, and I never made the same mistake twice.

I returned to my regularly scheduled mornings— a Peloton ride while I watched the sunrise over Atlanta. Time spent reviewing the markets and business news while downing a mug of coffee. After a shower and stepping into a new suit and uncomfortable dress shoes, I arrived at Miller Design before the front doors were unlocked. I was punctual, and I had a point to prove. I could roll with this change, let Miller play this game, think he's winning, and still get what I wanted.

I met Jenny, the receptionist, at the door as she unlocked it, then waited in the lobby for Esme to arrive. While I watched the clock and the parking lot, I reviewed the dog-eared and well-marked copy of the agreement draft. There was room for concession, but a few of the terms that Miller demanded were far different from those presented to Pops. It was nothing I couldn't handle, but it would not make Pops happy.

I stood from my chair and paced the lobby. The unforgiving, industrial concrete floors did nothing to cushion the sharp sound of my shoes clicking as I wandered from one end of the front office to the other. I hoped that I was bothering Jenny so much that she'd call back and let Miller know that I was waiting.

Esme's silver Jetta swung into the lot, coming to a stop in front of the building. She parked and climbed out of the car, pulling the straps of a leather bag over her shoulder. The sight of her in a form-fitting, knee-length grey dress and heels in a coordinating shade did things to me. I gripped the back of a chair and forced myself to breathe.

Inhale. Exhale. *Picked the wrong week to fall in love, bruh. She don't even like you.*

Esme rushed in, all smiles. "Mr. Pettigrew," she said,

extending a hand to me. We shook briefly; I reluctantly released her. "I'm sorry to be so late; I was not expecting traffic to be as bad as it was."

"Call me Trey. You should invest in a GPS device that will give you another route. Might save you some time."

She'd been elbow-deep in her bag, pulling out a mobile phone and a set of keys, but her head snapped up, and a look flashed across her face. Internally, I cringed. I didn't even know her, but I knew that look.

"Don't concern yourself with what I need to be doing, Mr. Pettigrew."

She turned on a heel and marched toward the locked door, whipping out a badge she swiped across the entrance pad. With a beep and a click, the door unlocked, and she pulled it open.

By noon, we had thoroughly irritated one another. Esme and I had come nowhere near agreement on any of the terms that Miller had defined. I was stoic in my arguments; Esme was aggressive in her defense.

"Why not go back to Miller with my proposal? Wouldn't it be easier than arguing every point to death?"

"If Miller was interested in your proposal, he would have accepted it. He wants a better deal, and the final purchase price is lower now. We are moving in the wrong direction."

She exhaled, dropped a pen onto her notepad, propped her elbows onto the table, and her forehead in her hands.

"You and I are going to waste a lot of time arguing the same numbers back and forth. My side isn't budging."

"And neither is mine," she shot back. "Non-negotiable means non-negotiable. Didn't you learn what words mean at whatever fancy school you went to?"

"I'm an idiot because Miller thinks his company is worth twice its actual value?"

"No, you're an idiot because you refuse to move on to items that we can talk about, like—"

"If we don't hammer out these greater details, the lesser items don't matter because we won't have a deal."

"Then I guess you won't have a deal, Mr. Pettigrew."

We had reached an impasse. More like a stalemate. I was tired of circling the same wagon. I'd had nothing but coffee since early that morning, and I was irritable.

I paused, looking for some balance, and pulling the tension from the room before it crackled like lightning. "Can we break? I need to call the office and check-in, take care of a few things. Maybe we can meet back here at—"

I flicked my wrist to bring the face of my watch around.

"Yes. Let's break. See you at one o'clock."

Esme pushed her chair back from the table and stood, grabbed her bag, and stalked from the conference room.

"See you at one o'clock," I mimicked, talking out loud to an empty room. I pulled my phone from my pocket and took her lead, leaving the conference room.

CHAPTER NINE

Esme

The aroma of baked bread drew me a few doors down from Miller to a sandwich shop. I ordered a bowl of vegetable soup and a grilled cheese sandwich and took a seat near the window. I pulled a book from my bag, and when my lunch was ready, a server brought it to my table. I settled in for a few minutes of peace with the third book in a series of thrillers from an author I had recently discovered.

O'Neal would never believe me, but I *was* trying to be nice to the man. It was just that my attraction to Trey was so... *unnerving*. Everything about him, including his striking sense of fashion, turned all of my senses on high. If I hadn't escaped that room, he would have caught me admiring how the custom-tailored jacket in midnight blue hung from his broad shoulders, and how the well-fitting slacks outlined the perfectly formed orbs of his ass.

I wasn't the type to spend a morning staring and daydreaming about running my hands over a man's body, but in the past week, thoughts of Trey Pettigrew had taken up more of my brain space than I wanted to admit. The only thing keeping me from throwing my self-respect to the wind was his insistence on pushing my buttons.

I was no pushover. He tried the cocky, confident man thing on me, and I rejected it. Now I could unclench, bring my shoulders down from around my ears and enjoy a few minutes outside of that windowless room and away from Trey Pettigrew.

I ate soup and took bites from my sandwich, my attention enveloped in *The Janitor*, the latest in a series based on a New Zealand serial killer. Despite every attempt to find him, he was playing mind games with the lead investigator. The weary and hardened detective had taken to confiding in a doddering, mild-mannered janitor at the precinct.

The sound of a chair scraping across the tile and a familiar scent wafting over the table thrust me back to real life.

"A thriller," Trey commented, scooting up to the table. "I figured you for a romance reader." He set an enormous plate of chicken salad sandwich and kettle chips in front of him. Without thinking, I moved my bowl so he would have more room.

Then I stopped and remembered: *He* was crowding *me*. I moved my bowl back to its original position.

"I do read romance. I also read thrillers. And biographies. And self-help, and business –"

"Versatile literary tastes," he interrupted, hiking his brows up at me with a smile. "I like it. A well-read Black woman is incredibly attractive."

Trey centered his plate on the edge of the table and plucked a chip from the overflowing pile. "I love kettle chips. Well, I stan a fried potato, but these? Hot, crispy, fresh from the fryer. Mmmmm." He winked as it disappeared into his mouth, then closed his eyes and moaned as he chewed.

"They're fine, I guess if you don't mind breaking a tooth.

Do you mind, though? I want to get back to my versatile reading habit."

He picked up one half of his sandwich and took a generous bite, licking residual chicken salad off of his lips as he chewed. I tried not to watch, but the way his mouth moved was doing strange things to me.

"Mmmph." He made noises, pointing at my book and chewing, then swallowed. "Let me save you some time because that book drove me crazy when I read it. The janitor is the serial killer."

I blanched, horrified, first, at the idea that the quiet, meek, helpful janitor could be the culprit, right under the nose of the entire investigative team. Then again at how frank Trey had been about giving me that detail. "How... do you know?"

"It's been on the bestseller list for over a month. I'm surprised that you're just now getting around to it."

"This is a new author to me. I wanted to read the other books in the series. Did you just spoil this book for me?"

"No, I gave you a clue. You don't know how it ends or why he's killing." He lifted and lowered his shoulders in a shrug. "Read it. Find out if I was right."

I flipped through pages until I got near the end, then thought better of it and snapped the book shut, tossing it back to the table. I put all of my attention on the bowl of soup and the sandwich, refusing to look up at him, though he was doing the most to get me to notice him.

Crunching chips loudly, he shoved his plate toward my side of the table which forced me to move my bowl.

"Would you stop? I'm trying to eat so we can get back to work."

I bit into my still warm sandwich, the cheese oozing out from the edges. "That looks good," he said. "Is it?"

I nodded, chewing the crunchy, toasted bread and spicy cheese. The cook used pepper jack, which gave the sandwich a nice kick.

"How long have you worked for Benning?"

I smiled as I swallowed. "Is that something you need to know to close this deal?"

"Nah. But since I know what's inside your wallet and your home address, I didn't think it was too personal. How's your face?"

"My face?" My eyes rose to his.

"Your face. Where that guy played rock 'em sock 'em upside your head."

"Do you have to be so crass about it?"

"Do you have to find a problem with everything I say? Damn."

He exhaled, then added, "I'm only asking how you're doing since your attack. You look good. You feel good? How is the swelling?"

"Do you see any swelling, Mr. Pettigrew?"

Trey said nothing for a few beats, rolling his tongue across his teeth, glaring across the table at me. "So…" I was hoping he'd given up, but no such luck. "Is it just me, or are you a bitch?"

My head shot back up. My glare matched his. "Mr. Pettigrew, I suggest you find another table. Otherwise, you're going to be wearing a bowl of hot vegetable soup."

He rolled his eyes, wiped his fingertips with a napkin, then balled it up, and dropped it onto his plate. "I was finished anyway. And by my watch, you have…" He flipped his wrist so the face was visible. "Seventeen minutes to meet me back in the conference room. Don't be late."

His chair scraped as he pushed it back. He stood, grabbed his plate, dumped uneaten chips into the garbage bin, and stacked his plate atop the others before pulling open the glass door and walking out. He passed me on his way back to Miller, but he kept his eyes forward, not daring to glance my way.

O'Neal would beat my ass for that conversation. Trey

brought out another Esme, the version of me that was argumentative and easily offended.

And violent. I had never threatened a person with a dousing of hot soup before.

I picked up my book again. Had he guessed at the ending? Was he teasing, trying to get under my skin? Irritated, I stuffed the book back inside my bag when I realized that he was right. I would have to read the book to find out if he spoiled the ending.

An employee made the rounds, cleaning up the tables near me. She offered to take the empty bowl and a half-eaten sandwich. I nodded, considering I needed to get back to the office.

"Your date was cute," she said with a smile. "Did it go well?"

I smiled up at her, admiring her neat layers of braids, caramel skin, and two deep dimples. "Honey, that was not a date."

Between Trey and Thomas, I was wearing out my heels. My feet ached from walking back and forth with questions, commentary, negotiations. They were getting nowhere. Slowly.

Trey was having more fun than I, peppering me with questions about myself instead of the contract in front of him.

"I'm an Atlanta native. Are you? Or did you transplant from somewhere else?"

"I am a native," I answered. "Rare, I know. Now, Mr. Pettigrew, the contract states you'll provide office space for employees above a job grade three- that looks to be project lead or manager level. Is that agreeable?"

"Do your parents live in the city? Or nearby?"

"My parents are somewhere in North America in an RV

that costs more than my car and is nicer than my house. Considering that I bought my childhood home from them, that's saying a lot."

We actually laughed together, then bent our heads over the contract again. "So, can we discuss additional benefits, like the environmental improvement rider that Miller wants to be included? He offers a stipend to employees who use ride share, carpool, or public transportation like MARTA. Miller was hoping to implement this policy in the new organization."

"That sounds boring," said Trey. "Where did you go to school? What did you major in?"

"My degree is in finance, from Georgia State. I went back for an MBA five years ago. Dare I hope that you want to discuss freezing and not dropping salaries?"

"Nah."

I laughed, finally succumbing to his gentle protest. I checked my watch, surprised at the time. "Oh, wow. It's late."

"It is. You hungry?"

I stretched, bobbing my head from side to side to work out the kinks in my neck, taking in the view of the room from the conference table covered in documents to Trey's notepad covered in doodles but no actual notes.

"Let's call it a night. Can you please come with a *yes* in your pocket tomorrow? It'll make things so much easier."

"I have *something* in my pocket," he quipped. I tried not to laugh but I knew it was coming as soon as the words left my mouth. He seemed the type to have a comeback to anything suggestive. "I asked if you were hungry."

"I have leftover pizza waiting for me." I paused, offering a small olive branch. "I should finish it up but thank you."

"Leftover pizza?" One side of his mouth curled up in mock disgust. "Only college kids eat leftover pizza. Let me buy you dinner. Payback for bugging the shit out of you all day."

"Thank you. Again."

"You don't like for people to do for you, do you?"

My hands, which had been occupied by gathering all of my notepads and pens, not to mention copies of the contract, stilled. "Do for me?"

He leaned in his chair, tipping so he was in a near recline. "You don't like for folks to be nice to you."

"Nonsense." I resumed packing up. "I don't *need* you to be nice to me. That's the difference."

I drew the lid down on my laptop and tucked away my copies of the acquisition contracts. We were on day two of this process, and Trey was being stubborn.

Pettigrew would employ a maximum of 15 Miller employees. Miller wanted guarantees for 20 employees and generous severance.

Miller wanted continued healthcare for furloughed employees because of the transaction. Pettigrew would only offer full benefits for the employees that were being brought over to Pettigrew.

Miller wasn't leaving anyone out in the cold. Pettigrew wasn't in the business of being benevolent, so the idea that he was trying to be nice was laughable.

"One of my boys from college opened this nice steak and sushi spot in Sandy Springs. It's close; on your way home." It bothered me a little that this man I did not know knew where I lived. "Would you care to join me?"

I picked up my bag. "Homemade leftover pizza is calling my name."

"Suit yourself," he said, standing. He walked to the conference room door and opened it, holding it for me. "Missing out on some great food."

"You're easy on the eyes. I bet you can find someone to join you," I shot over my shoulder. "I don't eat sushi anyway."

"Don't eat sushi?" His voice took on a high pitch. I walked toward the front door, refusing to turn around. "Who doesn't eat sushi?"

"Me. I don't eat sushi." I set the alarm, then pushed

73

against the front door to swing it open. The skies were dark, and the cicadas were out, making the evening a little noisy, full of nature sounds.

I twisted my key in the lock and double-checked to make sure the door was secure and that the alarm had switched on. Trey and I walked toward our cars, as we had parked next to each other.

"Why don't you eat sushi? It's good for you. Fish, rice, seaweed."

"It smells like standing water."

"It does not. Have you ever eaten it?"

I shuddered. "Have I eaten food that smells li—"

The tip of my shoe caught a crack in the pavement, and, too late, I tried to correct myself. For the second time in as many weeks, I was sprawled on the pavement.

"You have terrible luck." Trey bent over me, offering a hand to help me up, as he'd done the first time I was knocked off my feet. "Might want to ask the Universe what's up with your *chi* or whatever. Get some kind of aura cleansing."

Embarrassed, tired, ready to go home, I got to my feet without his help. I picked up my bag, which had, once again, spread my life out onto a parking lot. I collected several items and shoved them back inside, double-checking to be sure I had grabbed my wallet this time.

"You straight? I know you can take a hit, but I thought I would ask, anyway."

"I'm fine."

"Oh, wait. You forgot something." He bent to pick up a folded piece of notepaper. "A grocery list?"

Shit! My Never list! I'd thrown it in my bag the other night and now Trey was about to be nosy.

"I'll take that." I marched toward him, hand outstretched.

"Oh, it's not a grocery list. It's a bucket list." He read from the portion of the list that had been unfolded. "Ride a rollercoaster or Ferris wheel." His eyes rose from the page, sheer mirth in them. "You've never ridden a Ferris wheel? There's one right downtown. How old are you?"

"It doesn't matter. Can you... could you hand me that?" I reached for it, but he held it just out of reach.

"Is eat good sushi on this list? You've never had any if you think it smells like putrid water."

"Trey! Could I have that, please?"

"I need to see what else..." He began to unfold the rest of the page. My stress level catapulted to the catastrophic end of measurement.

"Mr. Pettigrew! Give that to me!" I screeched, knowing that my nose flared, and my eyes were wild, but *dammit*, I tried to be nice.

It worked. He folded it closed and handed it over. "Here. You call me Mr. Pettigrew when you get emotional."

"I'm not emotional. I'm pissed."

"Which is an emotion. You're shaking."

I was also in no mood to be psychoanalyzed by Trey Pettigrew. I turned back to my car, unlocked it and flopped inside, dumping my bag on the passenger seat.

Trey stood outside the car, watching me flounce around in anger. "You can call me Trey, you know. And try to be on time tomorrow. Don't take 75; hit the back roads until you get to−"

"You know what you can do, *Trey?*" I punched the ignition button. "Shut the fuck up. Okay? See you tomorrow."

I slammed the car into reverse, pulled out of the space, and changed gears, smashing the gas pedal so hard, the tires squealed.

CHAPTER TEN

Trey

I pushed back a plate of decimated bone-in, medium-rare steak and remnants of the best salmon rolls I'd had in years.

Back at Georgia State, I roomed with Ken Takagi, a biracial man with Black and Japanese heritages. On Saturday nights, our group of friends would find him poring over a carefully constructed imaginary menu, making additions and changes depending on the season. He preferred to cook, and I liked to eat, so our dorm suite always smelled like the most amazing cuisine. His southern fried chicken rolls and variations on ramen were still my favorite dishes.

Ken's complaints about the distasteful food at the Georgia State cafeterias were legendary, but they also spurred his dreams of combining the best foods of his cultures into a fine dining concept. He earned a business degree, then went straight to culinary school, landing a job as a line cook and worked his way up the chain at some of the nation's hottest restaurants while still critiquing food and still inventing dishes.

Tonight, I studied every finely tuned detail of Eito Sushi and Steakhouse. This location was his tenth restaurant opening, but the one that meant the most to him. I beamed with pride while I sat at the bar of thick black marble, ate a sumptuous Kobe beef steak and tangy broccoli salad off of vintage china dishes, sipped sake from a bulbous opaque glass, and monitored the evening's games from several TV's hung above the bar. Business was brisk, but not crazy. Ken was having a great night.

I nodded, more to myself than to keep time with the soft music that flowed from the speakers mounted around the room.

This is a guy that made his dream come true, repeatedly. It could be you, but you're playing.

"I take it you like my place."

I reared back with an outstretched palm and a wide grin for Ken. He glowed with pride, his chest puffed out so far that the buttons might pop off of his shirt. His sandy complexion betrayed a blush, and his dark-as-night eyes danced as they bounced around the room. Ken had traveled widely, building an Eito Sushi and Steakhouse everywhere he went, but Atlanta was home. He put roots down and opened his latest restaurant minutes away from the campus where we'd been roommates and his dream had taken hold.

"Easily my favorite meal this year. Give props to your chef. He's doing his thing back there."

Ken grinned wider, pumping as he squeezed my fingers in his palm. "I hire straight from culinary school and train them like I want them to cook. I don't like breaking bad habits."

I pointed to a plate that was practically licked clean. "He's doing a fine job. How is business?"

Businessman to businessman, I drained my sake, ordered a beer, and traded stories about running our businesses.

"The CEO look suits you," Ken noted, watching the bartender pour another beer from the tap and taking a sidelong glance at my dark jacket, slacks, and tie. "Never thought I'd see you out of khakis and a polo."

"At least I look good. And I'm not doing too bad of a job."

"Maybe you really can carry the Pettigrew mantle."

The lighthearted joke was an attempt to brighten the mood. It would have worked if my day had gone better. As it was, I was grumpy about the state of the deal with Miller Design and frustrated at having a wrench thrown into my plans.

"You could be closer to the truth than you realize," I mused.

"Oh? You had other things in mind, I thought."

"Still the plan. I'm… doing something else right now."

"How long are you going to be doing something else? This is a temporary thing, right?"

I fisted the beer bottle and poured a swallow down my throat before answering. "Pops is hinting like he might not come back to Pettigrew."

"Oh." His expression darkened.

I reassured him with a nod of my head. "He's fine. Healthy, looking good, getting stronger. But the business almost killed him, and Mom is pressuring him to retire."

"And he might take the bait, which leaves you in the driver's seat."

Ken's melancholy tone was a direct reflection of my mood. He understood that if I had to run the company, I wouldn't have time or energy to focus on establishing a new division. I didn't want to assign the job to someone, to have an employee report how well they carried out my dream. I wanted to set it up, to launch it, to run the first few jobs. I wanted to do it myself.

"Pops might have given me an out last week. I've stalled us on an acquisition. He mentioned bringing Vincent in to close the deal."

Ken's thinking pose was to cradle his chin in his palm.

"Maybe it'd be a good move. If he can close it, he can take over Pettigrew, and you can move to residential."

"Sometimes, I think that would be ideal. And then..." I paused long enough that he glanced over at me, the urge to finish my thought in his eyes. "Well, I can't do both, right? If Pops wanted Vincent to take the company, he wouldn't have pulled me from the field to run Pettigrew in his absence. I feel like this is a test."

"A test of what, though? To see if you're a Saul Pettigrew clone? You're not your father, Trey."

I'd been telling myself every morning, noon, and evening that I wasn't my father. If he didn't like how I did his job, he could come back to work.

"I need to see this project through," I told him. "I want to prove that I can do this. Once this acquisition is settled, I'll have his trust. Then I can make my move."

Ken offered a fist. I bumped it.

Not to mention, I told myself, that pulling off the acquisition meant spending more time with a woman that challenged me. I wanted to know more about her.

Now to devise a way to make that knowledge happen.

CHAPTER ELEVEN

Esme

I really hated to admit that he was right, but the shortcut that Trey suggested shaved twenty minutes off of my commute. That left time to swing through Brew Bar, a shop that only sold coffee and coffee-flavored confections.

As I pulled away from the curb with SiriusXM on blast, Drake's low and slow cadence cut out as a call rang through the speakers. The display on the dashboard read *Jewel Simmons.* I pressed the accept button on the steering wheel with the thumb of one hand while maneuvering the straw of my usual drink, a large hazelnut cold brew into my mouth with the other.

"Hey, Jewel," I called out, before sucking down a long sip.

"Hey, baby girl. Whatcha doin'?"

"What do you think I'm doing?"

"Don't answer a question with a question. I wanted to know if you were busy."

"You always call me early in the morning on a weekday and ask what I'm doing. I'm driving. What's up?"

"I should ask you. Were you going to tell anyone that someone mugged you?"

My jaw clenched so tight that my molars ground together. Nobody asked O'Neal to share that information. I'd hear from my parents within hours for sure.

"I was not mugged. There was an attempt, but I wasn't mugged. And why would I bother telling anyone? You seem to get your information just fine."

"I shouldn't have to hear about my sister getting molly whopped in the street in a WhatsApp chat, Es. What happened?"

I shared the highlights, allowing Jewel to groan and gasp at appropriate moments. "And then I got this enormous project at work, so I've been a little preoccupied. I wasn't trying to be secretive. I just forgot."

"Mmmhmm," she grunted. "Is this the project with the guy that came to the house, and you couldn't find anything nice to say, and now you two have to work together?"

I almost choked on the coffee I'd thought it was safe to sip. "O'Neal's mouth has been busy."

Jewel's laugh sounded so sinister over the speakers. "In more ways than one. So?"

"So what?"

"Don't make me cuss, Esme. Is he the guy?"

I laughed, maneuvering my way around two slow drivers and off of the highway, heading to the winding, tree line side streets that would take me to Miller Design.

"Really? You're married with kids and got your nose all the way in my business. You have nothing else to worry about?"

"No. My old, married-with-kids ass wants to know what's up. I assume he's a snack if O'Neal thought you should have been nicer to him."

"Yeah. He's the guy. And he is...."

I sighed, hating myself for even admitting it. "Snack-ish. I guess. He's corny, though. He laughs at his own jokes and everything."

"Esme, you need to learn at the knee of the Goddess Ciara. Corny is not all bad. I would take Russell Wilson all day. Corey could be a little more corny, come to think of it."

"That'll be enough of that, Jewel."

Corey, her husband, was a Math professor at Emory University. He also hosted virtual reality games and loved Math Olympics. He and their two pre-teens, Samuel and Georgia, spent their weekends holding trivia tournaments and epic D&D sessions. He was corny enough.

"You need to get you a big ol' chocolate nerd. O'Neal told us what happened at the restaurant. I mean with the chair. Why'd you have to be so mean to him?"

I felt my eyes pop, they grew so large, so fast. "Jewel. He was *rude*."

"He went out of his way to bring your wallet to you. That doesn't sound rude to me, Es."

I slurped more of the strong, sweet, icy brew before answering. I needed to fortify myself for a morning with Trey. "You're only getting one side of the story. And the side you're getting is the side that thinks I want to know him biblically if you know what I'm saying."

"Well…"

"Not an option. I went over this with O'Neal. I can't date him. I can't… *not* date him."

Jewel sighed. I could feel her eyes rolling. "Those books you read, full of perfect men? None of them are going to walk out of a book and into your life, Esme."

"I don't need perfect. I'm not looking for a fairy tale. I'm not looking for anything, actually."

"Maybe you should start looking. In the meantime, the snack might take care of a few things. Know what I'm saying?"

"I should ask a random man that I met last week to deflower me?"

"Ugh. Stop saying that word. But maybe. Nobody cares that it's your first time, but you."

"That's exactly why I will wait until it's right for me."

I turned the corner into the group of buildings that housed Miller Design. Trey's long-legged form paced the sidewalk in dark slacks and a collared shirt. I stifled the groan that wanted to pour from me, just watching his smooth gait, full of swagger.

"Ok, I'm pulling up to the building, and he's outside. I don't want to have this conversation through my car stereo system."

Jewel cackled. "You don't want him to hear us talking about bustin' it wide open, Es?"

I huffed. "Get your trash mouth off of my phone. Don't you have thirty pairs of eyes looking at you right now?"

In the background, a protracted bell rang. "I will, in a minute."

"Love you. Try not to ruin them kids."

"Love you. Don't be mean today, Esme."

"No promises," I muttered, then disconnected the call. I killed the engine, gathered my coffee and work bag. Before I could pull the latch, the door opened.

"That's correct." Trey was mid-conversation while pulling my car door open. "Vincent negotiated a deal on cement mix based on how much we order, so the price per unit should be lower than that. Check it against the contract, so we're forecasting correctly."

Since I hadn't moved, Trey bent over to peer inside at me. "Ms. Whitaker? You good?"

Don't be mean today, Esme said Jewel's voice in my head. I wanted to argue with her, just to be obstinate, but I didn't.

"I'm fine, Mr. Pettigrew."

I climbed out of the car and hiked my bag onto my

shoulder. He closed the door as soon as I moved away from the car.

"I need to go," he said, looking down at the phone. "My appointment is here. We'll pick this up later."

Trey slid a long finger across the screen, then dug a case out of his pocket. He removed two earbuds and tucked them neatly into the case, then slid it back into his pocket, followed by his phone.

"Never seen a man handle his business before?"

I blinked. Then realized I'd been watching him.

"Thought you might have gotten caught up."

"Caught up in... what?"

He nodded, but his long glance said that he'd caught me. He tipped his head toward the building, reaching to open the door. "Shall we? I have a yes in my pocket."

<hr />

Trey and I settled into the conference room. He set the attaché case that he'd picked up in the lobby on the table before settling into his seat.

The room was built to host eight to ten people around an oblong table. Like the rest of Miller Design's décor, it was plain and non-descript. Taupe walls, low-pile carpet, black leather chairs that were not only on casters that could glide across the floors but also tipped back so that a person could recline.

The benefits in Miller's offices lied in its technology investments—state-of-the-art software and equipment made for the industry. At the front of the room, the entire wall was a built-in digital monitor. On the table, several plugs and connectors, one of which broadcasted the working document from my laptop to the wall.

"You said you came with a yes in your pocket," I reminded him. I opened my notebook to the pages I'd marked up the day before, where we'd reached an impasse and called it a day. "What would that yes be about?"

"Not what you think," he said. He arranged his pens, notepad, and tablet, then laid his phone next to these items. Once he was set, he steepled his fingers, so the tips met.

"Not what I think? Is this a game to you, Mr. Pettigrew?"

"Could you call me Trey? Please? Only the bank and local PD call me Mr. Pettigrew."

It was my nature to argue, just to be petty. Instead, I inhaled a breath through my nose and gave a brief nod of my head. "Fine," I answered. "And call me Esme."

"Thank you. And no, this isn't a game to me. It shouldn't be a game to you, either. And I know it's not a game to Miller. There's a reason that he reached out to my father to begin talks about merging our companies. Miller wants to do more than medical facilities. Pettigrew wants to expand. We can do a lot for each other. So..."

Trey exhaled, then pressed the Home button on his tablet, bringing up an illuminated page of typewritten notes. "I've done some thinking, some projecting based on future business, and I'm willing to take some risks. But this will only work if you're also willing to take some risks."

"Me?" My brows shot up. I reached for my iced coffee and used the time I needed to suck down a gulp to search my brain as to what he could be referring to. "Any risks I take would be on behalf of Miller Design, and—"

"No, I don't mean Miller, Esme. I mean you. Personally."

He picked up a pen, holding the barrel between two fingers, then flipped it back and forth over his knuckles.

"Last night, I did a lot of thinking. Miller said it won't break him if he doesn't get to bid on this facility. Frankly, it won't break Pettigrew, either. It's found money if we get it, but we won't go under if we don't. But like I said, I'm thinking about the future. The end game. I know what Miller wants. I know what his company is worth, I know what he's willing to sell it for, and he won't get a better deal anywhere else."

"Mr.— Trey. I'm the middleman. I represent Mr. Miller and the best interest of Miller Design. If you want to have another meeting with him to have a high-level discussion, I'm happy to step aside—"

"We don't have time for that. And that's not what I want. What I want is some concessions from you."

"From me?"

"Yes."

He paused, then let his eyes travel up from the screen of his tablet to mine. Those dark brown orbs seemed to be swirling.

"What's in this for you, Esme? A raise? A promotion? A comfy office? Will Ethan Byron over at Benning M&A finally pat you on the head and tell you that you're a good little worker bee?"

My lips betrayed me by frowning. Trey chuckled.

"They taught us how to research at that fancy school I went to. Coincidentally, I also went to Georgia State. So, I dug into Benning and the deals they broker. They let you do grunt work, give you all of this responsibility so that you think you're essential, dangling the carrot of the corporate ladder and making your way up. You and I know that essential often means overworked, underpaid, and unrecognized. So, what do you get out of this?"

"The satisfaction of a job well done if Miller gets his way."

"And if he doesn't? Does that come back on you?"

He hummed, then slowly shook his head when I protested.

"Before you hitch your horse to that wagon, check into who benefits when the papers are signed. And what happens to you if they aren't. I'm doing this because my father wants it done, not because I believe in it. If it was me, Joe Owner, evaluating this deal, I'd have walked. Bringing you in was dirty. Miller knows it; that's why he sprung you on me and didn't allow me time to arrange an administrator on my end."

"So walk away," I argued, more like a challenge, but lobbed softly to mask the edge to the question. "If you don't like the terms and it won't hurt you to lose the bid, walk away."

Trey was contemplative for a few beats. Then he tossed the pen to the table, set the tablet down next to it, and leaned in.

"Real talk? Keepin' it a *hunnid*?"

I leaned in, conspiratorially. "Real talk. Whatever a *hunnid* is."

"I can't." He shrugged his broad shoulders, then relaxed again. "I'm looking at you, talking to you, but as far as Miller is concerned, I am my father. Saul Pettigrew is a giant of a man, not only in stature but reputation. There's so much more than money riding on this, the least of which is my father's opinion of me and my ability to do what he asked me to do. Which is to close this deal."

"Then I'm not the only one whose ass is on the line," I responded. "Real talk? I've been at Benning M&A for over ten years, but I had to almost sue to get the promised raise and promotion after I got my MBA. Ethan is pissed that they had to promote me. This assignment…"

I wrinkled my nose. "It stinks. I don't mean that it's terrible, but… something's off. Maybe they hope I'll fail so they have a reason to get rid of the troublemaker? If this deal tanks and they don't fire me, I doubt I'll be seeing any more negotiations. They'll kick me back to pushing paper in the same tiny cube on the low rent end of the floor."

I paused to breathe. And collect myself. Had I said all of that out loud? To a man that I didn't even know?

"Anyway…" I sighed, folding my arms and leaning onto the table. "I can't walk away either, Trey."

"So we understand each other. I've got an idea for how we

can make this mutually beneficial. I make sure you win. You make sure I win."

I let my head tilt a little, to let him know I was suspicious. But I was also curious, so I nodded, prepared to listen. "If it means that you'll pull out that yes you have in your pocket, I'm interested."

"Good. I don't want to get down to brass tacks in here, though." Trey glanced around the room, frowning at everything from the décor to the built-in screen to the plain slate grey table. "This room bugs the shit out of me. How do I know Miller isn't watching and listening?"

I tensed and sat up straight. Right. How did we know that he wasn't watching this entire exchange and monitoring the progress from some secret lair like a cartoon villain? Then I told myself that it was silly. This was a design firm. But still…

"Where do you suggest we talk? In the parking lot?"

"How about neutral territory?"

"Such as?"

"Do you trust me?"

CHAPTER TWELVE

Trey

I t took little arm twisting to get Esme to take a ride with me. Truthfully, I was hungry, I hated that room, and I hadn't prepared what I was going to say yet. I needed the extra time to gather my thoughts.

"Order whatever you like," I told her as soon as the hostess seated us at a small table in the corner of J. Christopher's, a casual breakfast and lunch diner with locations around the city. I'd frequented all of them. "You eat breakfast, right?"

"Yes, I eat breakfast." She glared, picking up the laminated, oblong menu. "Although, I'm more of a Ria's Bluebird kind of girl."

I knew the place. Ria's was the type of spot where you could get a stack of pancakes the size of your head with a side of eggs, bacon, and a hot buttermilk biscuit with fresh homemade jam for under ten dollars.

"Consider it an adventure. I'm starving, which is unusual for this time of day, but I eat when my body asks for food."

I watched Esme in my peripheral vision. She studied the

menu section by section, item by item. Meticulous, this woman. She scrutinized the menu like it was a contract.

"I've had everything here. The food's good, that's why I come here a lot. What are you in the mood for?"

"Uhm…" She laid the menu down on the table and lowered her hands to her lap. "Honestly, I'm out of my element. I'm wondering why we are ordering breakfast instead of working. Miller is paying a pretty penny for my time—"

"Don't worry about Miller's pennies or your timesheet. If this deal goes through, his bills become my problem. And it's my goal to make this deal go through."

A slim woman stopped at our table, a brown apron bearing the restaurant's logo tied around her waist. "Did y'all have time to check out the menu?" She asked, a southern twang accenting her husky tone.

I glanced at Esme. She shook her head. "I'm not hungry. But go ahead and order."

"Can I get you some coffee?" Asked the waitress. Esme nodded. I placed my order for a breakfast skillet with steak, eggs, fried potatoes and a glass of orange juice.

She rolled her lips inward, then took a slow look around the homely, country-style restaurant. It wasn't much to look at, but I ate at J. Christopher's for the food.

"Tell me why we're here, Trey."

"I will. First, though, let's talk about that piece of paper that fell out of your bag the other night when you left the office."

She chuckled, appearing calm, but I caught the slight dip of her head and tensing of her shoulders before she forced them back to natural position. "What about it?"

"Is it a list of stuff you want to do? Like a bucket list?"

"Bucket lists are morbid. But… similar. It's a Never list. Things I've never done. I want to make a huge dent in that list before I turn forty next month. What's it to you?"

"What's it to *you*? You're defensive and evasive about it."

"You're unusually curious about something that isn't your business."

"True," I acknowledged. "But it is important to you. Am I correct?"

After a beat, Esme nodded. "You are correct. So?"

"Why do you have a list of things you've never done that you need to?"

"It's a long story."

"I love a long story. I've got nothing but time. I'm waiting for my breakfast."

"Trey..." She sighed, thrusting herself back against the chair and rolling her eyes to the ceiling, dramatically. "Maybe I don't want to talk about it with a stranger."

"I've spent more time with you than I've spent with my mother this week. We are not strangers."

"I'll be more succinct. I don't want to talk about this with *you*."

"Ahhh." I nodded. "Now we're speaking truth. What if I say that I'm interested in helping you clear up that list?"

Esme froze. The temperature between us, which had been rising to a comfortable level, dropped like a rock. "You're interested in... *what?*"

"You heard me. Let's knock some items off of your list."

Esme tried to speak, but her lips flapped; no sound came out. When her eyes rose to mine, they were blazing, her bottom lip trembling.

"Uhm...I was just starting to like you, so please tell me that this *isn't* your cute way of offering to fuck me so I'll give in to all of your concessions on this contract. Tell me that, Trey, so I don't have to beat you upside the head with my damn purse."

My brain flurried with thoughts, rolling my words back to me, analyzing each syllable. I hadn't said that at all.

"Uhm, I was starting to like you too, so ok. This *isn't* my cute way of offering that. Why would you assume that was what I meant?"

"You said you'd like to help me knock some items off my list."

"Yeah. So... you think I'm the type of person to ask for sex to get what I want? This... this is what you think I'm about?"

"You saw the list, Trey!"

"I saw two lines. You threw your little tantrum and snatched it back before I could see more. What's on that list?"

"None of your business!" She snarled.

Gratefully, the waitress took that moment to bring Esme a ceramic mug and poured a steaming cup of coffee. She rambled about the progress on my breakfast skillet, either not catching the thick blanket of tension over the table, or not caring about it before leaving packets of cream and sugar and bouncing away.

"Look, I apologize," I blurted. "I didn't mean to insinuate that you should sleep with me for contract concessions. That wasn't what I was trying to say."

"What were you trying to say then, Trey?"

"I was trying to say that maybe we can help each other out. For every item that I help you cross off of your list, you help me cross off one of mine. I need Miller to do some serious retooling of his proposal. He's in his feelings about his company, and his numbers don't make good business sense. You have his ear. He trusts you."

"And you think that helping me clear my list will mean so much to me that I'll walk into Miller's office and fight for what you want?"

"Not in so many words. But if he budges even a little bit on half of the items that I need him to revise, I'll consider it a victory."

"This sounds very close to unethical, Trey."

Esme stirred cream and sugar into the dark brew and lifted the mug to thick, deep red lips. She sipped, then smiled, hummed a beautiful tone from the bottom of her throat, and sipped again.

"I know it sounds unseemly, and I don't mean it to be. I wanted it to be more of an incentive. A little give and take. Some back scratching. I'm not asking you for sexual favors."

She didn't say another word for a few minutes. Sat there and sipped coffee and stared at the empty sweetener packets next to her mug of coffee. There's no way she didn't hear me, so I didn't repeat the statement.

She ended the long pause by asking, "Why does it even matter to you?"

"Being honest? If it wasn't a big deal, you'd have told me to throw it away. You almost beat my ass to get it back. It matters to me because it matters to you. And I'm hoping that if I help you with this, that you'll —"

"Help you with this contract," she finished.

I nodded. Then leaned back as the waitress arrived to set a sizzling dish in front of me. The scent of a medium rare steak, crisp potatoes, toast, and two fried eggs wafted from the mini cast iron skillet, making my stomach rumble.

"Are you sure you're not hungry? I don't fuck with toast. You want mine?"

Without a word, she took the toast halves and laid them on a saucer, then poked through the container on the table for toppings. She chose strawberry jam and a pack of peanut butter, spreading one on each half.

"Let's say that I feel like risking my job to help you. How would it work?"

"I hadn't thought that through," I said, wielding a steak knife to slice my steak off of the bone. "But I'm serious about the reciprocity. I do something for you. You do something for me. If you feel weird about that, or it's not going to work, we can call it off now and go back to fighting each other in that conference room."

"That does not sound appealing." She bit off a piece of toast with peanut butter spread.

"Tell you what," I began, spearing a slice of steak and scooping a potato wedge with the edge of the fork. "Let's try a couple. One. See how it goes, all the way through. If you're not going to be able to change Miller's mind, it's a waste of my time and yours."

"Well, not mine." She smiled, holding the second half of her toast slice aloft. "I intend to clear that list, with or without you."

My brows shot up. "Go-getter, huh? Felt the need to remind yourself of all the life you haven't lived yet?"

Esme's smile was sneaky and small, but it was there. I ached to pry, but resisted, reminding myself that she didn't respond to aggression. I had to let her meet me in the middle.

After a few bites of toast from her and thoughtful chewing from me, she answered. "I wrote the list to humor my cousin, who thinks I haven't lived enough. I planned to bullshit through some of them, then let it go because my cousin is flighty. He'll forget. But the more I think about it?"

She bobbed her head side to side. "The more I feel like I need to do what I said I would do."

"So we'll give it a shot? See how it goes?"

"Sure." She popped the rest of the toast into her mouth and chewed, then washed it down with coffee. "It's worth a test run, at least."

"Good." I speared another slice of steak, then potato and paused before taking a bit. "Then the next question is... what do you want to tackle first?"

CHAPTER THIRTEEN

Esme

"Esme, wait! Back up! You are *where*? Doing *what*?!"
Jada had never been able to keep alarm out of her voice. If something bothered her, she couldn't hide it. Both of my sisters were tall, over 6 feet in heels. Both were an average size 14, and bottom-heavy like our mother. Both were chestnut toned women with pointy chins, chiseled cheekbones, and large, expressive brown eyes.

That was where the similarities between my twin sisters ended.

Jewel, the firstborn, was the cool, calm, and collected twin. She liked the blues end of Rhythm & Blues, the dulcet tones of smooth jazz. If Jewel showed an emotion other than irritation, shit was serious. Jada was younger by nine minutes, and it showed. She was excitable, sensitive, and emotional. She liked Drake and Tamia, but also Three 6 Mafia and JCole, and was very much an empath, as evidenced by the high pitch of her voice through the phone.

I was the one about to face one of my fears. I needed her to keep it together.

My phone had buzzed in my bag as we left J. Christopher's, but Trey and I were talking. Chatting, as if we were friends who got along, had gotten along the entire time we'd known each other, instead of snapping at one another. I didn't want to cut off the conversation or be rude as we rode into town. And, if it was Miller calling, I didn't want to talk to him, considering I'd just agreed to conspire against him.

Before I climbed out of the truck, I pulled the phone from my bag to peek at my messages, almost wincing with the expectation of a glut of missed calls and messages from Miller, but... nope. He must be used to employees dipping out for hours at a time.

Instead, it was Jada that had called, probably out of worry about the incident from last week. There was likely a mess of punctuated messages in the family WhatsApp group that I shared with my sisters and O'Neal, separate from the WhatsApp group we shared with my parents. Some things were not for the eyes of Jonas and Carol Whitaker.

Jada had left a message, demanding an immediate callback. She needed to hear your voice, to talk to you to know that you were ok. I dialed her back, and she asked where I was because it sounded like a carnival in the background.

"Funny you should say that. I uhm... I'm downtown. About to go on the Ferris wheel."

My eyes skimmed the parking lot, focusing on the mid-sized crowd milling around downtown Atlanta; some headed toward Centennial Park, some toward the Georgia Aquarium and the World of Coca-Cola. Most people, however, were gathered in the ticket line for the main attraction.

My eyes floated up toward the gigantic wheel in the middle of Skyview Park and the focal point of the area, especially at night when every light was illuminated. Every day when I drove past it, I entertained an irrational fear that it would somehow break free from its base and roll toward me, crushing me in the car.

I was about to break my personal rule of keeping one foot on the ground at all times.

O'Neal would have been so proud of me if I could reach him to tell him. He hadn't checked into the WhatsApp group since he left on his trip, and his phone was going straight to voicemail. Knowing my cousin, he was somewhere drinking Prosecco while being manscaped in an Italian spa. I was almost jealous.

"Hear me out," Jada was saying. "You got punched in the head last week, and now you're at the Ferris wheel, an object that makes you shake with fear. Tap one time if you're being held hostage."

I laughed because if I didn't, I might cry. "I'm fine. I promise. But I am about to get on this wheel."

"Are you sure you don't have a concussion? Brain damage? O'Neal said you didn't go to the doctor or anything. Who's the President of the United States?"

"Bill Clinton." I snickered.

"Esme!"

"Barack Obama is my forever president. I told you, I'm fine."

"You cannot be fine if you're about to get on that Ferris wheel! You hate things that leave the ground."

"I'm just, you know, being adventurous, I guess."

"Adventurous? All those times that we tried to take you on rides, and you screamed like we were trying to murder you? Now you're being adventurous?"

Trey was approaching, tickets in hand. He'd gone to pay for admission while I stowed my purse in the trunk. I wished I could have changed into flat shoes, but my Sam Edelman pumps would have to do.

"Hey, I've got to go. I'll call you later to let you know I'm alive."

I hung up before Jada could reply as Trey reached me. He'd been looking at me funny all day, like he wanted to ask questions but refused to do so. I expected him to pry into my business, but he didn't.

I shoved the phone into a side pocket of my bag, then pushed it back into the corner of the otherwise empty trunk. I stepped back while Trey fished his key fob from his pocket and pressed a button. The trunk closed, then latch on its own. He pressed another button, and the muted click let us know that the vehicle was now locked.

"Ready for this?" He asked.

"As I'll ever be, I guess."

We walked a few paces to the end of the line to get on the Ferris wheel. There weren't many people in front of us, and it was a nice afternoon, so the wait wasn't altogether unpleasant. It wasn't what I thought I would be doing with my afternoon.

We both stood, awkwardly glancing at one another. Like I did whenever I was nervous, I launched into inane small talk.

"Nice day," I lobbed.

"Mmmhmm," he responded, with a single nod.

"Seems to be warming up. Might be a nice day, not too hot."

"Might be."

He did not want to talk. So I didn't want to talk either.

But I was nervous, so I needed to talk, or sing or dance or take my mind off of the constant chant of *what the fuck am I even doing?*

"I'm a little surprised I haven't heard from Miller. Aren't you?"

"No," He replied, super casual and quiet. He stared ahead of him, eyes trained on some object in the distance.

"No?" I glanced up at him, using one of my hands to block the sun so I could see him. "Why not?"

"Because I told him we'd be offsite today. I told you not to worry about Miller's pennies." He glanced over at me. And smiled. "Or your time. You're about to earn your paycheck."

I groaned, my eyes catching the slow movement of the big white wheel with the enclosed gondola baskets that didn't look so sturdy. I was sure a person could fell out of one.

"Hey, I didn't mean to scare you." Trey grabbed one of my hands and tucked it into his elbow. "I'm sorry. I should be more considerate."

"I'm not fragile," I snapped. Then relented. "Sorry. It doesn't seem like a good idea. It doesn't look like it should work like it does."

"But it does work. You know that, right?"

"My brain does." My bottom lip crept between my teeth. I had to stop, or I would chew the Fenty right off.

"Have you never... *ever* been on one?"

"Not willingly."

"Not even as a kid?"

I wagged my head. "I'd scream if I even got near one. My family stopped taking me to fairs and amusement parks because the rides scared the shit out of me. I never did the jungle gym. I never climbed the ladder to go down the slide. One year, my family decided to treat me and my sisters to a trip to Disney World."

"Hmmm. Considering that you're still scared to get on this wheel, it doesn't sound like it went very well."

I shuddered, then told him the story that O'Neal loved to tell, that made me sound crazier and more dramatic every time.

"After the first day, if I closed my eyes, I could ride the rides that never left the ground. But those were boring, and my sisters wanted to do the big, scary rides. And my parents wanted to go on them, too. They had to take turns babysitting. Every few hours, they'd switch; one would do some silly kid thing with me, and the other would run the park with the other two. Or I'd follow them all around and hold the bags."

"I'm sorry. That sounds miserable."

"It was. We tried therapy, we tried talking, we tried exposure…"

I shook out my hands, realizing that I was shaking at the memories of my parents trying to force me onto rides. "Eventually, the therapist told my parents to leave it alone. That I would make my way toward certain things, activities places when I was good and ready. They never bothered me about it ever again. Or… anything else, for that matter."

"So the time to move toward certain things is now. Right now?"

I squinted up at the wheel. "I'm sort of second thinking, to be honest."

Trey slipped a hand into his pocket. His gaze had moved from a far off object to something on the ground. "I assumed your list was like a bucket list. I would never have suggested a tit for tat exchange with something so important. Do you still want to do this? You want to back out?"

My head rose, my gaze following. High...then *higher*, to the top of the Ferris wheel, then zooming in on the two-seater bucket that seemed to swing menacingly, back and forth with momentum, its occupants laughing and shouting, having the grandest time. I doubted I'd be doing any of that.

But I would get on that fucking thing. Today.

"Listen, Trey... I know we've been fighting for the last week and everything—"

"Water under the bridge. For real."

"I need you to promise that you'll hold my hand, and you won't let go, and you won't let me fall out of that bucket thing. And you won't laugh if I scream."

"Gondola. It's called a gondola, and you can't fall out of it unless you force the doors open."

"Whatever. I said what I said. Deal?"

"I cannot promise not to laugh if you scream." My eyes darted to his face, where the corners of his mouth were tipping up into a smile. His eyes danced with delight. "The rest? You got it."

Our turn came sooner than I'd been prepared for. We tucked into a small, contained space that was all windows except for the bench and the wall behind our heads. Thankfully, we didn't have to share it with anyone else. We sat back while the attendant, a friendly but loud, older gentleman gave out instructions before he locked the doors in place.

Unconsciously, my hand shot out for Trey's. His fingers wound between mine.

"Y'all good?" He hollered. "You in?"

"We're good," Trey answered. "She's got a death grip on me. We're not going anywhere."

"You not scared are ya, Lil' lady? It's a whole lot of nothin', just goin' round and round in this box, up and down about four times. This a date, or somethin'? Y'all are dressed real nice for this dirty ol' Ferris wheel."

"Impromptu change of plans for the day," Trey said. Then he gestured toward the doors. "We're ready."

My heart was in my throat, remembering the words *round and round, up and down.* "You know what? M-maybe I d-don't—"

"All aboard!" He stepped back and called out. Then he pulled the door shut. After a clang that made me jump and a shudder that made the entire car shake, the wheel began to turn, lifting us off the ground.

I couldn't watch. My eyes slammed shut, and I buried my face in the sleeve of his jacket. "Trey…"

"You're not going to throw up, are you? This jacket was expensive."

"No," I squeaked. "I'm scared."

"I'm right here." He squeezed my hand, enclosed in his. I squeezed back. He flinched, howling in my ear. "Ow! Damn, Esme! You don't need to dig those claws into me. I said, I got you."

"You know when I was on the phone when you came back to the car?" I rambled, trying to keep my mind off of this bucket swinging freely in the air. With us inside of it.

"Uh-huh."

"My sister called me. She runs a salon and day spa. Did you find that out, while you were doing all of your information gathering?"

"I wasn't gathering information on you. I was looking into your employer. Your sister runs a salon. Is it nice?"

"Mmmhmm. One of those spots where they serve mimosas and wine while you're getting a pedicure. Do you know what I mean? Jada's Boutique & Day Spa. It's in Decatur. Have you heard of it?"

Trey was quiet for a moment. He probably thought I was crazy. Then, quietly, he answered, "Can't say that I have, Esme. Does she have male clients?"

"Yeah. Men come in all the time. My cousin goes there. Anyway, she does my nails. And my hair. It's cute when it's not in a bun."

"She's responsible for these claws." I felt him lift our entwined fingers. He must have been closely inspecting the gel nails that Jada applied every few weeks like clockwork. "Both are nice."

"She guarantees the nails are unbreakable."

"I guess that's good for you, so they don't pop off when you break my skin. Seriously, ease up, Esme. I'm right here. You're not going anywhere."

I loosened my grip. A little. My face was buried in the smooth, decadent fabric of Trey's suit jacket. After I got used to the sensation and sound of the wheel climbing into the skies, I let one eye creep open and turned my head so I could see.

I couldn't help the gasp that escaped my lips. Though it was mid-day, the view from above the city through the clear glass front of the gondola was breathtaking. Below, the five

Olympic rings set into Centennial Park were remarkable. Straight ahead were the Westin Hotel, Peachtree Tower, the Promenade, the Equitable building, and other glass structures glinting in the bright sunlight amid clear, blue skies.

"Wow," I whispered.

"Imagine this scene at night. My favorite view of Atlanta is when I'm driving from my parents' place up north, and the downtown skyline comes into view. I'm never prouder to live here than when I'm driving through downtown at night."

I had barely taken it all in when the view disappeared, and the wheel dipped, making its first revolution.

"Made it through your first round," said Trey. He elbowed me a few times, knocking me out of my reverie. "How do you feel?"

I gulped, blinking away the fog and finding it easier to breathe. And move my head so I could look around at the view, as we were closer to the ground and heading back up again.

"I didn't die."

I felt Trey's light laughter. I shot him a dirty look.

"You said not to laugh if you screamed."

"I'm screaming in my heart."

"And I didn't promise not to laugh."

He pulled his hand from mine and dropped an arm around my shoulder. The imperceptible tremors that had been rocking my body since we'd climbed inside the gondola subsided. And I could breathe.

"See? You're good. We're good. A few more minutes, and we'll be out of here."

"Yeah, I'm good. I mean, I can't wait to get out of this little box, but I'm good."

"So, while I'm busy doing something for you, we could talk about what you'll do for me. And I mean that in the most business-like, not at all suggestive way possible."

"I know what you meant. So what do you want?"

"He needs to come down on his asking price."

"Trey!" I almost laughed in the man's face. "You're asking him to come down two million dollars. This little field trip is not worth that."

"Can he at least go back to what he agreed on with my father? He jacked up the price as soon as he knew I was taking over, and my nose is bent out of shape about it."

"I'll think about it. But I can't go to him off the strength of toast, coffee, and a Ferris wheel ride. Let's ease into this, Mr. Pettigrew."

"Here you go with Mr. Pettigrew again."

I giggled. Which… surprised me, because I'd never been on a theme park attraction and smiled, let alone laughed. I was a hundred feet in the air, in a tiny bucket next to an attractive man who had a protective arm around me.

Let me find out Trey Pettigrew was going to be good for me. I'd never hear the end of it from O'Neal.

"Alright. Something easy." He was quiet for a few seconds, then continued. "How about forty-five days of health and wellness coverage for the employees we have to let go. Now, that should include Employee Assistance like resume writing, therapy, budget counseling, and the like."

"Forty-five days *past* the minimum that you have to offer them by law if you end employment?"

Trey groaned, tipping his head back against the metal wall of the gondola.

"It's not an added benefit if it's something you legally have to offer. Miller wants ninety days on top of the legal requirement. I could talk him down to half of that number."

"Alright." Trey tipped his head forward again, then gave his best attempt at a side-eye. "You drive a hard bargain, Ms. Whitaker."

I wrinkled my nose. "I don't think I like you calling me Ms. Whitaker."

"Then, you need to drop that Mr. Pettigrew business."

The gondola came to a stop, and the doors slid open. "Y'all make it?" Asked the attendant, poking his head in and offering a hand to help me out.

"We made it!" I almost screamed. I stepped out, resisting the urge to drop to the pavement and kiss it. The ride wasn't bad at all. I still liked keeping both feet on the ground.

Trey climbed out after me, adjusting his jacket. "You good? How do you feel?"

"I feel...fearless." I sighed, stepping back to look up at the Ferris wheel. I was no longer afraid of that giant contraption. "At least for today, I'm fearless."

"Fearless enough to hit the rooftop at Ponce City Market?"

I paused. "Don't get loose. I rode a Ferris wheel. Now you want me to get on somebody's roof?"

Trey's shoulders bounced with the laughter that rolled from deep in his chest. "I'm not trying to kill you, Esme. I need you. But since we're out and we're already playing hooky..." He shrugged. Then smiled. "Might as well ramp up the stakes, start a war and bet that I can beat you at Skee-ball."

"Well, seeing as how I've never played Skee-ball, you probably could. I like to think I make a worthy opponent, but I'm not going to anyone's rooftop—"

"C'mon, Esme," Trey interrupted. "You said you felt fearless."

"In these shoes," I finished, kicking up a foot. "Besides, shouldn't we head back to the office?"

"Why? We're working."

"We're not—"

"You got me to agree to health care coverage for furloughed employees. I don't talk about work on my personal time, so we must be working."

"I mean, I guess. If you want to manipulate it that way. I'm just—"

"Worried about what Miller is going to say. And I told you to stop. Do you ever relax? Let go? Have fun?"

"Yes. When I'm not being paid to be at an amusement park."

"So, it's a no on a Skee-ball tourney, then?"

Trey was an immovable object, standing in front of me at the edge of the park.

"I am not dressed for playing Skee-ball, Trey. From my head to my toes, I'm dressed for the *office*. Which is where we should go. So I can talk to Miller about health care for his employees, which gets you one point closer to signing your deal. Tit for tat. That's the agreement. Right?"

He sighed, then his head dipped slightly, his eyes rolling up to meet mine. "Compromise?"

I returned his sigh. "What, Trey?"

"We go back to the office. We work or whatever. Tonight? Jeans and tees. Flat shoes. The rooftop at Ponce City Market. Drinks, food that isn't leftover pizza or sushi. I teach you to play Skee-ball. I might even let you win."

I shook my head. "Why would you let me win? Why wouldn't I beat you?"

"You've never played Skee-ball. No way you'll beat me."

"Uh-huh. And this would be another one of your tactics to get what you want from Miller? You use me, butter me up, I feel closer to you, I fight for what you want?"

"Nope," he answered. "Not at all. This would be off the books. A one-off. A hangout."

"A hangout." He nodded. "And I would agree to that... for what reason, Trey?"

"Because it's a theme. Because I'm trying to get to know you. And because you're doing things you've never done before."

CHAPTER FOURTEEN

Trey

W hen the idea to help Esme clear her list popped into my head the other night, I thought it was flimsy. Weak at best.

I expected to have to talk her into it, to prove the effort was worth her while. Her relationship with Miller seemed to be based on an immense sense of trust. I'd have to bring her over to my side, make her sympathetic to my point of view.

And I'd have to carefully toe the line between playing the game and manipulation. There was no business goal to asking her to have dinner, drinks, and play Skee-ball with me.

I honestly enjoyed her company. Which felt weird because... wasn't she *kind of* the enemy?

It was well after noon, and midday traffic was thick. Satellite radio weaved through road noise and the sounds of Esme's nails clicking on the screen of her phone.

"Oh, turn that up!"

I pressed the volume knob on the steering wheel. Gladys Knight and the Pips, Neither One of Us, blared through the speaker system. I grimaced and grunted my appreciation into the air, raising a fist.

"Whatchu know about Ms. Gladys and the Pips?"

"My parents take their era of music seriously. I know it well."

"Mine, too. Pops loves him some Gladys Knight."

"And Diana Ross, and Aretha Franklin, and Patti LaBelle... all of the usual suspects. Heard a lot of them growing up. My dad had this on reel to reel."

"Mine too! My mom had it refurbished for their 40th wedding anniversary this year. Those big ass speakers and everything. The sound is crystal clear. He'll bust it out in the summer when they grill out with friends or whatever."

"So, he's the DJ?"

"If you want to hear Midnight Train to Georgia at least three times—"

When the phone rang, I turned the volume down.

"It's one of my sisters. Do you mind if..."

I shrugged. "If you don't mind that I can hear your conversation. Just don't be telling lies about me."

"Hello?" She said, bringing the phone to her ear. "Yes, I'm alive." She laughed, but one of those low, giggly throaty cackles that surprised me. It softened her.

Then I rolled my eyes at myself as I realized that, indeed, the woman laughed. And maybe she hadn't laughed or smiled in my presence because I'd been terrorizing her since we met.

She continued her low conversation while I tried to focus on guiding the Acadia through traffic and tune out the sultry tone of her voice. It didn't work. Her low, dulcet tones permeated my ears and stuck there.

I pulled into the parking lot at Miller Design and parked next to her Jetta. She ended her call and slid her phone into her bag.

"I'm going to head over to my office for the afternoon," I told her, leaving the truck idling. "I've got work stacked up since I've been focused on this deal, and it's giving me anxiety."

"Uhm, Trey? Before you go..." She had one hand on the handle to open her door but had paused.

"You want to thank me for a thrilling afternoon of facing your fears, huh?"

Her eyes rolled as they did a lot when we were together. But she also smiled. It was a thin smile, but it was there. "Actually, yeah. I was talking to one of my sisters."

"The one with the salon? That has male clients?"

"Yeah. She wanted to make sure that I was Ok because they've been trying to get me on that Ferris wheel forever, and I've never gone." She shook her head, tipping at an angle and giving me a quizzical stare. "I don't know what it is about you, but I felt safe up there. Thank you for today."

"You're welcome. That's one thing off your list, right? How many things are there?"

"Ten," she answered. My eyebrows must have betrayed my surprise.

"Do I get to know what's on the list?"

She paused, pursing her lips. I had to stifle a growl. *Dammit, man, be cool!*

"No. I think it'll be more fun for me if I get to tell you what you'll be helping me accomplish."

"If that's what floats your boat."

"It does."

"You said *one* of your sisters. How many sisters do you have?"

"Maybe I'll tell you tonight. We're still on, aren't we?"

I'd been thinking of pretending that I'd never asked her to meet me. I wasn't sure that she'd even show up, and the last thing I wanted was to be stood up by a woman who seemed to wield a lot of power—not to mention my future — in her hands.

But the way she glanced over at me, eyes wide, brows raised, a bona fide smile on those thick lips...*yeah.*

"We are definitely on. Meet me at the elevator at Nine Mile Station at seven. Don't be late. Do you need me to send you Google map directions?"

She huffed, opening her door. "I have already told you to not be worried about what I do and how I get there, Mr. Pettigrew."

"See, there you go. You call me Mr. Pettigrew when you get —" She slammed the door in the middle of my sentence, but I was sure she caught my drift.

CHAPTER FIFTEEN

Esme

This is not a date.

Not a date, not a date, not a date.

I lectured myself all afternoon while I marked up copies of the contract to review with Miller, who was surprised at the progress we'd made while offsite. He agreed that getting out of the office and on common ground was an excellent strategy that I should use where applicable.

While I drove home, actually smiling at the Ferris wheel as I passed it on the freeway, I reminded myself to not get excited about having evening plans that had nothing to do with Shonda Rhimes' Thursday night lineup.

This is not a date, I told myself, as I pulled into my spot in the garage. Tonight's hang out with Trey was just that, a hangout. Not a date.

But I was nervous like it was a date. I wanted plenty of time to get cute like it was a date. I had flutters of excitement in my stomach like it was a date.

I showered, changed, fussed with my hair for longer than

usual, taking it down from the bun I usually wore and letting the shoulder-length curls fly free. My face was bare except for a tinted moisturizer and a swipe of gloss on my lips. I arrived at the agreed upon spot in a pair of tapered jeans that I bought off of Instagram, so I was thankful that they fit. I paired them with a graphic t-shirt and my favorite Vans. My feet were still throbbing from standing in heels all day.

I spotted Trey's casual stride in dark rinse, loose fit jeans, black Nikes, and a thin, Korean collar shirt in olive green. The sleeves were rolled up to his elbows, giving him a casual, *I'm just over here being sexy* vibe. Watching him, then noting how his expression changed when he caught me watching him made my heartbeat gallop.

Trey let out a low wolf whistle as he approached, giving an obvious up and down glance. "Got me singing Ginuwine, In Those Jeans. Evening, Ms. Whitaker," he said, extending a hand to me.

I slapped his hand away. "Knock that Ms. Whitaker bullshit off. You're only doing it to get on my nerves."

He stepped back, then made a show of giving me the up and down stare. "You dress down real nice. No suit, no bun, hair all... out here." He chuckled, taking in the curls that were probably increasing with the humidity. "No heels. I'm a little sad. I liked those heels."

"Do you plan on being this Quiet Storm guy all night?"

Trey laughed. "You don't like it?"

"You don't have to impress me. This isn't a date. You can be Trey."

"Fine." He sighed, dropping his shoulders, his voice climbing a few octaves. "I will be Trey, then. Are you ready to go up?"

"Up... as in the roof?"

"Yup. The roof."

"I guess," I said, not sure that I meant it.

"This isn't as bad as I thought it would be."

I clutched the bulbous globe of a bourbon glass tightly in my hands. I braved a look around at the spacious patio at 9 Mile Station, staying seated at our table mere feet from the edge.

In actuality, we were at least six feet from the edge. There was a steel barrier around the perimeter. Still, you never knew what could happen throughout dinner to make you leap six feet sideways and topple up and over the barrier, so I stayed in my seat.

Reservations were required, but they didn't matter, since Trey seemed to know everyone from the staff working the floor to kitchen help. He mentioned, offhand, that we'd like to sit out on the patio, so we were shown there and set up at a stainless steel high bar, set simply with a votive candle in a glass holder that flickered in the light breeze.

The surface was now dotted with china plates since Trey had ordered multiple appetizers— crudité, spinach and chickpea dip, and smoked trout croquettes. We each picked out a drink to try. I chose a smoky, chocolatey, locally brewed barrel-aged bourbon called The Tears of My Enemies. We both thought it was appropriate for what we'd agreed to do.

The drink made me warm. And loose. And *lusty*.

I'd known handsome men, particularly in my MBA program. Most were friendly, but once they figured out that the girl with the pretty face and wide hips wasn't handing out sex and blow jobs in gratitude for attention, they stopped showing up for study sessions. Men like those were hell-bent on attaining "cream of the crop" status that shouted a preference for a certain type of woman— thin, silky haired, fair-skinned women. They *deserved the best*, which didn't include a shy brown-skinned woman who hid her curvy shape under oversized clothes and wore a scarf over her hair to class.

I wasn't self-conscious with Trey. I never felt that I should shrink myself or cover up. He was working overtime to get on my good side. I never imagined what a turn on that would be. I was free to be myself, even if that meant that I was caustic and sarcastic.

I did, though, have to step outside of myself and wonder how the hell I ended up on some rooftop drinking bourbon, thinking lewd thoughts about a man that I worked with, and letting him satisfy more than the minor items on my Never list.

I squirmed in my seat while my mind wandered toward the possibility. I would need a man for sex. Here, right in front of me was a man. I'd bet anything that I wouldn't have to work hard to get him to agree to cross that line with me.

Keep it classy, Esme. He's using you to get what he wants, so make sure you get what you want.

"Do you come here a lot?"

His eyes flicked up from the menu and settled on my face. When he didn't answer right away, I clarified my question. "You seem to know everyone. You're a regular, or you work here."

"You could say I'm a regular," he said, sliding the leather bound menu back to the table. "Pettigrew developed this plaza. My parents became friends with the owners after they opened. This is one of my father's favorite spots—he'd have me meet him and his VP for a drink on Fridays."

"Oh. I heard that he had some health issues. Is he…"

Trey gave me a polite, closed mouth smile. "Alive and well. Getting stronger and crankier by the day."

"That's good to hear."

"It is. I want him to get back to work."

A waiter clad in an inky black t-shirt and black shorts brought an icy cold bottle to the table and set it on a napkin. He smiled and left as quickly as he came. Trey reached for it.

"So. Tell me something about you," Trey lobbed across the table.

Men thought that *tell me about yourself* question was interesting, but it was such a lazy way to get the woman to carry the conversation that I cringed when I heard it. It rated up there with *what do you do for fun*, and if I responded that I stab people who ask what I do for fun, suddenly the date was over, and I was a psycho.

I lobbed back my usual response. "What do you want to know?"

"What do you want me to know about you? What am I all the way wrong about? Where do I have you fucked up at?"

That... that made me laugh. "I think you have me pegged, actually."

"For real? I read you like a Buzzfeed article?"

"Buzzfeed has lists and quizzes like what kind of pizza you are."

"You..." Trey paused, then pointed a long finger across the table. "You're a homemade pizza."

"See?" I nodded. And giggled. *Giggled? Fuck this bourbon.* "You read me like a book I wanted to finish, but I can't because you spoiled it for me."

"I didn't spoil it," he argued. "Trust me. Keep reading."

"Whatever." I rolled my eyes up to the dusky evening sky and took a dainty sip of bourbon. "I don't want to read it now."

"Figures. I know you, huh?"

"Stubborn? Obstinate? Know it all?" He nodded, grinning wide while he held an Anderson Valley Hazy Sour Ale aloft. "You think you're smart, don't you, Trey?"

"I went to Georgia State too, so I am as smart as you," he replied. "But it doesn't take a genius to figure you out. You make it easy. You don't hide your feelings or your personality. Even with strangers, you exude Esme-ness."

"Esme-ness," I repeated. "Explain this."

"No nonsense. No bullshit. Bullet train to the point."

"Ah. My sisters will love that this essence of me has a fancy word."

"Sisters. How many?"

I laughed. "Two."

"Two? You make it sound like there's a whole bunch of them."

"They're a lot. Jewel and Jada. Jewel teaches eighth grade math."

"Older? Younger?"

"Older by ten years. They're twins."

"Identical?" I nodded. "Do they look like you?"

"I look like *them*. We all look like our mother. The hair, the eyes, the nose, the skin—"

"Mmmph!" He grunted, furrowing his brows and sipping more beer. "That's where you get that luminous mocha landscape from."

"You can tell that we are sisters. But I'm young and single. They're old and married."

Trey's head tilted. It made him look like a puppy. "And why—"

"Nuh-uh. If you ask me why I am single, I will throw you off of this roof. Don't."

"Esme, you're scared to get out of that chair, and I've got height and pounds on you. You're not throwing me anywhere."

"Stop knowing me! It's creepy!"

Trey laughed, then took a long, slow swallow. I tried not to watch his Adam's apple bob as he drank, but... well, he was right in front of me. I couldn't help it. I joined him, bringing my bourbon to my lips.

"No brothers?"

I shook my head. "I wasn't a planned baby. After I came, they tried again for a boy, but..." I shrugged.

"You're their little miracle, then."

"If you want to put it that way."

"I do."

"You strike me as an only child."

Trey laughed. "That's...that's funny. What about me says I'm an only child?"

"Petulant. Demanding to get your way, throwing a fit if you don't. Comfortable with silence. I could go on—"

"I get the picture," he said, nervously weaving his fingers through his beard. "I'm not an only child. I have an older sister, but we didn't grow up together. Long story." He waved a long fingered hand in the air, brushing the subject aside. "Missy would probably agree that I act like an only child, though."

"So, what do you want me to know about you, Trey?"

He shook his head. "I'm a guy with a job."

"Do you like your job?"

A shadow crossed his face; it was brief, but I saw it. His lips twisted to the side, and he averted his gaze.

"Don't answer that," I said, my words rushing out, so they were jumbled together. "Sorry. I... you looked like you didn't want to—"

"It's fine, Esme," he interrupted. "The job that I have is not the job that I want, but it is the job that I need to do to get the job that I want. Make sense?"

I bobbed my head. It did.

"You get one free answer. You have to work for the rest."

"Work?"

"Yeah, work. I'm not offering up my personality to you for free. You gotta win the rest. What are you ordering for dinner?"

"Aight, so."

Trey clapped his palms together, then rubbed them, giving me a grin that told me I was in for some fun.

"The point of this game is simple. Roll the ball up the hill, over the hump, into the numbered rings. The bigger the number, the bigger the point value. You win by accumulating the highest points. Do you want my tips for best play, or do you want to wing it?"

"Oh, I want tips. We need an even playing field. What do I get if I win?"

"You will not win, Esme."

"So says you, but let's say that I do."

"I don't know. I guess I have to share something about myself."

"What are you going to share when I win?"

"You aren't going to win. But uh… I'll tell you my actual name."

"What?" I whipped around to face Trey, who was pressing the buttons to make the balls fall. "Trey isn't your name?"

"Don't you wish you had done some background research on me?" He shot me a smarmy grin. "Don't you wish they taught you that, at that fancy school you went to?"

"Alright. Ok. It's on. I win, I get information. What if you win?"

"Then I win."

"No prize if you win?"

"I'm spending time with a beautiful woman on a perfect Atlanta evening. I'm full of smoked ribs, cornbread, and greens, and I'm about to play a game that I haven't played since college. I've already won."

It took a few beats, but eventually, I processed what he'd said.

And blushed. *Fuck that bourbon.*

"Trey… you don't have to flirt with me. I know this isn't—"

"I'm not flirting with you," he interrupted. "Flirting intimates that I aim to manipulate your emotions and increase your attraction to me for romantic purposes. I'm just stating facts. I am here, at this place that I enjoy with you, a woman who is beautiful on a clear, warm evening, full of food and drink. I don't need a prize for this game that you're not going to win if I don't give you my tips for best play. You want them or not?"

My eyes narrowed, and I did my best to scowl through the smile that spread across my lips. "These better be some winning tips, the way you're talking them up."

Trey taught me how to stand, the best way to throw, how to angle the ball so that it hits the ring I want to hit. Once the game started, however, the pressure was on, and I was a sorry Skee-ball player. My balls kept bouncing off of the side of the lane and rolling back down the slope until I picked them up and tossed them instead of rolling them.

"Hey! That's not how you play the game!" Trey called, easily rolling the balls up and dropping them, consistently, in the 75 and 100 score rings.

"Your tips suck! This is the only way this ball is making it into that ring!" I hucked the ball toward the 100 point ring. It landed, circling the ring. The machine exploded in lights and sounds. "I got one!"

"One," Trey repeated, smirking. I looked over at his score and shook my head. There was no catching up to his near 1,000 point score.

"Whatever. You picked a game that you're an expert in, so you'd have an advantage."

"Sometimes it be like that. Sometimes you walk into a situation that you thought you knew, and you get thrown for a loop because someone else had an advantage. Sucks to be on the other side of that, doesn't it?"

I paused play, slowly turning to Trey, who was still rolling balls next to me. "Is that supposed to be a dig at me?"

"No. But take it however you want to take it."

"Miller brought me in because you were impossible to work with, and he has a company to run."

"Like I don't?"

"Doesn't seem like it, since you spend most of your time at Miller getting on my nerves and arguing ridiculous contract terms."

"They're not ridiculous when it's my bank account that he's playing in. I owe it to Pettigrew to fight for every penny that I don't have to spend to acquire this company. If you were on this side of the table, you would agree. Don't pretend that you wouldn't."

A buzzer sounded overhead, and the machines went dark, ending play until we inserted more coins.

"I win."

"You didn't pick a prize, so did you win?"

"I got under your skin." He grinned. "Close enough. You feel like revenge?"

"Load 'em up. It's on."

Four games later, I won, though it was obvious that Trey was playing at less than half power so I could win. I didn't care. The way the machine lit up and spit out extra tickets to redeem for prizes, you'd have thought I won the lottery.

I clutched an oversized pencil and a bear with a t-shirt that read *I won this at Skyline Park Atlanta* under one arm and sipped a toasted coconut liqueur. Trey wanted dessert, so we went back to the rooftop, where he ordered skillet s'mores and two forks. We shared the dish and drank our sweet dessert drinks.

"You cheated, but I'll let you have your win."

"I didn't cheat. I was innovative."

"I don't think you'll ever be a professional Skee-ball player."

"Damn. Good thing I have a career to fall back on."

Trey's chuckle sat deep in his throat, barely audible over the noise from the tables near us. "You want your prize?"

"Hell yeah, I want my prize!" I shoveled a layered chunk of graham cracker, chocolate, and marshmallow into my mouth, trying not to hum my note of pleasure too loud. "What's your real first name?"

"My first name..." He paused, mostly for drama, but also, I suspected, to get on my nerves. "It's Saul. Not earth-shattering."

I paused. "Saul? Like your father?"

"Yep," he said, nodding, then going in for a bite of hot, gooey chocolate and marshmallow. "Pops is Saul Pettigrew II. I'm the third. They wanted me to carry on the name but also have an identity. They've called me Trey my entire life."

"Hmmm. How uh... I mean, do you harbor any feelings of resentment about sharing a name with your father and your grandfather?"

"Resentment? Nah. I do feel, though..."

Trey's voice trailed off, then he lifted his glass of liquor to his lips. I wasn't sure he'd pick up where he left off, but he went on. "My dad has these goals and visions for me, you know? He and my grandfather dreamed up Pettigrew. He built it from the ground up. It's a good, strong business with a great future. I'm proud to be a part of the legacy. And it's not that I hate the business. I just..."

Trey shrugged. And frowned, his brows knit together.

"It's the job you need to do to get the job that you want. It's why you can't walk away from this deal with Miller."

"Exactly," he agreed quietly. "I'm going to get it done. I have to. I don't have to like it, though. And I don't. Except for working with you." His eyes found mine and held my gaze for a long moment. "And being with you right now."

I didn't know how to respond to that. So I didn't. But I also didn't break the intense contact.

"Esme, do you trust me?"

"No. Why do you ask?"

"Liar."

I pushed out a breath, wondering what this would lead to. "Alright. Five minutes of trust. What do you need?"

"Do you hear the music?"

I turned my head, as though it would make me hear the strains of music more clearly. Now that I was paying attention, I recognized Smooth by Santana featuring Rob Thomas. The sultry Latin hit screamed up the charts while I was in college.

"Yeah, I hear it."

He stood, grabbing my hand to pull me up. "Come dance with me."

"I–"

"I know. It's the roof, and you might fall off. I won't let go. I promise."

He drew me tight against his body. I followed his lead, dipping one way, then switching it up. Despite the rooftop being about half occupied, he led me around the space like we were alone, his eyes half closed, his shoulders swaying with the beat of the drum, flowing with the whine of the guitar.

"Relax. I've got you," he leaned in to whisper, his mouth so close to my ear that his breath stirred the hairs on the back of my neck. Goosebumps cascaded down my body. "Feel the beat, move with me. Like that."

Trey's thighs were muscled, rock hard as he anchored his stance and moved us side to side. His hand slid from my side to the small of my back, pulling me into him, close enough to feel his thickness between us pressed into my belly. My body responded, moving in rhythm and time to him, not even tempted to pull back in shyness, because maybe he hadn't intended for me to know that he was hard.

Or… maybe he did mean to press into me, calling it dancing only because it was on the beat, on this hang out that seemed to be turning into a date no matter how many times I told myself that it was not a date.

Trey inched us back to our table as the song faded out, and another one began. He headed to his seat, then stopped and bent to kiss me.

Not a peck on the cheek. A licking and sucking my lips

into his mouth kiss. A *turning me into goo, setting me on fire, clit hardening, nipple pearling, making all of my body parts buzz* kiss.

When he pulled back, and I managed to pry my eyes open, he was grinning down at me. "*Now* I'm flirting with you, Esme."

I stepped back, regrettably out of his arms, tugging my t-shirt down and running my fingers through my hair. Anything to appear to have something else to do besides stare at him because *what the fuck just happened*?

And why do I want to ask him to follow me home and show me what that long, hard, thickness do? I sucked in a long breath and slowly, *slowly* let it out.

"Wow, look at the time. I need to head home. Do I owe you anything? For the drinks or… the game?"

Trey sat up in his seat, his eyes wide. "You're leaving? I'm sorry, I overstepped—"

"No!" I held up a hand to stop him before he said another word. "Don't apologize. Tonight was so much fun, but I need to leave; otherwise, I am going to make bourbon and liqueur induced decisions."

Trey's chin lifted as he inhaled deeply. Then he nodded. He got my point. "I feel you. I'll walk you to your car."

I wanted to insist that I could take care of myself, that I wasn't parked too far inside the deck and would be fine, but Jewel's words came back to me. Don't be mean today, Es.

"Sure," I answered instead. "I'd like that."

"I'll take care of the bill and meet you at the elevator. Don't forget your prizes. You won them fair and square."

With a wink, he picked up the folio with the printout of our bill and headed toward the line to cash out. I took one last look around the rooftop, smiling at the glistening lights of downtown, then grinning at the Ferris wheel making another revolution across the park.

I tipped the last of the liquor into my mouth and walked

back to the elevator to wait for Trey, pulling out a tube of lip gloss, since he'd just kissed all of mine off.

Today… was a day. I couldn't wait to talk to O'Neal.

Trey pushed his wallet into the back pocket of his jeans as he approached. Something about the way he moved, the way his shirt stretched across his chest and shoulders, the way he carried himself in such a casual yet self-assured way… shit.

Somebody struck a match and relit the pilot light.

"So, you made it to the rooftop."

"Twice!" I noted. The elevator doors slid open, and we stepped inside the cube.

"Twice. And you didn't die. How about that?"

"I also rode a Ferris wheel today. I don't know if you knew that."

"I had heard that. You were very, very brave, Esme."

I laughed, picking up on the shade in his tone. "Shut up, Trey."

"I'm serious. Fear knows no age. It defies logic. You can't talk yourself out of fear. You have to be brave; to decide that you want to work through it more than you want to give into it. You did that today. That's dope."

"You sound like you speak from experience."

"A little bit," he mused. "A little bit."

The elevator doors slid open, revealing the landing and the underground food court. Unhurried, we strolled past counter serve shops that sold snacks and beverages. Pizza, popcorn, hot dogs, what my father would call carnival food. He loved carnival food.

"I forgot to tell you that I spoke with Miller this afternoon. I told him that you had agreed to 90 days of health and wellness coverage for the employees that he'll have to release. He was pleased."

"There's nothing I love more than pleasing Thomas Miller."

"Sarcasm aside, he thinks our offsite excursions are a good

idea. And that I got you to budge on anything at all is nothing short of a miracle."

"He's right. I was so sure that I could wear him down that I wasn't being fair. It was more about trying to impress my father by brokering a better deal than the one he offered. I guess Miller went to a fancy school, too."

"Mmmmm. Wharton and then Savannah College of Art and Design."

"Oh. He's smarter than us, is what you're saying."

"But you know how some people have book smarts but not street smarts? That's Miller. He can't imagine any other way that this shakes out except to sit in a room and argue about it. The idea that we went off-site to negotiate is revolutionary to him."

Trey cocked his head back and laughed. "Esme, the idea of a red tie is revolutionary to him. He's the greyest man I've ever met."

I laughed along, realizing that I'd felt the same way since I met him.

Our footsteps echoed through the parking garage as we both headed toward my car, parked near the entrance so that I wouldn't have any trouble finding the car and getting out of the garage.

"So... look. I'm not just saying this. Tonight was nice. Thanks for meeting me. And trusting me."

"Thanks for asking me. I have things to mark off of my list now."

"You're still not going to tell me all the stuff on the list, are you?"

"Mmmmm..." I bobbed my head side to side, pretending to think it over. "Nah. It's more fun for you to not know yet."

"I need to ask you an inappropriate question about your list, given our working relationship."

I inhaled, wondering if he was going to ask, again, if sex was on the list.

And if I was going to tell him that it was.

"Given our recent agreement to exchange favors for contract concessions," I said, "I don't think I have room to complain about inappropriate questions."

"Aight, bet." He paused, making sure I was hanging on every word before he spoke again. "So… is having a man kiss the shit out of you in a parking garage on your list? Because if it's not, we might need to add it."

The thought of another pass of his lips brought a 'wave of heat that flushed through my body. I didn't think about it or argue against it or tell myself that this was not a date. In a few steps, I crossed the short span of distance, gripped the back of his neck, and relished in the feeling of him clutching my hips to pull me to him, angling his head slightly to the right as our lips met.

He growled low, slipping his tongue between my lips. Unlike the kiss before, it was sensual and slow, more intimate and intoxicating than a fevered, passionate smashing of our mouths together.

With a groan, and then a short exhale, Trey released my body and my lips. He swiped a hand across his mouth, frowning at the film of gloss.

"I thought women wore that paint stuff that doesn't come off when you kiss."

"I wore that earlier."

"I should have kissed you on the Ferris wheel like I wanted to."

"You wanted to?"

"Woman..." Trey let out a little chuckle, then reached up to scratch his neck while giving me a squinty smile. "I've wanted to kiss you since I asked if I could take your chair, and you damn near cussed me out."

"I did not."

"You almost called me everything but a child of God, as my mother would say."

"My cousin said you were flirting with me."

"Your cousin is right. But..." He shrugged, then balled one hand into a fist and punched it into the other flat palm. "I got what I deserved. I was rude. I hope I have more than made up for that."

I nodded. "I was rude too." I gestured to the arousal that had to be embarrassing, but he was calm about it. "And I know I've made up for that."

He stepped around me and reached for my driver's side door, but it wouldn't open until I slid my finger across the sensor. He pulled the handle and held the door open.

"You need to get into your car and drive away. Bad decisions are about to be made."

Amen, I agreed in my head. I slipped into the driver's seat and waited until he firmly pushed the door shut before I pressed the START button, and the car purred to life. The seat belt automatically moved to enclose me in the car. I reached for the gearshift and put the car in reverse, then backed out of the spot while Trey stood a few feet away, watching me pull out.

I watched him wave from the rearview mirror. I waved back and headed to the exit.

My body was on fire, but not from the alcohol. My mind flashed memories of the day, the evening, the kiss. And then the other kiss.

Somehow, I was supposed to get up the next morning and sit in that little room and look at Trey Pettigrew in the eye and pretend that my vibrator didn't get a workout as soon as I got home.

And that I was no longer trying to pretend that I wasn't thinking about Trey.

CHAPTER SIXTEEN

Trey

My phone buzzed its usual alarm, but I was already awake. Sleep had been hard to come by all night.

I'd come home last night, prepared to shower and crawl into bed, except... I wasn't tired. My brain and my body competed to see which could bounce me off the walls harder, first with elation at gaining Esme's trust, enough to get personal and up close.

In the next moment, I berated myself for making that move. A personal connection based on what I knew was a mutual attraction could cause problems and a conflict of interest.

Why couldn't I control my mouth? And my dick. It was a good thing that I'd had no plan to keep my attraction to Esme a secret.

I needed to expel some energy, so I changed into a pair of basketball shorts, a sleeveless t-shirt, and my biking shoes and hopped on the Peloton for the *Late Night Ride*, a hip hop themed HIIT cycle class. The instructor, Sharida, had a sculpted body that was a work of art, and the perfect bald head. She wore bangles and chains that made little ringing noises that rode under the sounds of J Cole, Big Sean, and Kanye West. It helped me stay in rhythm and on pace. I loved her class when I could catch it.

When I still wasn't tired enough to sleep, I tapped out a quick text, grabbed a racquet, and headed down to the basement of my building. Twelve88 Towers was a mid-rise condo complex offering safe and luxurious living in the heart of Atlanta. I walked through the brightly lit social corner that overlooked the pool and jacuzzi. The area was dotted with plush couches, oversized chairs, and bistro tables. One of two well-stocked bars had a few patrons, as they were about to wrap up the evening.

I passed them both, rounding the corner to the fitness center and racquetball courts. I keyed in my passcode and entered court one, letting the door slam shut.

I paced the wood floors of the oblong, glassed-in room, listening to my footsteps echo and bounce off of the windows, swiping the air with the racquet every few seconds. Behind me, the steel door opened, then latched closed.

"Well, well, well. Look who made it to midnight racquetball."

I didn't need to turn around to know that Ken was happy to find me in his favorite spot in the building. He'd played racquetball all his life, was so skilled that he had the chance to try out for a pro team. When he had to choose between culinary school or racquetball, he made the tough call. Still, he liked to hit the court every night after the restaurant closed. It helped him to decompress so that he could sleep, then do it all again the next day.

I knew a thing or two about that. I would explode if I didn't work off some extra energy.

"I thought I'd join you if that's Ok."

"You kidding? I'm looking forward to kicking your ass," he

crowed, pulling a few small bright blue balls from a bag that he kicked to the side of the court, out of the way. I heard the Velcro of his gloves as he tightened them, the squeak of his shoes on the freshly varnished wood. "I could use the competition. You look like you've got something sitting on your shoulders. Rough night?"

"Actually…" I mused, smiling to myself while gripping my Ektelon racquet and moving into place for Ken to serve. "It was a really good night."

"I can't wait to hear this."

"So, remember that deal that I'm fucking up?"

Whap! The ball whizzed past me and slammed into the wall at the end of the court. I ran to intercept, swinging to make contact and send it back. Then it was Ken's turn to race, diving to just barely lob it back.

"Yeah. What's up with that? Did you fix it?"

"Enough that Pops is off my back, for the moment." The hard rubber made a hollow sound as it hit the ground. I reached, easily sending it back to the other side of the court. "Thing is that my target hired a contract administrator. You know, somebody to work out the finer points of the deal. I guess I was being a pain in his ass."

"You? No, I don't believe it." *Slam!* Ken executed a perfect splat, sending the ball forward and to the right. I crossed the court, sending the ball with a nice back shot. "So it's some pencil pusher nerd?"

"Nah. It's a woman. Like… a *woman*."

Ken turned on a heel, the ball in one hand, racquet in the other, both propped on his hips. "Shit, Trey. Do not tell me what I think you're about to tell me, man."

I paused to catch my breath and wipe a bead of sweat rolling down my forehead. "What am I about to tell you?"

"You said you had a great night. I'm guessing it has something to do with this contracts chick—"

"Woman. Her name is Esme."

"This *woman*. Esme. So you had a late working session? Or... something sexier?"

"In between. We had a good working day, so we decided to hang out. She met me at Ponce City Market. We had some drinks and dinner on the rooftop at 9 Mile Station and played some games. Then we had dessert. Talked a little. Danced a little…"

"Danced? Hardly contract negotiation activity—"

"I kissed her," I interrupted, unsure why I felt like I needed to confess to Ken. Or why I instantly felt lighter and less frazzled when I did.

"Kissed her." Ken's blank stare said a lot.

"Twice. I couldn't help it. She's so… *fucking—"*

"Fucking is what's on your brain, why you're at the courts at midnight when I usually have to drag you down here because you need your princely rest."

"My job takes a lot out of me. And I'm up at sunrise, unlike you."

Ken laughed, then dropped one of the balls he was holding. He swung his racquet, bouncing the ball against the wall. "I'm not that far behind you."

I laughed. "10 AM is so many hours past sunrise, man."

"Anyway. You kissed her."

"Twice."

"I take it the feeling is mutual?"

"She kissed *me* the second time."

"And you think you can still work with this woman."

"It's not like I was the only one having a good time."

"She could play you to get you to agree with whatever Miller wants."

"Or I could play her to get what I want."

The sound of the ball hitting the wall stopped echoing into the ceiling. "You're playing her?"

"No, man. No one's playing anyone. But I *am* trying to get close to her. I don't want her to see Pettigrew as this giant conglomerate monster with no feelings. I'm not trying to eat Miller's company alive and spit out the bones. I want the best of both worlds."

Ken's eyebrows rose. "Kissing her gets your point across."

"Look, I know. It's dangerous ground. But..." I turned, pacing the room. "I don't care. Which is also dangerous."

"She must be an amazing woman for you to not feel Pops' breath on the back of your neck."

I slowed my steps, glancing back at him before I resumed pacing. Ken hissed a breath through his teeth.

"Wow, it's like that? What makes her worthy of thumbing your nose at the job you need to do?"

"That's the thing—we're actually getting work done. We came to terms on a contract point that Miller and I have been arguing over."

I filled Ken in on the background, stopping short of my deal with her to clear her list, mostly because I was still confused about it. While we talked, we casually served and returned a ball. Less strenuous play, more to keep our hands busy.

"So, tonight..."

"Tonight was strictly about being with a beautiful woman in a place where we could relax, be one on one. I had a good time. And I know she did too. I haven't felt...*this*...in a long time, you know? The urge was so strong, it was hard to deny it. She was hard to walk away from."

"Hence being down here looking at my sweaty mug at—" Ken lifted his wrist to eye level to check his watch. "Nearly 1 AM."

I lifted my shoulders, then lowered them and exhaled a cleansing, calming breath. "Anyway, I put her in her car before I could talk myself into thinking I should ask her to come home with me."

"So, knowing that you probably have to wait until this deal is done to act on your feelings, will you be able to look her in the eye, share the same air and working space with her? Pops won't be interested in this burgeoning love story, as romantic as it is. Can you be the pit bull you need to be to close this deal?"

"Most definitely," I told him. "But keep your racquet handy. I'm going to need to work off a lot of energy."

"Hell yeah." Ken gave the ball a hard bounce, then served. "Heads up!"

Ken and I slammed the ball around for over an hour. Then, drenched in sweat, so exhausted that we were weaving down the hall to the elevator, we headed back upstairs. Ken lived two floors below me, so he slapped me a high five and got off on the 8th floor. I climbed to 10 and got out, then traveled the hallway to my condo.

When I got inside, my phone, which I had left on the charging pad, lit up with text messages.

Good luck, man. Haven't seen you this crazy over a woman in a long time. Get the deal done first. I'll cater the wedding, ha-ha.

"Don't even play," I mumbled aloud. I set the phone back on the mat and headed to the shower, peeling off my clothing as I went.

I already knew though… the first opportunity to get closer to Esme that presented itself, I'd likely take it. Damn the consequences.

CHAPTER SEVENTEEN

Esme

I woke up tired. A good tired. A worn-out tired.

I drove home in a horny fugue, pulled off all of my clothes and fell into bed. I drifted to sleep while watching one of my favorite Black romance movies, Love Jones, for the millionth time. I watched the action on the screen, in my mind flipping the scenario with Trey and me, that he showed up at my door like Darius showed up at Nina's place. That I let him smooth talk my boy shorts right off my body, then rode my vibe on the highest level while I imagined Trey taking me to places I've never been. Literally.

The Roku screen saver lit the still-dark room with a purple glow. My sheets were rumpled around me, my nightshirt was bunched up around my hips, and my headscarf was on the floor next to the bed. Apparently, I had a fitful night of sleep.

Naturally, my mind drifted to the evening before. And that man. And, being honest, his dick, which I hadn't stopped thinking about since it made its presence known. And since I was beginning to consider letting him get very close to me, very soon.

Did Trey sleep naked? Did he let his erection fly free? Did he restrain himself with briefs? Boxers? Boxer briefs? Was he thinking about me, the muscles in his arms and chest rippling, his breath catching while stroking himself lazily in the bed? Or would he hop in the shower, breathlessly pumping to orgasm under the spray of water?

More importantly, when I saw him today, would he act like last night was an anomaly? A one-off? That those kisses never happened, that we weren't vibrating off of each other's energy and that both of us decided to go home because if the situation were different, we'd have had sex?

Or... were tempted and primed to have sex until he found out that I was a virgin. Then he'd pull back and beg off, insisting that we should just be friends because what grown ass man wanted to stumble through a virgin's first time?

"Stop it," I mumbled aloud, tossing the light comforter back and rolling out of bed. "You're getting ahead of yourself."

I paced myself through my usual morning routine: a few minutes of deep breathing and intention setting on the yoga mat, a shower, and a yogurt, berry and flaxseed smoothie.

And then two chicken sausage links because that smoothie didn't do anything for me but keep me regular. I'd be chewing off my arm by 10 AM, and Trey was probably not taking me to breakfast two days in a row.

I wondered if Trey could cook. He seemed to eat out a lot.

I dressed with care in a rose gold, drape neck shell, pairing it with a black, asymmetrical hem skirt and a short blazer. I fastened the ankle straps around a pair of low heel sandals that showed off a pink pearl pedicure and still looked fresh and grabbed my bag.

What was Trey wearing today? Did he take as much care in looking casually seductive as I had this morning? I liked him in blue. His undertone made him striking in shades of blue.

I hopped in the car, fuming at myself because I didn't leave time to go to Brew Bar. I could be late, but I hated lectures on being late. Besides, I prided myself on being a professional, which included arriving on time. I'd have to make do with the hot brown water that they called coffee at Miller Design. At least they stocked flavored coffee creamer.

Did Trey drink coffee? He never brought a travel mug or a to-go container with him. At breakfast, he'd had juice.

I turned into the parking lot at Miller Design with a few minutes to spare. Trey's dark maroon Acadia was parked right up front, clear of the trees that dropped flowers and branches on the other cars. His truck was spotless down to the rims and gleamed with the shine of a recent wax.

"Good morning, Jenny," I called, pulling open the front door and digging my security badge out of my bag. Trey wasn't in the lobby, as I'd expected him to be. "Is Mr. Pettigrew already here?"

"Yes," she answered, angrily pounding keys while cutting her eyes at the closed door a few steps away from the front desk. "He must get here at a ridiculous time because he's always waiting when I pull up. Then he paces in front of the desk, back and forth and back again, and takes calls on speaker, and pounds on his laptop until you get here. Yesterday, I gave him dirty looks until he took his phone call outside."

That made me want to laugh, but I stifled it.

"So today," she continued, "I let him back there to sit in the room you usually work in. He had a bunch of stuff with him anyway. I told Thomas that he's driving me crazy, and if they decide to keep me when they take over, I want a raise for having to deal with him."

"I'll see if I can work that into the deal," I told her, then swiped my badge across the reader. When it beeped, I pulled the door open and stepped through, waiting until it closed behind me to giggle.

I was still chuckling to myself as I approached the conference room that Trey and I used for our discussions. The scent of something wonderful almost bowled me over as soon as I walked in.

Two tall cups from Brew Bar were on the table, alongside a box of mini cappuccino muffins. Napkins, sugar, cream and stir sticks were piled on a short stack of small plates.

Trey was in his usual spot, his head bowed over his tablet.

I strode into the room toward the chair that I usually sat in. "You're wearing out your welcome with Jenny. She's threatening to demand a raise if you take her to Pettigrew."

"The goal was to be enough of a pest to get me back here," he said, not looking up.

"This is that only-child behavior that I was talking about." He didn't look up, but I did see his cheeks round with his smile. "Remember, she knows where the bones are buried. All the secrets of how the company really works. How the invoices get paid, who works the longest, the hardest—"

"Alright, alright. Point made. I'll be good."

"What's with coffee and muffins?"

Trey looked up finally, pulled a pair of drug store readers from his eyes, then flipped the leather cover of the tablet closed. Even if they were for fashion, he looked great in glasses.

"Yesterday, I noticed that you had coffee from Brew Bar. If I hit Peachtree on the way to Pettigrew, I pass them. I always wonder how their coffee tastes. Since you must like them—" He paused to level a questioning glance at me.

When I nodded, he continued, gesturing toward the little feast on the table. "I decided to give it a shot. I didn't know what you'd like, so I got vanilla. Everybody likes vanilla. They had mini muffins on special, and the girl at the counter caught me in a good mood, so I grabbed a dozen."

"A good mood," I crooned, reaching for one of the tall cups and a couple containers of cream. "Mr. Pettigrew is in a *good mood* today. So you're making this an easy Friday for me?"

"See, your sarcasm is ruining this moment."

I laughed. "This is very nice, Trey. Especially since I didn't get a chance to stop. I thought I would have to suffer through the coffee here."

I glanced up, grimacing. I caught Trey doing the same.

"That is not coffee," he said. His lips made the saddest but funniest downturn while he slowly shook his head. "That is…"

"Hot brown water," I finished, laughing. "I wasn't sure if you drank coffee because I never see you with a cup."

"In the morning before work. Any later than noon, and I'm up all night. Early on in our negotiations," he said, picking up the cup in front of him as he spoke, "I accepted coffee from Miller. Black, like I usually drink it at home."

He shook his head. "Mistakes were made. I vowed to never drink the coffee here again."

"Same," I said, using the stir stick to turn the brew into a creamy brown.

"I typically only drink coffee at home. I'm not saying I'm a connoisseur or anything, though I order my beans online and grind them myself. Coffee shouldn't taste like broken dreams."

"I have my beans ground at Kroger, but I agree." I took a sip from my cup and smiled. Perfect. "How do you like Brew Bar, then?"

"Not bad," he answered, sipping too, pleased that I smiled. "Agreement is a good place to start the day, don't you think?"

"Are we transitioning to work talk now?"

"Not before I tell you that you are fine as hell today, head to toe. And yes, I caught the toes."

I felt myself blush and dipped my head to hide the flush on my skin. "Thank you, Trey. But we should probably not talk—"

"Did you think about me last night?"

He lowered his voice to just above a whisper. Miller couldn't hear him if he was seated in the chair next to me.

"After you went home to your cozy south Atlanta home, took off those tight ass jeans and that cute t-shirt, and that bra that must have cost a fortune because it had your titties sitting up just right, did you think about me? Did you wonder if I was thinking about you? Did you *hope* I was thinking about you?"

"I—I don't know what—"

"Because I thought about you. All of you, from the tightest curl on your head to those hips that rocked the beat with me last night, to the very last painted toe, have been on my mind nonstop. I thought about you all night. All morning."

Either I was having a hot flash or it was the electricity in the room, but I was parched suddenly, and near breaking a sweat. Trey was barely audible, but my body heard him loud and clear. My thighs involuntarily clenched, and I prayed that the hardened nubs of my nipples weren't poking through my bra.

"Trey, we cannot have this conversation right now," I told him when I had gathered myself enough to complete a sentence. "Definitely not here. We have a job to do. Thank you for the coffee and the muffins. Let's get to work. I have an appointment this afternoon, and I want to make some headway before then."

"You're right."

He pushed back from the table and picked up his tablet, sliding the cover off again. The face of the device lit up with activity.

"Work conversation, boring chit chat. Safe. I get you but understand something, Esme Whitaker. I'm committed to getting this contract signed because when neither of us has an ethical obligation to stay away from each other, I plan to pursue the shit out of you. If you don't want that, I need you to let me know now."

I cleared my throat, then cleared it again. Still parched. I reached into my bag to unpack my laptop, notebook, pens, highlighters and a well-worn, dog eared, marked up, and sticky note covered copy of the contract.

"We really need to get to work, Trey. So we can get this deal done."

"Is that your way of saying you'd welcome a pursuit?"

My face blazed fire-hot, which was no match for my galloping heart and everything happening below my waist and in my head. I wanted this man to do *more* than pursue me. I wanted him to conquer me. To possess me. To make me his in a way that no man had ever done.

"Yes. That's what that means."

I swallowed hard, then sucked down a lungful of air. I gave this man the green light to come for me. Did he know how much of a head start he already had?

"Which section would you like to work on today, Mr. Pettigrew? Several points are ripe for discussion."

"We're back to that? You call me Mr. Pettigrew when you're—"

Boldly, I flicked my eyes up to his. In the seconds that passed, I watched his facial expression morph from amusement to... something else. I hoped he caught the tendrils of smoky attraction that I tried to radiate across the table.

Trey rolled his tongue across his teeth under closed lips and nodded. "I got you," he muttered quietly. Then at a normal volume, said, "Stock options. I think we're close to an agreement. I have a few notes that I'd like you to consider."

I strolled into Jada's Beauty Boutique & Spa at three o'clock on the dot. I never needed an appointment—the perks of being related to the owner—but I always gave Jada a heads up that I was coming through. I'd texted her earlier that morning, and she'd responded, *good because we need to talk.* I wondered what that was about.

"Aunt Esme!"

Jada's daughter, Layah, squealed as she hurried around the reception desk to wrap her arms around my neck. She was tall and slim, already 5'10" at fifteen. She also reaped the benefits of being related to the owner. Her deep brown skin was flawless, her brows and lashes immaculate, and a fresh set of box braids cascaded down her back.

I beamed. I hadn't expected to see one of my nieces today. "Hi, sweetheart. You have practice today?"

I stepped back to eye her uniform of black knee-length shorts and a sleeveless t-shirt with the Atlanta Women's Hoops logo in the center. Hoops was a privately funded, city team that gave Layah more opportunities than the basketball team at John Lewis High. The city teams play year-round, not just in the winter, and play wasn't tied to her grades or attendance, though Jada wouldn't let Layah play unless she kept both in line.

"Tonight. I told Mama I would help out this afternoon since we had an early dismissal."

"Did you really have an early dismissal, or did you get bored and leave school?"

Layah cringed. She had to know that I'd bring up that time my gifted and grown niece was so bored with the material being taught that she left school in the middle of the day. After that, Jada looked into switching her to advanced classes and put her in basketball—anything to occupy that enormous brain. Her brother, Courtney, was on the same path.

"Why you gotta bring up old stuff, Aunt Esme? Let it go."

"Because I'm your auntie, and it's my job." The phone trilled a ring throughout the airy, sunlit salon. I tapped Layah on the shoulder. "Get back to work. Where's your mom?"

"Out on the patio," she said, before picking up the line and crisply delivering the standard greeting.

I weaved through the salon, saying hello to Jada's long-time staff. Some were at their chairs creating art with hair, some were in the massage rooms working out stress, and some were at the nail bar. She ran a tight but fair and profitable ship, so she didn't lose staff often, and when she did, the seat didn't sit empty for long.

At the back of the shop was the business office, the storage room where she kept her stock, and the break room, which housed two washers, one dryer and a full kitchen set up. She was open six days a week, so she liked the back office to feel like home. There were many nights that I'd bring dinner, and we'd sit in the kitchen together and eat.

A set of French doors were propped open, white sheers fluttering in the afternoon breeze. I stepped out onto the stained wood deck that Jada's husband built behind the salon, turning an ugly, unusable concrete pad into usable space. Customers could wait up front or on the patio, grab a drink from the bar cart, and relax in the lounge area.

"Yeah, she just got here. I'll tell her."

Jada pulled her phone from her ear and watched me approach her spot at a patio table under an umbrella. A full glass and a plate of cheese and crackers sat in front of her, and she looked cozy casual in a grey Nike Sportswear shorts romper and sneakers.

I grabbed the mason jar and took a sip, frowning as I set it back down in front of her. "Vodka lemonade before you put your hands in my hair?"

A face that was more like mine than her twin returned my smile. "I always have a sip before I do your hair," she answered, flipping her own set of braids behind her shoulder. Hers had bubble gum pink hair weaved into the braids, and they looked amazing on her. Benning prohibited unnatural hair colors; otherwise, I'd be tempted to do the same.

145

"Mmhmm," I hummed. "Does your husband know you got your thighs out?" I gave her flesh a meaty slap then dropped into the seat next to her. "Tell me what? Who was on the phone? Your sister?"

I chuckled, reaching for two Ritz crackers from the sleeve she had opened.

"You haven't checked into the family chat since you got on that Ferris Wheel. The people need the update, and you haven't delivered."

"I lived, obviously." The buttery cracker melted in my mouth as I shrugged my shoulders. "I talked to you right after. What updates do the people need? And by the people, do you mean O'Neal, who hasn't answered any of my texts?"

"Oh, he got on another leg from Milan to Dubai, I think? Somewhere far away with no cell service for a minute. He'll probably hit you when he gets to wherever. Or back home."

"Weird how I live with him, and you know his schedule better than I do."

"It wouldn't be weird if you checked WhatsApp ."

I rolled my eyes and reached for my phone. I opened the app and scrolled. And scrolled. And scrolled. Random chit chat. Jewel was buying an air fryer. My mother was raving about Palm Springs— they'd pulled into the resort late the evening before and were settling in for the next few weeks. Jada asked about getting bubble gum out of towels. Kids loved to stick their gum in salon towels.

"What am I looking for, Jada?"

"Conversation! We just be talking in there."

I closed the app and put the phone away. "I don't have time for conversation."

"Don't even tell that lie. You have plenty of time for conversation between all those tv shows you watch and those books you read."

"Well, I might not have free time like that for the next couple of weeks."

Jada leaned back. Then leaned in again. "Is this a super casual way of updating me on the guy at work?"

"Maybe." I shrugged. "Ask me where I was last night."

"Where were you last night, Esme Whitaker?"

"The rooftop at Ponce City Market."

"The what?" Jada screeched. "You got on somebody's roof? After the Ferris wheel? Was Shonda Rhimes up there?"

"Y'all are gonna stop picking on my love of Shonda Rhimes shows like you don't watch them too."

"Don't change the subject. What were you doing on the roof?"

"I was on a date," I answered slyly, swiping more crackers. "With the guy from work."

"Aren't you—can you do that? Date him and work on the contract?"

"Not really." I shrugged. "We're not dating. We're hanging out."

"Unh huh. On rooftops and riding Ferris wheels and shit." Jada's eyes rolled skyward. "So, you think you like him? I mean, he got you up on a roof, so I guess so."

"Yeah. I'm... kind of thinking that he might be The One. I mean, I don't mean my soulmate. But I mean…"

"You're trying to decide if you're going to fuck him."

"I came to you because you're sensitive and romantic, Jada." Her belly laugh was contagious. I laughed, too.

"Hell, Esme. I have two teenage children. I haven't been romantic in about sixteen years. My husband sends his regards."

"Whatever. You two moon over each other all the time."

Jada smiled. Her eyes squinted like they always did when she talked about her husband, Joe. "He is the shit, ain't he?"

"Anyway, so yeah. I'm thinking that I might… you know."

"If you can't say the words, you can't do the deed. You're grown. You can say sex. Intercourse. Fuckin'. Dick in pussy—"

"Yeah, I got it. So, yeah. I might see if he's interested."

"In letting him hit that? Poppin' that cherry?"

I threw up my hands in frustration. "I feel like I'm talking to Layah right now."

"What do you want from me, Esme? Should I encourage you to go for it because you're about to turn forty, and now's as good a time as any? Do you want me to talk you out of it because it's something that should be organic? What do you want?"

"Organic isn't going to happen," I mumbled, coming back from my silly mood. "If I want it, I have to take control. Make it happen. Make sex happen."

There was the matter of a list and a contract and two businesses in the balance, but I couldn't really talk about that part of the situation.

"I don't think you'll have to work that hard, Es. Men like sex."

"Do they like sex with virgins?"

"Some do."

I huffed, balancing my elbows on the table and resting my head in my hands. "I want him to want me and want me to be ready. I want him to want me to have a good time and not be weird about it being my first time. I want him to make sure I come and not think less of me because I waited so long, and I didn't fuck him like a pornstar right out of the gate. Men don't like… instructing."

"You don't think— what is this man's name, so I can stop calling him the guy from work?"

"Trey. His name is Trey."

"You don't think Trey can be that guy? Tell him what you need. Can he deliver or not?"

I sat up, then. "So, today, he told me that when this contract is out of the way, he plans to pursue me. He asked if I wanted that, because if not, he'd back off."

Jada's brows rose. She urged me to continue. "And you said…"

"I said... I... would welcome his pursuit."

"Well, ok. You 'bout to bust it open!"

"Until he finds out that I'm a virgin. He's expecting sex and—"

"The whole point is for him to expect sex."

"I don't want to feel like I'm tricking him, like getting him to the point and then springing it on him. But I also know from experience that men fade away when you tell them that you don't have the same history that his last five girlfriends had."

"The women that came before you have nothing to do with you. They're none of your business. There's no wrong answer here, Es, but I promise you can make this happen without tricking him into sleeping with you. You're taking that step on your terms, and that's going to have to be enough for him. If it's not, he's not the last man on the planet. Alright?"

"Right." I nodded. "In the meantime? I still want him."

Jada grinned. "Tell me *all* about this man that got you on a Ferris Wheel and took you to a rooftop. Have you sampled the goods? You know what I mean?"

"Jada..." I laughed, shaking my head. "No. We kissed, though. Twice."

"But you're *not* dating. Hanging out, huh? He got skills?"

I huffed, fanning myself. "That shit felt like fucking with our clothes on."

"Because you know how that feels."

"I know exactly how that feels. We danced for few minutes. We were close enough that I... well, I got an idea of what he's working with."

"He's got a big ol' dick?"

"I don't know why I thought you'd be more sensitive than Jewel would be. She wants me to jump him already."

"So does O'Neal. Three for three. What do *you* want?"

I hesitated before answering because Jada knew me better than anyone. I had a great relationship with Jewel, and O'Neal was my best friend, but I had a special kinship with Jada, always had. She'd know if I was lying or holding back. I squirmed in my seat, twisting so I leaned close enough to say what I wanted to say without whispering.

"I want… him… to fuck the shit out of me." I nodded.

"Mmmhmm. Speak on it."

"Multiple times. In multiple ways. Just…" I formed a fist and pounded the table. "I need him to hit it hard, one good time."

"You probably need more than one good time, but I feel you."

"I'm serious, Jada. I was *on fire*. I almost asked him to follow me home last night."

"See, you need to be careful. Good dick will trap you. Turn you right out. That's how I ended up with that man and those hooligans you call niece and nephew."

"Jada, shut up. Joe chased you all the way through college."

"I let him think that. I'm hooked, honey. You find yourself a good man with a good dick, you don't let go. You got a picture of this Trey?"

I pulled out my phone again and scrolled to a photo that I'd saved off the Pettigrew Construction website. "It's an old picture," I told her, turning the phone around. She frowned, and I understood why.

Trey wasn't much to look at in whatever era that photo was taken, but since then, he'd had a glow up. "He's thinner now. Leaner with a beard and a nice cut. You heard O'Neal. He's working with something."

"If you like him, I love him. And you didn't scream once on that Ferris wheel? Didn't wail and demand they let you out of that thing like you did every fucking time we tried to take you to an amusement park?"

I locked the phone again and put it away. "I might have tried to climb out of that gondola before the attendant shut us in. And I also might have impaled his hand with these claws you put on me." I furled my nails toward her like a cat. "He's not a fan of these."

"Joe likes when I use them on his—"

"Mama?" I turned to find my niece halfway hanging out of the open space between the salon and the patio.

"Dammit, Layah. I'm trying to have a conversation with your Auntie! What?"

"My ride to practice has to pick me up early, in about an hour. Adam said he'd cover the phone."

"Alright. Don't leave this building without letting me know you're gone, little girl."

"Yes, mama."

"Mmmhmm. Yes, mama all day and then do what you want. You're one bad decision from losing your phone. I'm not playing."

"I hear you, mama." I felt Layah roll her eyes when she turned around to walk back to the salon.

"What is that about?"

"House rules, Esme. When they break them, they've got to feel the consequences. That one—" She pointed in the direction of the salon. "Acting like she's grown and out of my house like I don't pay a pretty penny for her lifestyle. She don't bankroll nothin'."

I laughed while Jada fumed. My phone buzzed inside my bag. I pulled it out and saw that I had a new incoming text. Trey and I had finally exchanged phone numbers if we needed to reach each other outside of Miller.

Or, in Trey's case, if he needed to send me texts that I read in his quiet storm voice.

Trey Pettigrew: *Hey, girl. How you doin'? Anyway, if you're not busy tomorrow night, we could do whatever scary thing you gotta do from your list...after you join me for dinner. Let me know.*

"Uh... hang on a second, Jada. I got a text. From... from

work." Why was I lying about Trey texting me? "Can I meet you at your chair?"

"Yeah. It got hot out here anyway."

I waited until Jada was back inside the cool shade of the salon before I opened my texts and thumbed out a reply.

Next on the list is an extreme sport. You up for that?

Trey Pettigrew: *I'm up for whatever. Extreme sport, though?*

You read me. You scared? :)

Trey Pettigrew: *Nah. I'm not scared of nothin but Pops. Can I pick the sport? I have some ideas.*

I guess. But I'm done with heights for now.

Trey Pettigrew: *No bungee jumping. Got it. Can I pick you up?*

I started to answer yes. Then erased it, to type that I could handle my transportation. Him picking me up would make it too much like a date. But then I argued with myself about my Esme-ness and went back to the app.

Sure. Since you know where I live. No sushi.

Trey Pettigrew: *Still missing out on a good thing. I'll let you know what time to be ready tomorrow. Can't wait to see you.*

My cheeks were flush and round when I closed the app and headed into the salon.

"Was that Trey on the phone?"

My eyes met hers in the mirror as I sat in her salon chair. Her lips twisted into a knowing smirk. "I don't know who you thought you were fooling. It's Jada, baby! Your whole face tells the story. Y'all doing some more *hanging out?*"

"Yeah, tomorrow," I admitted. Jada shook out a large black smock and circled my body with it, fastening the Velcro at the neck.

"Where to? Bungee jumping?"

"Hell no." My chest went cold at the thought of that. "I explicitly said no heights. I don't know where. He's planning it."

"A man that plans dates. I know the bar is on the floor, but as an old married woman, that's impressive."

"When men think they're going to get some, they work pretty hard."

"Any reason he should think otherwise, Esme? You said you planned to open the candy shop."

"Do you… do you have to put it like that?"

"Chile, I am grown and sexy. I can put it a lot of ways. And so can Joe."

"Isn't it time for my shampoo? I swear, I can't stand you. Did Joe cook, though? I'll be starving when I get out of this chair."

"He's grilling now. I was supposed to tell you that Jewel and Corey and the kids were coming over and that you were invited."

"The single, hungry bitch in me likes the sound of that."

CHAPTER EIGHTEEN

Trey

I used my sleeve to wipe a bead of sweat before it could trickle down the side of my face, but it was pointless. It was a hot, humid day, and I was working outside.

"I think it may be time to get a riding mower," mused Pops, who'd been keeping me company all day while I worked in the yard. Mom wouldn't let him do anything, but supervising was his strong suit, so he sat nearby in long khaki shorts that showed off muscular legs that needed sun and a thin t-shirt. Mom came out periodically with glasses of tea, a few snacks, and refilled my steel water tumbler.

"You need to hire a professional," I grumbled. "The trimming, the gardening, the mowing, not to mention the painting and repairs and minor renovations. It never used to be like this, but over the years of adding this and adding that..."

I wiped my face again, trying again to keep sweat out of my eyes. "There's too much going on here. You can't do it, and I don't plan to spend two Saturdays a month over here for the rest of my life."

"I know, son. We appreciate you coming to fill in."

"And I know you hate me picking on your baby girl, but Missy's arms and legs work fine. There's no reason she can't help, but when I call her, I get voicemail."

"Missy is—"

"Special. I know, Pops."

"In therapy on Saturdays, since you know so much. If you'd take the time to speak with her, you'd know her new therapist is working wonders with her. He has her on a whole new program."

I didn't have to look at him to know his face bore a scowl. It had been a nice day, near heat stroke notwithstanding. I opted not to poke the bear.

"I love doing it myself," he said, changing the subject. "It's soothing, and it gets me out of the house. You know your mother is picky about how things are done."

I looked up from the lawnmower, where I'd been detaching the bag that caught the clippings to dump them into a bin. I would drag that bin to a shed at the edge of the property where we kept compost materials. In the spring, Mom used that nutrient-rich mix for her new plantings. She swore by it and had been doing it for years.

"Yeah, I know. That's how I got stuck with your chore list."

"It's hard getting used to change. I keep thinking that I'll be back to full power soon, but full power almost killed me. I have to give up some things. I don't like that. I'm not used to giving up control."

I stopped myself from commenting about riding me on the Miller acquisition, among other Pettigrew projects. He knew his shortcomings and faults. It didn't mean he wanted them parroted back.

"You don't have to give up control, Pops. You're sitting in the yard watching me do your job. You're in control right now.

It would make it easier for you to stay healthy and have time and energy to do the things you really want to do."

His head bobbed with his nod. "You're right. I'll look into it. May have some companies come by this week to give estimates."

"I'll believe it when I see it. I need to cut out early today, so I'm not staying for dinner."

"Oh? Big plans tonight?"

"Hanging out with a friend, Pops."

"Oh. Well. Alright. I'll let your mother know that it's just the two of us for dinner, then."

He rose from his lounge chair, walked through the emerald green, freshly cut, weeded and trimmed yard and entered the house. I set about cleaning off the lawnmower, then dragging the compost bin to the shed.

He wanted to press for information, just because I was being cagey. I was thankful that he resisted because I didn't want to lie to him about having a date with Esme. We were calling it hanging out, but I wasn't fooled by that term. By the heat level of our last kiss, and the conversation in the office the day before, neither was Esme.

Besides, I'd made it plain that I was attracted to her and that I had every intention of following through with that attraction. And she made it clear that she was open to that.

More than that, he could never know about our side deal. It was working, getting me to make progress with Miller. And getting me closer to Esme.

Speaking of Esme, I pulled my phone from my pocket and navigated to the text app. She hadn't responded to any texts since the night before, and I hadn't expected any, but I was open to a surprise flirty text or two if she was so inclined.

I thumbed out a short text and sent it. *Hey, girl. How's your Saturday?*

The bouncing dots that said she was replying didn't appear right away, so I put the phone back in my pocket and went back to dumping grass clippings into the compost bin. A few minutes later, my phone buzzed.

Esme Whitaker: *Hi. My Saturday is great. Yours?*

Weird, but I heard her voice in my head as I read her words. *Yard work*, I responded. *Hoping we're still on tonight so I have an excuse to bail.*

Esme Whitaker: *LOL. Yes, we're still on. What time will you be here? And where are we going?*

Does 6:00 work? And you'll find out when we get where we're going. Still trust me?

Esme Whitaker: *6 is fine. You only asked me to trust you for a few minutes.*

Trust me for a few hours. It'll be fun. See you at 6.

I locked the phone and slid it back into the pocket of my shorts, then cleaned up my mess and put the bin back in its assigned space. I mowed my parent's property twice a month, alternating the front and the back of the house, so I didn't have to come back to this shed full of decomposing, disintegrating yard waste for another few weeks. I closed the door tight, then attached the padlock and slipped the key into its hiding spot.

I lifted a hand to wave at my parents, who were having afternoon tea on the patio and admiring my handiwork. I climbed into the Acadia and backed out of the driveway, debating a quick nap before the evening's events.

It had been a long day in the yard after a sunrise Peloton session. I was exhausted, sweaty and filthy. I was eager to get home and get right for Esme.

I pulled up to the resident parking gate at my building and climbed out, handing the key to the valet. I told him I'd be back down around 5:15, so bring the car back up then. As always, I stood back while he carefully navigated the ramp to the parking garage, then swiped into the building and punched the elevator button for the tenth floor.

By the time I crossed the threshold of my condo, I was

already halfway undressed, having shed my t-shirt in the hallway from the elevator. I was itchy and covered in grass, so I dropped my shorts and t-shirt at the door, kicked off my shoes, took off my watch and headed straight for the shower.

Minutes later, I breathed a sigh of relief as I stood in the spacious gray marble shower under a torrent of hot water. The day cascaded off of my skin as I scrubbed a soapy washcloth over my body, then used an exfoliating cloth and cleanser on my face.

Finally, I stood under the shower head, letting the cooling water rinse the suds away. The force of the water pounded onto my shoulders, which was relaxing. In the back of my mind, I remembered that it wouldn't be another chill night at home watching whatever sport I could find, sprawled across the couch or even driving out to Pettigrew because there was always a pile of work on my desk that needed my attention.

Tonight, I would be with Esme. More than one part of my body became excited at the thought of being near her, touching her, the light perfume she wore invading the fiber of my clothing so that I smelled her scent even when I wasn't with her.

I would watch her roll those deep brown eyes at my corny jokes and twist those thick, red tinted lips when I said something smart... or smile when I complimented her. Which, by the way, I planned to do a lot of. There was so much to compliment, and she was pretty when she blushed.

I hoped we'd get the chance to get up close and personal, in the most literal way possible. My mind began a journey that it had traveled many, many times since I'd met Esme. Wondering, imagining, daydreaming about the day when my fingers could glide along her skin, when I could cup her breasts in my hands and pinch her nipples before taking them into my mouth and sucking them to full, taut attention.

I groaned aloud, pumping my dick in one hand, holding onto the built-in shelf in the shower with the other, my thoughts and desires to feel every bend of her curves up against my body running wild in my mind. I shuddered, climaxing with a groan and a spurt at the mental image of her long legs locked around my torso while I plunged deep into her, then her thighs flung over my shoulders as I devoured her. I heard her moan in my mind; imagined how she would shake and writhe under my power.

Fuck, I wanted her. Like I had never wanted a woman before.

I regained my breath and balance and, though the water was cold, scrubbed down once more for good measure and hopped out of the shower. I grabbed a bath sheet from the rack off of the wall, and wiped the water away, spent a few minutes replenishing moisture with body oil, and did the same with my hair.

I checked my phone and was pleased to see that I had plenty of time to grab a cat nap before I had to head to Esme's house. I set the alarm, then stretched my limbs out on the bed.

Sated, clean, relaxed, I was asleep in moments.

E sme sat across from me, her head bowed over the menu at Two Urban Licks, a rustic, warehouse turned restaurant that featured rotisserie-cooked meats and seafood alongside fire-roasted vegetables. I had every reason to be looking directly at her, and I still felt like I was doing something wrong.

Her hair was piled high on top of her head in a messy bun with curls spilling out. Her black lace top, so sheer that I could see the dark bra underneath, put a tempting amount of cleavage and skin on display. It flared out at the waist, drawing my eye to the curves that I had thought about in the shower. Her worn denim jeans, cuffed mid-calf, paired with black matte leather sneakers, said she was ready for whatever I had in store for us.

"What's good here?" Her head rose, giving me enough time to bring my eyes up to meet hers. "Everything looks amazing. I don't know where to start."

I pointed out a few of my favorites on the menu, including the spicy turkey wings, the ribs and the crab lettuce wraps on the appetizer menu.

"You can't really go wrong with anything on the entree menu," I told her. "Red meat, white meat, seafood... they do it all really well here. And save room for dessert. Their peach pie hits me right after a good meal."

Esme laughed, cocking her head back a little so I could see all of her pretty white teeth. "You like food. I like that."

"Sometimes a little too much, but I got that under control."

"Trey. I have a confession."

Esme clasped her hands together, resting her elbows on the table. Her face looked bare, but I knew enough about women to know that a bare natural face took a lot of effort. The pop of color was her lips, coated in a berry tone that complimented her skin. I hoped it was that stuff that wouldn't come off when I kissed her.

"Confess away."

"I... I looked you up. I mean, I used Google. I didn't run a background check or anything."

"Fair," I commented, sitting back so the server could set glasses of ice water and wrapped silverware in front of us. When he left the table, promising to be back to take our orders, I continued. "I expected that. And what did you find? Anything surprising?"

"Well, I knew a lot about Pettigrew Construction. I did my research to put together Miller's counterpoints for the contract, comparing and contrasting the strengths of each company to demonstrate how you fit together like puzzle pieces. But this time, I looked deeper into the founding of the company, some of the bigger, more historical projects the company played a hand in. Like the Ponce City Market and Nine Mile Station projects, both pay homage to Atlanta's history and bring construction into the next millennium. Impressive."

Esme picked up her water glass and sipped, then licked her lips before going on. I was listening to her but also noticed that her lipstick didn't budge. Good.

"Then I got to Trey Pettigrew." She paused to smile. "Saul the third, though it's never acknowledged on the company website. Is that on purpose?"

I nodded. "As I said, I'm intended to be third in name only, in the hopes that I'll have a son and carry it on. But looking at how I've been running my dad's company in his absence, it may have more meaning than that."

Esme was nodding as I spoke. "Saul looks… well, certainly, he's a powerful man. He looks foreboding in his CEO portrait. Is he controlling?"

"Pops is a teddy bear," I said. "Until you don't do what he wants you to do. I don't know if it's controlling, so much as he has an idea of how things should be done and can't imagine anyone doing it any other way. It blows his mind. You sort of… fall in line."

I made a motion with my hands, of one moving after the other.

"Mmmmm," she mused. "And have you fallen in line?"

"Some. More than I planned to. More than I want to. It's a necessary evil but, I'm trying to do this job my way."

"You uhm…you look different in your website photo. I would have never believed it was you if you didn't look exactly like Saul."

I laughed, remembering that I hadn't had my images updated when I took over Pettigrew. It was a bone of contention with the web design team, but I'd refused so many times, they'd stopped asking. There was no reason to waste time and money on a photoshoot. Saul would be back in his rightful place.

Though, lately, I wasn't so sure about that.

"Heh. That photo tells a story about five years, fifty pounds, and months trying to get my beard to connect."

"It seems like it was well spent. You look great. Very handsome."

"Thank you, Esme. A genuine compliment from those lips means the world to me."

"There must be something about the mid-thirties, you know?" She said, moving her hands to her lap, relaxing against the cushion behind her. We'd been seated in the corner of the restaurant. I was in a regular chair on one side of the table; I gave the more comfortable booth seating to Esme. "I woke up at thirty-five, and every clock was screaming at me. My life was almost half over, and what was I doing with it? I'd wasted that time existing. Just… being here on the planet. It wasn't good enough anymore. That's when I started making changes."

"Like?"

"Well, a change of habits. New wardrobe. Letting my sisters play in my hair, making them take me shopping."

She fingered the delicate lace of her blouse. "I wanted to look better and feel better. I went back to school. An MBA meant I was eligible for a senior position at Benning. It also meant that I could compete in the job market. If this contract doesn't go through—"

"It will because we're making it happen."

"Well, you never know. Things like this can turn on a dime. I've seen it happen. But now I have confidence that I could step outside of Benning and make as much or more elsewhere. Hopefully, more."

"I feel you on that mid-thirty crisis." I reached for the glass of water in front of me and took a sip, sucking a few cubes of ice into my mouth. I crunched the ice between my teeth. "I hit thirty-four and felt the same. I started taking classes, too. Dabbling in a few things. I hated how I felt, the way I looked, so I spent time and effort on self-improvement. I still like to eat… obviously."

I sent a smirk across the table. She caught it and returned it. "But I don't miss a workout. And, I'm removing things that don't make me happy. Like that Marie Kondo chick says to do."

"The other part of that practice is to keep or procure what brings you joy."

"That's where you come in."

There it was. The blush, the sweep of her eyelashes when she closed her eyes briefly, then refocused her gaze on mine.

The waiter appeared at our table, a thin electronic pad in one hand. "What can I get you started with this evening?"

Esme and I both chose an appetizer, then placed orders for roast chicken and brisket. We each chose a different roasted vegetable and agreed to share. Then I ordered dessert ahead but asked for it to go. As the waiter stepped away, I saw the question in her eyes.

"We have to celebrate conquering your next fear. I celebrate with pie."

CHAPTER NINETEEN

Trey

I paid for dinner, drinks and dessert in cash, leaving a hefty gratuity, mostly to impress Esme, but also out of solidarity. When I wasn't working for Pops, I was serving, bussing tables, washing dishes, sweeping floors. When I say I felt weird in a suit and tie, I meant it.

When Pops pulled me from the field office to work in the corporate office, it didn't feel like a come-up. I felt stifled. I didn't mind calloused hands and work boots. But I also understood that Pops wanted someone in the role that could, someday, take his place. Why he felt Vincent wasn't that dude was a mystery to me, but I hoped that me being at the helm at Pettigrew wasn't on his five-year plan, because it definitely wasn't on mine.

I grabbed the handles of the brown paper bag with two servings of peach pie and walked with Esme to the car as the valet brought it around. He made sure we were safely inside, nodding his appreciation at the folded bills that I slipped into his palm as we shook hands.

"So!" I called out, maneuvering out of the parking lot. "Extreme sport."

"Yep. Do you mind if I change the music? There's a station I like."

"You don't like the SoulCycle channel? It's supposed to pump you up for tonight's adventure!" I laughed at the look she sent me. "You know I say shit like that to get you to look at me that way, right?"

"I just figured that out." She punched through the buttons on my dashboard, flipping up and down the dial.

"The channels with skinny, ugly rappers whining about not getting pussy till they got rich are higher on the dial."

She landed on a channel, then sat back.

I nodded my head to the beat as I pointed us north to our next destination. "What channel is this?"

"Heart & Soul. This is Rashaan Patterson. Do you know him?"

"Vaguely. You know when I realized that I'd hit that mid-thirties crisis? I started liking this adult R&B stuff. Turning down the hip hop, because it was so loud, and the bass was so heavy, and the lyrics are just... everyone's just whining about how hard it is to be rich."

"Not being able to find stark white Nikes in your size is an epidemic."

"When I started going to bed early so I could get up and work out?" I shook my head, frowning hard. "It was over for this kid. I could pretend before, but I was officially an adult."

"You know what I did today? I got up early, put on my mama's Aretha Franklin records—"

"I know what's coming," I broke in, already laughing.

"That's what Saturday was about at our house. Mama waking us up ass early, having me, Jewel and Jada in a headscarf scrubbing shit, doing laundry, cleaning our rooms."

"Now I spend my Saturdays at my folks' house doing yard work."

"When I got grown, I was going to sleep in on Saturdays. Then do whatever I wanted to do." She sucked her teeth. "I couldn't wait to get up this morning, strip the bed, mop the floors, clean the house top to bottom, especially since O'Neal isn't around to mess it up. I've become my mother."

"Maybe that's not all bad. She set a good example."

"That chick sleeps in now. Doing whatever she wants to do on Saturday."

"So we don't get grown until retirement."

We both laughed at that.

"Does your sister live here, Trey? You don't talk about her much."

I sucked my bottom lip into my mouth and chewed on it. I hadn't expected her to ask about Missy. I was never ready to talk about her.

"Missy..." I began but quickly gave up articulating any thought that she'd be able to understand. "The situation with Missy is complicated. I love my sister. We just... it's a lot. I'd like to leave her out of this for a little while."

"Oh, sure," she replied. "Sorry. Didn't mean to pry."

"Nah, don't apologize." I reached across the console and laid a hand on her thigh, giving her a few reassuring taps. "We're getting to know each other. You can ask whatever."

"Just not about Missy."

I glanced over at her and tried to soften my expression. I wasn't angry, but she was pressing on a nerve. "Not right now, Es. Alright?"

I saw her head bob in agreement. Then she propped her elbow up on the windowsill and rested her head in her palm. "Are you going to tell me where we're going?"

"It'll be obvious when we get there."

Esme didn't ask any more questions or make any more comments. We listened to the radio and watched the traffic as I headed north. After a few minutes, though, she moved her hand to rest on top of mine and then curled her fingers under my palm.

And then I could exhale because I knew then that she wasn't angry or feeling weird about how I cut off that conversation. My relationship with Missy had been a sore spot for too long. It was probably something I needed to see a therapist about.

I switched lanes, then turned into a parking lot. I slowed to a stop next to an activity center housed in a strip mall, then pulled into a spot. Esme sat up, then leaned forward, squinting to read the neon sign that flashed.

"Lunar Golf," she read aloud. "That doesn't sound very extreme, Trey."

"We're going over there," I said, pointing to the other side of the building. I watched her eyes grow wide as she read the sign.

"Laser Maze. What is a laser maze?"

"Ok, did you see Oceans 12? Remember the dude had to dance through that room, around the laser beams? If you break the beam, the alarm goes off. It's like that, but we're not in the middle of a jewelry heist."

"Ohhh." Esme paused. Then glanced at me and giggled. "This is my extreme sport, Trey?"

"You ruled out bungee jumping, so..." I shrugged. "They play Mission: Impossible music while you're in there. You can be Tom Cruise."

"Alright. Sounds fun." She clapped, then released her seat belt and popped open her door, making the dome bulb fill the interior with light.

"Wait, wait. Esme. Hold up."

"Yeah?" She paused, turning to me. The excitement in her voice matched the anticipation on her face.

"I know we're just hanging out, but... I'm dying to kiss you. Your lips, and that lipstick and the way you smile are just begging me to put my mouth on you."

There was always the possibility she would get out of the car and slam the door in my face. This was Esme, after all. Instead, she leaned toward me, lips slightly parted. I took it as an invitation and pressed my lips to hers.

But that peck, that chaste kiss was not nearly enough for me. As many times as the thought of this woman had brought me to climax in the last week, I needed more.

I teased her with my tongue, deepening the kiss. Esme purred. The sound brought me out of the trance that her lips had put me in. I pulled back in time to catch her breathy exhale while her eyes were still closed.

"I've been thinking about kissing you since the last time we kissed. And..." Esme opened her eyes, finding mine. "When you said you wanted to put your mouth on me... I wasn't thinking about kissing."

"Are you hinting, Esme?"

"Not at all." She shook her head. "A benefit of this big age is that I can be straightforward. You said you planned to pursue me. I'm letting you know how very open I am to that."

I didn't know what to say to that, honestly. No games, no subterfuge? Did I even know how to deal with a woman that didn't play with me, bat me around like a cat before going in for the kill?

"Let's go do a laser maze. I need to finish my list."

"The object of the game is to make it through the maze without breaking the beam."

Our mission guide was a kid who couldn't be older than 16. He took the tickets I'd printed out at home earlier and went over the rules of play with us. I'd paid for a private game, so Esme and I would be the only two players. If I wanted to pause the game to grab her and kiss her, I didn't want to be holding anyone up.

"However, you'll get two free beams. If you break a third beam, you have to go back to the beginning."

He opened the door to let us into a room that was pitch black and quiet. Then the room exploded in a burst of neon light that narrowed to dozens of thin beams. Overhead, the first strains of the Mission: Impossible theme poured from the speakers.

Esme's eyes danced, watching the laser beams form across the room. She grinned at me, then tucked her hand into mine. "Let's get our Tom Cruise on!"

We weren't so much Tom Cruise as Tom Greene. Esme spent a lot of time rolling around on the floor under high beams and making dramatic leaps to jump over relatively low beams.

"You don't need to do all of that, Esme. You're expending energy you might need later." I stepped over a low beam of light.

"I'm making it extreme!" She shouted, darting from one edge of the room to the other, then leaping over the same beam I'd stepped over. "You picked this. I'm making it worth crossing off my list."

I grabbed her arm before she could run past me again. "Aight. Let's make a deal."

"Another one? I can't wait to hear this one."

"If we make it through this maze without breaking another beam—because we already broke one, remember? You tell me what else is on your list."

Esme's face, or what I could see of it, went blank.

"Don't shut down on me. I'm half of this equation, Esme. I'm the one doing these things with you. Shouldn't I know what we're doing? What we're working toward?"

"I don't know if I'm ready to share yet. There's two…"

She huffed, throwing up her hands, then slapping her thighs in what was probably frustration. I couldn't blame her;

I was pushing hard. But I needed more. I needed her to let me in more.

"I wish you knew how much I'm putting myself out, Trey."

I pulled her to me by her hips, tucking her body up against mine. "I'm just asking you to trust me. I know I haven't done a lot to deserve it, but please give me a chance. I'm putting myself out, too."

"You're right, I know. I'm not ready yet. I will. But not yet. Can we get out of this room now?"

"Bet. But I'm not gonna stop asking. Just letting you know." I kissed her, then set her free. "Get your Tom Cruise on, girl."

We both blinked in the brightness of the lobby lights after being in that dark room for an hour. Esme pulled her bun out, absentmindedly running her fingers through her hair, fluffing it around her face. She was flush, but her eyes were bright, and her smile was wide.

"Whew, that was fun! I'd love to bring my nephews out here. They'd lose their minds. My nieces, too."

"You made it," I told her, slinging an arm across her shoulder and guiding her toward the exit. "Another checkmark on that list that you'll eventually show me. You proud of yourself?"

"I am. Not what I had in mind for an extreme sport, but it's done."

"You made it extreme. You were gangsta in there."

"I did that, huh?"

"And you were way sexier than Tom Cruise will ever be."

"You didn't do so bad yourself."

I unlocked the Acadia with the key fob. The interior lights illuminated, the running lights popped on, and the door locks clicked as they disengaged.

"Okay, I'll admit it. Laser Maze wasn't that extreme."

"It wasn't," she agreed, laughing. "I feel like Lunar Golf would have been more of a challenge."

"I thought it would be fun to see you jump over stuff. I didn't lose my planning privileges, did I?"

"Not at all. I'm happy that I let you plan."

"Because it wasn't bungee jumping?"

"No. Well, yes. And because you did it with me. That's kind of my favorite part."

She rose onto her toes to bring her mouth to mine. A pleasured groan rolled from the my belly as our mouths meshed. I inched her back against the side of the SUV, then maneuvered between her thighs.

Esme whimpered, which sent my dick into overdrive. She sucked on my tongue while moving her hands around to grab two handfuls of ass and pull me up against her. Her hips rolled against my growing thickness. I matched her rhythm, grinding back.

I slipped my hand under her blouse, exploring the velvet texture of her skin, traveling up her waist to the orbs encased in the dark bra that I'd been staring at all night. It didn't take long for my fingers to pluck a nipple poking through the fabric.

She jerked, inhaling sharply when I flicked my thumb across the taut nub, but when I pulled away, she grabbed my hand and moved it back to her breast. "Don't stop. I like that."

Esme panted hot breath on my neck, her pelvis rocking against mine. I ground out a grunt, my thrusts turning urgent, more aggressive. I marveled at the heft and shape of her breasts in my palms. I longed for the day when I could taste them, when those diamond tip nipples would rasp against my tongue.

A rhythmic, guttural sound accentuated Esme's movements. Those talons she called nails dug into my skin, but hell if I was going to stop her.

"Oh my God… Trey…"

She moaned into my ear, her breath hot on my neck. Then she hissed, sucking in air through her teeth. Her back arched, pressing her body into mine. I pushed us both up against the SUV, using it as leverage to buck my hips against hers until she let out a muffled yelp and I felt a full-body, violent shudder.

I closed my eyes, absorbing the sound and sensation of Esme in the throes of orgasm— shallow breaths, deep moans, tiny tremors.

Moments later, she visibly wilted, letting out a long, loud exhale. "Jesus."She wiped a palm across her forehead. "What was that?"

"You know exactly what that was." I moaned my appreciation into her ear, planting light kisses up her neck. "And it was sexy as fuck. Damn girl. I can honestly say I have never done that."

"Get your own list," she mumbled. Then laughed. Then her eyes popped wide open, and she gasped. "Shit, we're outside!"

I'd been so lost in her, so drunk on her that I had forgotten that we were standing with the passenger side door open. While the lot wasn't full, and we were on the opposite side of the truck, we faced a busy main road for the county. The line of trees between the chain link fence and the four lane arterial wasn't thick. Anyone stopped at a long red light could have watched that whole scene play out.

"Come on here. We don't want to get arrested for fucking on Cobb Parkway."

I stepped back, offering a hand to help her inside, then closed the door. Then I hopped in, snapped my seatbelt, and reached up to flip the dome light on.

Esme turned in her seat to face me, tucking a leg up under her. Her lips were swollen and puffy, her hair a wild mass of curls, her eyes at half-mast.

I love how a woman looks after orgasm. So satisfied. Esme looked satisfied.

"You straight?"

She nodded. "You?"

"I'm real good. You 'bout to cuss me out?"

She laughed. "No, Trey. I'm fine. I'm not ready for tonight to end yet, though."

"I feel you on that. You trust me?"

"Yes," she answered, her tongue thick. "Why?"

"Field trip," I answered, turning off the dome light and putting the truck in drive. "We need a place to eat our pie."

CHAPTER TWENTY

ESME

If my situation were different, i.e., I'd already had sex, I'd have demanded that Trey take me somewhere, *anywhere* and give me every inch of what I'd been grinding against until I was hoarse from screaming his name.

I was closer to the end than the middle of my sexual peak, but my hormones raged like a hot-in-the-ass co-ed who had her eyes on the sexiest piece of chocolate on campus. It was far from my first orgasm, not even the first with him on my mind, but it was the first that he'd been actively involved in producing and... *damn*. Even through two layers of clothing, that shit felt good.

He felt good. When he pulled me to him and held me by my hips, tipping his pelvis into mine... *Mmmph.* I reflexively clenched, adjusting in the seat.

Trey had wedged a hand between my thighs as he drove, so when I moved, he took his eyes off the road briefly, checking me out. "Do we need to stop? There's a Quick Trip up here."

I shook my head. "No. I don't…"

"You don't… need to stop? You don't… like Quick Trip?"

"I like QT fine. I don't use public restrooms." I knew he was going to laugh. I didn't expect him to put so much energy into it. "You know what? Fuck you, Mr. Pettigrew. I can't imagine what quirks you have that make you annoying."

"You've already discovered a few of them. I don't think I have quite so many, though, Esme."

"What an adventure for me. I guess I get to discover them all."

"An adventure indeed," he said. I liked the way his voice dipped low when he said that, like he was thinking about the same thing I was thinking about.

But probably not in the same way. My thoughts were consumed with the need for him to lay me down, to run those lips over every inch of my skin, to take his time introducing me to the world of sexual pleasure.

Being honest, I really, really...*really* wanted him to fuck me. To be the *first* to fuck me. I huffed, feeling my body begin to heat up again.

Trey squeezed the thigh gripped in his hand. "You alright?"

"Yeah. You like that thigh meat, huh?"

"This thigh meat?" He squeezed again. "This sexy thigh meat right here? These beans and rice that didn't miss ya? Yeah. I like it. That ok?"

I wound my fingers around his, tipped my head back against the seat, and closed my eyes. "That's more than ok."

I don't know when I fell asleep, but I woke up when we hit a bump in the road. It felt like we lurched a foot in the air. We weren't on Cobb Parkway anymore, a major thoroughfare through one of Atlanta's largest counties. And we weren't on the freeway.

Trey was picking his way across an unpaved road, around more bumps like the one that woke me up.

"Sorry about that. Fixing this road is up next on the list."

I sat up and yawned, then reached for my purse at my feet. While I unwrapped and chewed a piece of gum, I tried to get my eyes to adjust to the pitch black night. I couldn't see a thing except for whatever was illuminated by the headlights.

"Where are we?" I asked.

"Stockbridge. We're actually not far from your house. I wanted to show you something. A little side project."

We rode through a thicket of trees that gave way to an expanse of land. After a few minutes of total darkness, the road ended at a bare bones frame of a home under construction. Trey stopped at a spot in front of two wide open bays that I assumed would eventually be garage doors.

I knew he wouldn't answer, so I didn't ask what this place was. Trey was a man that liked to tell his own story in his own way. So I followed his lead, climbing out of the truck. He left the headlights on so that we could see.

"There's a little bit of power out here. The guys hung some lights so we could work after dark if necessary. Or if I need to sneak over here at night and check up on them."

He led me through the open space, lined with building materials stacked and organized along the walls. He pulled a set of keys from his pocket and keyed two locks, then swung the door open. A burst of cool air swept past me as I stepped inside. I listened to my sneakers echo across the wide boards that made up the floor. I heard a metal sounding switch, then a flood of light from a hanging construction lamp lit up the space.

Whatever this place was, it was going to turn out nice.

"We came from the garage, obviously. Mudroom over there," he said, pointing to a small alcove, then continued ahead of me, pointing out spaces where things like appliances and cabinets and counters would go. "I think I'm going to do granite countertops. I haven't picked it out yet, though. You like to cook?"

I smirked. "That depends on if you're going to ask me to cook for you."

He stepped into an open space and turned. "The gas range will go here. Built-in stovetop grill, double oven, microwave. One of those warming drawers. I don't know what that's for, but I hear it's good for resale value. Then over there," he said, pointing to the other end of the room. "Double sinks, those deep motherfuckers that you could practically bathe in. I'll probably never use it because the dishwasher will be over there too."

He made his way around the room, calling out different spaces: pantry, the alcove for the wine refrigerator, storage closets, and the power room where everything would be run and house a state-of-the-art security system.

"Over here is where things get interesting," he said, leading me to another part of the house. My eyes had adjusted to the darkness by now, but he turned on more lamps. The rooms were spacious, flowing from one end of the house to the other.

"These are windows?" I asked, pointing at the boarded up cutouts in the frame.

"Yep. The deck wraps all the way around this side of the house. Some doors lead to the outside from every room down here."

"A lot of natural light from both sides of the house."

"This is entertainment and living space. Kitchen, dining room, formal living room, family room, theatre room— that'll be nice. I'm looking forward to outfitting that. A big office with one of those doors that lead outside to the deck. Then outside, there's all this land. I have landscape plans for the backyard—definitely adding a pool eventually. I want to do something with the acreage without having to maintain it. I'm thinking about racquetball courts. Get my boy Ken out here."

He seemed to pop out of his monologue to remember that I was there with him. "Do you play?"

"I'm going to let you guess if I've played a sport where a rubber ball comes flying at my face."

Trey's laugh was warm as he draped an arm over my shoulder. He led me toward a set of steps that were plain wood. Not stained or carpeted. Freshly built.

"Bedrooms are upstairs—"

"Whoa, wait. Are these safe?"

"Nah. I plan to lead you up these totally unsafe steps. I thought you trusted me."

"I have terrible luck, remember?"

I followed him up the flight of stairs to a wide landing with several door openings. "I like open spaces. There are more possibilities for changing it up. I'll probably put the library up here, some nice leather seating. Get a camera, film some skin flicks..."

"Alright, now."

"Anyway, this spot will be a place to chill. The master will be over here," he said, pointing.

The only way I could tell that area would be a room were the spaced poles that framed it.

"I wanted a lot of space, room for a big ass bed, big ass furniture, a gas fireplace. The master bathroom will be laid out, too. Italian marble, soaking tub, double sinks. Everything premium. I'm not skimping on anything."

"So, this is your house?" I finally asked. He'd dropped enough hints to know the answer to my question, but I was sure that he wanted me to ask. And that he wanted to talk about it.

The pride that made his eyes glow in the dim light almost brought tears to mine. "Yeah. This is my place. Or, will be my place, once it's built."

"Well, you have a loan on it. It's yours. It's been yours."

He smiled. "I like how you think, Esme."

"When is it supposed to be finished?"

"I'm hoping to be moving by Christmas." He looked around, squinting, and bobbing his head side to side. "Might be tight. They'll likely still be finishing some things, but I want the big things done by then."

A breeze whipped through the open, unheated space. "It got kind of cold tonight, huh?" He pulled me to him, wrapping his arms around me and dropping a kiss on my forehead. I already loved being in his arms.

"I'm fine right now, though."

I felt his chuckle through his chest. "Let's go to the car. I can turn on the heat, and we can eat our celebratory pie."

Trey pulled the truck into the garage, turned on the heat and the radio, and lifted the hatch in the back so that we could sit in the trunk space behind the rear seat. Then he unpacked our individual dishes of peach pie, which were cold and congealed by now, but it didn't matter. I was happy to swing my legs and eat pie in the back of a truck listening to Jill Scott in the middle of nowhere.

"Why'd you want to show me the house you're building?" I asked, before sliding another slice of pie into my mouth.

"Because I'm proud of it," he answered, around a mouthful. "And because, you know, we talked about that glow up period when we both decided to be better people."

"Yeah. You said you started dabbling in stuff. You built a house?"

"I *designed* this house. You got an MBA. I got a Master of Architecture."

My jaw dropped. All of those jabs about him going to a fancy school suddenly seemed shallow and uninformed. Trey shoveled another forkful of pie into his mouth and chewed, grinning at me. I felt like shit.

"I..." I shook my head, still in surprised mode. "I'm sorry, Trey—"

"I forgive you for thinking I'm a pedestrian dude with a lil' four-year degree from a state school."

"That's not—"

Trey's laugh cut through the dark, quiet night. "Esme, really. I'm not precious about it. It was something I wanted to do, but I couldn't miss a lot of work. The University of Florida offers an online program. It's slower, and I had to fly down for some week-long seminars and group activities, but what else was I going to do with my time? While I was at it, I got LEED Certified. Now I can build green homes and buildings."

"But... your family owns a construction company. Did Saul say that you had to get another degree?"

"Nope. He had nothing to do with it. But it was strategic. This is what I really want to do: design and build smart, sustainable homes like this. This house is the prototype. It's everything I wanted, and I needed to know that I could dream up something that could be applied to modern design. I needed to draft it, to plan it, then contract it to be built."

Trey shrugged. "I'm not trying to flex, but I make good money being a Pettigrew. Every assumption you probably have about me is true. Saul Sr. left me a little trust fund. I work for my father at a well-off business that I'll probably inherit. By the time it mattered, I was a kid with rich parents, living with a lot of privilege, even though I'm Black. I'm spoiled, and I'm not used to hearing 'no.'" He paused to lob a self-deprecating grin in my direction.

"Pops instilled a lot of real-world common sense and work ethic, though. He made sure that I knew the value of a dollar and the meaning of hard work and responsibility. I've had dirty, calloused hands, an aching back, a crew that didn't respect me. I own work boots. And when it came time to bring me up the line, he did that. Which comes with expectations of continuing the line."

"How does Saul feel about the architecture degree and you designing your own house?"

"Well…" Trey inhaled, sucking in a long breath through his nose and furrowing his brow. "He's proud that I did something I wanted to do. I set my mind on a goal and didn't let anyone or anything stop me. That's Pettigrew shit right there. Business-wise, he thinks it's a waste of time and money."

"He doesn't want you to run residential?"

He sucked his teeth. "Woman, we ain't got no residential division."

"So start one!"

"He's never been a proponent of residential design and construction. Too many variables. When he asked me to run Pettigrew while recovering, I told him that my agreement came with strings. He knows what the strings are. That's why I can't fuck up this deal with Miller."

I understood, at that moment, what the acquisition meant to him, and what hung in the balance. If he screwed up, an opportunity to fulfill his life's dream would dissipate like vapor in warm air. He'd have to leave Pettigrew and strike out on his own, which would probably break Saul's heart, and, given his health struggles, Trey wouldn't do that.

I also understood that The Never List played a part in this game. And seemed like a petty pawn to play.

"Trey." I elbowed him to get his attention. He sat with his back against the seat, one leg bent so that his elbow rested on his knee. "We don't have to keep doing the list, just to get concessions on the contract. If you make reasonable efforts to negotiate, Miller will work with you. He wants it to happen. He's just not giving up his company without a fight."

"I appreciate that you offered but helping you with the list isn't about the contract."

My brows shot up. "It's not? What's it about then?"

"Really, Esme?" He laughed a little, then gave me a long stare. "The list is about you, Esme. About spending time with you one on one. Finding out what's important to you. How you think. What makes you tick. What holds your attention. What brings you fear. Contract concessions tied into it is... honestly, to make the tedium fun."

He pushed out a short puff of air and shook his head. "We can't even really mention this deal to anyone."

"I haven't said anything."

"Me either. I need this to fly through."

"It will. Because we're making it happen. Right?"

Trey didn't answer. Well, he didn't answer in words. He leaned over to kiss me, his lips lingering on mine for a second longer than usual.

"I really, *really* like you, Esme. I shouldn't, because you're mean. I guess I like that in a woman."

"I am not mean, Mr. Pettigrew. I am assertive. I have to be. People will walk all over you if you let them. I got tired of people seeing a frumpy girl and thinking they can treat her any old kind of way. Use and abuse her and make her think she should accept that because she's lucky that anyone paid attention to her."

Trey set up and pulled back, angling his head so that the light from overhead illuminated my face. "Wait, abuse? Who do I have to fight? Did somebody hurt you?"

"No... no." I pulled him back to me. He was warm, and the late evening chill gave me goosebumps. "A turn of phrase, I guess. A lifetime of immature men that don't want much but a wet hole and somebody to make him a sandwich."

"You make good sandwiches?"

"Really, Trey?"

"On a serious tip, I'm glad you were assertive and served up your worth because now you're here with me. And I have a chance to be your man. Right?"

"Yeah," I admitted, nearly under my breath. He heard it,

though. "I like you too, Trey. I shouldn't because you called me mean like you didn't try to take that chair from my table."

"I am never going to live that down. You'd been sitting there by yourself for an hour. How was I supposed to know you had a date?"

"Hell if I know. But I was pissed."

"Did you ever hear from that dude?"

"The investigating officer said that he got bailed out. I closed my dating account that night, and we never exchanged phone numbers. Something about being cold cocked after being stood up was enough for me."

"It was rough to watch," he said quietly. "Everybody saw it. And they... sat there. Watching. I was mid-sentence when I noticed what was happening. Jumped up and ran out there."

"And knocked him right out."

He chuckled. "Those games of racquetball come in handy. I had a good swing."

"Racquetball should have been my extreme sport."

"It can happen. I'll add it to your list."

I tapped his arm, then gave him a reassuring squeeze. "I had a good time tonight."

"A good time, Esme? Like we went to a movie?" He sucked his teeth, slowly shaking his head. "Out here acting like horny teenagers."

My giggle came out as more of a snort. "I need to add *dry hump a guy up against his car in view of a busy street* to my list. It can, for sure, replace a sailboat ride."

"Nah. We can do it all. You tell me what you gotta do. I'll make it happen."

I tipped my head up, brushing my lips against his cheek. He turned his head so that I got his lips. I kissed those too. Then I shifted so that I sat on his lap, straddling him. His hands automatically flew to my ass and molded to my shape.

"Hey, girl," he mumbled, his lips brushing against mine.

"Hey." I rested my arms across his shoulders and scooted

close so that my breasts pressed into his chest. "Did you have a good time tonight?"

"I had a real good time. I hope I'm not done having a real good time."

"No, I mean... did you *have a good time*?"

Silence from Trey. And then, "You want to know if I came?"

"Yes. Did you?"

"Esme——" Trey's mouth dropped open, but no other sounds came out. I took that to mean that he didn't.

"Do you want to?"

"I mean...always. Do I want you to make me come?" He chuckled, the sound coming from deep in his throat. "In so many ways. In due time, I hope. I'm not asking for that from you tonight."

"It's only fair, Trey. I got mine."

"I got mine, too," he protested. "You feel good to me. Anyway, I get to touch you, I'm winning. I'm straight. Really."

"Ok, what if..."

I drew my bottom lip into my mouth, catching it with my teeth before releasing it again, while I held his gaze.

Bold, Esme. Make it happen. Get what you want.

"When we danced together the other night, you were hard. I cannot stop thinking about it. I've been imagining and dreaming and, honestly, getting off on those thoughts and dreams, and after tonight, I want to see you. I want to touch you. I want to taste you."

"And you want to do that right now? Out here."

"These trees make good cover, unlike busy Cobb Parkway. What, you need perfect lighting and presentation to show me your dick?"

"Nah, I'll whip it out——"

"So do that."

"You want this because you came and I didn't. I'm not keeping score, Esme."

"I want this because you got a big ol' dick, and I want to see it."

That made him laugh. "Is this a thing on your list?"

"No!" I laughed with him, then cupped his face and kissed his lips. "I'll tell you when it's a thing on my list. I'll drop it if the answer is no."

"It's not no. It's never going to be no. You don't have to, though."

"I know. But I want to. So… yes?"

Trey sighed, trying hard to sound like getting head was going to be a chore. He stretched an arm to the edge of the trunk, behind the seat he leaned against and flipped a lever. He did the same behind the other, then pushed both seats back, so they laid flat.

I took the hint, dismounted from his lap, and moved further inside. He reached for the door latch and pulled the rear hatch closed. The dome light turned off, dunking us in nearly pitch black darkness. Trey reached up to press buttons and turn the low interior lights on, then stretched out next to me.

"I want to see you, but I can turn it off, if—"

"It's fine," I murmured.

In moments, I was enveloped in his scent as he pulled me closer to him. His lips brushed across mine softly, gently a few times. He worked his way across my jaw to my ears, nibbling the lobe for a few moments before leaving a trail down my neck and across the exposed skin of my chest.

"Esme," Trey whispered, while he tucked a hand under the hem of my shirt. He palmed a breast, his thumb resting on the tip of a raised nipple. My breath quickened with the anticipation that at any moment, he would rub his thumb across the hardened nub.

"Mmmmm?"

"Am I supposed to be able to see your bra? Like through your shirt, because I've been trying not to stare all night. "

I giggled. "Yes. It's part of the outfit. I thought I was being sexy."

"Oh, you are. You very much are."

His thumb whispered over the fabric of the thin bra, bringing a wave of electric pleasure that made me writhe and squeal even while he kissed me, swirling his tongue around mine before pulling back with a deep, lusty groan. Trey moved his hand to my waist and pulled me up against him. His erection was present and accounted for.

"Feel this? Feel me?" He tilted his pelvis so that I felt him, all of him. "This is what happens when I'm having dinner in one of Atlanta's finer restaurants, staring at you because I wish I could take that bra off and put your nipples in my mouth."

"You should have said something." I sat up, grabbed the hem of my blouse, and pulled it over my head. "I would have whipped them out for you."

When I pulled my hands behind me to unclasp the bra, Trey went to work unbuckling his belt, then undoing the button and zipper on his jeans. He stopped there, leaving them open to expose a dark pair of briefs because the moment the clasp was released, my breasts dropped.

He reached over to cup a breast in the palm of his warm hand. He only had to tip forward to swirl his tongue around an areola before closing his mouth around one, then the other nipple. I hadn't felt the rasp of a tongue across my skin in so long that I'd forgotten the pleasurable sensation, but it rushed back to me, and I didn't want him to stop.

"Damn," he said, following up with a groan.

"Is that a good damn?"

"That is the best damn. You taste like brown sugar. You feel good in my mouth."

His pants were open, so I went for it, sliding a finger under the band of his briefs, then daring to go further until I felt him, thick and smooth. And warm. So *warm*. Trey made it easier for me, easing his briefs down so I could pull his dick out.

I estimated about eight inches of manhood jutting from his body, angled up toward me. I danced my fingers along the length, then ran the tip of my index finger across the head, smearing the creamy evidence of his arousal around the tip. He responded with a deep-throated moan and bucked his hips.

"Damn," I mumbled, making my best Trey Pettigrew impression.

"That better be a good damn."

I smiled up at him, adjusted so I was level with him, and took him into my mouth until I could take no more, then pulled off, then took him again.

"Oh my... fuck yeah..."

Trey pushed his jeans and briefs down so he could kick them off. I moved to sit between his legs, encouraged by the nonstop sounds coming from him. I pulled almost all the way off, then took all of him again and again. Slower, then faster, using a hand to squeeze him at the base, then swirling my tongue across the sensitive head.

I rolled my eyes up to meet his before taking him again.

"Fuck." His voice sounded tight, taut. Full of emotion, but he was holding back. "This feels so good. You...your mouth is amazing. Is it good for you, baby? You like that?"

I moaned, still full of him, still moving my mouth and my hands on him, building a rhythm to take him higher. He hissed, rolling his hips in sync with me for a few moments before he sat up, cupped my chin, and pushed me back.

Trey took his dick into his own hand, pumping with a roughness that I was too ladylike to perform, but I took mental notes in case I ever got the chance to duplicate the technique.

"Ahhhh!" He cocked his head back, the sound of him filling the interior of the SUV.

A warm spurt hit my chest and splashed up to my chin.

"Oh!" I yelped.

He tipped his head up at my sudden sounds, then his eyes widened. "Oh… shit! I'm sorry! I didn't mean to—"

"No! It's ok! I'm... I'm in the line of fire. I should have... realized...." I started laughing, taking in my view of Trey with his dick in his hands, still seeping from the tip, and my bare chest covered in ejaculate.

"This… is funny?"

"This is hilarious!" I shrieked, laughing harder.

Trey chuckled along, but eyed me, probably in case I was laughing maniacally and not genuinely amused.

"I might not be able to hang out with you anymore. Three new things in one night is a lot. Do you have any napkins?"

"Yeah. Hang on."

Trey sat up, reaching to press the button to open the glove box, where a curiously large assortment of napkins, ketchup packets, and silverware in plastic wrap was stuffed inside the compartment.

At my wide-eyed stare at his stash, he shrugged. "I used to work in the field, on job sites. Those guys eat a lot of fast food and food truck fare. I always save the extras. Never know when you'll come on a girl's face and need a handful."

I grabbed a few napkins and swiped the already cold wetness from my chin. He helped, dabbing at my chest before I took the napkins and finished the job.

"You mad at me?"

"No." I laughed, shaking my head. "I'm having so much fun with you."

"Es, I just came on you."

"You did." I bent forward to kiss him while pressing the soiled napkins into his hand. "So now we're even, and I'm happy."

He sat up, then crawled to the rear of the truck and popped the hatch open again. He reached for his boxers and pants and climbed out.

"I need to get right. Give me a minute."

When Trey came back, he was pulling his t-shirt down over the band of his jeans. I'd put my bra and blouse back on and had moved back to the front seat. Trey reset the back seats and closed the hatch again, then got into the driver's seat.

"How you doin'?" He asked, leaning across the console.

"I am real good." I met him halfway for a kiss, then leaned back. I laid an arm across his shoulder, then asked earnestly, "How are you, Trey?"

"If you're real good, I'm real good."

He reached for the gear shift, backing away from the house, then made a wide turn to head down the road we'd taken when we came to the house.

"It's been an eventful evening Ms. Whitaker, but I'm taking your exhibitionist ass home before you get me arrested."

CHAPTER TWENTY-ONE

Trey

Sixteen ounces of spiced vanilla flavored coffee from Brew Bar gave everything I needed. I'd arrived at the office early, while the building was still dark, and settled in at my desk without being bothered by anyone on the way in. I sipped, nodding appreciatively at both the report waiting on my desk and the hot, creamy brew that had quickly made me a fan.

Esme and I had fallen into a habit of switching off days picking up coffee and muffins from Brew Bar when we met at Miller Design. I was fine with plain French roast or vanilla and didn't like to get fancy. Esme loved whatever sweet swirl of flavors they tossed together that sounded good. Chocolate raspberry almond was her current crush.

Unfortunately, I'd had to cut my mornings at Miller to a few times a week. Esme and I were making great strides on negotiations, and Miller seemed particularly agreeable as of late. Pettigrew was working against Atlanta's upcoming cold and rainy season. At this time of year, the race was on to make progress on outside work so that crews could spend time inside when the weather wasn't agreeable.

A loud *tap tap* sounded at the closed door. "It's open," I called, raising my head to greet Vincent, who blew into my office, holding a copy of the same report that I'd been staring at for an hour. "Look who learned how to knock."

"The progress report is out," he said, ignoring my joke and dropping it onto my desk.

"I'm reading it now," I told him, showing him my copy. "Maybe getting to the office before noon would be a good habit to get into."

"It's only 9 o'clock, young blood. When you clock out at, what? Five, six o'clock, I'm still here. I put in my hours." Vincent took a seat and assumed his usual position, ankle resting on a knee, a hand restlessly tapping. "Tell me about the report, since you have a head start. Do you think the fourth quarter projections are accurate?"

I flipped back through the pages, referencing my notes on the projects that Pettigrew had slated for the last quarter of the year. "We have three builds in final phases, so those are automatic wins. Four in progress, a few of which just broke ground, but it looks like the crews are moving on time. We'll need to ride the project leads to keep them on schedule, or we'll end up with overtime, especially if we're supposed to run wire by December. We've got a couple that are behind schedule, but…"

I sipped more coffee, giving the pages one last brush before closing the report and relaxing in my chair. "Nothing to worry about yet."

"You know Saul would—"

"Yeah, I know. Pops would shit a brick at this report. But then I'd come behind him and reassure him. Seeing where the crews are, we're in good shape. Let's evaluate the situation in two weeks, though. A lot can change in that time."

"What the hell are you drinking?" Asked Vincent, his

mouth screwed into a scowl. "It smells like those candles my wife burns all the time."

"Coffee," I answered. "Spiced vanilla from a shop that's not far from me."

"Trey..." Vincent shook his head. "I have never known you to drink coffee."

"Well, I do," I responded with a laugh. "I didn't drink it at the office."

"And... now you do."

"Yeah." I hadn't even noticed that I'd started drinking coffee at the office every day, and not only at Miller Design. I smiled to myself at a small but meaningful change since I'd met Esme. I tipped the cup up to Vincent in a mock toast. "Now I do, I guess."

"Whatever. Another piece of news, besides your recent foray into coffee, is that the bid grapevine is rumbling again. We're looking at two, three weeks at the most."

I sat up, suddenly very alert and trying to swallow my heart, which had leaped into my throat. "Vincent, why didn't you say that when you walked in here?" I set down my coffee and reached for my cell phone. I had to call Miller.

And Esme.

He chuckled. "Honestly, I like watching you scramble. I hope you've made it over the hump to Miller's good side. How's his administrator that hates you?"

I mumbled, scrolling through my phone. "Making excellent progress, actually. And she doesn't *hate* me."

Not anymore, anyway.

Esme and I were getting along very, very well, though we had taken a small step back from hanging out. We hadn't been out since the night I took her to my half-built house, and we did things that we could probably get arrested for. I'd seen her at the office, and we spent at least an hour a night on the phone talking or watching the same movie. With the contract hanging over both of us, Esme wanted to concentrate on her job. We wanted that contract out of the way as soon as possible, using the anticipation of being able to move forward together as a reward to work harder.

It was working. I couldn't wait to be alone in a room with Esme naked as the day she was born, a bottle of wine, and nothing but time.

"We would be further along if Miller didn't want to argue every line and add an addendum to include his terms. I'm calling a meeting. We need to move quickly. It still has to go through the lawyers."

"Yeah, well…" Vincent pushed himself up from the chair, grabbing his copy of the report as he turned to leave my office. "Let me know if you need a closer. If we get the bid, we need to hit the ground running and break ground as soon as possible."

I picked up the phone at my desk and started dialing, waving Vincent out of my office. The line rang in my ear, and then picked up.

"Thomas, it's Trey Pettigrew. I need to meet with you and Ms. Whitaker. The bid is maybe a couple of weeks away. If we're doing this, we need to move."

By the clock on the wall, my watch, and the knot in my stomach, it was nearing 7 o'clock. I'd arrived at Miller, after rushing through my morning meetings, after noon. We immediately went into a closed-door session to define the remaining contract terms.

Per Vincent, I was under orders to be amicable and generous but not give away the whole store. Whatever it took, within reason, to get the deal done, I was authorized to approve. If Pops got mad, he got mad. He'd get mad all the way to the bank, once the project was complete.

Miller didn't get the same memo. Though he'd come

forward on a great many sticking points, he dug in his heels on the others. Which was why, seven hours later, I was irritated that I was still in a drab, grey conference room staring at an eerily calm, collected Thomas Miller.

And a flustered, frustrated Esme in the middle. I felt bad for her, but this was the job. This was what Miller hired her to do. Besides, I was the one being nice.

I scrubbed a palm down the side of my face, then cupped my chin in my hand. "I've hit a wall. I'm starving, I'm tired, and I feel like we're talking in circles. Can we table this? I feel like I'll have a better head on some food and sleep."

"Maybe you're right," he said, once again agreeable, but not where it mattered. "Let's round up in the morning."

Thomas stood, pushing his chair away from the table and, without a word, walked out of the room. His crisp white dress shirt still looked ironed, a testament to how he never folded his arms or even rolled up the sleeves. The guy was eerily calm all the time. Even when I called him to inform him that the hospital bid was coming in as few as two weeks, and we were nowhere near ready, he had no emotion for me. There was no sense of urgency.

There was a lot about Thomas Miller that got directly under my skin, and the more time I spent with him, the less I wanted to do business with him. If Pops wasn't chomping at the bit to acquire this firm, I'd have walked away a long time ago. This was not work that a CEO would typically be involved in, and I resented being put in the position. If it were not for Esme, I'd have turned this process over to Vincent. Or an underling.

Esme's strong, brave front collapsed as soon as Miller left the room. She listed to one side, leaning on one elbow with her head cradled in her palm. Her eyes were closed, showing off her expert eye shadow application, and she appeared to be breathing deeply.

"You straight?" I asked her quietly.

DL WHITE

Her eyes fluttered open, then settled on mine. "I'm *also* tired. I'm *also* starving. And that man—" She whispered the last two words, pointing one of her long nails toward the open door. "Is on my last nerve. There's no reason he can't revert to the original sale price that he and your father discussed. The company isn't worth any more or any less today than it was six months ago."

"Really?" That struck me as odd. "Like... value is flat? Pettigrew rises and falls depending on the season, how much work we have contracted, what the economy is looking like. His numbers have never changed?"

Esme shook her head. "Not that I have seen. The numbers that Miller gave me have stayed static since the agreement was first drafted earlier this year with Saul."

She reached for a stack of spreadsheets that we used for reference. "No adjustments for seasons, no ups, and downs. No projected salary increases, no adjustments for expenses that vary like taxes and insurance and materials."

She flipped through more pages, her brow becoming more wrinkled with each page. "I know we don't need exact figures, but these numbers look artificially good. Do you know what I mean?"

I knew exactly what she meant.

"I don't know why I never noticed that before."

"Miller is friends with your boss over at Benning, I'd bet. Golfing buddies, probably. They showed you what they wanted you to see," I said. "Anyway, his finances aren't your concern. The contract is written around agreed upon numbers. But as soon as this deal closes, his bills become mine. And if he's using dummy numbers, that could be a problem for Pettigrew."

Esme's eyes flicked up to mine. She was picking up everything that I was putting down. "We need to get out of this room," she mouthed.

I couldn't agree with that sentiment more. I picked up my

bag and began packing. Esme did the same, sliding her stack of notes and her laptop into a bag in seconds.

I walked out behind her, pulling the door to the conference room closed behind us. She swiped us out of the office suite, then out of the front door.

"Meet me at Brew Bar in a few minutes," she tossed over her shoulder as she walked to her car.

"Whoa." I grabbed her by the arm, forcing her to stop marching away from me. "What's up?"

"I don't want to talk anywhere near here. And I don't want security cameras catching us chatting it up out here either."

"So, we're going to have coffee and muffins and chat like I'm one of your sisters?"

"Well, do you have a better idea?"

"A hell of a better idea." I pulled out my phone and sent a text to hers. "Meet me there at 8 o'clock."

She pulled out her phone and stared at the text, then raised her head to land a quizzical stare at me. "Where is this?

"My place. Drop your car out front, tell the valet that you're visiting me. Go up to the tenth floor. I'll text you the code to unlock the door."

"Where will you be?"

"Picking up dinner. You'll get there before I do, so make yourself at home. Do you want me to order something for you?"

"Trey, I—"

"You know what? There's this new chicken dish on the menu that I think you'd like. I'll get that and some rice and vegetables. See you at eight."

I walked away before she could argue. When I got into my SUV, she was in her Jetta, setting the phone in its dashboard mount and tapping through screens.

GPS. Good.

Tonight's Stupid Human Trick: get through the evening without trying to sleep with Esme.

CHAPTER TWENTY-TWO

Esme

Meeting Trey in midtown at 8 o'clock meant flying home to take a lightning-fast shower, fluff my hair, refresh my deodorant and perfume, not to mention my Fenty lip color, then shooting back up I-75. My saving grace was that it was after rush hour and mid-week. And that O'Neal wasn't home to slow me down.

I swerved into Twelve88 Luxury Condominiums with minutes to spare. The valet was pleasant when I dropped my car out front, but I noted the rise in his brows as he took my key and handed me a tag to retrieve the car later. I walked inside and went to the elevators and the tenth floor.

I arrived at 10028 and pressed the buttons on the door in the order that Trey had texted me. The lock clicked, then whirred. The door swung open to reveal dark grey tile in the entryway leading into an open concept living area. The kitchen, dining room, and living room were one big space, with floor to ceiling windows from one wall to another.

"Well, alright, Mr. Pettigrew. This is nice."

I dropped my bag on a saddle leather couch the shade of an almond, kicked off my flats, and walked across the spotless off-white handwoven rug to stand in the window. Trey had an enviable view of the pool and patio below. His floor was high enough to get a view of the city lights at night.

I pressed buttons; lights turned on and off, dimming and brightening. I pressed another button, and the electric shades lowered and then rose again.

The dining room wasn't much except for a small round table and 4 tufted chairs sitting around it. A bright yellow vase held an explosion of colorful silk flowers. The kitchen was sparse but tidy with stools lined up against one counter, stainless steel appliances, and glossy, granite countertops. A glass carafe French press sat in a corner, next to a black lacquer box that I assumed was for bread, because next to that was a toaster oven.

It was a nice place, but… impersonal. Chic and upscale, but there was nothing about this condo that screamed Trey Pettigrew, except for the smattering of family photos in frames along the mantle above the fireplace. The decor was more corporate apartment than a grown man in his domicile. I knew him as a man with a casual, laid back style. This condo was pretentious and stiff. No wonder he was building a house to call his own.

I headed back to the living room, where I investigated his bookshelves filled with business books, mysteries, and architecture manuals. I sat down on the couch and dug through my bag, unpacking the materials that I'd brought with me— my laptop with database access to Benning systems and my notes from our discussions. I thought Trey was right to trust his suspicions. I needed to find a way to prove him right before Pettigrew got too far in.

By the time I heard rustling in the hallway, I was elbow deep in spreadsheets. I got up to open the door and found Trey holding several brown handled bags. His grin when I stood in the entryway to his place burned a warm glow in the pit of my belly. I should not have been so giddy to him smile, but I was.

"You found me. Good."

"You seem surprised," I quipped as he walked past me. I closed the door and followed him to the kitchen, where he was already pulling plastic containers out and lining them up along the counter.

"I thought you might let your Esme-ness take over and not show up. Suffice it to say…" He paused, his arm deep inside a brown paper bag. "I'm happy you're here."

"I decided that I was hungry, and I'd let you buy me dinner."

Trey pulled a square container out of the bag and held it, reverently, in his hands. "My boy Ken said hello, and that you will love the dish he created specifically for you." He handed me the container.

"This Ken guy knows who I am? And made my dinner?"

"He was my roommate at Georgia State. The best food you've ever tasted comes from his kitchen."

"He's the guy with the new restaurant you mentioned."

"Yep. Got a surprise for you. Open it."

I groaned, fighting a frown. "I'm scared. I feel like this surprise involves food that smells like standing water."

"Would you open it? Damn."

I removed the lid and peered inside at beautiful rolls, all lined up and nestled close together. "Something smells good in here."

"These are teriyaki chicken sushi rolls. All cooked. There's chicken, cucumber, and rice rolled in sesame seeds." He pointed to a few others. "There's nothing raw. Vegetables, smoked salmon, cooked shrimp."

"Oh. I thought sushi was like...raw fish."

"Sushi can be anything you can roll in some rice and

sesame seeds. If you still don't want that, I also got some stir fry chicken and vegetables and a ton of rice."

"It looks amazing. And it smells delicious. Thank you for arranging this for me."

I tipped my face up to his. He met me halfway and gave me the first kiss he'd given me since he dropped me off at my house more than a week ago. Because it had been so long, I went in again for another, longer kiss.

"Is it sad that I've missed your lips?" He asked.

"If it is, then I'm sad, too." I kissed him again, then pulled back to catch his eye. "Trey, did you peek at my list?"

"What? I haven't seen it since the day you dropped it. Why?"

I turned around, marched to my bag, dug around in the side pocket, and pulled out the well-worn, folded, unfolded, scratched out, and heavily edited list. Without unfolding the bottom half, I walked it over to Trey.

"Try an exotic dish," he read aloud. "Sushi is exotic?"

"If jumping over lasers is an extreme sport, sushi is exotic food. It counts."

"Aight. I guess we're crossing off another item on the Never list."

It was not lost on me, as we pulled out plates and forks and glasses for wine and settled in for our meal, that we were approaching the bottom of the list. There were a few fun things left and some big ones. I wasn't sure how I'd approach them. Or, more to the point, approach Trey about them.

He didn't seem the type that could be scared off. Trey was the type to be gentlemanly and decide that the privilege of deflowering a woman, however performative, should not be granted to him.

And then I'd be frustrated and, honestly, pissed because by now there was no one else I wanted to touch me.

"What are you thinking?"

Trey and I sat on the floor between the couch and the coffee table. Paper plates, plastic containers, and bottles of sake and plum wine filled in the spaces around my stacks of paper and notebooks.

"I'm thinking that we need Miller's true financials."

"We do. Do you think he cooks his books?"

"Maybe not cooked. Definitely heavily finessed to make Miller Design look more appealing."

"Wouldn't he be more agreeable if he was trying to dupe me into buying his company with fake numbers?"

"I think it's a reverse psychology thing. If he tries hard to keep his company from you and make it harder to acquire him, you might want it more. You might push harder. You might give in where you'd normally fight."

"Miller isn't a traded company, so his financials aren't public."

I set my wine glass down on the table and pulled my legs under me, then turned to lean an elbow on the supple leather of the couch. "I can access them."

Trey blinked, then ran his tongue between his lips before asking, "Like... through Benning?"

"Yes. We have platforms that we use to research potential and current clients, monitor the market, especially for comparison. It pulls financial statements, investor information, credit reports. If there's something to see, it'll find it."

"I get the feeling, though, that logging into Benning's system to look up their client wouldn't be received well."

I pondered that. "Probably not. Maybe that's why I haven't logged in yet. But I have a username and a password for a reason, and if there's nothing to hide, there's no reason to be angry at me for logging in to take a look. You need accurate, updated numbers to decide if acquiring this firm is in your best interest."

"True. But I'm not about to ask you to risk your job, Esme."

"If you ask Miller for updated numbers, do you think he'll give them to you?"

He bit out a short laugh. "No. I know for sure he wouldn't give them to me."

"So then I'm not waiting for you to ask me to run the numbers."

"It's not your job to save me from acquiring a lemon of a company. You could be fired, and you know it."

"Then I'd be fired for doing the right thing, and any company that would fire me for that doesn't deserve me as a valuable employee. If he's hiding something from you, it's unscrupulous and could be grounds for a lawsuit if you were petty enough. And think about what Saul would say."

"He'll have something to say, one way or the other. If I sign the papers, and Miller turns out to be a dud, I'll hear it. If I don't sign these papers, I'll hear it."

"So, what do you want to do?"

I appreciated that Trey appeared to take his time and consider that question. Once I logged in and started looking, there was no turning back. He shifted his weight, turning his body toward me, his bottom lip caught in his teeth, then reached over to grasp one of my hands, clutching it in his, sweeping his thumb over my skin.

"It's crazy how much I've missed you."

I smiled, recognizing the sharp turn in conversation topics. "You've seen me, Trey. Several times. We talk every day."

"I miss you in between. I miss being alone with you, being able to speak my mind about how goddamn sexy your thighs look in those leggings."

He leaned in and brushed his lips across mine, so light and airy that it made me twitch with the longing to kiss him until I pressed my lips to his. "I'm starting to see why you invited me to your place."

Trey kissed his way from my mouth to the spot below my ear that made parts of my body stand at attention while the rest of me went soft. "I'm still not asking you for sexual favors." He pulled back, but only long enough to look me in the eye and add, "Are you offering?"

I laughed. "Not... yet."

"Yet? So you might eventually?"

A few beats later, I answered. "Definitely eventually."

A long, loud groan rolled from him as his body seemed to overtake mine. I cackled in laughter as he urged me back until I was lying on the handwoven rug that I'd admired earlier. Trey hovered above me, then lowered his body to mine. My body seemed to move without my brain urging it to; my arms and legs closed him in, holding him in position.

"You seem to always be erect, Trey. I'm starting to feel some concern for blood flow through the rest of your body."

"It's only when you're around." We kissed, sharing a long, slow, romantic moment. "Or when I think about you. Or when I'm on the phone with you, and your voice is doing that husky thing—"

"What husky thing?"

"When you're tired, your voice is like... lower. Kind of gritty and smoky, like a sex line girl. It hits the lower register. It hits *my* lower register if you know what I'm saying."

To emphasize his point, Trey ground his pelvis against mine. All it took was a whimper and a thrust in kind to make Trey sit up, then pull me up with him.

"What? What's wrong?"

"Nothing. You trust me?"

"You always ask me that when you're about to suggest some fuckshit. I'm not going to the roof."

"No fuckshit," he said, laughing. "Do you trust me?"

"Yes. Why?"

"Come with me." I let him help me up, then he grabbed

both of my hands and pulled us through the living room, the dining room, and the kitchen.

"What about all this stuff we left out?"

"I know how to clean up."

"I wanted to help, though…"

"No need. You're going to be busy."

We passed a few closed doors and turned into a darkened room. Trey released one of my hands to tap the light switch. Two bedside lamps turned on, bathing the room in soft light. The bed, clearly the centerpiece of the room, was a wide king covered in a black goose down comforter and coordinating beige and cream accessories. Thin, sheer curtains obscured picturesque windows.

"Ooh, you have a Peloton."

"Yeah. I ride every morning. And some nights, if I can't sleep."

I walked over to the sleek exercise bike positioned in front of the window. The screen, which looked like a large tablet, was dark. I tapped it, and nothing happened.

"Really? You want to play with the bike right now?"

"I've never seen one up close. Can you turn it on?"

Trey reached behind the small tablet affixed to the machine and pressed a button. The tablet came to life, the *Peloton* brand emblazoned across the screen. He pressed a few buttons, then turned a lever to lower the seat.

"Hop on. Let's see if Sharida has a class that's up."

"Who the hell is Sharida, Trey? Is that your girlfriend?"

Trey laughed, waiting until I climbed up onto the molded seat. "She's my Peloton girlfriend, yeah." With a few taps, he pulled up a class and pressed the start button. "Ride to the beat, adjust your strength with the knob under the screen. She'll pump you up, keep the energy going, let you know when you should be working hard, and when you should go all out because cool down is coming up."

"Neat." I was already huffing, trying to keep up with the class riding to The Jackson 5.

"She's got a live DJ tonight. These are fun rides. Like a party."

Trey stood next to me, watching the screen with his arms crossed, nodding his head to the beat. A gorgeous, bald, bronze bombshell was upfront on her bike, barking out commands over a headset mic with a smile.

"Uh, huh…"

"They make special shoes so that your feet stay secure on the pedals—"

"Ok." I hopped off of the bike before I broke a sweat. "I'll stick to yoga. Let's uh…" I nodded my head toward the extremely comfortable looking bed. "Let's talk over here."

"Ain't gotta tell me twice."

I climbed onto the bed on my hands and knees, then flipped over and laid back. Trey followed, stretching out beside me and already working his fingers under my t-shirt.

"Trey, I have a question that I want to ask you."

He cupped a breast in his palm and gently squeezed, then released and moved to the other one. "Go for it."

"What kind of women do you usually date? Do you have a type? I didn't see any pictures of women that don't look like family on your mantle."

He paused his motions, but only for a moment before resuming squeezing and kneading, flicking his thumbs across my nipples.

"Are you trying to see if you measure up? Or if I'm upgrading?"

"Sort of. I'm curious."

"Well. I try not to be too shallow. I like her to have arms and legs, hair, and teeth."

"See, why can't I get a serious answer to this question? Why don't you want to tell me?"

He laughed. "I like Black women, Esme. Black women

with thick hips and meaty thighs and juicy breasts and—" He leaned in to kiss me. "Pillow soft lips like these right here."

"So, you're not going to answer?"

"I *did* answer. What do you want me to say? You want me to call out a bunch of shit that doesn't describe you, so you can wonder why I like you? Why I want you? You are exactly the kind of woman I like. That's why I like you. Among other reasons."

"Other reasons like what?"

"Like…" Trey paused, staring somewhere above my shoulder for a moment before answering. "Scruples. You give a damn about me, about my company, even when you're paid to care about the other guy. You're offering to risk your job to make sure I don't get fucked over. By your client."

"It's the right thing to do."

"Some people—like me, for example, might argue that it's not your job to do that. But I recognize that you want to, and I appreciate that you're willing to do that for me. It means a lot to me."

I cupped his chin, bringing his lips to mine. "Thank you. That was a very sweet, kiss-ass answer. I'll take it."

"Good. Because it's true."

"You don't want to know what kind of man I like?"

"Nope," he answered quickly. "You're here with me, at my place, on my bed. I'm pretty sure I fit the description."

"I feel like you think it should be that simple, but you know women aren't that simple."

"Neither are men, to be honest. There's a lot of pressure to be the perfect guy. But this?" He moved his hand between us to indicate both of us. "This is good. I like how it feels to be attracted to someone, to know that somebody feels the same way about me. I'm not trying to question it or talk myself out of wanting it. You bring me joy."

I grinned. "So, I get to stay?"

"For as long as you want to be here."

He rolled on top of me, settling inside thighs that instinctively opened for him. I willed myself to relax and enjoy him. I was soon lost in the heady sensuality of his mouth, his tongue, his lips, and the ripple of muscle under his skin when I gripped his arms or ran my hands down his back.

Trey sat up, resting on his knees. He'd changed into a t-shirt and shorts when he came home, but now he was pulling them off, tossing the clothing over the side of the bed. I followed suit, pulling off my t-shirt, leaving the bra on underneath. Then I tugged my leggings down and tossed them in the same general direction.

My clothing choices, down to my lingerie, were strategic. He'd already seen me all dolled up. Now he could see me dressed down. I knew we wouldn't be able to resist each other, so I chose a provocative, retro-inspired burgundy satin and lace set. My skin glowed against the deep color of the panty, and my breasts were just barely contained in the bra.

I felt irresistible. By the fire in Trey's eyes, he agreed.

Wearing only his boxer briefs, he lowered his body to mine and took my mouth swiftly. Without missing a beat or a swipe of his tongue, he took my hands in one of his and pinned them above my head. He slid the other to my thighs and pushed them open, then cupped me, using a finger to stroke my rigid bud through the thin satin. My body responded in kind with a deep flush of heat and lightning. My hips rolled in rhythm with his strokes, but it wasn't doing much but driving me crazy.

As if he could read my mind, he tucked a long finger under the band, emitting a groan and a hunch of his hips when he felt the pool of slick wetness. "Shit," he muttered, between bouts of sucking on my tongue. "You're so fucking wet. Is that for me?"

I could only whimper, mentally willing him to stroke harder, faster. I hooked a thumb in the band of my panties and pulled them down until I could kick out of them, then splayed my thighs to give him full access to a freshly waxed pussy that was ready for... *whatever.*

Especially if *whatever* meant the sensation of his fingers inside me. I shuddered, unable to contain the vibrations that rocked me. No man that I'd even contemplated sex with had ever tried to find that spot that made my body arch up off of the bed and a yelp of pleasure tear from my throat.

No matter what happened with Trey and me, I'd already decided that if it didn't feel like this— if I didn't crave him, If I didn't think about him constantly, if the sound of his voice didn't bring a visceral, pleasured reaction, then it wasn't it for me. All I had to do was moan, and Trey would respond.

Whatever happened tonight, I'd decided I was going to let it happen. I was so damned tired of staring at the TV, of dreaming about the romances I read about, imagining the sizzling scenes from Zane novels with my vibrator and a rotating list of Black porn sites. I'd explored my body and the lengths to which I could experience sexual pleasure independently. I was more than ready to top anything I could do for myself.

The only thing standing between me and copious amounts of sex with Trey was that damn contract, which wasn't even worth the paper it was printed on.

Trey released my lips, only to move his mouth down my body, dropping kisses at strategic places like the rise of each breast, then light snaps of his teeth at the nipples encased in satin, then moving south across the soft roundness of my belly. He moved further down until he was eye level to my core, then slid his arms under my body to hook my thighs over his shoulders. He kissed the inside of my right thigh. Then sucked the inside of the left.

With a long, flat tongue, he tasted me. He made sounds that made it clear that he was pleased. For that matter, so was I. I grabbed a pillow from the head of the bed and shoved it under my neck. I wanted to watch when, without hesitation,

Trey took my whole clit in his mouth, rasping the length with his tongue.

"Oooh… shit…"

Involuntarily, my pelvis jerked. I could hear how wet I was, which only made me more aroused. Trey was undeterred, setting his cadence and varying pressure until I held his head in my hands and writhed against him, riding him. He flicked his tongue across my clit and inserted two eager fingers into my slick center.

Moans that weren't quiet to begin with rose until I was shrieking. I pulled the pillow from behind my neck and put it over my face to scream into it.

"Mm-mmm," he hummed, grabbing the edge of the pillow and throwing it across the room. "Don't hide. I want to hear you."

He went back to his task, working two long fingers inside me and stroking my clit with his tongue until my gasps came quicker, accompanied by moans and, finally, a gut level scream. As I pulsed around his fingers, I released an explosion that left him soaked to his wrist.

"Good girl."

"Oh my *fucking* God, I never came that hard before!" My chest heaved with my breaths as if I'd actually done miles on the Peloton. I fell flat against the mattress, lightheaded with limp limbs.

"I'll take that as a compliment," he said, dipping his head one last time to press his lips to my clit. I was so sensitive that it was a sweet kind of pain. "Be right back. Don't move."

He crawled off the bed and disappeared behind a closed door. I heard the water running for a few minutes, and then he was back, the scent of body wash wafting around him and a towel in his hands. He used the warm cloth to wipe me clean before he took it back to the bathroom.

Trey chuckled when he returned and stretched out next to me again. "You really did not move."

"I... don't think I can," I said. My voice came out weak. Dreamy. I was high. "I want to reciprocate with some bomb ass head, but I can't... right now."

"You don't need to reciprocate. I've been daydreaming about that since I met you, so I got mine. You just need to recover and tell me that you had a good time."

"I had a good time," I replied, then stretched, cat-like. "That was so...*so* good."

"Yeah? You'd like more of that?"

"I'd like much more of that, please."

"I think I'm going to be able to make that happen."

My eyes slid closed in a post-coital fugue, but I forced them open. "Trey. You didn't answer my question earlier. About running Miller's numbers."

He didn't respond for so long that I thought he'd fallen asleep. But then his voice rumbled beside me. "I don't want you to risk your job for me. I'll find a way to get the information I need. At least let me ask Miller. You know, try to get them legitimately."

I rolled my head toward him but ended up staring at the side of his face. "You said you didn't think he'd give them to you."

"I don't," he replied with a frown and a shake to his head. "But I can ask and go from there. I want this closed as much as you do. I want to be with you, but I need to do this guilt-free. Whatever I can do to keep you safe, that's what I want."

"But so you know, I'm gangsta outside of the Laser Maze, too. I'm willing to do it."

"I know. That's why I like you."

He sucked in a long breath through his nose and stared, wide-eyed, at the ceiling. The tension was palpable. I didn't envy his position. If he disappointed his father, he would lose any chance of getting to open and run a residential construction division. If he went forward with the transaction on faith, it could bankrupt Pettigrew.

"You feel like getting in the shower with me?" He asked, another sudden topic change. "I have those rainfall shower heads, and it's all marble inlay. It's almost as cool as the Peloton."

My eyebrows hiked in interest. "Maybe I'll get a second wind."

CHAPTER TWENTY-THREE

Esme

Trey's body ran like clockwork, so he said.

His circadian rhythms were set to 5 AM, so no matter what time he went to sleep, that was when his eyes opened. My body clock was not in alignment with his. After a luxurious and eventful shower the evening before, and a mutual body oil rubdown, Trey lent me a t-shirt from his collection and I passed out.

When he got out of bed to get on the bike before the sun was even up, it woke me up. I rolled over to watch the muscles in his back move through the white sleeveless tank he wore before I drifted back to sleep. He woke me up again after he finished.

"Come on now. You can't go to work in my t-shirt." He had a point, so I got up and searched for my clothes.

Now I yawned as I packed my bag and slipped my shoes on.

"Sorry about this whole walk of shame thing you gotta do."

"Sorry? For what? Bringing me dinner and wearing my ass out?"

Trey folded his arms cross his broad chest as he leaned against the counter behind him. He'd showered and stepped into a pair of briefs to walk me to the door. If I didn't have to go to work, I'd drag him back to the bedroom by the bulge that was taunting me.

"Since you put it that way, I don't have anything to be sorry for. I'm actually quite proud."

"Besides, I'm a grown woman," I added. "There's no shame in having several orgasms, returning the favor, then passing out." I looped an arm around his neck when he pulled me close, giving me an extra squeeze and a kiss at the door.

"I'll see you later this morning. I hope your client feels agreeable today."

"I'll try to prime him before you get there. Should I bring coffee?"

He shook his head. "Let me. You go home and get ready." He kissed me again, then opened the door and gently pushed me out to the hallway with the tips of his fingers. "If you don't leave, I'm going to convince you to play hooky so we can repeat last night. Go."

I frowned because that sounded like an excellent idea, but I turned and walked toward the elevator. When I didn't hear his door close, I peeked over my shoulder to find Trey lingering in the doorway, his head tilted down. I could guess that his eyes were on the generous roundness of my ass.

I turned the corner, then pressed the button for the elevator.

Since I was moving against traffic, the drive home was pleasant. When I pulled up to the house and saw lights on, I knew that O'Neal was home. All of that talk about being unashamed to go home in the daylight in the clothes I wore last night stuck in my throat.

I entered through the kitchen and hung my key on its

hook. O'Neal leaned against the counter in a sleeveless t-shirt and plaid lounge pants with one of my mother's gigantic stoneware bowls balanced in his palm, likely full of cereal.

"Look who just walked in this door at—" He leaned over to check the time. "7:30 in the morning? Looking smug and satisfied, too." O'Neal spooned a mouthful of cereal and spoke while crunching Cheerios. "I cannot wait to hear this shit. Where have you been, Esme?"

I set my bag down on the seat next to him, then headed straight for the coffee grinder. "I should really ignore you because it's none of your business."

"I will troll the shit out of you. Don't try me, Esme. Where. the hell. you been?"

"I was with Trey. Alright?" I poured beans into the grinder, then ground them and tapped out a few tablespoons of ground coffee. I turned the stove on under the kettle to boil water for the French press, then turned to face him. "We worked late. I stayed over. When did you get home?"

"About midnight. They delayed my flight in Istanbul, so we didn't get in until late, then I went out with the crew. So when I got home, and you weren't here, I pulled up the Find My Friends app. Somebody's fast ass was in midtown. When you still weren't home this morning, I checked the app again and saw that you were coming this way."

"What are you doing up, if you just got home?" O'Neal would typically have a day off after a long trip.

"I got a call to cover a flight. I'll take the hours. Stop stalling and tell me what's up."

"There's nothing up. Seriously. We just… are hanging out."

"Hanging out. All night. At his place in midtown." O'Neal tipped his head to the side. "Y'all fuckin'?"

"No. We are not fucking."

"Y'all doing everything *but* fuckin'?" That… I couldn't lie about. O'Neal knew me too well, and I couldn't hide the truth if I tried. "I don't even know why I asked, actually. Y'all doin' something; it's all over your face. I thought you didn't want anything to do with him?"

"I know what I'm doing, O'Neal."

"Do you, Es? Explain it to me."

"O'Neal, you told me to get with him!"

"I told you to *fuck him*. I don't want you to get into a drawn-out entanglement, get your heart dragged behind a nigga taking from you like he's your man, but calling it hanging out. We are too old for that shit, Esme."

"That's not what's happening, O'Neal—" A whistle from the kettle interrupted. I turned the knob on the stove to remove the heat, then poured the boiling water into the press and put the lid on the carafe.

"You said you know what you're doing. So, explain it."

So, I explained it, while I waited for my coffee to brew. The remnants of Honey Nut Cheerios grew soggy in the puddle of milk at the bottom of O'Neal's cereal bowl.

"Es, if anybody was watching you, they'd assume you were already sleeping with him. May as well go on and do it."

"I know. But between us, we want to say we didn't and not have to lie."

"You like him, then? I mean... you must, rolling in here the morning after."

"Yes. I like him. I don't know about a forever kind of thing, but he's definitely getting this first round."

"Is he asking you to risk your job for him, Es?"

"No," I shot back, vehemently shaking my head. "He would prefer that I didn't. He's dead set against it."

"But you're going to do it anyway."

I poured myself a cup of coffee, added cream and Splenda, and stirred. I avoided O'Neal's gaze because I knew what his reaction would be.

"Esme..."

"*I know*. But *you* know how it's been at Benning. It wouldn't be a terrible thing to never have to face Ethan again. It would be so much easier if Miller would be an upstanding guy here. He could provide updated financials, and I wouldn't even have to consider going behind his back. Trey could make an intelligent, informed decision instead of walking into this situation blind."

"He's not even the man you're paid to care about."

"The thing is that the man I'm paid to care about may not be worth caring about. And the man I do care about? Is worth getting fired to protect."

I shrugged, picked up my coffee mug, and headed toward the stairs. "I need to get ready for work and head down there. What time is your flight?"

"Almost noon," he answered. He got up to empty his bowl but turned before I got out of earshot. "Make sure he thinks you're worth protecting. And start logging into WhatsApp and updating us. I'm tired of asking your sisters what's going on with you."

"I'm tired of providing entertainment for y'all. These are not the Awkward Adventures of Esme Whitaker anymore. This could be real, and potentially something very good for me. And y'all are too nosy."

O'Neal fake sniffled as I walked away. "My little Esme is all growed up."

Inside my bag, my work phone buzzed. I pulled it out, expecting a cute note from Trey about how much he already missed me, or that he was looking forward to seeing me today, or asking what flavor of coffee I wanted from Brew Bar.

Instead, it was a message from Reese, Ethan's Executive Assistant: *Report to Benning this morning before going to Miller Design. Ethan needs to speak with you. Please acknowledge receipt and report ETA.*

Fuck.

I sat in a guest chair in front of Ethan's desk and set my bag near my feet. My nerves were so shot that my body vibrated. I tried crossing one leg over the other to appear super casual. My right leg trembled so violently that I opted to sit up straight, both feet flat.

I'd dressed to impress at least, in an olive-green scoop neck dress that clung in the best places and draped over others, with Weitzman suede pumps dyed to match. I was no longer dressing only to impress myself. I knew somebody that would look and would enjoy getting an eye full of thigh visible through the deep side split.

The thought of Trey ramped my nerves up even more. What if Ethan was pulling me from the project? What if he was planning to replace me with someone who didn't "give a damn"?

The door to Ethan's office opened, and he rushed in, sliding his laptop and a stack of files on his desk. "Esme," he said in greeting. "Thanks for coming in."

"You say thanks as if you gave me a choice. It surprised me to receive a summons to the office today. Is there anything to be concerned about?"

Ethan situated himself at his desk and arranged it the way he liked it. Laptop to his right, files and notes to his left, stacked so that they were only organized to him. His desk was otherwise bare, but he kept a few utensils in a cup on the credenza behind him, between framed photos of his family. At least, I assumed the people in the photos were his family. He hadn't swapped them out in the entire time I'd been working for him.

"Always with the smart ass comments, Esme." He scowled, punching keys on his laptop while he spoke. "I received a concerning phone call from Thomas Miller this morning. Pettigrew is pushing hard on a few terms of the contract, and he's unsatisfied with the progress. He doesn't feel like you have his back in this negotiation."

My jaw dropped open. Was Miller throwing *me* under the bus?

"I want an update, and I don't want to hear the party line that everything is on schedule. What's happening out there, Esme?"

"Well, I have to disagree with Miller. At every turn, my conversations with Mr. Pettigrew have led with Miller's needs in mind. I've been clear that there are reasonable concessions to be made on both sides, but Mr. Miller does want to come to terms. He will not give away his company. Mr. Pettigrew understands that —"

"Then what's the problem?" Ethan was more of a menacing, low talker, not a brash man, but today his tone was sharp. "This should have been open and shut. Nothing to fuck up, just process the contract. Easy work, that's why I gave it to you. Now, Miller tells me that you and Mr. Pettigrew seem friendly. That you often spend time together away from the office—"

"That little room that Miller gave us to work in is a hole, so yes, we take our meetings offsite, where I plead Miller's case and get Pettigrew to come forward. And when I return to the office, I bring something that Miller can agree to. You told me to get this job done. I'm trying to do that."

"Mmmhmm. I bet you are."

My eyes narrowed. "What… what does that mean?"

"Miller suspects something is going on between you and Pettigrew. Frankly, I don't care if it gets the contract signed. Pettigrew is pushing to involve legal and asking for financial statements that he doesn't need. If you're close to him, find a way to get him to sign. This deal has to go through, Esme. Fuck him if you have to but wrap this up. Whatever it takes, or it's your ass. Am I understood?"

I wanted to laugh.

I wanted to cock my head back and scream in laughter. Did my boss just suggest that I do what I've been trying not to do? I was being set out like a sacrificial lamb. Whatever it took to get Miller Design sold, Ethan would do it.

After the transaction was processed, Ethan would have a reason to fire me.

I swallowed my seething, roiling anger, grabbed the straps of my bag and stood. "Understood," I bit out, then walked out of his office.

I hustled to my car, got in, and sped away.

I had to talk to Trey. And not at Miller Design.

CHAPTER TWENTY-FOUR

Trey

A phone call broke through a monotone modern rap hit with bass that thumped so hard, I felt it through the steering wheel. It was too young for me, but I was too lazy to look for a new station. The dashboard display read *Esme Whitaker*.

I'd just picked up our coffee and was headed to Miller Design. She would either have news to share—maybe she had worked miracles to bring him around—or she'd be calling to tell me how much she was looking forward to seeing me.

"You miss me, huh?" I called out as I picked up the line.

"Trey, it's Esme."

I hadn't known her long, but I knew when someone's voice held an unusual edge. "I... know. That's why I said– anyway, what's going on? Are you at Miller already?"

"No. And I don't think you should go there either. We need to meet."

"I'm at Brew Bar, on my way to Vinings."

"I really need to talk to you before you go out there, Trey. And I won't be there. Can you meet me at Pettigrew?"

"Uhm sure. Yeah." I was confused, but I didn't think Esme would redirect me without reason. "Park in the lot and wait at the front desk. I'm on my way."

"I'm already here."

I redirected to the southbound lanes, headed toward Pettigrew. I parked in my spot between Pops and Vincent, then rushed inside the three-story, bright yellow group of buildings overshadowed by the Pettigrew Construction sign.

Esme was waiting in guest seating. The sight of her shapely body in a dress and heels, hair in bouncy curls and her stern, concentrated stare into the atmosphere made my heart leap. I'd kissed her goodbye a few hours ago, but damn, it was good to see her.

I called out to her, catching her attention. She hopped up, picking up her bag. I laid a hand on her shoulder and dipped my head to catch her gaze. "Hey, what is going on? Why are you here?"

"I'm fine. I didn't mean to make you worry; I have a lot on my mind. Can you take me to your office? I need to speak to you in private."

I signed her in and escorted her to the executive suite, then into my office.

I'd refused to take over Pops' office, mostly because I believed in my heart that he would be back. His assistant guarded his space like a German shepherd. I also hated his furniture and had become accustomed to my office suite. And my view.

I handed her the coffee that I'd picked up for her, which had stayed impressively warm, but she didn't seem to notice, taking large gulps from the cup. I sat on a corner of my desk and waited until she was ready to talk.

"Thanks for this." She said, holding the cup in both hands. "So, I got called into Benning this morning. Ethan tore into me about the progress on the contract. Miller had called him, pissed because he felt like he was being pressured to sign the contract early, that you were pushing him to sell his company for less than he wanted to take for it, and that he felt like you and I were working together against him."

"We kind of are. But I'm not trying to tank this deal. I did email him this morning to request updated financials. I said my team wanted to take one last look at the numbers before it heads to legal."

"Well, that started a shit storm. Ethan said something about you demanding financials that you don't need. Miller told Ethan that he thinks there's something going on between us and used it to encourage me to do what I had to do to get you to agree to his terms. His exact words were, fuck him if you have to."

"Oh." I felt my brows hit my hairline. "That's... not ok."

"Yeah. And not that the thought didn't cross my mind—"

"Or mine."

"But that's what we've been trying to avoid, yes? The appearance of impropriety? Anyway, the cat is out of the bag where you and I are concerned. We apparently don't hide our affection for each other well."

She couldn't help but smile. Neither could I. I didn't care if Miller knew that I had feelings for his contracts administrator. Those feelings in no way affected my mission to acquire Miller Design.

"But it feels like Ethan is setting a trap to fire me. No matter what happens with this deal, I'm on the chopping block. Miller is pushing him, so he's pushing me. And I figure that there must be a reason that he doesn't want you to see actual numbers."

"We agree there. But that means that—"

"I'm going to lose my job anyway," she said, her brown eyes wide and brows raised. "And if they don't fire me, I'm going to quit. At the very least, I won't have to work for a man who tells me to fuck a guy to push a deal through."

She paused, pushed out a harsh breath, and continued. "So. I ran the reports that I needed to run while I'm still employed. That you need to be able to close this deal."

I hung my head, slowly releasing a loud, hissing breath. "I really didn't want you to do that, Esme."

"I know, Trey because it means risking my job, but my job is already at risk. I may as well go down in flames. It's the right thing to do. Besides, it's not like it's illegal. It's not that I can't, or that they have forbidden me to. I hadn't because those reports were all provided to me. I took them at face value. Did Saul ever run his own Dun & Bradstreet report?"

D&B was like Experian or TransUnion, a credit reporting agency but for businesses. Like consumer credit agencies measured my worthiness to open a credit account or take on a loan, D&B measured and monitored the same for a commercial entity. That report would answer every concern an acquiring company might have."

"By the time I came on board, they were signing papers. When I took over, Miller revamped the contract and raised his purchase price. Like you've said, we received a portfolio of documents from Miller's accounting firm. The report was in there. I don't honestly think he ran a single report."

"That's interesting because it's one of the first steps in setting up a customer profile at Benning, but I wasn't directed to do so."

Esme handed me her coffee cup, then turned to pull some folders and her computer from her bag. She flipped open the folder, revealing a neat stack of pages and notes clipped inside.

"This is the D&B report that Miller provided to Saul and Benning. As you can see, there are a few blips, but it's relatively clean. It's also quite aged, not current at all. Few companies have zero debt and no marks. This looks standard for a ten-year-old company, as reports go."

She opened her laptop, then pulled up a report.

"Take a look at this report that I pulled an hour ago when I was sitting in the car. A delinquency score measures how likely a business will be to have severely late payments. It goes from 101 to 670, with 670 being the highest. That's like having a perfect credit score. Miller scores 209, which means they probably pay some bills on time, but for the most part, they're frequently more than 90 days late on more than one account."

"That means Miller is hiding some debt somewhere, then?"

"Probably," she confirmed with a slow nod. "If he had the money, he'd pay the bills. Firms in this position struggle to keep the lights on and make payroll, pay taxes, and keep benefits current, then hope for the best with everything else. He might get a large down payment on a job and make a balloon payment to bring him current, but then he'll fall behind for the next four months while the job is progressing, then catch up when the final payment hits the bank. He might pay installments on a loan for drafting equipment, but he'll be late on software renewal. Or let machinery almost be repossessed before they'll make a payment."

"Can you forward that to me?" I stood, walking around my desk and picking up my desk phone. "I need Vincent to see it."

"Sure. I'm sending some other reports to you from our platform, but they'll confirm what the Dun & Bradstreet report says. Miller Design is failing. It'll go under without a buyer."

"**U**nbelievable. Un-*fucking*-believable."

It was the only word that Vincent had been able to utter since I'd called him into my office, laid out the entire situation with Miller, and showed him the reports that I'd pulled off the printers.

And introduced him to Esme, who was in the process of saving our asses. He stared at the printouts, flipping page after page, his head moving back and forth and muttering the same word over and over.

I swiveled in my chair, having long since shed my jacket and tie. Esme and Vincent were in the guest chairs in front of my desk. Esme looked exhausted, but also at peace, for someone that just took a huge risk for us and was on the verge of unemployment.

It wasn't the outcome that I wanted, but I could not have been prouder of her.

"What does this mean for us, then?" Vincent asked, finally looking up from the printouts, directing his question at Esme. "What should we do?"

"Your current contract with Miller, the one he's pushing Trey to sign, anyway, stipulates that Pettigrew assumes ownership of all assets. In this case, we're mainly talking about equipment needed to run the business. Now that makes sense, considering you're both in the business of design. He's likely leasing the equipment, which means you'd have to assume payments. I don't know much about drafting and architecture, but I don't think Miller would be using old and outdated machines. We're talking state of the art, cutting edge... so he's in for a large sum."

"We took a tour when we began negotiations," said Vincent. "He's got a nice shop over there. Brand new, updated, shiny. That's what we liked about them."

Esme nodded, showing that she understood.

"Given that, and his delinquency score, he's probably more than 180 days behind on loans on those machines. He might be hoping that a big payday gives him enough money to cover that debt and bring him current. And then they become your problem, your bill to pay."

"The question, Vincent," I interrupted, sitting forward, "is if Miller is still a good target. He's got no room to play. We know the real deal, so if we still want this company, we can probably get it for a steal. Call that office a Pettigrew satellite and swallow it up."

"Something to think about, for sure. But son…"

His gaze landed on me, and I knew what he was going to say. I averted my own eyes, so I didn't have to watch him say it.

"It's time you talked to Saul. I know you don't want to, and had hoped to avoid it, but he needs to know what's happening. If we kill this acquisition, he will not be pleased. I want him to understand why."

When I told Esme that the only thing I was really afraid of was Pops, I meant it. It wasn't a physical fear but an emotional one. I didn't want to tell him that I'd failed to do what he specifically set out for me to do.

Begrudgingly, I nodded. And braced. This was going to be a tough conversation.

———

E sme had offered to come with me, as had Vincent, but I'd declined both offers. I had to do this, to stand on my own two feet. Pops made me responsible, and as the man in charge, standing in for the man in charge, this was my task.

That didn't make the task any easier. Neither did walking into my parent's house to see my sister sitting at the kitchen island, watching my mother cook.

"Trey!" My mother called out, a bright smile breaking out across her face. I bent toward her so that she could drop the customary kiss on my cheek. "So nice to see you on a weeknight. Should I set a place for you for dinner?"

"No, thanks, Mom. I'm actually here to talk business with Pops. It's important."

Her joyous expression dissipated, replaced by a frown and a furrowed brow. "He put you in charge for a reason, to make these decisions with Vincent. Now you rush home to discuss everything with him, get him all worked up, and then I'm the one that has to live with him. Whatever it is, deal with it on your own. Don't involve him."

"Can't really do that, this time. It's bigger than me, and at the end of the day, it's his company. But I do appreciate his health, and I'll try to keep him calm. Where is he?"

She sucked her teeth and shook her head but pointed in the general direction of a corner office. "In his study."

I turned to leave, but another voice stopped me. "Hello, little brother. Nice to see you. Thanks for acknowledging me. Love you, too."

I suppressed a sigh, turning to face her. "Hello, Missy. Sorry, I'm… busy."

"Mmhmm." Her lips formed a surly frown. "You always think your shit is more important than anyone else's."

"Are you serious right now, Missy? I'm actually working, and I'm here to see my boss. I don't have time to cater to you."

"Fuck you, Trey!" She spit from across the room.

"No, fuck *you*!"

"Melissa! Trey!" My mother's sharp tone cut off whatever Missy had planned to say in response. "That's enough! You two do nothing but fight like cats and dogs, and I'm done with it! Trey, go talk to your father."

I left the room, escaping the heavy blanket of tension. Missy and I hadn't had a good conversation in a very long time. I recognized that, like my approach with Esme, I wielded certain personality characteristics like weapons. However, they didn't always serve me well. Once this mess with Miller was over, I vowed to make that therapy appointment that I'd been telling myself to make.

I turned into the study, rapping my knuckles on the open door. Pops lounged on a dark chocolate leather couch, feet up on an ottoman, the TV blaring SportsCenter. A loud burst of laughter ripped from his throat as he pointed at the television.

"That Stephen A. Smith is a fool. I tune in to watch him stick his foot in his mouth." Pops reached for the remote, muting the sound. "Hey, son. Didn't expect to see you. You saw your sister?"

I had to fight to not roll my eyes. That wouldn't go over well with Pops. "Yeah. We spoke."

"You spoke?" He chuckled. "Sounds like you picked a fight."

"Pops, I actually had something I needed to talk to you about. Can I pull up?"

He gestured toward the couch, but I opted for the chair opposite him, made of the same leather. Uneasy, I lowered myself into it, exhaling a long breath.

"Sounds heavy," Pops commented. "What's going on?"

"Well, what's going on is that uh… I'm not sure that the acquisition is going to move forward."

I watched his expression change, growing darker. He was seething inside, obviously holding back.

"Miller hasn't been forthcoming with the financial status of his company. Today, we ran the reports that I think we should have run on our own to protect our name and reputation. And it's a good thing we did. The outlook is not good."

"I'm not surprised. He was trying pretty hard to get me to buy his company. What are you getting at? He cooks his books?"

"I don't know that his books are cooked so much as the numbers that he provided to you at the beginning of this process are no longer current. He's deeply in debt, likely pretty far behind with no hope of catching up without an infusion of cash, but his stance during negotiation is…"

I shrugged, puzzled even as I said the words. "Pops, he acts like his business has an A rating and that it's worth millions. It's just not. He likely owes far more than he brings in—"

"Like I said, Son, what the hell do you think an acquisition is about? It's taking the best and leaving the rest. That's what I told you to do."

"I understand that, Pops. But the deal that you drew up with Miller is different from the deal he's presented me with. This new deal says we take everything. Income, liabilities, expenditures. Debt."

Pops paused. "How much debt?"

"Not sure yet. We need actuals, and no one answers the phone at the accounting firm he says represents him."

A line of confusion formed across his forehead. "How do you know that he's in debt if you don't have updated numbers?"

And now I had to come clean about the entire ordeal with Miller.

How, when I'd rescued Esme from being mugged, it threw a wrench into the process and changed the game. How, when she was introduced into the equation, it became more about getting Miller to bend my way than to close the acquisition. How, after getting to know Esme and feeling the spark of something real and meaningful for her, I dreamt up a plan to get Miller to agree to my terms. And when I expressed concern about the project, she'd offered to run the reports.

How, despite not wanting her to risk her job, she had done so, and revealed important information that I wouldn't have known until the papers were signed. And that she was likely now unemployed over her decision to help me.

Pops quietly fumed, breathing deeply and evenly as he listened. His jaw was tight, and his eyes cut at me at various points of the story, but he waited for me to finish, sit back against the soft leather and await his response.

"Just to be clear," he began, "I asked you to close the loop on a deal that should have been cut and dry. That's all I asked you to do. Correct?"

"Yeah, Pops, but—"

"That was a yes or no question," he said, his index finger in the air. "That's what I asked you to do, right? Just to be clear."

Yeah," I sighed, dejected. "Yes, Pops. That's what you asked."

"And then you decided to do your own thing and *fucked it up!*" The last three words roared at a decibel that I hadn't heard since before Pops' heart attack, and frankly, it scared the shit out of me.

Pops stood, so I stood too. He had a few pounds on me, and we weren't quite eye to eye, but I stood my ground.

"I asked you to do one thing, Trey. One thing! For the future of this company. You come to me with your hat in your hand about how you fucked it up, running after a woman! Am I supposed to be impressed? Am I supposed to be *proud*?"

My mother appeared in the doorway. Her jaw was set, and her lips curled.

I raised my hands in surrender. "I didn't— I told him what was going on and he—"

"Trey, why don't you go ahead and go?" My mother waved a hand toward me, gesturing me out of the room. "Let him calm down. Call tomorrow. Or… something."

"Mom, I can't just leave when things get uncomfortable. We have decisions to make."

"No, *I* have decisions to make!" Pops roared, moving toward me. "*Vincent* has decisions to make. *You* have no more decisions to make, Trey. You want to run your own division, but you couldn't complete this simple transaction, and now we have no chance at that bid."

He waved a hand in my face and turned away. "Trey, just go."

"Pops, I get it. You're pissed. But we need to—"

He turned on a heel and ended up back in my face. "Get. Out!" He bellowed.

Missy snaked around my mother, flew into the room, and grabbed my arm. "Let's go, Trey," she muttered under her breath, pulling me out of the door. "Give it a rest."

Stunned, I allowed myself to be escorted out, straight through the house to the front door. Behind us, I heard my mother talking to him, using calm, soothing tones.

By the time we made it to the front door, I had regained clear thought and yanked my arm from her grasp. "Why did you pull me out of there? I still need to talk—"

"You need to go home. Or to work. You need to let him think. You need to let him calm down. He can't make rational decisions in a heightened state. Ask me how I know."

I glared at Missy, but where I expected animosity, there was exhaustion and a knowing expression. Finally, I nodded and reached for the door handle.

"Fine. I guess I'll go wait for my punishment."

"Trey." Missy's voice stopped me, yet again. "You did the right thing. He doesn't see it yet but give it time."

An eyebrow rose. She smirked. "I'm nosy. So is Mom. We listened at the door."

She lifted her shoulders in a shrug. "I'm always jealous of how Pops has so much faith in you. He took you into the business and showed you the ropes and let you run his company while he was out. You can do what I can't, and no matter what he feels right now, I know he's proud of you. And I know we don't get along, but I'm proud of you, too."

She frowned, then. "Not that you care."

"Missy, don't… don't say that. I *care*. It's just that we—"

"No, it's fine, Trey. I honestly don't need well-meaning platitudes and I don't expect much more than I get from you. You're a dick," she said, adding a laugh that I knew she didn't mean, but it helped to lighten the mood. "But...in a little brother way. And you're the only person real enough to be a dick to me. You're never fake nice to me. Everyone puts on kid gloves like they're afraid I'm going to grab a knife and go at them. I'm not an ax murderer."

I almost laughed. Then I actually did laugh, because Missy burst into laughter.

"I guess I'm glad you can laugh about it."

"Gotta find joy somewhere, right?"

"Right. So..." I glanced around, noticing her Mini Cooper parked on the street in front of the house. I'd been so focused on talking to Pops that I hadn't noticed. "What are you doing out here, anyway? I thought you had like... therapy."

Missy shook her head slowly, sucking her teeth while she leaned against the doorjamb. "I live a whole life that you know nothing about, Trey. I got a job, actually. Mom was making dinner to celebrate. It's part-time, but it's work."

My jaw dropped. "What? For real?"

She grinned, nodding. She seemed proud. "The grifter got a job!"

Now I felt even more like shit. "Missy..."

"Whatever, it's fine. The place where I used to go to therapy needs someone to answer the phone and direct people. I can do that. My therapist recommended me. After he transferred me to another therapist."

"Transferred you." I folded my arms over my chest, suddenly protective, responding to a flare of emotion on her behalf. I remembered that the therapists at Brownwood moved her from therapy to therapy, doctor to doctor. "What's that about?"

"Oh, it's just a better therapist. A whole new routine and different meds and intensive treatment and weekly sessions. So far, it's working. When Pops had his heart attack, I got really, really scared. It must have changed something for me. It's sticking so far. So, I'm going to ride the wave."

"Good," I replied. "Really good for you. Stick with it, if it's working. If you need anything, you have my number. I know you have it because you send me to voicemail when I call you to come to help me with this yard."

She chuckled. "You might regret telling me to call you."

"Let me worry about that." I hugged her, probably for the first time in double-digit years. "Love you. I'm headed back to the office to see if Vincent has any ideas on what to do next."

CHAPTER TWENTY-FIVE

Esme

"Yep. Let's do it."
I was covered in a smock in Jada's salon chair with
the Beauty Boutique logo across the front, a towel catching
drops of water from freshly washed hair. I gave her a
confident nod in the mirror, though I was still very close to
changing my mind about dying my hair.

"Wait, do you think I shouldn't?"

"Honey, it's up to you," she said, holding a container of
purple-tinted wax. "It don't matter a bit what I think."

"You've been trying to get me to dye my hair forever. Now
I want you to, but you're hesitant. Am I too old for purple
hair?"

I scrutinized my face for signs of old age—crow's feet,
wrinkles, a dull pallor— knowing full well that I would not
find them. I had the supple, flawless, youthful skin of a woman
with an expensive skincare regimen and, like my mother and
sisters, would continue looking young far longer than I would
ever appear old.

"I am over fifty with pink hair, so I'm not hearing that, but you marched in here bright and early and demanded that I dye your hair purple. Right after you marched in here, talking about Ferris wheels and dancing on rooftops. I'm checking that you haven't lost your damn mind."

She had a point. I *was* acting a little crazy lately. "Jada, I'm good. Promise. I want to do it. It'll be cute. I think."

"Will your man like it? That is the question."

"Mmmmm. Good thought. If I had one, I'd ask him."

Jada's jaw dropped. She screwed the container open and dropped the cap on the counter in front of me. "What happened to Trey? Did you tell him about—"

"No," I said, cutting her off. "I haven't told him. And nothing happened to Trey. He isn't my man."

"Did you or did you not roll up to the house at sunrise after being with him all night? He said he wanted to pursue you. Sounds like serious pursuit to me."

"I did do that. And Trey did say that. It's probably still true, but nothing is official, and I don't want to get caught up. Anyway, we're not at a point where I'm not going to dye my hair purple because he might not like it."

I craned my neck around so I could see her face. "Do you care if Joe likes your hair?"

"Joe is obsessed with me. He likes everything." She shrugged, then grinned.

"You two make me sick." I turned around again. "The color of my hair doesn't matter anymore, so let's do it."

"So, yeah. Let's talk about you quitting your job, young lady. What the hell is going on over at Benning?"

While Jada worked the wax through my towel-dried hair, I gave her the rundown on the last few weeks with Benning, Miller Design, and Pettigrew, including the enormous reveal that Miller was probably hiding debt and trying to get Pettigrew to buy his company before they found it. I hadn't heard from Trey since he sent me a text late the evening before. His conversation with Saul didn't go well, and he'd been talking with Vincent most of the night.

My heart grew heavy reading those words. I sent him back some encouragement, but he didn't respond. I'd hoped that his father would understand that he had Pettigrew's best interests in mind and that it wasn't that he couldn't or wouldn't close the deal.

I also couldn't help thinking that there was no longer a barrier between Trey and I growing our relationship, a thought that both exhilarated and terrified me. Trey was different from the men I'd dated before. I got past the second date before he demanded sex and didn't act put out when I could have given in and didn't. Instead, we made it work, openly showing affection and exploring each other in the best way possible.

I didn't want to scare him off with my feelings. Or the assumed meaning assigned to my virginity. I wasn't presenting him with a precious gift. I didn't want my time wasted, and I wanted my first time to be enjoyable for both of us. I had a feeling that Trey could give me the experience of a lifetime that I'd been purposely waiting for.

"You know Ethan is a dick, been a dick, always gonna be a dick," I told Jada, rounding out the story. "I am fine with using my savings so that I never have to look that man in the face again. I'm honestly more worried about Trey."

"His family is rich. What are you worried about him for?"

"He said his dad is pissed that the deal didn't go through. I know he feels bad that he let his father down. And he needed this deal for his dad to let him do some other things with Pettigrew. That's pretty much dead now."

"What, like to prove himself? It's not like his father will fire him. Right?"

"I don't know Saul at all. Trey paints him as a tyrant that is benevolent when he wants to be. I'm sure Saul is upset, but did he really want Trey to blindly sign those papers and commit Pettigrew to a ton of potential debt?"

"Probably not. Maybe he needs to regroup. Tell me that you love this purple so far."

Jada had pulled the tinted wax through half of my hair. I tossed my head from side to side, watching the tint catch the light. Ethan would *lose his mind* if he saw me.

And, in fact, he might.

I'd typed up and emailed my letter of resignation, effective immediately, then turned off my business mobile phone and powered down the laptop. I still had to go to Benning and clean out my cubicle. On my way home from the salon, I would drop off the company assets, clean out my workspace, and happily never set foot in that place again.

"It's *amazing*," I said, swooning. "I love it! What do you think, Jada?"

She stepped back, nodding and smiling while looking at it from all angles. "It suits you. You're giving me Justine Skye vibes. You know her? Layah listens to her. Young sangin' gal."

"Yeah, with the purple hair. She's why I wanted to try it."

"Ooh, hang on a second, Es." Jada left and came back with a jar of bright pink wax. "What do you think about mixing some pink in there? Maybe on the bottom, a little in the front, give it an hombre look?"

I shrugged. "I can do what I want, and this stuff washes out in a few days, right?"

"Sure does." She unscrewed the lid, scooped wax into her hands, and began to work it through sections of my hair. "So, you haven't talked to Trey about... you know. The conversation y'all need to have?"

"Not yet. But I have to do it soon. Since there's no contract holding us up, his expectation is going to ramp up. He hasn't been pushing, but now there's no reason to say no if he does. And if he doesn't push, I will. I don't know how much longer I can hold out."

I felt my phone vibrate in my pocket, so I dug it out to check the screen. The way I smiled when I saw his name, and my shoulders relaxed the tiniest bit? *You in trouble, girl.*

Trey Pettigrew: *Hey, girl. How you doin'? So sorry for the radio silence. Been crazy over here. You good?*

I'm good, I typed back. *You?*

Trey Pettigrew: *Rough. I'm struggling. I know it's late notice, but are you free tonight? I need to see you.*

A few short weeks ago, I would have had to check my show schedules to see what was airing that night. Then I'd have to decide if I wanted to watch it live and decline an invite, or if the company was good enough to watch it back on DVR. My, how times change.

Yes. What did you have in mind?

Trey Pettigrew: *Honestly, I'm exhausted and stressed. Feeling down. Those lips of yours would make me feel better.*

Trey Pettigrew: *Need to rub on your booty and tell you that you're pretty.*

That made me laugh so hard I almost dropped the phone.

That would make you feel better?

Trey Pettigrew: *Almost immediately. Please?*

Come over. I'll cook. You'll chill.

Trey Pettigrew: *Bet. What time is good for you? What can I bring?*

7? Let me know you're on the way. Just bring that booty so I can rub on yours too :)

Trey Pettigrew: *Ain't gotta tell me twice. Text you later.*

"Speaking of not being able to hold out, somebody finessed an invite to Netflix & Chill."

"Chile, you'd best go on home and shave the cha-cha. I'll be surprised if you're still a virgin tomorrow."

"From your lips to his dick." I sighed without realizing I had done so while I tucked the phone away. When my attention returned to the room, I found Jada's smirk in the mirror.

"Know who you remind me of? Myself when I met Joe. I was stone cold nuts about that boy." She closed her eyes and let out a light grunt. Then her eyes popped open again. "Did you know he made me wait for sex?"

"No! For how long? And why?"

"Six months of hand holdin', and cheek kissin', and dry humpin'. His family is religious, you know. Strong church upbringing, and he felt like he should wait. I was climbing the walls. I was well and good in love with him by the time we got down to business, and maybe that was the point. It was nice, though. I never so much as looked at another man, to tell the truth."

"Have you had... *the talk* with Layah? And Courtney? What do you tell them about sex?"

"The truth," she answered. "It feels good, it's a good thing, but you need to be ready— heart, mind, and spirit. Me and Layah have had a couple of good conversations about what to expect. The boys and the girls at her school have wild hormones, but she's got a good head on her shoulders. And you know she's like her Auntie Esme. She has researched the subject of intercourse from A to Z."

I smiled. It was nice having a little protege.

"Courtney..." Jada sighed, her eyes rolling. "He knows biology and anatomy, but the boy giggles if you say breast. He can't even point to pee in the toilet, so..."

I cackled at that.

"He's nowhere near ready for a mature conversation, and that's fine with me because I'm not ready to have that conversation with him. Trey, though? He's old enough to have the conversation. Are *you*?"

"Yes! But there's such a stigma about virgins. Like... they get easily attached to that first guy and never explore. And... I feel myself getting attached. And I don't want to explore."

"If I set aside twenty years of saving myself, it better be for somebody good and for a good reason. And he better make sure I get mine. You know what I'm saying?"

"I know what you're saying. That hasn't been a problem, so far." Smug, I winked at Jada in the mirror. "I get mine every time."

"Ooh, you hussy!"

I saw her about to land a playful tap on my shoulder. "Nuh! That wax. You better not."

She glanced at her hands, covered in bright pink. "But I *want* to hit you. We're sisters, Es! Best friends, even! You ain't told me nothin'!"

"And I'm not about to start. I already told O'Neal that the Esme Whitaker Comedy Hour is over. I've got something good, and I want to keep it to myself. Mostly."

Jada resumed her work with my hair. I saw the dejection all over her face in the mirror. "Fine. But call me when you do the do. One tap for *it was aight,* and two taps for *it was hella good.*"

"Trust me. I will not need to tell you."

"If he got a big ol' dick, I want you to be ready to be walking around like you just dismounted a mustang. Stroll past the shop windows. I'll know by how you're walking."

I laughed so hard, tears sprang from my eyes. "Finish my hair, Jada!" I shrieked, wiping tears from my cheeks. "I have shit to do."

Jada's nails gave my scalp a relaxing massage as she continued to smooth and pull the wax through my curls. The manipulation gave me volume, and the color gave me a dramatic style. She pulled out the blow dryer to finish the look, then added some oil to my roots and edges.

"Leaving my salon fine as hell."

When I stood to hug her goodbye, I caught myself in the mirror and stopped to admire my hair in a ray of sunlight. "I can't believe I waited so long to do something daring with my hair. I totally love it."

"Seriously, Esme… you think Trey will like it?"

"You are not the only person around here with a man that loves everything about her." I handed her my usual tip, hooked my bag in the crook of my elbow, and slipped on my shades. "Trey will love it."

After I left the salon, I headed to Benning M&A Consulting for what I hoped would be the last time. I parked in the lot and walked to the building, carting a box for my belongings, my purple hair bouncing with each step. At the front entrance, I swiped my badge and waited for the door to open, but the LED light flashed red.

I swiped again, but nope. Red. Ethan already had my badge turned off, the petty bastard. I pressed the security button and held it until it buzzed.

"Can I help you?" Asked the faint voice over the intercom.

"It's Esme Whitaker. My badge is turned off. Can you buzz me in?"

The door clicked, then released, and I walked in, but I was met at the front desk by a member of security. "Ms. Whitaker? Mr. Byron asked that you not be permitted upstairs. If you wait here a moment, I'll get someone to help you."

If I wasn't so over this job, this company, and my boss, I'd cry. But as it was, I was sick to death of Benning, so I happily trotted over to guest seating to wait.

After a few minutes, Reese came downstairs, carting a box.

"Esme, I'm so sorry that you're leaving us," she whispered, handing me the box as I stood. "Ethan asked me to pack up your desk. Actually, he said, put her shit in a box and get it outta here." She frowned, then continued. "I think I got everything but let me know if you're missing something."

I opened the box to check it. Everything seemed to be inside: framed photos, my favorite coffee mug, a personal calendar, and a sweater that I kept around if the building's cooling system was running on overdrive.

"All good. Thanks, Reese."

I handed her my phone and laptop and the access badge and key for Miller Design. I instantly felt lighter, like an elephant had been lifted off of my shoulders. I had spent over ten years of my life at Benning. It wasn't altogether a waste, but I could have done so much more if only I'd been allowed to flourish. I'd have quit years ago if I knew it would feel like this.

"For what it's worth, Reese, I enjoyed working with you. I don't know how you manage to work for Ethan, but I can't do it anymore. See you around."

I waved goodbye and turned to leave.

"Esme!"

I stopped, then turned to face her. A flush was blooming its way up her lithe, runner's body, making her skin glow pink. "I want you to know that I think you did the right thing. I mean, I don't just *think*... you did the right thing. Ethan had to go out to Miller Design this morning. That negotiation is in flames. Ethan's boss is *pissed*."

Good, I thought, with every bit of deserved sanctimonious attitude. I could only hope that they now had to deal with Vincent or Saul. The time for softball was over.

"They haven't killed that contract yet?" I asked. "Is Pettigrew still in the game?"

"Apparently so, though the terms have changed drastically. Ethan was on the phone with one of the other contract staff to get a major rewrite out. Anyway," she paused, her face reddening. "I'll miss you, Esme. You're an amazing talent with a bright future. I hope we cross paths again."

"Thanks, Reese. It's nice to hear someone in this building say that."

"Also? I love the hair. I wish I could do that."

"You can. When you quit." We exchanged a brief hug before I stepped away and walked out of the building.

I never looked back.

I 'd decided to make lemon chicken, a recipe that I knew by
heart because I'd had it all my life and made it often. Still,
I was nervous, and when I was nervous, I made mistakes, so I
took great care in perfecting the baked chicken, angel hair
pasta, and spinach salad on the side. I made vinaigrette
dressing and pulled a loaf of Italian bread from the freezer to
toast.

After checking dishes and taking a long shower, slathering
my body in decadent, silky body butter, fluffing my hair, and
spending too much time picking out a dusty rose tank dress
with a deep round neck, I whipped through the living room,
not even silently cursing O'Neal. He'd been home long
enough to leave shoes, magazines, a copy of the Atlanta-
Journal Constitution, and other items sitting around like the
house wasn't spotless when he got home. He was gone again,
off to Madrid, leaving me to clean up his mess.

By the time the doorbell rang a little after 7:00, I was
ready. Still nervous, but excited and *ready* for whatever this
night brought me.

"Hey," I said, pulling open the door with a wide smile at
the tall, brown-skinned, handsome figure that took up most
of the doorway. As usual, he made casual look sexy in navy
blue sweatpants and a thick, stark white t-shirt. He smelled
good as hell, like always— sandalwood and laundry
detergent.

"Hey, girl," he said, stepping inside and immediately
sliding both arms around my waist to pull me to him. I looped
an arm around his neck and tipped my face up to his. He
dropped his lips onto mine, landing a groan-filled kiss that
communicated with me.

I felt his fatigue, his heartache, but also the sense of calm
that overcame him when we laid eyes on each other. When the
kiss slowly and regretfully ended, he stepped back, then

narrowed his eyes, tipped his head, and pulled his lips in until his mouth formed a thin, straight line.

"What?" I asked, immediately patting the wild pink and purple mass that my hair had become. "You… you don't like it?"

So much for not caring what he thought of my hair.

"Do you?" He asked.

"Yeah," I answered, pulling my hands from my hair, throwing my shoulders back, lifting my chin. "I do."

Yeah. Find your confidence and fuck him if he don't like my hair.

But also, I hope he likes my hair.

"That's all that matters, right?" Then a moment later, a smile burst through his solemn demeanor. "It looks real good on you, baby. Especially with the dress. It picks up the pink." He nodded. "Nice."

"Really? You like it?"

"I love it." He cupped my chin and pulled me to him for another kiss, then straightened to sniff into the air. "What do I smell? Chicken? Garlic bread? Don't let me find out you can burn, Esme."

Trey had seen the house twice before, so I didn't feel the need to give him a tour, but both times, he'd stuck to the living room. This time, I led him into the kitchen, where dinner was laid out on the island, alongside plates, silverware, and napkins.

"I don't know about burn, but I can cook. I thought we would eat in the living room, maybe watch a movie?"

"Sounds good to me. I had a burger about eight hours ago, so I'm starving." He leaned in to nuzzle my neck below my earlobe. "You might put my new stove to good use after all."

"I feel like I'm competing with Mrs. Pettigrew's cooking. This is my mama's recipe, and this is still Mrs. Whitaker's kitchen."

"Well, alright, then. Let's get it crackin'." He slid a hand across my ass, then gripped a cheek, his fingertips digging in just enough to make me flinch. "Booty rub for luck," he said, before grabbing a plate to hand to me.

"I'm fixing your plate? Something wrong with your hands, Mr. Pettigrew?"

He smirked, aiming a playful side-eye in my direction. "I was letting you go first, Ms. Whitaker. Damn, I'm not even all the way in the door, and here you go."

I began plating my dinner, waiting for Trey to load up before we headed back to the living room to settle in front of the widescreen plasma TV that O'Neal insisted on buying, then was never home to watch.

"So, the office has been rough for the past couple of days?"

"I'm being light when I say rough."

Trey perched on the edge of the couch; his dinner plate balanced on his knees. I'd opened a bottle of Chardonnay to go with dinner and he'd already taken a few generous sips from the glass that sat in front of him on the coffee table.

"Vincent was out there most of today. That's Vincent's wheelhouse, though. I should have turned the whole thing over to him in the first place, but I let my ego run the show."

"I went by Benning today to drop off my computer and phone and get my stuff from my desk." I nodded at the box that still sat by the door, near the steps. I'd unpack it, eventually. "Ethan's assistant said he had to have a new draft of the contract drawn up."

Trey nodded, his jaws working on chewing a large bite. "Yup," he offered, after swallowing. "Vincent said Miller gave us the sob story that he was cool until a project that he was halfway into went bankrupt. He got his customary deposit upfront, but he was never getting the back half of that, and he was counting on finishing that job to stay above water."

Trey bobbed his head side to side while he chewed another bite of dinner.

"It was a good deal until Pops had a heart attack. When I took over, he got greedy, thinking that I would just accept the revised terms, and he would get the money he needs."

I chewed thoughtfully, listening to Trey. I'd heard the same story so many times over the last ten years with Benning. "But you're Saul's son, so of course you didn't just accept."

"Not with my neck on the line and Vincent watching. I hope that dude doesn't think I don't see him pretending not to gloat. This is what he always wanted; for me to fail and to prove that he should succeed Pops. Fuck it, man. He can have it."

I finished my salad and sipped wine. Then I asked, "They're still going after Miller, then?"

"Not in the same way. Pettigrew will mentor to Miller. He needs to get a loan to cover his shortfalls, which will be hard with his credit, so Vincent is walking him through that. They're setting up a Joint Venture, so they bond together to complete and file the bid, maybe work together on a couple of projects while the powers that be decide who gets the work. If they get the bid, the provisions in the agreement provide for payment to both companies. Miller owns his company, Pops owns his. They work together for special projects where Miller's firm has the upper hand."

"That sounds like it might work."

"Yeah. That's why I should have turned it over to Vincent all along. Maybe he was right. I'm not equipped to run this company. Not the way Pops wants it to run. But it's not like I haven't been saying that. And it's not like I didn't tell him that I was only doing this job in the interim, on the sole condition that he was coming back, and that I'd get to do my own thing when he returned."

"And… what is the chance of that happening?"

"Right now?" He bit out a short burst of laughter, chuckling deep in his throat while he inhaled another bite.

"Not likely. I'll bide my time and my money and jump to my own thing."

"Keep hope alive."

"Always."

Trey set his plate on the coffee table in front of him, then picked up his wine glass and scooted back, settling into the comfort of the microfiber couch. He laid an arm across my shoulder, then pulled me close and laid a wet kiss on my temple.

"Dare I hope that I'll get to spend more time with you?"

"No need to hope for that, Trey." I set my plate next to his and leaned into him, angling my face up to get a kiss on my lips, too. "Unless you confess to murder or something equally heinous, I'm not going anywhere."

"One time, I stole a pack of gum from the corner store. How heinous is that?"

"You fucking criminal. Did you get away with it?"

"Hell no. My mama did not raise a petty thief. I had to return that gum, apologize, and work for that store owner for a month. Not to mention the lecture: *we work for things, Trey. We don't just take what we want.*"

"I like Mama Pettigrew."

"Because she's mean?"

I reached up to stroke the stray hairs in his beard. He leaned in to kiss me, letting the kiss linger longer than normal before opening his mouth and taking the kiss deeper. When I came up for air, Trey set his wine glass down and angled his body toward mine, easing us back so that he was snug between my thighs.

"I probably taste like lemon chicken and garlic toast. I'm sorry."

"Don't be. I see you enjoyed dinner."

"It was terrible," he mumbled, tipping his head to nibble on my earlobe, then kissing his way down my neck and across my shoulder and back again. "Really awful, Esme."

"And you call me mean." I clicked my tongue. He kissed my lips. "In my house, laying on top of me with your dick rubbing on me while you taste like the dinner that I cooked."

"I'd rather taste like pussy, if we're keepin' it a buck."

"Don't threaten me with a good time, Trey."

"Oooh." Trey's eyes grew wide at my response. "I sense a shift in your approach to my lewd suggestions. Half the fun of making them is knowing that you'll roll your eyes and pretend they're inappropriate."

"They were! But they're not anymore. I don't work for Benning. You're out of the contract negotiation. We're free and clear to do…"

I ground my hips up and into his. "Whatever we want."

I watched his Adam's apple bob as he swallowed, then his mouth dropped open when he sucked in a gasp. He started to sit up, but I caught him with my thighs. I cupped his face, a hand on each cheek.

"Don't go. Tell me, I can take it."

"It's just, I was thinking, right? This thing between us has been a lot. We met under strenuous circumstances. We started off fighting because you're mean."

I scoffed. "Assertive."

"Then I won you over with my charm."

"Because you act like an only child."

"And now, we can direct this whichever way we want to go. All of that before was preamble. Foreplay. Precursor. Now we get to the show."

"And the show is sex?"

Trey lowered his gaze to the rise of breasts peeking out of my dress. His lashes, long and lush, seemed to brush his cheeks as he bent to kiss them, lingering for a few moments on each. "At my place, you said definitely eventually, and I figure if I hang around, eat more of these delicious dinners and if I may be inappropriate, more pussy…"

"Trey…" I pretended to protest, but the mere mention of his mouth on me lit me up.

"Then I will get to that *definitely* part of the show. We still have Never list items to cross off, right?"

I knew that I'd know when the time was right, and with every exploding nerve in my body, I knew that it was time to tell him about the last two items, the ones that I needed his help to cross off.

And I prayed that he would be willing to cross them off with me.

"Let me up a second? I need to show you something."

Trey sat up, grabbing at his crotch to rearrange himself. I hopped up, headed straight for my bag, the same Louis Vuitton that he'd saved from a certain fate, and dug through the side pocket. I pulled out the list. I normally kept the very bottom two obscured, but this time I unfolded it all the way.

I sat down on the couch next to him and handed him the scrap of paper, worn thin by now.

He glanced at me, eyebrows raised. "The whole list?"

"The whole list."

"Wow, ok. Let's see what you've got here. Take a flight. Whew, girl." He shook his head. "But after the Ferris wheel, you're ready." He read on. "Go sailing. Cool. Swim in the ocean-we can do those together. Pet a cow?"

He glanced at me. "Really? A big, stinky cow, but you won't eat sushi?"

"I don't have to eat a raw cow."

I shrugged. Then swallowed hard. My heart pounded, knowing he was getting to the few blank lines, and then the two at the bottom of the page.

Have sex.

Fall in love.

"Uh…" He stared at the page, then dipped his head, blinked a few times. Then his head rose, but he didn't look at me. He stared into the open air of the living room, head tilted to the side for longer than I felt comfortable.

"Trey." I gripped his hand. He didn't grip me back. "Please... *please* don't be mad."

Finally, he turned to me, his eyes wide, mouth hanging open, brows riding high on his forehead. "You've really never had sex? Is this a joke? Are you punking me right now?"

"Not a joke. I've really never had sex. Well, intercourse."

"Uhm..." I watched his Adam's apple bob a few times as he swallowed.

"Trey, talk to me. Are you mad? Do you... feel like I lied to you?"

"Uh, surprised," he answered. "That's a better word. Surprised. We just never talked about... I mean, you don't seem like...."

"Like a virgin?" I smiled, almost laughing. "How does a virgin seem? Prim and proper? Scared of men? Doesn't know what an orgasm feels like? I don't seem virginal because I sucked your dick, and let you eat my pussy, and definitely had an orgasm on Cobb Parkway, and my vibrator knows your name?"

Trey's mouth hung open. Then, I swear I saw that man blush. "Yeah. A lot of that, I guess."

"I've done most everything but engaged in intercourse with a human male. And I want to. Tonight."

"With... me."

"With you."

Trey exhaled, loud and long, then settled himself back against the couch. Repeatedly, he swiped his hand across his mouth and then weaved his fingers through his beard. Slowly, his head began to wag back and forth.

"This... Esme, this changes everything."

I was genuinely shocked, and more than a little disappointed. So I hadn't let myriad men take something that meant a great deal to me… why would that change anything? We were going to have sex anyway, right?

Maybe I should have never told him.

"How? Trey, your dick tells me that you want me. My pussy is screaming loud and clear. I'm thirty-nine. I'm mature, and I'm ready. Don't pretend you care about virtue. You don't give a shit about that when I have your dick in my mouth. The only reason we've waited was because of the contract, and…" I pursed my lips, tossing up my hands. "It doesn't matter anymore."

"Es, I'm not saying—"

"Look, I'm not going to beg you to fuck me, ok? But I'm not a starry-eyed co-ed. I'm not an inexperienced woman who doesn't know her body, doesn't know how to ask to be pleased. I'm pretty sure you come every time, so I know a little bit about pleasing men. I'm not going to lay there like a dead fish while you do all of the work, and if that's what you think it'll be like, think about all the times we've already been together, and you had no idea—"

"Esme! Damn!" He laid a heavy hand on my thigh and squeezed me, laughing softly. "Can I get a word in here?"

I understood that Trey had to yell to interrupt my stream of consciousness rant. But he didn't have to laugh.

"I'd planned on… well, I brought condoms because I figured you wanted to get down tonight."

"You figured right. I thought you would, too."

"I do. I just don't want our first time to be some random Tuesday in September."

"You—" I blinked, running that back. "You what?"

The shy smile on his lips was adorable. He set the list down on the table. "Baby, I'm just thinking something different. I want our first time to be special if this is the situation."

"You don't have to pretend that you don't want to stumble through a first time experience. If you don't want to have sex with me now, it's fine to say it. It's not my first time hearing it."

"Let's phrase that differently. Do I want to tear off that dress and fuck you into a stupor? Immediately. I want you. Today, tomorrow, early and often. Yes, I still want to have sex with you."

"Ok! We agree on something. Let's do it!"

His eyes found mine and held that smoky, intimate gaze for a long beat. "Do you trust me?"

"*Fuuuuuck.*" I groaned, throwing myself back onto the couch. "Now we have to have sex in a gondola on a roof or something. What?"

Trey climbed on top of me, lowering his body to mine. "Go away with me. Let's get out of here, take a long weekend somewhere."

I lifted my head, frowning in confusion. "Go away?"

"You heard what I said, woman. We'll cross off some items on your Never list. Fuck it, let's cross off all of them."

"Well…" I blushed. "Maybe not all of them."

"Oh, no." He nodded his head. "*All* of them. Cause if I don't make you fall in love with me, I don't know what I'm gonna do, Esme Whitaker. I'm into you. Figuratively. And if you let me play it right—"

"Lord."

"Come on, you know what's coming…"

We finished his sentence together. "Literally."

My laughter bubbled from me like a spring. I drew my arms around his neck and asked, "When are we taking this trip?"

"This weekend, if you can swing it. I've got to get out of Atlanta. Clear my head. Make some plans. Give Pops and Vincent some space to work out this agreement. It's a perfect opportunity to take my girl away and show her a *real good* time."

"Well. I am jobless with purple hair. I'd love to go

wherever it is you're going. But..." I poked out my bottom lip, hoping I looked extra pitiful. "We're seriously not having sex tonight?"

"Don't worry this pretty mouth about that," he told me, brushing his lips across mine. "We're going to have a *real good* time tonight too."

"I think I can get with that." I pulled him to me, squeezing him in a hug. He burrowed into me, burying his face in the swell of my breasts. "So... I'm your girl?"

"Yeah," he answered, his words muffled. "You've been my girl, in my head. Have I been your guy in your head?"

"Yeah." I nodded, thankful that Trey couldn't see my eyes filling with happy tears. I blinked them back, feeling symbolically official for the first time in... I couldn't even count the years.

I tightened my grip around his shoulders and kissed his temple.

"You're my guy, Trey."

CHAPTER TWENTY-SIX

Trey

I fell asleep.

Esme put on a romantic comedy about two couples falling in love against their friend's advice. Halfway through, the rough work week and lack of sleep, plus dinner, then brownies and ice cream for dessert took me out.

When I woke up, the TV was off, the living room was dark, and I heard noises in the kitchen.

I sat up, scrubbed my palms down my face, and followed the sounds. Esme was loading the dishwasher with her earbuds in. I walked past her phone, which was lit up on the counter. She was listening to The Janitor, the book that I had spoiled for her by revealing a major plot point.

When Esme bent over to close the dishwasher door, I snuck up behind her and palmed a generous ass cheek.

"Shit!" She screamed so loud the neighbors were probably dialing 911, slamming the door closed, and whipping around to face me. She ripped her earbuds out, then came at me, both hands clenched into fists.

"I'm sorry! I'm sorry! I'm sorry!" I tried not to laugh while bobbing and weaving, steering clear of her fists.

"Are you–" She punched me in the arm. Hard. "Are you laughing? Fuck you! You scared the shit out of me!"

"Baby, I'm…" I sucked in a breath, then tried to stop laughing, but I couldn't. "I'm sorry," I gasped.

"Ugh!" She flailed, her hair flopping around her. "I wish I knew karate. Or Ju-jitsu. Or… a *fuck-you-up* sport!"

"Yeah?" I moved in, grabbed her by the waist, and pulled her to me. "I'm 6' 5", 220lbs. You're shorter and lighter. You think you can fuck me up? What… *exactly* do you think you could do to me?"

She punched me in the arm again. "That!"

"Stop hitting me, with your mean ass. That shit don't even hurt. You left me all alone in the living room." I pouted, stepping closer to her. "I was scared. I came to find you…"

"Rubbing my ass while I'm listening to a thriller. Great idea, Trey. He just got to the part where he killed that woman in her kitchen."

My brows shot up. "Oh, damn."

"Oh, damn!" She glared up at me, her eyes extra wide. "So, you deserved those punches."

"I really did. But now I'm sorry. Kiss me? Make it better?"

"You walked up on a single woman at night and rubbed her ass. *You* kiss *me*."

I laid a hand on her cheek, my fingers tucked into a wild mass of curls, and pulled her face to mine. I gave her a long, meandering, sensual kiss. By the time I pulled back, she was smiling. And so was I.

I was also wide awake. And erect.

"All better?"

She nodded. "You're not leaving, are you?"

"What do you think?" I answered, grinding myself into her.

"Then let's take this upstairs."

She turned out the lights, put her phone on the charging mat, and led me up the stairs. "That's O'Neal's room. He's never here," she muttered, passing a closed door. "O'Neal's bathroom," she said, passing another. At the end of the hall, she opened a door and stepped inside, flipping up the light switch as she did so.

"This is my domain. Welcome."

"I'm honored."

Esme's bedroom was... very much Esme. Bold and bright, and catered to everything that amused and interested her. A cozy reading nook near a window, full bookcases, a flat-screen TV, king-sized bed, a mountain of pillows and walls the shade of a bright summer's day with large prints of aspirational sayings written in fancy calligraphy in silver frames. On two nightstands were stacks of books, phone and watch charger, and a few framed photos of people who looked exactly like her. The Whitaker genes were strong.

"Yellow is a bold choice for walls." It was bright, but I was already getting used to it. Besides, if Esme was in a room, it didn't matter what color the walls were painted.

"My mother loves yellow. I don't have the heart to paint over it."

"Oh, that's right. You bought this place from your parents."

"Yep. Keep it in the family."

"And where are they?"

"Palm Springs. Some retirement village for a few months. They'll be back here around Christmas."

"What a great way to celebrate your freedom. Sleep in on Saturdays."

"Come here, Trey."

She sat on the bed, then patted the spot next to her. I sat, knowing a serious talk was coming. I'd had to process my surprise quickly and on the fly. Everything I thought I knew about her, everything I'd dreamt of doing with her, I sent through this new filter of information and… it was a lot.

"Please tell me how you really feel right now. And I know it might not be complimentary."

"What do you mean—"

"Trey." She looked at me, her eyes pleading. "I'm a 39-year-old virgin that's been pretty forward with you. You have thoughts, I'm sure."

"I mean… I'm confused. I don't get it, and I don't mean your virginity. I mean that I don't get a man not doing what he needs to do to get close to you."

I pushed out a breath, puffing my cheeks out while I laced my fingers together.

"I don't understand why you've waited, and I don't have to. But you want to explore that now, and you made a choice to move forward. I guess I wonder, out of all of the men you've ever dated, why none of them ever made you want to take that step with them. Not one of them ever—"

"Made me feel the way you do," she finished. "I consciously waited to meet a man that wanted to *know* me. You dragged that contract process out so ridiculously long so that you could get on my nerves all day. When you offered to help me with my list just to spend more time with me…"

She licked her lips and shifted, turning toward me. "Maybe it was a game for both of us, but you made that game fun. You made me want you. You made me think about being with you in a way that I wasn't used to thinking about men. You made me feel like you want me. And that's all I've ever wanted."

"So now I get to turn you all the way out."

She blushed, looking off with a dreamy expression. Was she thinking about it? Because I was.

"I want my first time to be fun. Not reverent. It's not a ceremony or a rite of passage; it's just some fun, but I want to be with someone that I can explore with and learn from without being shamed about what I don't know. I don't want to wake up the morning after with regret like I wasted the experience. When I read about first time sex, too many women regret not waiting. Too many women didn't even come. And I appreciate you wanting to take me away to make it special, but I don't need all that, Trey. All I need is you."

I scooted back on the bed, angling my head for Esme to follow me. She crawled across the bed, stretching out next to me and reaching for the band of my sweats.

"Why are your sweats blue, Trey?"

"Huh?" I watched as her hand slid below the waistband, then felt her warm palm wrap around me, her fingers grip... and then squeeze. "What do you mean?"

"Grey sweatpants are the thirst trap. You didn't know that?"

"Uh. Yeah, I knew that. I was under the impression that I had already trapped you."

"Oh, and you have. But I like looking at nice things."

She stroked, her hands expertly squeezing, gripping, pulling. Then she slid closer, right up against me so the heft of her breasts rested on my arm. She leaned into drop feather-light kisses down my neck.

"You're trying to tempt me into sex tonight, huh?"

"Guilty." She grinned, pulling back. "I kind of love this role reversal. Is it working?"

"Actually..." I laughed. "Yeah. It's not happening tonight, though, babe."

She huffed, poking her bottom lip out. "I do not believe you're making me wait."

"Too bad." I rolled to my side, slipping a hand between her thighs and working my way up. "I have plans for that ass. In the meantime..."

I wiggled my brows at her and bit her pouty bottom lip, gazing down at her with what I hoped was more seductive than half asleep. "You won't be deprived. I think you should introduce me to this toy that knows my name."

Minutes later, her deep brown skin was on full display, and my ears were full of Esme's moans and whimpers.

———

I awoke to the sensation of a warm, wet mouth.

It felt like a dream, but way more real. Real breasts pressed against my thighs, real breaths whispering against my skin, and real moans coming from beneath Esme's crisp sheets and thin summer comforter.

I lifted those covers and got an eyeful of Esme with a puff of purple and pink hair tied into a ponytail at the top of her head and a scarf wrapped around the rest of her hair. She rolled her eyes up to mine, with the tip of me in her mouth.

"That is a way to guarantee a good morning."

"Mmmmm?"

She sank down again, this time deeper, then slowly, slowly came up again, her lips applying just the right amount of pressure to make my eyes roll back in my head. Over and over and over again. I writhed, feeling it in my toes.

My jaw dropped as I angled my head back to moan. "Fuck. Yes."

I laid back, spread eagle in the middle of her bed, against a pile of Tiffany blue pillows and cream and blue striped sheets. I would have never imagined myself right here, right now, when I met Esme.

Dating was not ever easy for me. Despite being rather privileged, I didn't feel *enough* for a woman, not the kind of woman I craved. A man needed a lot of money to overcome an average appearance. And once I examined who I was vs. who I wanted to be, put myself through the wringer and came out on the other side a man that I was proud to be, my tastes and desires evolved too. I wanted more than a casual hookup or the occasional fling with pretty but vapid women hunting for muscular, wealthy, and cultured men; arm candy whose only job was to fund her lifestyle, fuck her, eat her pussy, and leave.

I wanted more than that.

Esme wasn't interested in me at first sight. Or second. Or third. She was aware of my Executive position at Pettigrew, saw the cut of my suits, my expensive watch, my silk ties, the brogues, the luxury SUV.

She didn't give a shit about any of it.

Making her mine became my life's work. No man had come before me, and that she wanted me — *chose* me to be the person to cross that line with her made me feel some kind of way, in the best way possible.

I wanted to fall in love with Esme Whitaker the moment I met her. The morning head I was getting was making that happen in a hurry.

"Baby…" I flipped the covers back, revealing Esme naked, with my dick in her mouth. "You're gonna make me come."

She moaned something that sounded like "Mmmhmm" but didn't pull off. Instead, she sucked me in deeper, then used her nails to clutch my balls and squeeze.

"*Fffff….uck!* Yeah, don't…don't stop, I'm coming!"

I cocked my head back as my body convulsed, pumping into her mouth until I was spent. Then I relaxed, every muscle turning to Jell-O. I felt my dick slap against my thigh as Esme pulled off. The bed shifted, and I sensed her getting up. I found the strength to prop myself up on my elbows.

"What are you doing?"

"I'll be right there," she called from the bathroom. I heard the water running, then a buzzing sound I recognized as an electric toothbrush. I chuckled. She came out of the bathroom with a towel in hand.

"You don't like pubes in your teeth?" I asked, watching her

approach me naked, her full breasts tempting me with their side to side sway at every step.

She smirked as she sat next to me, then rubbed a warm towel over my genitals and between my thighs. "I wax for you. I'm just saying."

"You do, and I love that."

I dipped to take a nipple in my mouth, sliding a hand between her legs to stroke her in appreciation. She gasped, leaning back, her hips already rolling. She laid a hand over mine and guided my rhythm, adjusting the pressure on her clit.

A ragged, sultry cry tore from her throat before her pelvis began a sinuous gyration. A flush colored her skin as she shuddered through her climax.

"Watching you come is my favorite thing."

Esme heaved a lung clearing sigh and rolled toward me. Her hair was still in that purple puff on top of her head. Her face was bare, a satisfied smile on her lips. I leaned over to kiss her.

"You're beautiful in the morning. I probably look like some kind of wolf." I pawed at my beard, which probably needed a fresh lineup.

"Mmmmm, no. Fine as hell, like always. I'm still trying to impress you, so don't get used to me waking up like this."

My eyes narrowed. "Should I not get used to morning head either?"

She grinned. "That all depends on how you feel about morning pussy."

"Message." I nodded.

"Would you like some breakfast, or do you have to leave?"

I sighed. "I would love breakfast, but I need to change, then head to the office to tie up a couple of loose ends since I'll be out Thursday and Friday. That's ok, right?"

She shrugged a shoulder. I took the opportunity to put my

lips on her once more, brushing my lips across her skin. "Unemployed," she reminded me. "Are we flying?"

The way her lip curled up was adorable. I sat up, then looked around for the clothes I wore. She pointed to a neatly folded pile on the nightstand, atop four books with post-it notes hanging out of them. I reached for the pile, pulling on my boxer briefs first.

"You know the guy that owns 9 Mile Station? Friends of my parents?"

She nodded. "They live in Florida, but they do business in Atlanta, so they bought a jet. They charter it out when they're not using it and offer it to me all the time. I'm taking them up on it. Flying is a little easier when it's private."

"I'll take your word for it."

"You'll be fine." I pulled on my t-shirt, then my sweats. My shoes were downstairs at the door. I sat down again, then bent to kiss her, dragging it out because I didn't want to leave.

"Trey?"

"Yes, baby."

"You need to brush your teeth before you go so I can kiss you like I mean it."

"Damn, you're mean." I laughed, though. "Do you have a spare toothbrush?"

"O'Neal brings me travel kits from everywhere. I don't know why, because I don't travel. I set one out on the counter."

"We're changing that no traveling thing," I called out, on my way to the bathroom. "Once you get used to flying, we can go anywhere."

"Yeah, we'll see about that." She rolled off the bed and pulled on a long, silk floral robe and tied it tightly around her. "I'll meet you downstairs."

I brushed my teeth and headed down, not registering that I heard more than one voice in the kitchen.

"If I knew you were home, I would have… you know what? I wouldn't have."

"Just nasty, all night long. *Oh! Oh my God, Trey!*" Shouted a male voice, pitched high to sound like a woman. *"Yes! Right there! Oh my God!"*

"You done?" I heard Esme ask, through laughter.

"No. Cause your dude was all *unh, Esme! Yeah, that's good. That's so. fucking. good.*"

I squinted, a little bit offended. Was that supposed to be his impression of me?

"Boy, shut up," said Esme. "You're supposed to be in Madrid. That's a 22-hour flight, round trip."

"I switched with another flight attendant since I took that other job through Turkey, then turned around and took another shift the next day."

"So what time did you get home?"

"Early enough to hear everything. We need to devise some kind of system, if you're gonna have men over—"

"First of all, this is my house. You pay rent. Sometimes. Second, I'm not going to have *men* over. It's *one* man. Third, you act like I don't have to wear earplugs when you entertain. You don't give a shit if I'm home while you're—"

"Uhm…"

I stepped into the kitchen, which stopped all conversation. Both heads turned in my direction. I'd met O'Neal once before, the night I brought Esme's wallet to the house, but once she walked in the room, other people ceased to exist. I vaguely remembered the man that stood at the kitchen counter, clutching a large stoneware bowl.

The Whitaker family resemblance was strong. He and Esme looked a lot alike, and that was to say that her cousin O'Neal was one of those pretty dudes. His friends probably hated his ass, drawing attention from all of the women all of the time.

"Hi. I'm Trey." I offered a hand to shake. He set down the bowl and crossed the room to shake my hand.

"We met," he reminded me. "But I wanted to shake the hand of the man that pulled the stick out of my cousin's ass. She was getting on my nerves."

I wasn't sure if I should side-eye this dude or not. "You're... welcome?"

"He's making me fly, O'Neal."

His jaw dropped, then he laughed. "Nuh-uh. Yeah?"

"Yeah," I answered. "Thursday. Out to South Carolina. It's a short flight."

"You'll get on a plane for a man you've known for a month, but not for me? I see how it is."

"Whatever," Esme said, casually picking up a magazine to flip through. Her hands were shaking, though. "I'm not on the plane yet."

He turned back to me, then smirked. "Look at her. Already shaking like a leaf. You might have to knock her ass out."

"I'll keep that in mind." I hooked a thumb toward the front door. I'd already put on my shoes and had my keys in hand. "Baby, I gotta run. I'll call you later with the details for this weekend."

"I'll walk you to the door."

"You ain't gotta leave. You can do all that noise-making and humping right here in the kitchen-"

"Shut up, O'Neal!" Esme yelled, pulling me through the living room.

CHAPTER TWENTY-SEVEN

Esme

This time, O'Neal and Jewel lounged across my bed, eating popcorn and watching me move from the closet to the open suitcase and carryon bag like it was the best movie they'd ever seen.

"It's so weird," said Jewel. "Isn't it weird?"

"Isn't what weird?" O'Neal asked.

"Esme is packing to go on a trip. It's weird."

"You act like I never leave the state." I frowned at them both, feeling deep lines of confusion across my forehead.

"You don't. You don't go anywhere. You meet some guy and let him take you everywhere we tried to force you to go. If he takes you on rides at Disney world, I'm disowning your ass. You go with family first."

"I've *been* to Disney with family."

"What if they go after they get married, though?" Asked O'Neal. "Then he's family." "Then they have to take us, obviously."

"Would you two shut up with that shit?"

Jewel, Jada, and O'Neal had been calling me Mrs. Pettigrew for two days, since O'Neal busted into the WhatsApp chat to gossip, not realizing it was the wrong damn chat.

Now my parents demanded information about Trey, and wanted to how long did I know him, and where was I going with him, and *oh my God, you quit your job over him?*

I was mildly furious at O'Neal since I'd had to spend the evening assuring my parents that I'd planned to quit Benning anyway and had built a nice savings cushion in preparation. And that Trey was an upstanding young man who did not want me to quit my job over the mess with Miller. Though he was grateful, I did that all on my own.

I flapped my fingers at both of them and went back to the closet. "Which of these should I take?" I pulled out two sundresses; both were flowy and frilly and made me feel extra feminine.

"The blue one," said Jewel, pointing to the dress on the left. "Shows off that nice rack."

"Do you not have anywhere to be, Jewel? Where is your husband, your children?"

"Away from me together. Math Olympics or some nerd shit. How is this my life?"

"I don't know, math teacher who married a man with a Ph.D. in math. However did this happen to you?"

O'Neal dumped a handful of popcorn into his mouth. "So, where is he taking you? South Carolina?"

I nodded, frowning at the kernels of popcorn I was going to have to clean up. "Myrtle Beach. He knows of a cute place on the water, near a farm. I uh… need to pet a cow. And ride in a boat."

"You what? Is that some kind of pre-sex ritual?"

"Is what a pre-sex ritual?" Jada walked into the room, her hair cornrowed with blonde strands weaved through the braids.

"We just walk into the house now. No knocking or ringing the doorbell?"

Jada took a seat near the window in my comfy reading chair. "I used to live here, and I still have a key. And the garage code is the same. You don't try very hard to keep us out. Stop pretending you don't want us to meddle in your life and let us meddle in your life. Is what a pre-sex ritual?"

"She has to ride a cow."

"Pet a cow, O'Neal. I actually have to just touch it... wait, hold on."

I opened a drawer and pulled out the infamous, worn list that I no longer needed to carry around with me. I handed it to O'Neal.

"Remember when you told me to make a list of ten things I was scared of? Ten things holding me back? I took your advice. Sort of. I wrote a Never list. And Trey has been helping me cross them off."

"Oooh." Jewel's face lit up as she scanned the page. "That's why you rode the Ferris wheel. And got up on that rooftop."

"Yeah. Kinda. Trey gave me the support I needed, I guess. In return, I was supposed to talk Miller into more reasonable terms. We decided that we would wait on the physical until the contract was signed so that no one could say I slept with him to make it happen. But we couldn't resist each other and I—"

"Caught feelings, and some self-respect, then got the hell on up outta Benning," recited O'Neal. "So these last two items? He knows?"

"Yeah."

"And... this weekend is... *the weekend?*" Jewel asked.

"Yeah," I answered again.

"Oh, girl. Hell no." Jewel shot up, waving a hand at Jada and heading for my closet. "Come on, Jada."

"What's wrong?"

"You gotta repack. We might have to hit the mall."

"Why?"

"Because you packed like y'all are an old married couple, not two lovers about to fuck up some sheets at the Marriott! Where is that little red dress that you bought when we went shopping last summer? That's *first time we're fucking* worthy."

"*First time a man is taking me away* worthy," added Jada.

"*First time a man is blowing my back out* worthy," finished O'Neal.

I groaned, flopping back on the bed.

"**E**sme, you're going to be fine."

"Mmhmm."

"Seriously. It's an hour, tops. You'll be comfortable like you're in your living room."

"Trey, can you stop talking? It's making me more nervous if that's possible."

"Ok, baby. But can you please unclench your talons from around my damn arm? I lost circulation ten minutes ago."

I heaved a breath and let go of Trey's arm, scooting back in my seat. We were at PDK Airport, a private airstrip in Atlanta, waiting for the jet to arrive for us to board. I was nervous. as. fuck. I couldn't stop the whole body tremors from thinking about getting on an airplane.

"You know what? I can't. I can't do this, Trey. I can't."

"Es. Look at me." He clutched my arm. "*Look*. at me." I looked up, into his face, into his eyes. "I've got you. You're going to be fine. Do you trust me?"

I swallowed, audibly gulping air. My heart slammed around in my chest. "I want to."

"I know. This is a big one, but when we land, you get to cross this off of your list. I need you to find the Esme who got on that Ferris wheel. Find the Esme who danced with me on the rooftop. She's fearless. She's a badass. Is she in there?"

I sucked in a breath, then blew it out. Then sat up straight and picked up my bag from where I'd dropped it because I needed to sit down. "The badass is in."

I watched a small jet fly into PDK airspace, then land and glide into place.

"Good. That's us. Are we doing this?"

"Yeah. Before I change my mind."

We went through a brief TSA baggage check, and then I forced myself onto the plane with Trey at my back. We settled into two of eight seats on a cozy Gulfstream. The cabin was small, with four seats grouped together and four seats more spread out. More passengers boarded, idly chatting amongst each other as they chose their seats and fastened their seatbelts.

I tried my belt again. Just to make sure I was strapped in. Trey reached across the armrest to hold my hand, winding his fingers between mine.

"Remember the Ferris wheel? How you had to close your eyes until we were up, then once you felt ready, you could look around? Why don't you try that?"

"Because I want to see us take off," I said, leaning over to peer out of the tiny, oval window.

"Alright. We're not getting off of this plane, you hear?"

"Ok."

"Seriously, Esme. We're not taking a train or driving to Myrtle Beach. We're flying. It's an hour long flight. Alright?"

"I hear you." I shifted my weight, leaning in for a kiss, then I squeezed his fingers weaved between mine. "I trust you. Don't let go."

"Never," he whispered. "Never letting you go."

I leaned my head back and closed my eyes, holding onto Trey for dear life as the plane began to push forward.

"That wasn't bad at all," I said, stretching my arms, then my legs. Passengers around us were unbuckling their seatbelts and chatting as they headed toward the exit. "That was only an hour?"

Trey unbuckled his seat belt, then mine, cutting his eyes at me. "All of that drama at the airport, for you to fall asleep. You only woke up because touchdown was a little rougher than normal."

"Well… I didn't sleep all night, worrying about this flight. I guess I passed out." Trey glared. "Wait, did you *want* me to scream and shake and cry?"

"No. But… I wanted to feel like I was here for you." He fake sniffled.

"Aw…" I leaned over to kiss his cheek. He softened up a little. "I'm sorry that you made me so comfortable that I fell asleep."

"Unh huh. Tell me anything." He pointed, gesturing for me to get up. "Let's go. Welcome to Myrtle Beach."

We deplaned, grabbed our baggage, and hopped into a shuttle to pick up our rental car. In an hour, Trey was loading our suitcases into the back of a midnight blue Range Rover sport.

"Oh, this is cute." I slipped my hands over the butterscotch leather interior, breathing in the scent of a brand new, clean car. My Jetta was paid off, but I could be tempted away. "Don't let me fall in love with this car. I don't have a job."

Trey laughed. He pushed buttons, flipped levers, turned the wipers on and off. "You want me to buy you a Range Rover, baby?" He pushed the ignition button and pulled out of the rental car lot.

"Hey, guess what?"

"What?"

"You flew today. In an airplane. You feel good?"

"Yeah." I grinned. "I feel really good. And I'm excited about this weekend and all the things to come. So to speak."

"No pressure. I'm the one that has to perform."

"Sex is a symphony, not a solo. We perform together."

"What if I'm not the world's greatest lover?"

"How would I know?" I answered with a shrug. "I chose you because I like you. Are you nervous?"

Trey didn't answer for a long, quiet few minutes. He stared ahead and drove, heading for the highway.

He sighed, then reached across the center console to tuck his hand between my thighs. "Actually, yeah. I'm nervous."

I curled my fingers around his. "Are you going to make me comfort you when I'm the one who's never had sex?"

"Nah," he answered. "I'm good. Just… excited. So let's go pet a cow."

Trey headed to the ramp to Hwy 501 and turned up the satellite radio. We rode in comfortable silence, listening and singing along to old school R&B. The GPS called out directions until it told us to turn right. The sign along the side of the road read Thompson Farm & Nursery.

Trey pulled into a parking spot near the entrance. "All the animals you can touch, right at your fingertips. They even have a petting zoo."

"Trey. Wait." I clutched his arm before he could open his door. "I didn't hurt your feelings or anything, did I?"

His brow furrowed. "When?"

"When I asked if you were nervous and you said yeah."

"Oh." He shook his head, lifting a shoulder in a shrug. "Nah, not really."

"Not really? Or yes, a little?"

"Yes, a little. But it's not a big—"

"It *is* a big deal. I'm sorry. I don't mean to minimize your feelings."

"We're good. I'm thinking about ways to make this a good weekend for us. Even if you say you don't need anything special, it's still our first time away together. I still want it to be nice. Plus, it's your first time. You'll remember your first time."

"Do you remember yours?"

He laughed. "Uh, yeah. It was like that move *Gone in 60 Seconds.* Not my best work. And I'm not trying to repeat it this weekend."

"You better not." My eyes slid closed, then reopened. "I've been looking forward to this for so long that I forgot that it's about more than me. Forgive me? With my mean ass?"

Trey gave me half a smile, then leaned across the console. I brushed my lips across his once, twice, then a third time before he opened his mouth and his tongue snaked out to meet mine. We sank into a long, unhurried kiss before he groaned and pulled back.

"If we don't go pet these damn animals, I'm gonna fuck you in the backseat of this Range Rover." He pulled the latch, popping the door open.

We walked around the entertaining, delightful little ranch, watching the children run screaming from one field to another. The farm boasted a variety of animals, including buffalo, donkeys, sheep, goats, alpaca, and even a 105-pound tortoise.

"There's the cattle over there." Trey pointed to a field where cows grazed openly.

"Baby goats!" I pointed toward the petting zoo near us. "I'd rather pet a baby goat."

Trey shrugged. "It's your list. Go pet a baby goat."

We walked through a field to the petting zoo entrance. Donkeys, sheep, and goats wandered around, bleating and showing off. A little black goat wandered over to us.

"Look at this little dude," Trey said, squatting next to the fence. I kneeled next to him. "Or gal. I don't know how to tell without getting up close and personal. It'll probably let you pet it."

The goat poked its nose through the slats in the pen.

"Hi, little one," I cooed. I stuck out my hand and rubbed its little nose. It was wet and twitching as it sniffed. I moved around to its ears and rubbed the soft surface of its head.

The goat let out a low bleat and licked the air, then bounded away to join its friends frolicking in the field. "I guess he's done with me. How cute, though!"

"See, livestock is not scary. You want me to buy you a goat, baby?"

I laughed, looping my arm around Trey's. "Are you going to offer to buy me whatever I like?"

"That's the plan. Gotta keep my girl happy."

"Then can you buy me some lunch? And a shower? I smell like a goat."

"That's it? That wasn't that bad." Trey turned to lead us away from the petting zoo.

"That's it. Another one bites the dust."

CHAPTER TWENTY-EIGHT

Esme

"Trey."

He put the Range Rover in park, then unhooked his seat belt. "Esme."

"This is us? Right here? This house?"

He looked up at the two-story home painted an adorable sea foam blue, bordered by lush green grass. When we got out of the car, the sound of ocean waves crashing onto the shore was almost deafening. I already never wanted to leave.

His head swiveled back to me, and he smiled. "Like it?"

"Love it. Will you buy me a beach house?"

"Yup. Let's get our bags."

Trey pulled a key from the lockbox on the front door and pushed it open. The air inside smelled like lemon Pine-Sol, Windex, and Glade plug-ins.

"Wow," I whispered, taking a self-guided tour through the house. Bright, airy, spacious. Wide, deep couches, big TV, bigger windows. The kitchen seemed to be mostly countertops, bookended by stainless steel appliances. There were three bedrooms, four bathrooms, a game room, a family room, plus outdoor living space, and a path that led straight to the private beach.

I opened the sliding doors, stood at the deck railing, and listened to the sounds of the surf rushing in and out. Footsteps sounded on the deck. I caught the scent of his cologne before Trey slid his arms around me.

"Hey, girl."

"This is so nice, Trey. Is this yours?"

"Nah. I know the owners, though, so if the place is available, I rent it. I was going to put us at a hotel, but they had a cancellation for this weekend. It was meant to be. Besides..."

He used his hands to twist me around so that I faced him. "I wanted privacy. You know, so we can do what we want, go where we want."

I smiled. "Make as much noise as we want?"

"That too." Trey inhaled, his chest barreling with the depth of his breath. "Uhm. Do you mind if we run things down, real quick?"

"Sure."

"How are you feeling? You change your mind or anything?"

I shook my head. "Nope. I want this."

"Good. Five days. We're here to relax. To build a little cocoon of sexy, sweet good times. Good food, good wine, good sex."

"Yes. I like that."

"Birth control?"

"Took it. Haven't missed a day in years."

Trey nodded. "Cool. I have condoms like you asked."

"Thank you. Next week, I can pull up my STD test online."

"Same. So, I figured we could hit the grocery store, get some essentials like water, juice, coffee... whatever. Maybe some quick stuff to cook during the day. There are some nice places I want to take you to, especially on the beach, so we can eat dinners out."

"Sounds amazing. I'm excited."

"Me too." He dipped his head so that our foreheads met. "Baby?"

"Yeah?"

"I said that I wouldn't ask, and I'm sticking to that. I want you to be in control, so that kind of leaves it up to you to let me know when you're ready for me to—"

"Tear that pussy up?"

Trey inhaled deeply through his nose. "Exactly."

"Well, shit." I pushed him backward toward the house. "I was ready three days ago. You're the one that wanted to wait."

We made it past the threshold of the sliding doors, long enough to close and lock them before our mouths met with desperate whimpers and grunts, our hands restlessly groping and feeling, pulling at each other's clothing.

We wandered across the house, aiming for the bedroom on the first floor, falling across the bed while hurriedly pulling clothes off of each other. I tugged his short down; he pulled off my shorts, my shirt and bra, leaving me in wispy, lacy black panties. Trey took off his t-shirt and gravitated back toward my warm and trembling body.

He rolled on top of me, his erection pressing into me so hard that I couldn't help but gyrate against him. He responded in kind, grinding against me, licking and sucking my nipples until they were standing on end and puffy.

"Lick me. Please. I want your mouth on me."

With a gentle push, I directed him south until his face was buried in my mound. He nipped at my clit through my panties, which drove me crazy until he hooked his thumbs under the band and pulled them down. The cool air of the room felt good in the seconds before his warm tongue bathed my clit, the texture and roughness sending fingers of lightning up my back.

"Fuck, *yesss*!"

I locked him there, holding onto the back of his head while I bucked against his tongue. I was frenzied and frantic, on the verge of climax when… suddenly he was gone.

"No!" I opened my eyes and sat up, reaching for him. "Why'd you stop? Where are you going?"

"Hang on, baby. I want to be inside you when you come."

He left and came back with his bag, then dug out his shaving kit and pulled out several condoms, keeping one and tossing the others onto the nightstand.

"Ambitious, aren't you?"

Trey grinned. He ripped open the packet and removed the ring, tossing the wrapper to the nightstand as well. "I'm hoping you enjoy yourself and want to do it again. And again. And again."

He rolled the condom on, checking to be sure it was secure. His sheathed penis was…tempting. Never before in life had I felt so ready for a man to lay me down and have his way with me. I reached for him, grabbing his face to bring him to me to take his lips before this moment.

"I want you to have a good time, too. Don't stop until you come."

"I've done this before. The whole point is for *you* to have a good time." Trey bent to kiss me while reaching down to spread my legs.

I should have been nervous. With every other previous attempt, I'd been scared out of my mind. I even got to the naked, *condom on, legs spread* stage and backed out, crying and shaking and ready to throw up. That guy never spoke to me again. I took that experience as a sign that I wasn't ready. I put a hold on sex until I knew that I was ready.

Now… I was ready.

Trey was slow, sweet, and gentle as he worked his way in,

pushing in, pulling back, working more of himself inside me with each thrust. I concentrated on feeling every movement, loving the sensation of him sliding in and out, filling me. Despite not wanting a big moment, the moment was pretty damn special.

Trey exhaled, then relaxed, lowering himself so that we were chest to chest. I wrapped my arms around him as our lips met.

"You good?"

"I am so, so... *so* good. You feel... I wish I could think of a better word than amazing." I giggled at feeling my body clench around him. "Oh!"

He grinned. "That's me, baby."

"Wow. I mean, wow like... you feel so fucking good, wow."

Trey began to rock his hips, moving deep inside, then pulling back. "Esme," he whispered, his voice already ragged. "I really wanted this to be romantic, you know? Some music, some wine..."

He bit down on his bottom lip.

"Then I ruined it by jumping you?"

I felt his laugh vibrate through his body to mine. "Nah, you didn't ruin shit. If you're having fun, it's perfect. We can do romance later."

"Because we're definitely fucking again."

"The house was part of the plan. So we could make noise, really have a good time. You feel me?"

I grinned. "You want to hear me come."

"I want to hear *everything*."

"Trey..." I wiggled underneath him and locked my limbs around him, then dropped my tone into the phone sex line register. "Fuck me, so we can make that happen."

"Woman..." His eyes narrowed. He ran his tongue over his bottom lip and slowly shook his head. "Ain't got to tell me twice."

Trey dipped his head to my neck and let his mouth, his

tongue, and his dick do the talking. He pushed into me, building to a steady rhythm. I rolled my hips, meeting his thrusts, not at all bashful about shouting my pleasure into the air.

A flicker sparked in the pit of my belly and spread. My body began to quake; I felt myself gush. Trey's moans grew deeper, more like grunts. His thrusts were deliciously forceful, met with the crash of my body against his.

"Trey! I'm…right there! Don't stop!"

"No chance," he said, his grin wide. "I want to hear it. Come for me, Esme."

I bit my bottom lip and closed my eyes, putting all of my strength and concentration on the sensation of being full, being stretched, being pleasured… *sexually*.

I rolled my hips, moving with Trey as he picked up speed. I clutched his torso and arched my back. "*Shhiiiit!*"

"Comin'?"

Every nerve I possessed exploded at the same time. I was simultaneously stiff and limp, pulsating, and jerking. "Yes! Yes! I'm coming!"

My limbs instinctively closed around him like a trap. I clung to him, hunching against him to eke out every spasm while his name ripped from my throat.

Trey rode it out, not missing a stroke, pushing himself up for leverage to thrust harder.

"Fuck… right behind you," he grunted, through a locked jaw, working his hips like a piston. His body tensed, his skin turned a deep red pallor beneath his dark tone, and I felt him pulse. He let a breath out in a thin hiss. His hips jerked against mine, eliciting rhythmic grunts.

He opened his eyes, seeming surprised that I'd watched him.

"That was the most erotic scene I've ever watched. Beats porn any time."

His body came to rest. He kissed my lips before lowering

his forehead so his touched mine. "You should watch yourself come some time."

He stroked my hair, pushing my sweat soaked curls back from my forehead. "Esme..." He paused, only beaming a tired smile at me.

"We had sex," I finished, giggling.

He nodded. "And more importantly, you..."

"Have had sex!" I shouted.

Trey laughed with me. "Another adventure off of your Never list. You good?"

I sighed, grinning into the air, at nothing and everything. "Shit. I might be good for the rest of my life."

"Well, I was hoping to have more, *better* sex with you."

My eyes spun in their sockets with giddy joy. "It gets better than that? I *have* been missing out!"

"Perfecting sex is the fun part." He dropped a kiss on my lips. "This is exactly... *exactly* how I wanted it to be with you. I'm so happy right now."

"Me too, Trey."

"I mean it, Es. I'm *happy* with you."

"You're still inside me. I would be worried if you weren't happy right now."

"Well, yeah, but later, when we get up and shower, or tomorrow when we're hanging out together, or next week when we're back in Atlanta, I'm still going to be happy with you. I need to know that that's what you want. Because I'm pursuing you. With a vengeance."

"A vengeance," I repeated. "So, you're on a mission."

"I am. I need you to fall in love with me, at your earliest convenience. Like ASAP."

My heart bloomed in my chest, so big I thought it might burst out of my body. Whatever I did to get him, if keeping him involved sex, I was willing to do it.

"I think I can make that happen. So, curious—what happens when I fall in love with you?"

"New mission. Keep you in love with me. We roll it forward."

"I like that. I really like that."

I sighed, then suddenly felt the cool air in the room since we'd come down. Trey's stomach growled, giving away his extreme hunger.

"We should probably shower and go to the grocery store, before I make you fuck me again."

"Not that that's a bad idea…"

We could not stop giggling. At random moments, like while we held hands on the drive to the grocery store or stood in the pasta aisle arguing about elbow or rotini, or while waiting for the clerk at the meat counter to grind fresh turkey for me because I was being picky, we would look at one another and laugh.

If sex made you giddy and touchy-feely and gave the illusion of walking on a cloud, then I always wanted to be having sex. I was in the mood to go again, but responsibilities like stocking the cabinets for a tall, very hungry man and his girl loomed.

"Do you think we got enough food?"

"I eat a lot." Trey glanced at the backseat and the trunk overflowing with plastic grocery bags. "Maybe we went overboard, but I'd rather have too much food than have to keep coming back."

He started the car, then his hand migrated to the usual spot. I loved that his hand had a usual spot.

"You good?"

He glanced over at me as he pulled out of the parking spot. The sun was on its descent toward the horizon, giving the beach town a pinkish wash.

"I'm real good, baby. You?"

"If you're real good, I'm real good. Are you sore?"

I let out a snort. "You think highly of yourself, don't you?"

"I'm aight." He shrugged, then looked over at me again. "Seriously, though. Do you need a drugstore or anything?"

"No. I feel fine."

"I mean..." He shot me a sideways glance. "I hit that pretty good. You should be feeling something."

I cackled. "Fine. That big ol' dick tore me up. Wore me out. I'm bowlegged now. Is that the hit that your ego is looking for?"

Trey grinned. "That's the hit I needed. My big ol' dick is happy now."

"Well, tell him to suit up. He's not done working."

"You said you didn't want to feel like you wasted the experience. I did good?"

"You're a very good lay, Mr. Pettigrew. Not a waste in the least."

I glanced over at him, then laughed at the pride in his smile.

He squeezed my thigh in his palm. "You're not so bad yourself, with these wrapped around me. I'm definitely looking forward to the repeat. You know what we should do first, though?"

"Before we have sex again? Nothing."

"We should swim in the ocean. Might as well cross it off of your list." He glanced at me to find that I was shooting daggers in his direction. "I think I created a monster."

"A mean ass that wants to fuck you. Yes. You did that." I turned my face toward the warm glow of the waning sun. "I do kind of want to get in the water."

"Let's do that then."

The house was steps from the beach, so after we put our groceries away, we changed into swimwear and headed down the path of wood slats to the edge of the water. The sand was soft, not rocky when I bent to dig up a scoop and let it run through my fingers.

"You've been to the beach before, right?"

Trey stood next to me, his molded chest and taut belly bare. His barely-there swim shorts were a source of endless amusement to me. I wore a two-piece that I picked up at the last minute when my sisters dragged me to the Swim Shoppe at Phipps Plaza, otherwise known as the Uppity Mall. Nothing in there cost under $100 besides socks.

Swim Shoppe had cute suits in sizes that would hold my breasts and cover my assets, though, so I felt amazing in a navy blue twist front bikini top and matching bottom. I tucked my hair into a swim cap and I picked up a floral cover-up that hung to my knees to give an extra layer of security if I needed it. So far, it was folded over my arm.

"Tybee. St. Simons Island. I just never get in the water."

"What is it about ocean water that scares you?"

I stood at the edge of the waterline, watching a wave come in from a mile off, slowly rolling toward us. It crashed onto the beach in front of us, washing over our feet, then moving back out.

"Maybe the strength of the current. I feel like it's going to carry me out, and I won't be able to get back. All those stories about people drowning at Lake Lanier..."

I shuddered.

"Ok. Do you want to try walking out with me? Then we'll float while the waves come in and go out. I won't let go. I promise."

I stuck my hand out and tossed the coverup back onto the sand. Trey and I clasped hands as we stepped into the waves that gently lapped at the shore. I matched him, step for step until we were waist deep.

"I think if we take this approach to everything that scares me, I'll be fine."

"I do it with you? I wouldn't mind that."

"You hold my hand; you distract me with these lips..." I kissed him before I went on. "And then you promise me sex when we're done."

Trey laughed. "I definitely created a monster."

"Do you like this monster?"

"I *love* this monster."

The waves rushing in grew louder. I stepped in closer and wrapped my arms tighter around him. "I got you," he soothed, holding me close while the wave washed past us, disturbing the bed under our feet, but leaving us standing as it rushed back out. When the water was calm again, I exhaled but didn't let go of Trey.

I never wanted to let go of Trey.

After a few minutes, we ventured further, past waist deep waters and I took my first ocean swim.

When the sun had sank well below the horizon, we walked back up the path and peeled off our wet swimwear, hanging them over the deck railing to dry. We had sex again, this time slower and sweeter. Seductive, not a frenzied afternoon fuck after dancing around each other for weeks. Trey serenaded me with the romantic playlist he'd created. We drank wine and ate decadent dark chocolate cupcakes and enjoyed every last inch of each other.

I fell in love with being a sexual woman, with feeling safe and open to exploring, with calling out my wants and desires with a man whose singular goal was to see me happy.

When we got back up, it was late, but we were starving, so I made peanut butter sandwiches, and we both ate out of an open bag of chips as we sat at the kitchen island.

"Trey..." I crunched while he wolfed down half a sandwich in one bite. "I have a question I need to ask you."

"Why do you tell me that you need to ask me a question?"

"I want you to be prepared. And I want you to be truthful with me. Lies breed resentment. Don't spare my feelings."

"Ok." He chewed and swallowed, then gulped down a few swallows of bottled water. "I won't lie."

"Would it... does it..." I sighed. How could I ask this question that was sitting in the front of my mind without sounding clingy and... like a virgin?

"Would what? Does what? Just ask."

"I've never been the type to date around, and I don't want to start. I don't want to sleep with anyone else right now. Or... maybe ever? I don't know, that's how I feel right now. Do you feel uncomfortable that I care about you like that?"

Trey bit into the second half of his sandwich and stared at me. I knew he heard me, so I waited him out.

"Es," he finally said, after he swallowed. "You remember when we had that conversation at my house, and we said we liked each other? And when I said I planned to pursue the shit out of you?"

"Yes. That was before you knew I was a virgin."

"That didn't change shit for me, except knowing that I had to be on my game today. I told you *today* that I need you to fall in love with me, like ASAP."

The burn of my blush was hot under my skin. My insecurity showed its ugly head at stupid times. This was a stupid time.

"So, how do you think I feel? You care for me, and you don't want to be with anyone else?" He leaned over to nuzzle my neck and nip my earlobe. "How do you think I feel about that, Esme?"

"Good," I whispered, trying to hide my shy, stupid smile.

"Woman. Listen." He shook his head. "If it's one thing you're going to learn about being with me, it's that I love being with you. I like every room that you are in, even that bright yellow bedroom. You're the only person I want to be with, so hearing that you only want to be with me? I'm good with that."

He leaned over to brush his lips against my temple. "Are you done having this moment, Esme?"

"Yes," I answered quickly. "Thank you for indulging me."

"No problem. I was hoping I could fall asleep watching a movie with my girl. But my girl is badass Esme, who knows who she is to me. She's fearless and bold."

"And mean."

"A little." He smiled. "Is she in there?"

I gripped Trey by the chin and pulled his face to mine so I could kiss his lips. "The badass is in. Thank you for reminding me who I am."

"Any time, beautiful."

CHAPTER TWENTY-NINE

Trey

I *fucking* loved Esme.

I fought the feeling, the very thought of it, because... Bruh, what?

But I had to be honest with myself. I *wanted* to be in love with her, so I gave up, gave in, and let myself sink into that warm feeling when I thought about a life with her.

Potentially. Because Esme was in love with me, too but getting her to say it?

I had to remind myself of the first few weeks of knowing her. I would need to keep reminding myself that I was a patient man. Esme was not the type of woman to jump into forever based on fun dates and nice dinners. We were going to do the dance, play the game, wait to say those words to each other because it was so soon, and it was so good that it couldn't possibly be real.

But it was real. Very real.

It was real when she woke up the next morning to my face

between her legs, while we ate breakfast and watched the local morning news, and walked the beach looking for seashells.... it was real.

I happened to glance over at her while we waited at the marina for the sailboat that I chartered to find her eyes on me with that dreamy smile. I had to just... decide that it was cool for us to know it because, in true Trey and Esme fashion, it wouldn't be a random moment that we said it. It had to be special.

I was looking forward to that moment.

"This is probably the best vacation I've been on in years," I told Esme. She looked over at me, her curls blowing in the wind under a wide-brimmed straw hat. The pink and purple had washed out, so it was her natural, dark brown color.

"It's only day two, Trey."

"Yeah. And I'm saying it's already the best. Normally I'm alone, or I drag Ken. He only wants to find a racquetball court or stalk restaurants or watch cooking shows. So I end up hanging out by myself in bars or sitting at the house. I always have to bring work, so at least I can hear the ocean while I'm pounding away at reports."

I waved a hand around the expansive sand, the ocean waves, the marina, the restaurants and shops around us. "This time, I didn't even bring my laptop. And I brought my girl, who I much prefer over Ken, by the way."

"Do you now?"

"You don't snore. And you have a lot less back hair."

"Thanks, Trey. Thank you for that."

"I am having a good time with you. Even though it's only day two."

I leaned in close and waited for her to drop those lips on me. She grabbed my chin and pulled me to her so she could kiss me. I loved it when she did that.

"Same. My vacations have all been with people pissed that they had to drive because Esme won't fly and pissed that they have to do boring shit because Esme doesn't like rides and pissed that Esme won't get in the water if we go to the beach. And pissed that they can't go to a sushi restaurant because Esme won't eat that. I'm tired of holding myself and everyone else back from having the maximum amount of good time. Clearing my list has been so good for me."

"I feel that." I nodded. "You've grown a lot in the last month."

"True. I could argue that it's because I found somebody amazing that I care about, who cares about me."

"Care, huh? We *care* about each other."

"Yeah," she answered, after a long, meaningful stare. "A lot. We care a lot."

Her eye caught the long vessel that moored into the marina. The driver cut the rumbling engine, leaving echoing sounds of water splashing against the hull of the boat. "Wow. I hope that's ours."

"Think so." I stood, pulling her up with me. "Let's go sailing, baby."

We spent four glorious hours on the ocean and inlet cruise. The trip on the thirty-nine-foot yacht with eight other passengers included a light lunch and a wine flight. Except for Esme's thin, white sundress constantly catching the wind so that she had to clutch fists of it in her hand, and her beach hat flying off of her head, it was a perfect sail.

We got off the boat slightly drunk, so we decided to grab ice cream cones and walk the beachside attractions. I got chocolate, Esme got strawberry cream, and we held hands while we wandered.

"You really didn't bring your computer. That seems like a big deal."

"It is. I never go anywhere without my work machine. Always something to do, some fire to put out. So, it's weird to have nothing to do."

"Saul didn't fire you, did he?"

"No. Not yet, anyway."

"Do you think he will?"

"Nah." I licked my cone, trying to be a positive thinker, but the reality was that Pops very well could fire me. "He can't admit when he's wrong, but his habit is to find a way to come around. I hope the last few days of riding Vincent on this revamped deal have shown him that I was right."

"Especially since Miller basically admitted to everything we suspected. Deeply in debt, hiding it, hoping you would sign the papers before you found it and were stuck."

"Right. It's best, in these situations, to…" I swiped a hand in front of us. "Get out of his face. All the way. No calls, no email, don't even be around. I heard that he was going to try to come to the office for a few days, so I took those days off."

"You don't feel like you're hiding?"

I shook my head. "No. I know Pops enough to know to stay out of his way. My sister—"

I halted, realizing that I was about to tell Esme about Missy, a woman I never talked about, had avoided talking about so much that I was putting off therapy because I'd have to talk about her. The only person I'd really confided in was Ken, and he was sworn to secrecy.

That I was about to share something so… sacred to me, and that I almost had no qualms about that spoke volumes.

Esme caught a drip of ice cream from the side of her cone with her tongue. I felt that in my groin. "You don't have to talk about your sister, Trey. It's ok."

"I uh… I don't mind, actually. Missy said something to me when I was at the house, and Pops blew up. She said I needed to give him some time because he couldn't reason in a heightened state. Then she said something like, *ask me how I know*."

"Hmmm…" Her forehead wrinkled as she took another lick of her cone. "What does that mean, you think?"

"Missy has Bipolar Disorder."

I glanced at Esme, looking for adverse reactions in her demeanor. My family history meant baggage and not anything I could easily unload. Esme seemed unbothered, deeply concentrating on finishing her cone before it melted.

"Uh... anyway, she spent her teen years at an institution in Alabama. It was the best place to manage her lows and highs, but she didn't want to stay, so she checked herself out. She's inconsistent with her medication and therapy. She hates the way Lithium makes her feel, so as soon as her moods stabilize, she stops taking it, and then—"

"The cycle of trying to get her back on medication."

I nodded, relieved that she understood. "She's heavily dependent on my parents. They bought her a place. They pay her bills. I'm bending over backward, trying to please Pops, and not bring him stress. Missy.... Missy is all stress."

My shoulders sagged with the heavy emotion that came over me when I thought about Missy. It was such a delicate situation. Pops thought that he could love and spoil the mental illness away when I thought Missy needed a stronger hand and to be more independent.

What the hell did I know, though? I wasn't doing so well in the *not stressing out my father* department.

"Do you think she might be saying that she's more like Saul than anyone knows?"

I pondered that, admitting to myself that it was something I hadn't wanted to think about.

"Maybe. This disorder can be hereditary. I'd like to talk to her more about it if we can have a conversation without fighting. She can't help the way she is, so it's up to me to change. I promised myself that when I got back to Atlanta, I'd see a therapist. I need to handle my relationship with her better than I have. That's because of you, you know."

"Me? We don't even talk about her—"

"No, I meant that I want to start dealing with things that I hold in, stuff that holds me back. I want whole and healthy relationships. Someday I want to be a great husband. A great father. I don't want anything standing in the way of that."

"Mmmmm," Esme hummed, her expression thoughtful. "I like hearing that."

"Yeah?"

"Because no matter what, the goal is to be the best person possible, but it's dead sexy to want to be that so that you can enrich someone else's life. I like that about you."

"Good answer."

I let the silence between us hang like a weighted blanket. The surf, the sand, the crowds all added to the atmosphere. Esme could change the conversation if she wanted to. Or forge ahead. Whichever way she wanted to go, I was game.

"And because..." She added, after a few minutes. "We've been dancing around this thing between us like it won't eventually lead to those discussions."

"Better answer. Do you think about that? With us?"

"I didn't used to."

Esme stopped walking and tossed the last bit of her cone in the nearby trash bin. My half-eaten cone followed. The local Myrtle Beach shops were nowhere near as good as Bruster's handmade ice cream.

I moved to stand in front of her, tucked my finger under her chin, and tipped her head up to see her eyes. "Didn't *used* to," I repeated. "So you do, now?"

Esme bobbed her head side to side. The expression she wore was... pained. Tortured. That wasn't the reaction that I expected. Or wanted.

"You don't want to talk about it?"

"Not right now."

"Cool. Zero pressure, baby."

I dropped an arm around her shoulder and guided her back toward the parking lot.

I could wait.

It had only been a few days of sleeping next to Esme, but I was already so used to sharing a bed with her that I noticed when her spot was empty. I sat up, blinking to adjust to the predawn darkness. Though I'd normally be wide awake at 5 AM, the sea breeze had been so relaxing that I'd been sleeping in. Getting back on the Peloton was going to be a struggle.

I pulled on a pair of sweats and stumbled through the kitchen. The red light on the coffee pot was on. A shadow outside caught my eye. Esme was sitting in one of the deck chairs facing the surf, her hands wrapped around a coffee mug. Her silk robe fluttered in the breeze.

I stepped out onto the deck barefoot. She watched me slide a chair over and sit next to her.

"Hey, girl."

"Hey. Did I wake you up?"

"My body missed you. What's up?"

"I was tossing and turning. I decided to get up."

"Two things Pettigrews are known for: a big nose that can smell what's for dinner, and big ears that are good for listening."

She smiled, almost laughing.

"Ok, the nose thing is true, but I lied about the ears. You don't want to talk to me?"

"I love talking to you. I just... I have *feelings* that I'm sorting through."

"You're up before the sun, sitting in the dark, staring at the ocean. It might help to talk. Is it about me?"

"A little," she admitted, her tone husky. I heard her swallow, then go on. "We've built this cocoon that we've been living in for five days. I have sex every day. I hang out with my guy, who thinks I'm amazing. I eat good food, I drink good wine. Did I mention that I have sex every day?"

"You mentioned that. Life's been good this week."

"So, we go home today, and I've been avoiding thinking about the real life that awaits me when I hit city limits. It's like I'm coming down from a crazy high, and I have to deal with whatever the hell I did while I was freewheeling."

She huffed a hard breath through her nose, shaking her head.

"I've been doing the most insane shit, things I would never do. I quit my job, Trey. I dyed my hair purple. I had sex with a man I met a month ago."

When she put it that way, things did look a little wild. But wild was not a bad thing.

"None of that is bad, Esme. And I mean... I have a real life to go back to, too. But maybe we don't dismantle the cocoon when this vacation ends. We take everything we built during this time together, and we keep it going. You're still with a guy that thinks you're amazing. We can still eat good food and drink wine and have sex. I'll help you look for a job. We'll make a new list of insane shit to do together."

"Trey..."

"Look, do you regret anything from the last month? Anything you wish you *didn't* do? Do you wish you never got on that Ferris wheel? Or danced with me on the roof? Did you *want* to stay at Benning? Didn't you *love* your purple hair?"

"I wouldn't undo anything I've done, for sure. I just... I really thought that the balance of my life would be me living my best Auntie existence. Maybe I could overcome my fear of flying enough to travel. I could stop being afraid of men enough to enjoy sex and have relationships. I thought my list would free me from that prison of fear so I could be different, I guess."

She paused for a beat, her face turning toward mine before she lost her nerve and dropped her gaze to the mug in her lap. I reached over and tipped her chin back up with a finger.

"Your list did free you, Esme. And you *are* different."

"To what end, though?" She coughed out a laugh. "I mean… I met a man that makes me want nothing but to be his, and *only* his. He wants to be a father. It never occurred to me that I don't even know if my body will do that when I'm ready. And even if it can, I've known him for a *month*. It is crazy to be thinking about planning for the future when I've only known a person for a month."

"Does the passage of time matter? Do you not feel what you feel, no matter how long you've felt it?"

"What if I'm just caught up in someone new, and the magic fades, and the cocoon goes away, and we fizzle? What if I lose something that I really like having? What if I get the chance to have things that I told myself weren't for me, that I realize I've wanted my whole life? I'm terrified to want these things, because what if I can't have them?"

"Esme, baby…" I moved closer, wrapping my arms around her. "How long have you been up, torturing yourself with this? Who said you can't have it? You have never been here before, and that's okay. You're not alone. I'm not putting timestamps on us. If you want this? If you want me? I'm here."

"I just…don't want to be selfish," she said her voice, not even a whisper. "Not about you, not with your time and what you want. My feelings for you are so strong, Trey. So strong that I want to be fair to you. Having children after 40 is a risk, and I'm scared that maybe the mature choice would be to—"

"No."

I was a little louder, more forceful than I wanted to be, but that stream of consciousness could not continue. I wouldn't hear of Esme making sacrifices for what she thought I wanted.

"I'll stop you right there because any scenario that doesn't have you in it is not better. It is not more mature. We are both young and healthy. We have time. We have options. We don't even know what the situation is yet. We could have twins by next Christmas, for all we know. Let's chill on worrying about things. And when we come to that bridge, we'll cross it together."

I pulled her up with me as I stood. "We're going home today, but right now, we're still in the cocoon, so let's take advantage of these last few hours. Ok?"

She seemed to breathe a little easier. At least she smiled when she walked past me. I grabbed her arm, though. "Whoa, sexy. Where you going?"

"In... in the house. You said..."

"I didn't say we had to do that inside."

She laughed, but I could hear the undercurrent of interest. "Trey...out here? It's the middle of the night."

"So it's perfect." I pulled her to me, holding her body close to mine. "It's me, you, and the ocean. A couple of seagulls. You mind if they watch?"

She tipped her face up to mine and smiled. In any light, Esme was beautiful, but in the moonlight, the smooth landscape of her skin seemed as delicate as porcelain.

I returned her smile, then pulled at the strings tying her robe closed. The two sides fell open, revealing the red silk gown she'd put on after we showered together. I already detected two peaks poking out of the thin fabric. I made them stand at attention, grow firmer when I rubbed the back of my hand against them.

I stepped back, running my gaze from her head to her toes, admiring every delicious curve of her, from the roundness of her breasts under the thin fabric to the flare of her hips, to the point of her knees, even her white toenails that seemed to glow in the dark.

"Like what you see?"

"More than anything I've ever seen before."

Esme rose up onto her toes, her mouth open and ready to meet mine in a passionate, breathy kiss. A moan curled from me as my body came to life. I moved, holding Esme by her hips and walking us back toward the railing that ran the length of the deck.

"We have to be a little quiet out here. Sound on the beach travels."

Esme giggled. "You've spent four days saying *louder, tell me louder,* and now I have to be quiet? Not sure that I know how."

"Practice for when we're fucking while your cousin is home."

She slapped a hand across her mouth to muffle a gust of laughter. My fingers were busy playing with the knee length gown, pulling it up far enough to slip my hand underneath. Esme wasn't wearing panties. She was slick. And warm to the touch.

"Do you have any idea how sexy you are?"

Her lips tipped up in a wicked, seductive smile. "You make me feel like the sexiest woman alive."

Her eyes slid closed, and her mouth dropped open when I slipped two fingers inside her, angling my thumb to run circles around her clit. It was like rolling a marble in oil.

"Mmmph…" She gripped my forearms and rocked against me. "God…" She gasped. "Trey, that feels good."

"Making you feel good is my new favorite thing."

"Uunh!"

"Shhh," I whispered, gripping the back of her neck. I found her mouth again while my fingers worked until she was bucking her hips. She hooked a finger into the band of my sweats, pulling them down my hips. My dick bobbed, growing harder in the sea air.

"What do you want? What do you want me to do?"

"Fuck me," she hissed. "Right here, right now. Fuck me, Trey."

I pulled my fingers from her, grabbed my dick, and smeared her juices across the head. She turned around, placed both hands on the railing in front of her, and looked back at me, her bottom lip wedged between her teeth.

"Goddamn. I don't see how I can say no."

I moved behind her, flipping up her robe and gown to take in the generous roundness before I guided myself into her. I reached around to palm a breast, gripping and kneading, flicking the nipple. I pumped my hips against her, my mouth buried in her neck to muffle the noises that I couldn't stop if I wanted to.

She pushed back against me, then reached for the hand that had her by the waist and moved it to her clit. I stroked, enjoying her warmth moving against me.

"Have I mentioned that I love this pussy?"

Esme moaned, long and low.

"Is this pussy mine, Esme?" I hissed into her ear. "You saved this, just for me, huh? Is it mine?"

"Take it! Take it, it's yours."

The slap of skin on skin, alongside the hushed tones of two people in the throes of ecstasy, trying not to make noise was erotic to me, like an open secret between us, the ocean waves adding background music to our symphony.

The pre-orgasmic trembles rocked Esme a few moments before she squealed my name and ground her ass against me. Her pussy clenched violently, pulsing and squeezing. I thrust harder, faster, to try to come with her. Finally, my orgasm crashed through, and I tossed my head back, gripping her hips and clenching my teeth to grunt a muted *"Fuck!"* into the night air.

Breaths heavy, hands shaking, she broke from my grip and turned around. Then she placed her hands on my chest and pushed us back to the chairs we'd just abandoned. I backed up until my legs hit the wood slats and dropped into the seat.

Esme wasted no time in lowering herself onto me. She rolled her hips and pulsed her pussy walls to pull me further inside. I gripped two handfuls of her and held on, alternately drawing one, then the other nipple into my mouth while she rode me.

"You feel so fucking good, Trey. How... how do you feel so good..."

"Babe, shhh..."

"I can't!" She tossed her head back and laughed into the night air. "Fuck! I love your dick!"

I laughed. "Es!"

"I don't care! This feels too good!"

I dug my fingers into her ass and spread my legs, scooting up in the chair so that I had some leverage to match her thrusts. The chair began to thump against the side of the house since we had worked our way across the deck.

"Come for me, baby."

She giggled. "Now you want me to be quiet."

"If you don't care about the neighbors, I don't either. I want to come, though. Waiting on you."

"Ok, I'm gonna...I'm..." She bit down on her bottom lip, her face a study in concentration. Her body moved like a piston, her breaths beginning to match the rhythm. A gut-level grunt ripped from her throat. I felt her thighs tense, her back arch, and her inner walls pulse with an intense climax, which took me over the edge.

"Fuck! I'm coming!"

"Me too!"

I released a burst of air, my release coming swiftly, and bringing immeasurable relief.

We spent a few moments catching our breaths. I glanced around at the homes on either side of us. No lights came on, no curious onlookers passed by.

"You..." Esme panted, deliriously giggling and lightly slapping a palm on my chest.

"Me? Nuh-uh, baby. You jumped me."

"No...I mean...you... are some kind of man, Mr. Pettigrew. I can't believe I waited so long to have sex. But I'm kind of happy I waited so long to have sex."

"Worth waiting for?"

She hummed happy sounds, sounds of pure pleasure as she wrapped her arms around me, her lips finding mine for a deep, passionate kiss.

"So worth it."

When she stood, I did too and pulled my sweatpants up. We went back to the bedroom, where I pulled the robe from her shoulders, lifted the silky red gown from her body, dropped my sweatpants where I stood, and took Esme back to bed.

We still had hours before our afternoon flight. I wanted to spend as much of that time as possible making slow, sweet love to her.

CHAPTER THIRTY

Trey

"Well, well, well. Do my eyes behold the ghost of Trey Pettigrew at midnight racquetball?"

I didn't even turn around so Ken could get the benefit of my sheepish grin. I bounced the rubber ball against the wall while I waited for him to get his petty gloating and ribbing out of the way.

"I mean, it couldn't be the actual likeness of Trey Pettigrew. I haven't seen him since he busted into my restaurant and demanded that I make a sushi dish that is not actually sushi. He doesn't answer the phone, he doesn't return texts, it's not like we live in the same building or anything—"

"Alright, alright, alright." I turned around, both arms extended, a racquet in one hand, a rubber ball in the other. "I am sorry. I didn't mean to ghost you. You're still my dude, jealous fool. I've been crazy busy."

"Is it Esme? I'll forgive you if it's Esme."

"Man..." I gestured at him to serve. He did, sending the ball into the wall for me to send it back. "It's work. It's the house. It's Esme. It's... a lot. I haven't been sitting at home, staring at the wall."

Far from it. At Pettigrew, I managed a full portfolio of projects, grinding to stay on Pops' good side and be available to Vincent while he stepped up to run Pettigrew. I didn't feel nearly as left out and dejected as I thought I would feel, knowing that I wasn't at the helm anymore. I honestly felt relieved, but still pensive. If I was going to spend the next ten to fifteen years being an underling – an executive underling, but an underling nonetheless— then I was going to have to make my move to run my own show.

If I wasn't in the office or at a Pettigrew site, I was micromanaging my house build. I wanted major construction to be complete, finishing up interior details by December. The walls were up, concrete had been poured, wire pulled, fixtures were going up, and the flooring and other materials had arrived. Ideally, I could wake up in my own house on Christmas Day if I had my bedroom, the kitchen, a bathroom, and at least one room downstairs walled, floored and powered. I'd put my condo up for sale, and Esme and I had started packing.

I spent the balance of my time with Esme. The cocoon that we'd built up over our vacation kept us solid. We preferred to stay in our cloud of newfound, giddy love. Good food, good wine, good sex, made easier since she didn't have to go to work.

Job hunting was going well, though. Her assumption that her MBA would let her play well in the market was correct; the response to her resume and years of experience with Benning netted calls and emails immediately. In fact, she had an early interview in the morning, so we'd had some dinner, some wine, some sex, watched a show, and then I cut out early so she could get to bed and be well-rested.

But I couldn't sleep, because sex with Esme didn't relax me; it wound me up. I'd become used to sharing a bed with her, coming down from the highs of orgasm together. When I got home, I texted Ken, though I had been ignoring him for weeks. I'd miss being close enough to get in a quick game. If I wasn't going to be having sex on the deck of a beachfront home in the middle of the night, I'd settle for getting my ass beat.

"So, the last I heard, the bid was toast. Are you still playing CEO?"

"Nah," I answered, returning a weak serve. I gave him a look and slammed it back at him. He had to run to catch it and send it back. "Vincent is acting CEO, and I'm actually happy about that. He and Pops have been running the company for thirty years. They finish each other's sentences. I should have known better than to think I could do it."

"If I remember right, you did know better. And you told him that you knew better, but he insisted on giving you the job."

"You know how it goes when I try to have those *I told you so* conversations with Pops. You have to let it play out. The good news, though, is that he's not furious about the bid anymore. Especially since they got to submit anyway. I'm holding out for that promise he made me."

"Pops has been fighting you on residential for a while. Think it'll pan out?"

"It would be a great way for him to say he's sorry for not trusting me. We would have lost our asses if I'd signed that contract. Now he feels like he's doing something good by acting as a mentor, bringing a young pipsqueak up in the world."

My eyes rolled involuntarily. "Miller is smart, but he's also a smarmy, sneaky motherfucker. The shit I've given up, that Esme gave up behind his shady ass?"

I seethed, slamming my anger into the ball. It bounced off the wall and came flying back, but Ken couldn't run fast enough to catch it.

"Piece of work, that guy."

"I have more insulting words for him. I don't like him, and I'm glad we don't have to absorb him into Pettigrew."

"Heads up!" Ken served. We slammed the ball around the room for a half-hour of rowdy play before taking a break to hydrate and breathe. Ken paced, sucking down water from a sports bottle. I did the same but sank to the floor with my back against the pane of glass.

"So, you're not going to spill any juice about Esme?"

I fought the smile that always popped up whenever anyone brought her up. Vincent had become insanely curious about her ever since she spent the afternoon at Pettigrew and risked her job to save our asses. Now he was asking after her, too. How she was doing? Did she find a job yet?

I got it. She was beautiful. Engaging. Assertive. But also a warm, sweet, sensuous woman. A person got a very good idea of what they were getting from her by spending a little time with her. I was obsessed with her too.

"What kind of juice are you looking for?"

"The usual, man. Maybe you're rusty on the rules. In this friendship, we talk about the women we date. You tell me you like her; I tell you that you're an idiot. You tell me all the simp shit you do for her; I tell you that you're whipped."

Ken paused for a moment, then grinned. "And then I go back to my place, pick up my phone, and hop back on Tinder because I'm jealous of what you have." He stood over me, offering a hand to pull me up. "Let's grab a basement beer before the bar closes down."

Basement beer was what we called getting a drink at the bar in the basement of the building. We often slid in just before the last call. Considering that it could be the last basement beer I'd have with Ken, I let him pull me up, then followed him around the corner to the bar.

A few minutes later, we were posted up with frosty bottles

and a bowl of salt and vinegar corn nuts, our usual basement beer combo.

"You seem different this time, man. I mean it."

I shook my head, my mouth in a downturn. "I'm no different. Same soup, just reheated."

"If that's the case, your woman is heating things up in a whole different way. Did you take her to your spot in Myrtle Beach? How'd that go?"

"Was nice."

I bobbed my head, smiling at the memory of five long, blissful days with Esme. Late nights on the deck listening to music, playing spades or UNO. Early mornings in the bed with her, starting the day off right. Sunset walks on the beach, hand in hand while we just... talked. Laughed. Played.

Easy. It had never been so easy.

"It was great to get out of the city, get some alone time with her. You know, spend some quality time together, figure out who we are outside of all of this work stress and family stuff."

"I bet. By quality time, you mean..."

"Come on, man. I've never been that dude. That's all you."

I was never the type to kiss and tell. I never had much to tell. Now I had something I wanted to tell the world, but it was precious to me. I couldn't see sharing what was intimate and meaningful between us for Ken's amusement.

Besides, Ken's worldwide exploits were infamous. Funny, because he always claimed to be jealous of the few more serious relationships I'd had.

"You're no fun anymore, Trey. You're not giving me anything?"

"I'll give you something," I said, leaning forward. I tipped my beer to my lips and took a long fortifying swallow, then set the half empty bottle back on the bar. "This woman? Esme? She's changed my life. My whole world, my whole outlook in like… six weeks. I can't remember what life was like before I met her. I don't want to think about going back to being without her. I love her. I'm in love with her."

"Damn." Ken whistled, pretending to wipe sweat from his brow. "That's heavy. Does she know? Does she feel the same?"

"Hell yeah, she knows. And she feels the same."

"So, I really am catering your wedding?"

"Man, keep the calendar open, you know what I'm saying?" We laughed together, then I picked up my beer again, and before I took another sip, said, "I mean… I haven't said the L-word to her yet. And she hasn't said anything to me yet."

"So, how do you know she knows how you feel? And how do you know she feels the same?"

I shrugged. "I know. Mark my words. Until then, I'm playing it cool. Being there. Loving her. Enjoying being in her world. It's a nice place to be."

"I guess. I can only hope to find the same sometime."

"You'd have to sit your ass down somewhere first."

"Actually…" Ken's tongue flicked out to moisten his bottom lip as his gaze dropped to the table, his skin gaining a pinkish tone. "I met this woman the last time I was in New York. Remember, I went up there to scout restaurant locations a few months ago?"

"I remember. She lives there?"

"Yeah. A waitress at the restaurant in the hotel I stayed at. I came in right before closing. Force of habit, I guess."

He chuckled, flashing me a shy half-smile. "I talked her into letting me sit down, said I'd take whatever they had left that was prepared, and I'd tip her well. She said she was saving something, and if I wanted it, I could have it. Turned out, she'd ordered dinner and was going to take it home. I felt bad taking her dinner from her, but she said she'd rather have the money. So I paid her double for it. Then I shared it with her."

"See, you talk about the simp shit I do. You sap."

"Anyway, we ended up sitting in the closed bar, talking and eating cold lasagna til like... I don't know... 4 AM? I've eaten frozen lasagna that tasted better. But she... she was nice. I got her number. We talk here and there. I'm uh..."

Ken sat up, then smoothed his palms down well-muscled thighs. "I'm thinking about taking a trip up there. You know, long weekend, some time to relax. Maybe run into her." He looked up at me and caught my eye. "Or whatever."

"You should probably make plans to see her and spend time with her like an adult, you moron."

"What, you're the Oracle now?"

"I'm in love with a woman that can't get enough of me. My advice is probably better than just showing up and expecting her to drop her life for you. Even if you're Ken Takagi, owner of Eito Worldwide, nobody gives a shit about your social status if you're a dick."

He nodded his head. "Maybe you're right."

"I know I am. Another piece of advice, and then I'm taking my ass to bed. 5 AM comes early." I stood and stretched my already tight limbs. "NAKED condoms. Buy a lot of them. They're pricey but worth it."

"You uh..." He pointed at me. "You two use them?"

"We did. We both tested clear for STD's and Esme is almost 40 and on the pill. At this point, if she gets pregnant, it's meant to be. I'll be happy as shit."

"You as a dad? Now that's a weird thought."

Ken stood, drained his beer, then dug into his pocket for his wallet. He left a few dollars on the table. I added to it, and we walked together toward the elevator.

"For what it's worth, I'm glad you met somebody. I really hope it works out for you two. And I'm watching. It's long past time for us both to grow up, you know?"

"Thanks for coming in, son. Good to see you."

"Sure, Pops. Surprised to see you in the office."

I was still recovering from the shock of walking into Pettigrew at my normal time of 7 AM, a cup from Brew Bar in hand and the residue of Esme's lip balm on my lips to find Pops in his office. He wore a dark, tailored suit, collared shirt, and tie with a pocket square, even shiny wingtips like he hadn't been out of the office for months.

His physique showed it, though. His eyes were bright, but the lids were hooded. He'd lost some hair, and he'd slimmed considerably, making him appear even taller. More foreboding. He perched in a tall leather chair, rolling it up to his desk, the surface of which had been clean for months. We hadn't used his office, and his Executive Assistant made it a point to keep it dust-free.

An 8 AM meeting popped up on my calendar as soon as I settled in at my desk. I had been summoned to Pops' office.

"You won't see me here often," said Pops, "but I am trying to get out of the house, ease back into business. It's no longer relaxing to sit at home and let other people run my company. I'm under strict orders to be home no later than 5 o'clock."

I let my deep nod show my understanding. My mother was not a tall woman, but her personality was a beast, and she was not to be ignored. Pops would vacate the office at the agreed upon time, or else.

"Anyway, Vincent is still in control, so I planned to have an easy day. Check up on progress, get a feel for how the business has changed since I was gone. I'd like to run down the current projects, discuss the forecast for next quarter and project into the first quarter of next year. A baseline, just to get your thoughts."

I... was not ready for this conversation.

I had the information in my head, of course. It was my job to know those numbers forward and backward for such a time as this. But this would mark the first time that Pops had called me into his office and asked me such detailed questions about the business, listened to my thoughts and assumptions, and offered opinions without starting a sentence with, "See, that's why you're here to learn."

I didn't feel like a pup anymore.

After a few minutes of polite back and forth business-speak, Pops leaned back in his chair and folded his arms across the belly he had left. "What do you think about carving out time next year, maybe first or second quarter, to float a pilot of your division? I'm thinking about that space on the second floor, in the southeast corner. It's got room for about four people to have a dedicated workspace. You don't need more than that to get started. Do you?"

I sat up, unsure that I'd heard what I'd heard. I wanted to be dramatic and pretend to clean my ears or turn my head toward him and ask him to repeat himself, but Pops wouldn't find that funny. Vincent would, though.

"Uhm...Sir?"

"Vincent has convinced me that this would be a great move for you. He thinks you've earned the opportunity and his respect. I am inclined to give you both the benefit of the doubt. I expect you to stay up on your current workload until the new division begins to demand more of your time. We aren't going through the effort to replace you, then shuffle people around if it doesn't pan out."

"Understood, sir. I appreciate this opportunity. I want to say that I won't let you down, but..."

I let the long pause float in the air between us.

"You've never been a disappointment to me a day in your life, Trey," said Pops. "You're a hard worker, with a sharp mind. Your business sense is impeccable, and I was wrong to question it. You got it from me, after all."

I wanted to roll my eyes. The fight to resist was valiant, and I won.

"The house you designed? I took another look at the plans you showed me a few years ago." He gave me a solitary nod. That was a lot, coming from him. "I understand that you're building now?"

I nodded, swallowing hard. I hadn't shared any housebuilding updates with him. I didn't want him to disregard them like I was a petulant teen who thought I could become a Grammy-winning rapper. I had knowledge, skills and a goal. It wasn't a silly pursuit, and I wouldn't give him another chance to push it down.

"It's almost up, actually. I'm hoping to be in it by Christmas."

"Mmmmm. I'm anxious to see how nice it looks in real-time. How's..." He shrugged, opening his hands to show his palms. "You know... construction?"

I shifted, feeling myself grow more at ease in this room, in the shadow of my father. I felt more like we were colleagues, not father and son. It was gratifying. Also terrifying, but I was ignoring that feeling.

"It's honestly about the same. Riding rough on the project manager, having somebody out on-site running the show, keeping the budget in line. Watching it come together is still like magic. It's very much... artistic. Know what I mean?"

"Mmmmm," he hummed, stroking his beard the same way I did. "I do. I cried at the first finished Pettigrew build."

"See, I might cry when my house is done. I'm not going to feel bad about that now."

We laughed together, a pitter-patter of polite chuckles.

"How's the lady?" He asked quietly. I hadn't brought up Esme, either, since she played a part in the contract negotiations flying off the rails. Though I shouldn't have been surprised that he was asking about her.

"Esme..." A smile broke out. Though I wanted to remain professional, her name on my lips made me happy. "Esme is great."

"Is she working again?"

"She had a great interview yesterday at a spot she really wants to jump to. They called her back already and offered her the job. Almost twice what she was making at the old spot. So...yeah, actually."

"Good." He tapped the desk and gave a resolute nod. I hadn't realized he was so invested. "I'd like to meet her. So would your mother. More than you realize, probably."

"I'm sure you'll get the chance soon."

"Oh? It's serious?"

"Yes," I admitted. "It's serious. I'm in love with her."

"Well, why don't you bring her by this weekend? Your mother hasn't had a chance to show out in the kitchen in a while."

"Uh...it's her birthday weekend. I've got something special planned. But maybe we'll swing through."

"Excellent." Pops smiled. Not a fake business smile, but the kind of smile a man has for his son. "Let us know. And... tell her that I said happy birthday."

He tipped his chair forward again and reached for his laptop to flip the cover open. That was his usual signal that the conversation was over.

"You'll report to Vincent, of course, on the residential business. I'd like you to set up some time to discuss the launch. And go down to the second floor to scope out the area. That's all the space you're getting for right now. Make it work."

"Yes, sir. I'll do that."

I hopped up from my seat like I'd been electrocuted and shot for the door. I wanted to get out of Pops' office before he changed his mind.

I still had to make plans for Esme's birthday, and we had one last adventure to complete.

CHAPTER THIRTY-ONE

Esme

"Happy birthday, Aunt Esme!"
"Thank you, sweet Samuel!"

I bent to let my nephew give me a kiss on the cheek and held out my arm to fold Georgia into a hug. Having fulfilled their required greetings, they rushed past me to the living room to say hi to O'Neal and their cousins, Layah and Courtney. Joe and Jada were making lunch, and Corey and Jewel took their time walking up the front sidewalk.

The Whitakers didn't need any excuse to gather, but birthdays were a family affair. We were only missing my parents, but we'd probably Skype with them once everyone sat down to eat.

I was giddy, knowing the family had set aside time to celebrate me. O'Neal made sure he was home, Jada took the day off from the salon, and Corey and the kids took the weekend off from trivia challenges and Math Olympics activities.

This wasn't any old birthday. It was my 40th. I had been

alive for four decades, nearly half a century, and I was still learning, still growing, still becoming me. At my big age, I was still doing things for the first time, making career moves... and falling in love.

Aside from O'Neal, none of my family had met Trey. He was coming over for my birthday lunch, and I was nervous, not that they wouldn't like him, but that they would be themselves.

I'd already warned Trey about them. He admitted to being jealous that I'd had what seemed like an above-average childhood and a great relationship with my parents, siblings, and cousins. Therapy was stirring up all sorts of feelings for Trey. He'd already helped me over so many hurdles in the weeks since we'd met. The least that I could do was lay next to him in a dewy, post-coital heap and listen to him process the thoughts that kept him awake at night.

I didn't picture myself as one of those women that put a lot of stock in a sexual relationship and how it changed a connection with a person, but... man was I wrong about that. The instant that I crossed that line with Trey, so much changed for me. I wanted more, needed more, and felt that I deserved more.

And right there with me was a man willing to give me more. I wouldn't be true to myself if I didn't give him a chance to give me more.

Jewel and Corey had just made it into the house when Trey's Acadia pulled into the driveway behind Corey's Jeep. I rushed out of the front door and down the sidewalk and shot my arms up and out to pull him into a hug.

He was casually sexy in a pair of dark, relaxed fit jeans and a long-sleeved t-shirt since autumn had officially arrived in Atlanta, and the air carried a crispness to it. He'd shown up the night before with a cut and a nice beard trim. Now he had a fresh face and appeared well-rested, though I knew full well that he was not. Neither was I.

"Hey, girl," he said, his mouth muffled against my shoulder, squeezing me as I squeezed him back. He lifted his head, and I turned mine. Our lips met in a long, sweet kiss that left both of us groaning.

I finally pulled back, smoothing my arms down the soft cotton of his shirt until I held his hands in mine. "Hi. It's good to see you."

"Back at you." He brushed a thumb across my cheek, then leaned in for another kiss. "It's almost like I didn't just leave here a few hours ago."

I giggled aloud at us earlier that morning, trying to get in a few minutes of what we thought was quiet sex before he had to leave to meet his parents and sister for breakfast. After I walked him to the door, I went back upstairs to find O'Neal standing in the middle of the hall, pulling earbuds from his ears.

"Look here, Cousin," said O'Neal, his voice gritty from sleep. "I need some kind of warning if y'all are gonna fuck like sailors on shore leave before sunrise."

"You know what, O'Neal? I have a lot of time to make up for. If Trey's vehicle is in the driveway, we're gonna fuck like sailors on shore leave, whenever we like."

I marched past him into my bedroom and shut the door in his face.

"Are you ready for this?" I asked Trey.

"I've already met O'Neal. How much worse could they be?"

"It's O'Neal times four. They literally have no chill. I want you to know that you're a big, strong man, and you can take it."

Trey dropped an arm over my shoulder and began walking up the driveway with me. "I think I'll be Ok."

We stepped inside the house to find everyone in the living room, not even trying to hide that they were all watching at the window and waiting for us to come inside.

Since everyone was standing there, I made quick introductions.

"So, this is Trey. My dude, my guy, my partner in doing dumb shit we could probably get arrested for." I glanced at him, he glanced at me, and we laughed, knowing we were both thinking about that night at his half-built house where we really got to know each other.

"Uhm... this is... my bond," I told Trey. "My strength, my guidance, my wisdom, my fun. Everything that I am, they made me. I mean, my parents gave me life and whatever, but my sisters and O'Neal are my heart."

Trey got long, tight hugs from my sisters, daps from the kids, and a head nod from O'Neal. Joe and Corey came forward to give Trey strong handshakes and slaps on the back.

"What about your brothers in law? We're not your heart?" Joe's long, thin face bore a constant serious affect, but I saw the mirth in his eyes. He worshipped the ground my sister walked on, and I loved him for it.

"The brothers I never had."

"You said *I* was the brother you never had," O'Neal grumbled.

Jewel started waving us all to the dining room. Lunch smelled delicious — grilled herb and garlic salmon, lump crab cakes, and crisp lemony vegetables with cheesecake for dessert was my request, and I was ready to eat.

"Come on, y'all, before we start fighting about who Esme loves more. I don't really want to go up against Trey on this one."

A few hours later, we all found a spot to recover from having eaten every piece of food available on the table. Joe was magic in the kitchen and had handled most of the meal himself. Jada made the crab cakes, and Jewel brought dessert. In the middle of the meal, we'd stopped to Skype our parents in Palm Springs. Trey met them digitally but promised to meet them properly when they returned to Atlanta before Christmas.

"When do we tell Aunt Esme about the surprise?" Courtney, who was on his second serving of cheesecake, blurted as he walked out of the kitchen.

"Boy, I told you to hush!" Yelled Jada.

"Uh, no. Courtney should say more. What surprise?"

Trey sat up. I'd been leaning against him, tucked into a corner of the couch while we watched an old episode of Bernie Mac on Def Comedy Jam. O'Neal lowered the volume on the TV.

"I guess that's my cue."

"What's your cue? What surprise?"

"First of all, baby... I lied to you."

I sat upright, fully upright, on the edge of the couch. "When? About what?"

"I've met your family. Your sisters, at least. Don't you recognize Jada's skills on my hair? My beard?"

He leaned over to let me look like I cared about his hair at a time like this.

"Somebody better say something to me. What are y'all talking about?"

"I went to Jada's shop about a week after we got back from Myrtle Beach. I wanted to meet her, but I didn't think you were ready to introduce us. I asked her not to tell you that I stopped by, but I wanted to set up a meet with me, her and Jewel."

My eyes narrowed as I bounced my eyes from Trey to Jada and back. "Unh, huh..."

"Anyway, we all met last night. To talk about...well, today."

"Oh. So... lunch and everything?"

"Yes. Lunch with everyone that loves you, including your parents. But we have another surprise for you. Can't tell you what it is, but... do you trust me?"

"**O** h, *hell* no!"
      After an hour and a half of driving, Trey exited onto a service road that wound up into the Tennessee mountains. And after a few miles on that road, followed by my sisters and their families in their vehicles behind us, Trey turned into the parking lot of a small ramshackle building set in the middle of nowhere. I wasn't so much concerned about the building, but the sign that loomed over it filled me with fear:

ADVENTURESOME! Balloon Rides, Bungee Jumping, and Zip Lining.

"What do you mean, hell no? "

"Exactly what the fuck I said, Trey! Hell no!"

"After all of those things you crossed off of your list, you're going to punk out at this?"

"Are you serious? I rode an elevator to the roof. I jumped over kid lasers."

"You also flew in an airplane and rode a Ferris Wheel."

"Which of these insane, daredevil activities did you sign me up for without asking?"

"Bungee Jumping."

"The one thing I always ask you not to set up. I am not in the mood for this."

"Es, you said you trusted me. This is going to be like all of the other things we did together. It's going to be like getting on the Ferris wheel. And dancing on the roof. And swimming in the ocean. And riding on a sailboat. And petting a cute baby goat."

"Except it's not," I shot back. "Except this one is actually extreme and dangerous, and legitimately scary."

"I get that. But you were scared before, and you didn't punk out. I'm here, and we can do this together. Your whole family is here."

Trey pointed out of the window on my side of the car. I looked up to see my sisters, my brothers in law, my nieces, and my nephews standing outside the vehicle waiting for us.

"You're not going to let them down, are you?"

"So, you told them that I was going to do this?"

"I told them that I was bringing you here. And that not doing it was going to be your choice, but I would be here to do it with you if you chose to."

"And did they tell you I would cuss you out because you're out of your fucking mind and you need to turn this vehicle around and drive me back home?"

"Yes, they did. And I told them that my girl was a badass that would eat this bungee jump for lunch."

I glared. "How dare—you bring up Badass Esme when you want me to do some fuckshit like jump off of a bridge."

"You know what, Es? Remember when we went for breakfast, and I asked you about your list, and you said that you were going to finish with or without me?"

"Back when you didn't encourage me to jump off of a bridge?"

"I got a little twinge in my chest when you said *with or without me*. I felt *a way* about you doing something that terrifies you or gives you a second thought without somebody there to support you. Hype you up. Tell you that you can do this shit. Somebody by your side to show you that I care about you and that I am always going to be here for you."

"So you brought me here to do a thing I would never do?"

Trey reached across the console for my hand. For some reason, I let him weave his fingers with mine instead of reaching for the steering wheel to drive me home.

"You haven't finished your list, Es," he said, his tone much softer than before. "Number three on your Never list was Be Daring. You remember? Would you really never let us be joined together, step out there together, jump together? Never?"

I had hoped that he wouldn't notice that I had one last adventure to complete. I'd already accomplished so much, above and beyond the list. It was no longer meaningful to me, so much so that I'd already put it in a scrapbook, where I'd probably not see it again.

"Trey…"

"Es. I'm doing this. Your family is doing this. Are you going to sit in this truck and watch us do it? Or are you going to put away everything you were afraid of, let us surround and support you, step out with us, and conquer this one little thing?"

"I fully resent you calling it this one little thing. It's literally jumping off of a bridge."

"With me."

"You want us to die together, then."

"Baby, I've got you. Have I not had you this whole time? Everything on your list that you've had to do, I've helped you. Right?"

I almost laughed out loud. I knew what he thought he was doing, planning this event and inviting my family, knowing that I'd probably work up the nerve to just do this.

Was I actually thinking about it? *Sneaky motherfucker.*

"I know you're scared, baby. Actually, I know you're terrified. Your sisters said you would probably punch me in the forehead, and I'm not a huge fan of jumping off of a bridge, but... why don't we both be brave and give it a try? Why don't we walk up there and check it out? Why don't we let them strap us into the tandem harness? Why don't we keep putting one foot in front of the other, because we're both scared as shit, but life after will be so much better than it was before the jump?"

I'd been fuming, staring hard out of the windshield, but something caught my attention. I rolled my head in his direction. "Tandem harness? We really go together?"

"I don't want to do this without you. I don't want you to do this without me."

"We aren't talking about bungee jumping right now, are we?"

He shrugged. "We could be talking about several things, Esme. But let's handle one thing at a time. I'm getting out. In about five minutes, we're headed to the bridge. I'll let you decide if you're coming or not."

Trey pulled the latch to his door and stepped out. The door thumped closed behind him. I watched him walk around the front of the vehicle and greet my family. I sat in the stuffy vehicle, watching him get along so easily and effortlessly with the people that I loved, that loved me back.

I could admit to myself now that Trey belonged in that group.

I sucked in a deep breath, my chest barreling with the intake to my lungs. Trembling, I reached for the latch, but the door popped open before I even touched it.

Trey held out a hand. "You coming?"

"Yes. I'm coming," I answered with a thick tongue to loud, rowdy cheers.

I let Trey help me from the truck. The door slammed shut behind me, and then we were walking hand-in-hand toward the entrance to check-in.

Was I terrified? Absolutely.

Did I think any of these people around me, behind me, would let me fail? Absolutely not.

Trey and I stood on the edge of a bridge that overlooked a lake of still water. Toe to toe, we faced each other, strapped tightly into a tandem body harness. Our Jumpmaster passed back and forth, giving instructions, checking each team's harness, and collecting the waivers we had to sign before jumping.

Now, he gave last minute instructions.

"Lead with your head; your head should be the first thing

that leaves the platform. Those of you in a tandem harness make sure that you hold tight to each other to stay out of the way of the cord and the carabiners. Tuck your chin in and your head down until you have reached the bottom and begin to bounce back up. When your jump is complete, hang tight."

He paused to chuckle. "We will pull you back up to the bridge. At that point, you can jump again if you like. Some of our customers like to try one facing front, and then one jumping backward. "

"I'm only doing this shit once, " I muttered.

"Bet," he shot back. "This is some one-and-done type of shit." He bent so that he could rest his forehead on mine. "You good?"

"Yeah. You?"

"I'm good if you're good. I feel like you might beat my ass after this, though."

"If we live, I might." I laughed and tipped my lips up to meet his. "Trey, before we jump off of this bridge together—"

"Don't make it sound so dramatic, Es."

"I have to make it worth crossing off of the list. Hush, I have something to say."

"Always."

"Anyway. I set out to cross ten items off of a list before I turned forty. Seven of them were silly. One of them, I had every intention of skipping." I rolled my eyes up at Trey. He had the good sense to wince, then smile. "Two of them were things I really wanted, but I honestly never thought I'd even get close. You took on my list like it was yours and made sure I never had to do any of those things alone, even the easy ones. I flew in an airplane. I quit a job I hate. I have an amazing sex life."

Trey's head bobbed side to side. "Mine's pretty good, too."

"I'm turning 40 tomorrow. I made it. *We* made it. We crossed off every item."

"Sure did."

"Including number one."

Trey's grin spread across his face like wildfire. "Yeah?"

I returned his smile, just as wide, just as bright. "Yeah. I love you, Trey. You already knew that, though. I was scared because it's early —"

"It's not," he said. I almost cried, watching his eyes gloss over. "You said by your 40th birthday, and here we are. It's right on time. I love you, too."

"You do?"

"Woman...yeah. I've been in love with you since you chose me to share something so deeply personal and then didn't want to share it with anybody else. I want to be the only person to share that with you. And I can't wait to find more absolutely terrifying shit for us to do together."

"Can we make this the last time we jump off of a bridge?"

"We can definitely make that a rule. But uhm... what do you say we get this over with?"

I nodded, then closed my eyes and tucked my head into his chest. I tightened my arms around him and stepped even closer. Trey's arms closed and locked around me. I heard his voice in my ear and fought back the trembles that wanted to climb up my legs. I was with Trey and my family. They would never let anything happen to me.

I loved them. I loved him. I was safe.

"Okay, baby. Here we go. Three... two..."

With a sudden jerk, Trey shoved us off of the bridge, and then it didn't even feel like a free-fall. It was like floating on a cloud, except everyone on the cloud was screaming, including Trey and me. The fall was over way too soon. A violent jerk of the rope rebounded us before we hit the surface of the lake.

I opened my eyes to take in the upside-down view of the wooded hills, the cloudy brown lake below, the peeling green paint on the bridge, my sisters, and everyone cheering with arms in the air.

"I love you, Esme!" Trey screamed while we swung side to side.

I laughed. Suspended from a bridge on a very springy rope strapped to a man I was deeply in love with, I was laughing.

"I love you, Trey!" I screamed back.

We had nothing but time until the Jumpmaster pulled us up, so we spent it lip-locked in a fiery kiss that gave me every indication of how the impending evening would go.

The Jumpmaster began to pull our rope, bringing us up to the surface, then helping us back onto the bridge.

"Esme," Trey began while stepping out of his harness. "I'm never doing this shit again."

"That wasn't that bad." I stepped out of my side of the harness and handed it to the Jumpmaster.

"Never."

"Maybe it should be your turn. Make a list of ten things you've never done. This can be number ten!"

Trey held out a hand. I slid my palm across it and wound my fingers between his. "Being honest? I love you. There's not much I wouldn't do if you were there to do it with me."

"I love you too, and being honest?" I rose up onto my toes to kiss him. "I'm never doing this shit again, either."

We stood back to watch the others make their jumps, cheering Jada and Joe, then Jewel and Corey as they had cheered for us. O'Neal and each of the kids decided to do a single jump, so excited and energized that they were bouncing off of each other when they came up.

"I think we're going to take the kids to ESPN Zone," said Jada. "Let 'em run around and burn off some of this energy, then get some dinner. Y'all coming?"

"Uh…" Trey glanced over at me. I saw the look in his eye. "It's your day, baby, so…"

"Nah," I said, winking at Trey. "We have to go be old and boring on a Saturday night."

"Ok, but..." Jewel shook her head. "Esme, you're the baby."

I pulled both of my sisters into a hug, muttering low so they both could hear me. "It's my birthday, and my present is dick. Tap motherfucking tap. Don't call me. I'll be busy."

"Alright, baby girl," said Jada. "Don't hurt him."

"I hope y'all are staying at Trey's tonight," O'Neal grumbled as he walked past us. "I have an early flight tomorrow."

"Wish granted." I grabbed my man by the arm and tugged him away. We climbed into the Acadia and waited for the system to readjust itself to Trey's presets.

"We gotta go be old and boring, huh?"

I grabbed his hand and tucked it between my thighs, where he liked it. Where I liked it too.

"Mmmhmm. We gotta listen to grown folks' music on satellite radio. Go get some sushi from Ken's spot—"

"And that chicken dish you like," Trey added.

"And fall asleep to Love Jones after you fuck me into a stupor on my 40th birthday."

"You know what I always say."

Trey slipped a pair of shades over his eyes, then leaned over for a kiss before putting the Acadia in drive and pulled out of the parking space.

We both finished his usual saying. "Ain't got to tell me twice."

EPILOGUE

Esme

I couldn't see over the cardboard boxes stacked on the counters and in the corner of Trey's new kitchen. The house, and everything in it, still smelled like milled wood and plastic sheeting and the fumes of painted walls and freshly laid carpet.

Trey sold his condo right before Thanksgiving, but the house wasn't move-in ready. The crew needed another month, at the very least. His plan had been to bunk with Ken, but I pouted so hard that he changed his mind. He'd been staying with me for a few weeks, much to O'Neal's annoyance.

When the house was finished enough to occupy, Trey was like a five-year-old on Christmas. Joe, O'Neal, and Corey showed up to help him move his things from storage. The place was a sea of boxes, but Trey couldn't be happier. His goal had been to wake up in his own house on his birthday, Christmas Day.

It was Christmas Eve. He'd made it.

"Babe, where is the box with the..."

Trey shuffled into the kitchen shirtless, a pair of cotton flannel lounge pants riding low on his hips. The Italian tile and wood floors were cold, so he wore slippers. He held his phone in both hands and tapped rapidly with his thumbs.

"The box with the what?"

"The coffee beans, the grinder, the French press? I put them all in one box."

"Mmmmm. I'll look around," he said, not looking up from his phone. "Maybe it ended up somewhere."

"It said kitchen on it. Where else would O'Neal have put it?"

When Trey didn't answer, I turned from a stack of boxes to find him chuckling and typing. "Are you texting your Peloton girlfriend to tell her why you haven't been in her class?"

I snickered, knowing full well that his late nights with me didn't make for early mornings on the bike. I didn't hear Trey complaining. Besides, the bike had been in storage for over a month, and though it made it to the new house, it wasn't up and running.

He laughed. "Nah. It's Ken."

"Ooh, with his girlfriend?"

"Yeah. She's coming to Atlanta with him, actually."

"Seriously?" Ken had made several trips to New York and had been up there for the last week, but she hadn't come to Atlanta yet. This was huge.

"They're at JFK right now. Eito has that big thing tonight, and he can't miss it, but he wasn't ready to say goodbye, so…"

Ken's restaurant was closed for a private dinner that would be a tour of Western and Japanese cuisine—seared steak, pork, mesquite chicken and turkey, a cornucopia of vegetables coupled with rice, noodles, and grilled or tempura-battered meat and seafood. Trey had been looking forward to it for weeks, and since it was his birthday, I was going, but I warned

him that I was not going to be talked into eating food that
smelled like standing water.

"She was off for Christmas anyway, so he bought the seat
next to him."

"A first-class ticket? On the fly?" Trey nodded. I smirked.
"And he talks about you being a simp."

Trey cocked a half-smile. "This dude goes from a girl in
every city to falling for just one woman, then flying her
around."

"Must be the Trey Pettigrew effect. Maybe you can have
the same effect on my cousin."

"Nah. O'Neal is an unrepentant fuckboy."

"Ok, well, could you at least have an effect on that box? I
need coffee. Brew Bar is too far away, now."

"Oh." He set the phone down and wandered away.

I went through the boxes again. "I don't get it. The storage
unit was empty, so we didn't leave it. It must be somewhere—"

"I found the box."

I tossed up my hands and rolled my eyes to the ceiling.
"Great. How did it get in the living room?"

I grabbed the kettle from the box I'd packed it in, rinsed it
in the sink, and set it on the stove. It took a few seconds to
figure out how to turn the gas burners on the professional
cooking range, but a blue flame finally licked at the steel kettle.

I turned around to find myself still alone in the kitchen.
Really?

"Trey! What are you doing?"

I marched through the dining room and around the
corner to the living room. "If you're on the phone while I am
suffering from caffeine withdrawal, I—"

I froze. Trey was still shirtless and in cotton lounge pants,
but he sat cross-legged in front of the bare Christmas tree. We
were supposed to spend the day decorating it.

In his palm, he held a black box tied with a white bow.

I gasped. "Trey. You... you're not... are you?"

"It's not Christmas yet, I know. I was supposed to wait until we decorated the tree, so it could be romantic. And it's actually *my* birthday, so you should be giving me a gift, but…"

He held out his hand, the box in his palm. "I can't wait."

"Trey. What…what is *actually* happening here?"

"Good things. Promise. Come sit." I sat next to him, and he handed me the box. "Open it."

I pulled the bow, then pulled the top off of the box. Nestled inside was a ring, white and rose gold with a polished ice matte finish and a band of diamonds around the edge. It was just enough.

"Oh, Trey!" I gasped again, this time with a smile. "Baby, this is gorgeous."

"Glad you like it." He took a breath, and I knew what was coming next. "So, you're funny when you don't want to be proposed to yet."

"No, I want to be proposed to! It's just…"

"Early."

"Not that I don't want to marry you. Definitely eventually."

"Baby, I have no doubt. It's coming, but it won't be a random Tuesday in December. And I haven't talked to your parents yet."

"You really don't need to talk to my parents, Trey."

"I know that and you know that. We also know that my mother will lose her mind if I don't talk to them first. *Do it right, Trey.*"

I relented once I realized that he was right. I already loved Pamela, but she was set in her ways and quite old fashioned. My parents would laugh at Trey asking for my hand, but they would also find it endearing. He needed all the help he could get since they were still a little raw that I quit my job over the deal between Miller and Pettigrew. Never mind that my new job was much more rewarding.

"I just barely met them and now I want their daughter to

be my wife." He shook his head. "I still wanted to get you something nice for Christmas, though. Something that twinkles and glistens in the light."

I smiled, because now I knew engagement was imminent. The anticipation of when he would ask was going to kill me.

He gestured to the ring still in the box. "You like it? Jada said you'd like it, so if you don't—"

He didn't get to finish his sentence. I squealed, bowling him over, climbing onto his lap and raining kisses across his face. When I pulled back, we were both grinning like idiots and overheated.

"Let's put it on. Then I can watch you overuse that hand all day, waving it around like you women do."

He pulled the ring from the box, then slid it onto my finger. The fit was perfect, nice, and snug.

I held my hand aloft and took in the view. "Jada did a great job. I love it so much."

"I love *you* so much." He leaned in to press his lips against mine. "Oh." He pointed to the box that was clearly marked *kitchen—coffee stuff* tucked behind the tree. "There's that box that I hid from you, so you'd come to find me."

"Oh, thank God," I said, as the kettle began to whistle. I climbed off of his lap, then. "I'll make the coffee. You can watch this ring twinkle and glisten in the light."

Trey followed me to the kitchen, then set the box on the counter and unpacked it. I took the press and set it on the counter. He pulled out a few bags of beans and the grinder, already measuring enough for both of us to have coffee.

I poured hot water into the carafe and attached the lid. I had to wait for the coffee to brew before pressing the plunger anyway, so I turned, leaning a hip against the counter. Trey did the same across the kitchen, crossing one leg over the other.

"Well, O'Neal *y'all are fuckin' too loud* Whitaker will be happy that you'll be living here, eventually."

I giggled. "I think he regrets telling me that I should check you out."

"O'Neal wanted you to check me out?"

"That night, when you brought my wallet to me, and I ran you off?"

"After I said you had a stick up your ass?" He clicked his tongue and glanced, wistful, into the chandelier. "That was such a romantic night for us."

"Mmmmm. Something about how I reacted to you... he knew. Everybody knew. They kept working at it until I saw it, too. And then I couldn't stop thinking about you."

"Girl. Same." He shuffled across the kitchen to stand in front of me, slid his arms around me. "Now here we are."

"Here we are," I said to him, tipping my face up for a soft, lingering kiss.

"So, about when will... *we* be...where we are? Where we are, being this house."

I laughed. "When am I moving in? You don't want to live in your own house by yourself for a while?"

His face folded in utter disgust. "No! We've spent every night together for the last three months. I've been living with you for the last three weeks... hell no. I do not want to live here by myself for a while. I want my girl here with me. I need Badass Esme here."

"You know I like it when you call me that."

Trey shrugged his shoulders. "I won't push, but I had a key made. It's at the bottom of the box that the ring was in. Use it when you're ready, but as far as I'm concerned, this place is ours."

"I..." I had to close my eyes and breathe; otherwise, I'd cry. "I will go pack my shit right now. I'm serious."

He laughed, then leaned in for a kiss, then stepped back. "Let's have coffee first?"

I slid two mugs over to him so he could pour, then carried them to the island. Trey settled onto the high bar stool next to me. They'd been delivered the day before, so new that we hadn't even taken the plastic off of them yet.

I sipped from my mug, shuddering at the strong blend. "Ugh. I need to make a grocery list. You need coffee creamer."

Trey stood, then walked to the refrigerator, pulling open one side of the shiny steel monstrosity. It was built for a person that entertained, that needed room for platters and rows and rows of food. The way Trey cooked, it would sit empty.

Then again, I thought with a smile, the way I cooked, it could potentially be full all the time.

He plucked a bottle from a shelf and brought it over. I brightened when I saw him twist the cap open and pour cream into my coffee.

"*We* have coffee creamer."

Trey caught my eye, holding my gaze for several beats before recapping the container and walking it back to the refrigerator.

"Thank you, baby."

"Mmmhmm."

I swiveled around, reaching for him as he came back to his chair. He stopped, stepping between my legs, and took my face into his hands, leaning in to brush his mouth against mine. He took his time, languidly caressing my lips with his, then went deeper, our tongues swirling. The kiss ended slowly, then he pulled back so we could see each other, eye to eye.

He was so damn beautiful, from his full brows to the tight line of his beard along his chin to his deep brown skin tone and molded body.

Trey Pettigrew was so worth the wait.

"You wanna know something?"

"Yes, Trey. I wanna know something."

"So, there's Badass Esme, right? And I love her. But there's another part of you that I'm fond of. She's soft. Very... *very* soft. I am *in love* with her."

"Soft? Me?"

"Mmmhmm." He moved his hands down my neck, across my shoulder, down my chest to palm the heft of my breasts through the cotton nightshirt that I'd slept in. He leaned in to kiss me again, whispering, "These are soft," against my lips.

He moved lower, rubbing his hands over the span of my hips and across my thighs. "These..." He chuckled, his head nodding appreciatively. "Yeah, these are real soft. I love these. They're almost my favorite part of you. *Almost.*"

He smoothed his hands up my thighs, pushing my nightshirt up, then pulled, scooting me to the edge of the chair. I leaned back, clutching the edge of the chair for balance, letting him push my legs open further.

Trey was already pulling the band of his pants down when he moved in closer and bent over me, possessing my mouth and my pussy. He lifted my legs and hooked them over his arms. I locked them around him, holding him in position while he thrust into me with hard, fast, deep strokes.

"Shit, baby," he ground out, his jaw clenched with the effort to maintain control. "You are soft. So soft for me. I love all your soft parts."

"Yessss..."

A long, needy moan curled from him. He alternated between sweet, whispery kisses and nibbles that almost hurt, moving across my shoulder and neck.

I began a grinding circle to match his strokes. With his moans as a gauge, I sped up my movements, taking us higher until my head rocked back, and my body pulsed.

"Oh my... shit that's good...so good. Right there..."

"Yeah? You glad you waited for me?"

I laughed. "I didn't wait for you, Trey."

"Sure you did," he replied, grinning down at me while not missing a stroke. "I came along and it was over for all them bros."

"Trey…" I wanted to laugh, but I wanted to come more. "Please… please fuck me…"

"You close? I want to watch."

I wrapped an arm around Trey and clung to him, smiling at our rhythmic moans and hunches of his body against mine until he was still.

"Shit," he panted, pulling out after a few quiet seconds. He helped me re-balance so I didn't fall off of the chair. "What was that?"

"Really?" I grinned. "You know what that was. And it was sexy as fuck."

"I'm glad we left the plastic on the chairs."

"We should leave it on until we've christened every room in this house."

He let out a salacious grunt, pulled up his pants, and bent to kiss me. "I like the way you think."

"I love you, Trey. I am excited to live here with you. And to definitely eventually marry you."

"I love you, too, Esme."

I sighed, stretching my limbs before I cramped up. "I'll warm up our coffee. We need to decorate your tree—"

"*Our* tree."

"*Our* tree," I corrected with a smile. "Then we can talk about when I can tell Jada about the engagement ring that I want you to surprise me with."

"Bet." Our lips met in a soft, slow kiss. "Let's get the rest of our lives started."

I hate writing. I love having written.

— DOROTHY PARKER

This is that feeling, right? Dragging yourself to the writing desk or the chair or the couch, or the cafe—when we could drag ourselves to the cafe— to write. To slog out the words, to worry over every sentence, to laugh at the funny bits and cry at the sad ones. We sludge through all of that to get to THIS point right here.

Done. Writing your acknowledgements, (which are actually really hard, and I've been so paralyzed by them as to just not do them because I will leave someone out and they won't think I am grateful... to be a writer is to be very neurotic).

So, this is technically my 12th or 13th book, but there are a few that I don't count. My goal was always to have ten books in print, on sale, available. The Never List makes book ten. Almost didn't make it, y'all. I started this book so long ago that I can't remember why I started it, or where it came from. My old blog is gone, and Anemia turned my brain into Swiss cheese, so I have no idea where these people came from. But I'm so glad they're here.

I have lots of people to thank, and I will forget half of them. I am sorry. But here goes:

My BetaReaders, who are the only reason that I feel my books are getting better with each release!

KMiller, whose dedication to making a book shine is so appreciated and does not go unnoticed.

Tina, for kicking my tail and giving me the side eye when I said I wasn't writing. Your turn!

Shelly, who hasn't blocked me from her twitter DM's or her email, thank goodness. I've got two shoulders to lean on when you need them!

All of my friends who harass me by asking when the book is done HEY THE BOOK IS DONE ! LEAVE ME ALONE FOR APPROXIMATELY FOUR WEEKS, THANKS. :)

My Brunch Boos (it's our ten year anniversary!) who pretty much started it all, kiss kiss. Love you all!

My PDubs, my BlackGirlTime gals, my Improperly Coiffured, Trollops, my Author frands, my fellow creatives: I am never alone. Thank you for your friendship and companionship and camaraderie. Writing is never lonely.

I can't ever, *ever* go without thanking my new and seasoned readers and staunch supporters. Y'all are the real MVP. The reason I slog to the writing desk and make the words is because readers are nice enough to reach out and let me know that they appreciate my books and love reading them. Sometimes those notes come exactly when I need them and I *absolutely love* hearing from you, so please don't hesitate to reach out with your kind comments to authordl@booksbydlwhite or hit me in the DM's on twitter or Instagram!

I have earned many books and lots of naps. And cheese!

xoxo,

Author DL White

CREDITS

Cover Image courtesy Dreamstime.com ID 118386148
Proofreading by KMiller
Formatted with Vellum

ABOUT THE AUTHOR

Atlanta based women's fiction and romance author DL White began seriously pursuing a writing career in 2011. She harbors a love for coffee and brunch, especially on a patio, but her real obsession is water— lakes, rivers, oceans, waterfalls! On the weekend, you'll probably find her near water and if she's lucky, on an ocean beach.

When not writing books, she devours them. She blogs reviews and thoughts on writing and books at BooksbyDLWhite.com. Grab a book by DL White and *#Putitinyourface*.

Join her newsletter at Booksbydlwhite.com/newsletter

Join our book loving community on Mighty Networks at BooksbyDLwhite.com/community.

ALSO BY DL WHITE

BOOKS
BY DL WHITE

Select titles available in ebook, paperback, and audio at
booksbydlwhite.com/books

FULL LENGTH NOVELS

Brunch at Ruby's

Dinner at Sam's

Beach Thing

Leslie's Curl & Dye

The Guy Next Door

A Thin Line

SHORTS

Unexpected, A Holiday Short

Second Time Around, A Potter Lake Holiday Novella

The Kwanzaa Brunch, A Holiday Novella

CPSIA information can be obtained
at www.ICGtesting.com
Printed in the USA
LVHW032023251120
672678LV00005B/1137